The Play's

the

Thing

MORE BY THIS AUTHOR

Historical Fiction

The Testament of Mariam

This Rough Ocean

The Chronicles of Christoval Alvarez

The Secret World of Christoval Alvarez
The Enterprise of England
The Portuguese Affair
Bartholomew Fair
Suffer the Little Children

The Fenland Series

Flood
Betrayal

Contemporary Fiction

The Anniversary
The Travellers
A Running Tide

The Play's the Thing

Ann Swinfen

Shakenoak Press

Shakenoak Press
ISBN 978-0-9932372-4-9

Cover images
The Grafton Portrait (Possibly the young Shakespeare)
Swan Theatre Interior 1596

Cover design by JD Smith www.jdsmith-design.co.uk

To the Memory of

William Shakespeare

King of Playwrights

1564–1616

Chapter One

London, 1591

I shivered. Outside the window, which faced east, the sun shone with an intensity of fire almost unknown in England. The brief summer shower that had fallen on the day of my return to London was the first rain the city had known for weeks, but it was a brief respite. As I had walked this morning from my lodgings along the south bank of the river toward St Thomas's hospital – just minutes ago, it seemed – I had noticed that the river was exceptionally low. Great plains of glistening mud stretched out from either bank, the Thames a sluggish stream meandering between them. The impish mudlarks of Southwark were splashing about in the slurry, searching for any treasure which might be revealed by the shrinking of the river. Only yesterday a lad had found a Roman coin and run with it to some lordling, who paid him well. The sun, hot as molten copper, burned through my physician's cap, springing forth beads of sweat in my hair. The occasional birdsong was desultory, as though the very birds were exhausted by the heat.

But now I shivered.

It was not the biting cold of a Muscovy winter that froze me, an assault, a siege from without, which could be battled with furs and spiced mead and heated stones. The cold came from within. I could see no means to resist it. Barely aware that I did so, I rubbed my arms and stared across the desk at Superintendant Ailmer. I could find no words to answer him.

Ailmer was clearly unhappy. He would not look me in the eye, but stared down at the papers on his desk, running a quill

1

between his fingers until the feathers, shredded away, fell down like snow.

'I regret having to tell you this, Dr Alvarez,' he said finally, when the silence had stretched out too long, 'but the matter was taken quite out of my hands. Of course, if Sir Francis had still been with us . . .'

His voice trailed away. Sir Francis Walsingham, my employer and patron since I was sixteen, had been dead more than a year now. Sir Francis had found me a place here at the hospital, even before I had qualified as a licensed physician. No one would have dared to countermand his wishes. But Sir Francis was gone.

'I do not understand,' I said. I understood well enough. I was merely stalling for time.

'When Dr Wattis came to us in May of last year,' he said . . . He cleared his throat. 'When he came, I know that it was agreed that he would undertake your duties until your return from Muscovy, when he would take up his appointment in the household of the Archbishop of York. That was to be at Easter this year.'

'You will remember,' I interrupted, 'that I was unhappy about the appointment at the time. Howard Wattis had just finished his theoretical studies in medicine at Oxford. He had no practical experience whatsoever. To put him in charge of both the lying-in and children's wards, where lives can so easily be lost—'

'Had Dr Colet not agreed to return from retirement to supervise his work, I am sure the governors would not have agreed to the arrangement,' he said.

'But you tell me Dr Colet is dead.'

'Alas, that is so. He was a good man and a conscientious physician. I fear he over tasked his strength.'

Over tasked it, no doubt, in making up for the mistakes and ineptitudes of that boy, I thought, gritting my teeth. I had not met Howard Wattis, yet I could only think of him as a boy. He had taken up his duties the week after I left for Muscovy. He was but a year older than I, without my seven years of practical experience in hospital medicine, starting as a fourteen-year-old apprentice and assistant to my physician father, a distinguished

2

man in his profession, once a professor of medicine at the University of Coimbra in Portugal. This fellow Wattis had possessed nothing but university book-learning when my patients had been entrusted to his dubious care.

'You say the Archbishop no longer wants him?' I said.

Little blame to him, I thought, but why should that affect me?

Ailmer shifted uncomfortably in his chair, gave me one swift glance, then resumed shredding his quill.

'It appears that Dr Wattis was appointed to the Archbishop's household through the good offices of an uncle,' he said.

Wattis was fortunate in his army of uncles, I thought. It was another uncle, a deputy governor of the Muscovy Company, who had put him forward as a substitute in my place at St Thomas's last year. That way he could gain some practical experience by molesting my patients before taking up his lucrative private post in York. Unfortunately, I am seriously lacking in uncles, with or without influence.

'Does this preferment no longer hold?' I asked. I was still stalling.

'After Easter had come and gone, without your return from Muscovy, the Archbishop sent word that he had been obliged to make another appointment. By then Dr Colet was seriously ill. Dr Wattis was working alone.'

'But it was always the case that I was unlikely to return to London before this year's Company fleet sails back from the north. That will be in September!' My anger was beginning to warm me. 'I did not travel to Muscovy willingly, as you know, but at the behest of certain great men. And I have made my way home to London myself, three months earlier than the fleet, having fulfilled my mission. Rescued Gregory Rocksley and brought back the report of certain affairs in that country.'

I drew a deep breath.

'And now I am to be turned out of my post here at St Thomas's?'

I was beginning to shake uncontrollably. I had arrived that morning assuming I would take up once more my care of the expectant mothers in Whittington's ward, and the sick pauper children in the adjacent ward. The two wards of which I had formerly been in charge. I had come with a joyful step, relieved to be back doing the work I loved, away from that terrible country which had consumed a year of my life. Now I was cast out, that fellow Wattis having been given my place. It made all too clear to me just vulnerable I now was, with Walsingham gone.

'Is there nothing I can do?' I said at last, dully.

Ailmer looked at me, pity in his eyes.

'I am afraid there is not, Dr Alvarez. There are no physician posts vacant at the moment. And as you know, money is always tight here in the hospital. We cannot afford to appoint extra physicians. I am sure you noticed the scaffolding on the west side of the building. We have barely enough to pay for essential repairs, merely to keep out the wind and rain.'

Indeed, I knew very well that money was always lacking here at St Thomas's, just as I knew that – despite his admitted respect for my skills – Ailmer would not put his budget at risk by taking me back as a supernumerary.

'Do you know whether there is anything available at St Bartholomew's?' I asked. It was at Bart's that I had trained with my father. The governors there had once valued me, but men in power have short memories.

He shook his head. 'I have not heard so, but indeed you might ask.'

I gave a slight nod. I would ask. I had little hope. Twice, now, this had befallen me. Two years before, when I had been out of the country on the Portuguese expedition, my father had died and our positions at St Bartholomew's had been filled by others. Now it had happened again, despite the promises of Sir Rowland Heyward, governor of the Muscovy Company, that my post at Thomas's would be held safe for me till my return. Alone, without any great man as my patron, I would have no redress against him or against the governors of St Thomas's.

Ailmer offered me a glass of wine, as though that might somehow compensate for the loss of my livelihood, but I refused. Instead of making my way cheerfully to the wards, greeting the mistress of the nurses, Alice Maynard, and Goodwife Appledean, in charge of the midwives, I found myself once more in the yard, where the cobbles were as hot as bakestones under my feet. Dust from the stonemasons' workshop drifted through the heavy air, blending with the summer stench from the river, which was worse than usual with the heat and the exposed refuse on the mud banks.

It was so hot that the gatekeeper, Tom Read, had retreated inside the cool of the gatehouse instead of taking up his usual post on a stool in front of his door. I blinked in the darkness of the single room on the ground floor, where he lived and cooked.

'Dr Alvarez!'

His voice came out of the gloom. I could make out his figure, as my eyes adjusted. He was seated at the table and was busy draping a wet cloth over his head to cool it. My heavy physician's robe seemed a mockery now, and I began to peel it off in irritation. His old wolfhound, Swifty, and my dog, Rikki, raised their heads, but were clearly too overcome by the heat to rise to their feet and welcome me.

Tom's greeting had feigned surprise, but I knew him too well to be taken in. There was little that happened at St Thomas's that did not reach Tom's ears within minutes, or at most half a day. I dropped on to a stool opposite him, rolling up my robe and laying it on the table.

'You knew,' I said. It was not an accusation, merely an acknowledgement. 'You knew, when I left Rikki with you this morning.'

He nodded. 'It weren't my place to say nothing.'

He got up and poured us both ale into a couple of his rough wooden cups. I was about to refuse this, like Ailmer's wine, even though Tom could not be blamed, then I realised how thirsty I was. My throat felt as dry as if I had been talking for hours, though I had hardly spoken in Ailmer's office. I drained the cup in a single draught. When I set it down on the table, Tom filled it again.

'They didn't ought to have done that,' he said. 'That fellow Wattis, he's trouble.'

I knew I should not discuss my fellow physician with Tom, but he was an old and loyal friend, who had cared for Rikki all the time I had been away. Besides, what loyalty did I owe St Thomas's now?

'Trouble?' I said.

He frowned. 'Upsets the sisters. There's allus one or more of 'em crying. The children are scared of him. I won't say he beats them—'

'What!' I was shocked. My little Southwark waifs!

'Nay, nothing like that. But he's one of them Puritans, the ones think they're better'n the rest of us, specially chosen by God. So he's allus talking hellfire to the little uns, till they're so frightened I swear it makes 'em more ill than when they come in. Then there's the babes.'

'What of the babes?'

My hand was clenched around the ale cup and I realised I had drained it a second time. I shook my head when Tom offered to fill it again.

'Well, now.' He was avoiding my eyes, as Ailmer had done. 'There's been a lot of babes died this last year in the ward, more'n three times the usual number, so Goodwife Appledean says.'

I realised I was not the only one speaking out of turn. If the senior midwife, who was generally discretion itself, had let this information slip to Tom, things must be serious indeed.

'That's bad,' I said quietly. 'And with this heat . . . there will be the bloody flux and all manner of summer diseases, worse than ever, even if we are spared the plague.'

'Aye. And that Wattis, he don't let the poor mites stay while we feed 'em up, like you do. Sends 'em off as soon as maybe. Happen they'm back again in a week or two.'

St Thomas's was not merely a hospital for the injured and sick, but a place of succour for the destitute. It was part of its duty to care for the paupers of Southwark, many of whom lived much of their lives on the very borderland of starvation. I felt my anger rising, and my frustration with it.

'A'nt there nothing you can do?' he said.

I shook my head.

'I have no influence here now, Tom. As you see, I am turned away.'

'One of your great friends?'

I gave a bitter laugh. 'Which friends would those be? With Sir Francis gone, I have no great friends any more. I am nothing but a poor jobbing physician, without employment.'

'Nay, don't put yourself down. There's no one here as likes Wattis. They want you back.'

I shrugged. 'The governors have made their appointment. There is nothing you or I or anyone else can do about it.'

I got to my feet and tucked the bundle of my gown under my arm.

'I'd best be off and not keep you from your work. I can hear a wagon stopping at the gate.'

'Aye, that'll be the new roof slates the builders are wanting.'

He got to his feet and I noticed that he moved stiffly. He had grown older while I was away. We left the gatehouse together, Tom to direct the delivery of slates, and I, with Rikki at my heels . . . to go where? I had never felt so desolate since my unhappy return from Portugal two years ago. My hospital post was gone. My work as code-breaker and agent had ceased with the death of Walsingham. How was I to live?

I wandered down to the river, just short of the Bridge, and stood watching the Southwark lads scrambling about in the mud. One of them had found something and the others had gathered around him. They were filthy, covered with stinking Thames mud from head to toe, but they seemed happy. Rikki leaned against my leg, sensing that all was not right with me.

When Gregory Rocksley, Thomas Edgewick, and I had reported to the Muscovy Company the day after our return to London, Sir Rowland Heyward had welcomed us warmly, relieved that Gregory had survived and had brought a report detailing all that he had discovered about the treacherous dealings of Boris Godunov, the *de facto* ruler of Muscovy, with our Spanish enemies. Gregory and Thomas would remain in the Company's employ, while I was thanked effusively for my mission to that country. Heyward made no mention of the loss of my hospital position then. He gave us each a heavy purse of coin. Afterwards the three of us had dined together, but I had not seen Gregory or Thomas since, as we each took up the threads of our former lives.

The money provided to me was welcome, but hardly a generous recompense for a year of my life, considerably less than I would have earned at St Thomas's during the lost year. And cruelly inadequate now that I understood how that mission had also robbed me of my professional post. Before I realised what had happened at the hospital, I had paid my landlady, Goodwife Atkins, three months rent in advance, thinking it best to ensure the roof over my head before I was tempted to spend the coin. Will Shakespeare, who had occupied my room while I was away, had found other lodgings, but Simon still rented the room below mine. If I was careful, I could probably feed myself and Rikki for another two or three months, but when winter came I would need fuel for my fire as well as victuals.

So Wattis was a canting Puritan. I wondered whether that was the real reason for the Archbishop's withdrawing the position of household physician from him. I knew nothing of the Archbishop's theology, but I strongly doubted that he favoured the Puritans. Perhaps word had reached him of Wattis's leanings toward Geneva, so my absence from St Thomas's had provided a convenient excuse for his dismissal. Whatever lay behind it, the facts remained unaltered. I had no employment and little money.

The only person I could think of who might be able to advise me was Dr Nuñez. It was time I visited him in any case, for I had been back in London for three days. My whole entanglement with the Muscovy Company had begun with a casual conversation over Ruy Lopez's dinner table, where Dr Nuñez and I had been present. That had been very soon after Walsingham's death, a little over a year ago, but it felt like a lifetime gone past.

With Rikki following somewhat reluctantly behind, I headed toward the Bridge. Encumbered by his thick coat, he must be exhausted with the heat, but I felt I could not leave him with Tom, although he had offered.

'Anytime, Dr Alvarez,' he said, 'I'm glad to have Rikki. He's good company for me and Swifty.'

I might need his help later, should I manage to find employment where I could not take a dog with me. Moreover, it was one less burden, thanks to Sir Francis's generous gift, that my horse Hector had free livery at the Walsingham house in Seething Lane. With a twist to my heart I realised I might need to sell Hector in order to survive.

The narrow roadway between the houses lining the Bridge seemed more crowded than ever with bad-tempered people pushing each other aside. The air was stifling, thick with the stench of unwashed bodies and river sewage. Even the cheapjacks and entertainers who plied their trade here barely had the energy to shout their attractions. Little wonder, when none of the passersby paid them any heed. The passageway under Nonesuch House provided a brief moment of shade, though the air was even thicker within its close confines. Several people had simply taken refuge here from the sun, sitting on the cobbles with their legs stretched out, to the annoyance of everyone who passed through. I saw one man give an old woman's ankles a sharp kick, at which she swore like one of the Queen's troopers.

At last we were across the river. I barely had the energy to walk the short distance to the Nuñez house in Mark Lane, but I had nowhere else to go, so I plodded on. Sweat was trickling down my back and my shoes had begun to pinch my feet, swollen with the heat. I fear I presented a sorry spectacle when I knocked at last on the door of the Nuñez house. It was answered by one of their black servants, a young girl called Milly (a stumbling English attempt to pronounce her difficult and alien name). Her parents had been African slaves from a captured Spanish ship, turned loose in London to survive if they might. Some had found work as servants or labourers, some had simply vanished. Milly, born and reared in London, could have been taken for any local girl, but for the colour of her skin and her tightly curled hair.

She showed me into Dr Nuñez's study, where he had coached me fiercely for my examinations at the Royal College. It was cooler here than outside, being a corner room, with windows facing in two directions. There was scarcely any movement in the air outside, but what there was passed through from window to window and brought a little welcome relief from the heat.

'Kit! How good it is to see you!'

Dr Nuñez had risen from his usual cushioned chair and came towards me, both hands outstretched to take mine. Like Tom, he had aged noticeably in the year since I had last seen him. Indeed, I thought he looked fine drawn and quite frail. Nevertheless, when we embraced like father and son, his arms around me felt firm. Despite myself, I was aware of tears threatening. Since the death of my own father, Dr Nuñez had become near enough his replacement, but I could see that he would not be with us much longer. He had never fully recovered his strength after the horrors and near starvation of our ill-fated Portuguese expedition.

'Milly,' he said, 'tell Mistress Beatriz that Dr Alvarez is here. I am sure he has not yet dined. He will join us.'

As the girl left, he turned to me, looking uncharacteristically anxious.

'I presume too much, Kit. Perhaps you have business elsewhere and have no time to dine with two aged folk like us?'

I smiled. 'I have not dined. And nothing would please me better than to dine with you both. You do not mind Rikki?'

'Of course we do not.'

He stooped stiffly to stroke Rikki's head.

'And besides,' I said, 'I have no business elsewhere. No business anywhere. I am come to ask your advice. I am turned out of St Thomas's.'

'What is this?' He motioned me to a chair. 'What do you mean, "turned out". They must be relieved that you have returned.'

'My place has been given to Howard Wattis. The governors have appointed him and I am without employment.'

He was clearly shocked at the news, which I had thought he might have heard already. Together with Walsingham he had found me my position at St Thomas's, then urged the Royal College to allow me to take the examination for a licence, even though I had not attended a university. He had invested much time and care into my future, so, I reflected now, the action of the

10

hospital governors was an insult to him as well as to me, for although he was old he was still a physician of high standing, a Fellow of the College, a former Censor there, and personal physician to Lord Burghley.

I recounted briefly the substance of my conversation with Superintendent Ailmer.

'There is no hope that the governors will reverse their decision,' I said, 'even should they wish to, which I do not suppose they would. It would mean a loss of face. Nay, it seems Howard Wattis has fairly wormed his way into their favour. Although,' I added with some bitterness, 'it appears he is unpopular with both the nurses and the patients.'

'It is unforgivable,' Dr Nuñez said. His hands were clasped in his lap and I saw that they trembled slightly. 'The hospital governors have betrayed their promise. And so has Governor Heyward. He arranged for his deputy's nephew to assume your duties merely until you returned. Then you were to take up your post again. It was all agreed before you left. I shall see whether I can–'

'Nay,' I said. 'I did not come to ask you to intervene. It will cause nothing but grief and trouble. I wanted your advice on where I might look for work. Now that Sir Francis's service is disbanded, and I am thrust out from St Thomas's, I have no work, neither code-breaking nor medicine.'

I gave a somewhat shaky laugh.

'I am afraid I must eat. And so must Rikki. Do you know of anywhere in need of a physician? I suppose there is Bridewell, or even Bedlam . . . or perhaps somewhere beyond London. Other towns must need physicians.'

My spirits sank even as I spoke. I did not want to leave London, newly returned as I was. I had known no other home since I was twelve. Like all those who have lost their first home, I clung all the more passionately to what I knew.

'I am afraid I know nothing of other towns, Kit,' he said, 'although I can make enquiries. Such a move might prove costly in many ways. You might find it much more difficult, living at a distance, to seize any chances when they arise here in London. I can offer you some help, however. My health has not been good this last twelvemonth and I should be glad of assistance with my own patients. What do you say to relieving me of part of my burden of work?'

'I think you are making the offer out of kindness,' I said. 'I cannot deprive you of your living.'

He laughed at that. 'My dear Kit, I make my living, by far the greater part of it, from my dealings as a merchant. I can sit here in my office and earn more with a few strokes of my pen than I can ever do toiling about the City in this terrible heat, listening to the imagined ailments of rich merchants' wives in Goldsmiths' Row. You are young and healthy, and more patient than I have become in my crabbed old age. You would be doing me a great kindness.'

We argued it back and forth, I thinking at first that he was acting merely out of pity, but gradually he persuaded me that he wished truly to unburden himself of some of his day-to-day work. He would retain his noble patients, amongst whom by far the greatest were Lord Burghley and his younger son, Robert Cecil – now newly made Sir Robert by the Queen. What Dr Nuñez had in mind was that I should assume the care of a number of the great merchant families of London – the merchants themselves, and above all their wives and children.

'For,' he said, 'though the husbands are much occupied with business, their womenfolk often find the long hours of the day are tedious when they are not visiting the shops in the Royal Exchange or dining with friends. They have no real occupation. They must find something to fill their time, so every small detail of their health, and the health of their children, assumes great importance.'

'I think such patients will be very different from my Southwark workmen and whores and paupers,' I said, somewhat ruefully, not altogether happy at the prospect of these wealthy ladies.

'Indeed they will. On the whole you will find them in better health, though even the rich are not spared when disease walks the city. However, although they are not great in number, you will find the remuneration will go some way to compensate for the many pointless summons and wasted hours you must endure.'

12

When he mentioned the fees I should charge, I was speechless. After one look at my face, he laughed.

'Fear not. There is no likelihood that you will become rich. I have taken on fewer and fewer patients in recent years. You will earn something from our arrangement, but it will not compare with your salary at St Thomas's. It will amount to barely half that. It will help you a little, but you will need to find other work. I shall keep my eyes and ears alert for anything likely to suit you.'

He rose and beckoned to me to follow him to the dining parlour.

'Is there no code-breaking work for you to do? I cannot believe that our enemies have ceased to plot against us, even though Sir Francis has been taken from us.'

'Everything had fallen into a shambles before I left London last year,' I said. 'There seemed to be no clear successor to Sir Francis, though it appeared at the time that the contest would likely be between my lord Essex and the Cecils.'

'Everything is still much the same,' he said, opening the door to the dining parlour and ushering me inside. 'My lord Burghley has assumed Sir Francis's position of Chief Secretary as a temporary measure, as well as continuing as Lord Treasurer, though he has told me he hopes that Her Majesty will appoint his son as Secretary before long. I heard a rumour that Essex is attempting to build a rival service of informants, with the assistance of Anthony and Francis Bacon. Though I doubt he has the patience for it. He will want some quick and spectacular victory to impress Her Majesty.'

'Nothing in that surprises me,' I said, 'except for the involvement of the Bacon brothers. Surely . . . are they not Lord Burghley's nephews?'

'Indeed they are. But perhaps they have no part in his plans, where his son Sir Robert takes precedence.'

'I would not hook myself to Essex's star,' I said. 'He will be off on some new madcap scheme before long. I have been trying to trace Thomas Phelippes. I do not suppose you have any word of him?'

He shook his head. 'Certainly I have not heard that he is working for Lord Burghley.'

'He seems to have disappeared.'

'I know that one of Sir Francis's men has joined Burghley, and has already been employed on missions to the Low Countries. The man Poley.'

I shuddered. 'Then my lord had best watch him. Sir Francis and Phelippes were ever suspicious that he served two masters. Francis Mylles was certain that he was paid by the Queen's enemies.'

'Poley has a slippery reputation.' He turned as the door opened again. 'Ah, Beatriz, my dear, look who has come to see us, fresh from those strange foreign lands in the frozen north. Kit, you must have much to tell us.'

Throughout our meal, neither code-breaking nor medicine was mentioned again. Instead I entertained them with a graphic account of my time in Muscovy.

When I left the Nuñez house, it was mid afternoon. I had promised Simon I would meet him at the Theatre in Shoreditch after the players' performance and my own day's work at St Thomas's, which I had expected to finish about the same time. Apart from Simon, I had last seen the players when we parted at the island of Wardhouse off the North Cape last summer. After a season of performances for the garrison and town there, they had returned home with the fleet which had taken us north. They were all eager, Simon said, to learn what had befallen me after I left them. We would take supper together at one of the nearby inns, and as the payment for entertaining them, they would stand me my meal. It seemed that today at least I would save the cost of my food, and Rikki would probably pick up sufficient scraps to supplement the meal Tom had given him in the morning.

Despite lingering over my meal with Dr Nuñez and Mistress Beatriz, it was as yet too early for my meeting with the players. They would still be strutting forth upon the stage. The good weather meant that they had been able to perform every day for weeks, Simon told me. And the heat had meant good audiences, as apprentices and even respectable craftsmen had downed their tools in preference for a lazy seat in the playhouse, adorned with a straw hat against the sun and equipped with an orange to suck against thirst.

In the past, I had often wondered how the players could endure such a chancy life, when bad weather meant few performances or an outbreak of disease meant the closure of the playhouses altogether. If they did not play, they did not eat. Now, it seemed, I myself had joined the ranks of those who must count themselves lucky if they had the chinks for a meal.

Since it was too early to go to the playhouse, and I was close by Seething Lane, I decided to visit my horse in the stable there. I had gone there the first morning after arriving back in London, and found him pleased to see me. His condition was as good as one might expect in such trying weather, for he was a favourite with the stable lads. I could spend time today grooming him while sounding out Harry and the other lads about the gossip concerning Essex, his wife Frances Walsingham, and any of my former friends in Sir Francis's service. The stable lads usually managed to know much of what was afoot in London. I hoped that they might be able to tell me where to find Phelippes. I still had the copy of Gregory Rocksley's report which I had intended to give to him, though I now wondered whether I should hand it to Lord Burghley instead.

Hector gave me a whicker of greeting, and I ran my hand down his nose to the soft velvet of his upper lip. I think there is nothing softer on any animal. Mankind is a coarse creature by comparison.

Harry came into Hector's stall with a bucket of water.

'You wouldn't believe the water they get through, this weather, Dr Alvarez,' he said. 'We have to watch 'em and dole it out small, or they'd blow theyselves up something monstrous.'

I picked up a curry comb and began to work over Hector's coat while he drank. The hairs had clumped into sweaty ridges.

'Aye,' I said, 'it's a worry. It's good that the house has its own well.'

He nodded his agreement and sat down on an upturned bucket, happy to see me doing his work for him. 'I'd not like to give them river water this summer,' he said. ''Tis no better'n a sewer at the moment.'

'I'd no chance to speak to you the other day,' I said, 'when you were getting Dame Ursula's coach ready. So what has been afoot while I have been away?'

He clasped his hands around his knees and considered.

'Well, Lady Frances was brought abed in January. A fine strong boy, she had. They've called him Robert Devereux, like his father.'

So Essex had an heir. I wondered whether fatherhood would steady him, or whether he would continue to behave like a spoiled child.

'That would be in Essex House?' The grand mansion on the Strand.

'Nay, the babe was born here. Lady Frances is more often here with her mother than in her husband's house. Reckon he's hardly there either, always dancing about the Queen with his winning ways.'

His tone dripped scorn. Unlike most Londoners, the servants here knew something of the real Earl, and did not idolise him. They had not been pleased when the daughter of the house, widow of the much loved Sir Philip Sidney, had been married off to Essex, whose reputation for the treatment of any women other than Her Majesty was dreadful.

'From what I hear,' he said, lowering his voice, 'he uses our Lady Frances badly. 'Tis no wonder she wants to be here with Dame Ursula. He has the morals of any stray tom cat. Why Sir Francis ever thought–'

He broke off and shook his head.

'I think he wanted to provide for her,' I said, 'for his own service to the Queen had consumed most of his estate. There was little enough to leave to his wife and daughter.' I had learned as much from Francis Mylles, Walsingham's chief secretary, but the poor nature of the great man's funeral must have made the situation clear to anyone.

Despite my words, I remembered all too well that hasty marriage to Essex, where I had been an unwilling witness.

Frances Walsingham had wept as she stood at the altar. I thought we should move to safer subjects.

'Have you any news of the others who worked here with me?' I asked. 'Nick Berden? Francis Mylles? Arthur Gregory? Thomas Phelippes?'

'Nick Berden has set himself up in a poultry business,' he said, ticking my fellow agents off on his fingers. 'His father was a poulterer, times past, it seems. He says it's a quieter life than working for Sir Francis.' He laughed. 'And he is no common poulterer, but supplies the Court.'

He considered. 'Master Mylles is living on that estate he bought from Sir Francis. Somewhere up near Oxford, I think it is.'

He scratched his head. 'Who else? Arthur Gregory. I heard tell he is working for a printer in Paul's churchyard.'

'I think he started out as a printer's engraver,' I said. I began to comb Hector's tail, though he kept swishing it from side to side, as though he thought I was one of the troublesome flies which had come with the hot weather.

'Then there's that scoundrel Poley,' Harry said, although I had not asked about Poley. Perhaps it was as well to learn what he had heard. Know your enemies better than your friends, Sir Francis used to say.

'Poley?'

'Aye, nasty fellow. He's working for Lord Burghley now and giving hisself airs. You'd think he was new made a courtier. Out of the country, last I heard. Somewhere in the Low Countries.'

That was what Dr Nuñez had said. It was something to be thankful for.

'And Thomas Phelippes?' I asked.

'Ah, Master Phelippes,' he said, 'I did hear that he had some sort of position in the Customs House, though I dunno what he would do there. Clerking, mebbe. Seems a strange place for him.'

It did. What a waste of one of the sharpest brains in England. I wondered why he was not working for Lord Burghley. But if our suspicions of last year were right, and it was Poley who had broken into the Walsingham house while we were all at the funeral, then it was Poley who had stolen all Sir Francis's secret files and all our precious ciphers. If he then presented them to the Cecils, it would have earned him a privileged position in their service. I had understood that the Cecils were (on the whole) honourable men, but possession of those documents and ciphers would have represented a victory over Essex, and spiery is at best an amoral business. The end of preserving England's and the Queen's safety justified almost any action.

If that was how matters stood, Phelippes could hardly go a-begging to the Cecils. Yet Poley, sly informer and sweet wooer of the Queen's enemies though he was, had no skills as a code-breaker. Why had the Cecils not sought Phelippes themselves? Our ciphers would prove useful for a time, but sooner or later new ones would be devised, and what then? No secret service could exist without code-breakers. The idea of Thomas Phelippes working as some kind of government clerk in the Customs House was baffling.

When Harry had gone off to attend to the other horses and I had finished grooming Hector, I heard a nearby church clock striking five o' the clock. The play would be over, the players changing in the tire-room. If I set off now I could meet them almost as if I came from St Thomas's. I would not pretend to them that I had kept my post. They might have some idea of what work I could find, for – like the stable lads – the players kept abreast of London gossip. Guy Bingham, I knew, would suggest I join him as a musician, but I had no taste for public performance. Once, at Whitehall Palace, and in Sir Francis's service, had been quite enough for me.

Chapter Two

I had a warm welcome at the Theatre, of the usual sort that I had come to expect from the players. Dick Burbage threw out his arms in an extravagant gesture and struck the heroic pose he used when playing one of his most dramatic parts.

'Behold!' he cried. 'A wanderer from distant lands! Does he bring treasures of the Orient? Pearls for my lady's ears? Silks to wrap her beauteous limbs? What? I see no white bear furs, no wolf skins!'

'I do own a pair of wolf skin mittens,' I said mildly, 'but find them somewhat hot in this weather.'

Dick thumped me on the shoulder.

'Even though you come bearing no gifts, Kit,' he said, 'it is good to see you safely returned from that terrible land. Wardhouse was bad enough.'

Christopher Haigh grinned at me, through a mouthful of pins, for he was mending a tear in a pair of canary-coloured hose. Goodwife Blakely was in charge of the players' costumes, even those they owned themselves, but they could all turn a hand to minor repairs like this.

'Who is that lord speaking to Master Burbage?' I asked, indicating with a nod of my head. James Burbage was standing at the far end of the stage, in earnest conversation with a grey-bearded gentleman whose clothes and demeanour marked him out as a courtier. 'The elderly lord with the beautiful young wife?'

The girl, whose lustrous black curls fell about her shoulders in an abundance unsuited to a married woman, was about my age and my colouring, but there any resemblance ended, although my hair had once had that same rich fall, before it was cropped short. She was as richly dressed and bejewelled, almost, as the Queen herself. She was also showing a lively interest in the playhouse, and indeed the players. For a moment a pair of intelligent eyes met mine, but I dropped my gaze at once. It was unseemly for a young man, such as I pretended to be, to gaze frankly upon the wife of such a lord.

Guy, who was sitting cross-legged next to Christopher tuning his lute, looked up and chuckled softly. 'You are mistaken, Kit. That is no wife. The gentleman is Lord Hunsdon, the Lord Chamberlain, first cousin to Her Majesty on the Boleyn side. The – ah – lady is Aemilia Bassano, his mistress.'

'Bassano?' I said. 'I think I have heard that name before.'

'I am sure you have. There is a whole tribe of them. A musical dynasty from Italy. Jewish converts to Christianity. A clutch of brothers brought over by King Henry. Our good king was a great lover of music and had heard of their talent. Talented indeed, for they survived his reign with their heads still on their shoulders.'

'She is too young–' I said.

'Oh, the lady belongs to the next generation. Her father was the youngest brother, I believe. Her mother was an Englishwoman, though the girl was orphaned long since and brought up in the households of the Countess of Kent and the Countess of Cumberland.'

'You know a good deal about her,' I said, curious.

'Ah, all we musicians of London know each other.'

'She is a musician?'

'Like all of them. Sings like an angel, plays more instruments than I do. Reads Latin and Greek.'

'I heard tell she is a bastard,' Dick Burbage said scathingly. 'Which explains her profession.'

Guy shrugged. 'Perhaps, perhaps not. What I heard was that the parents had a hand-fasting, which is as good as a marriage.'

'Well, it seems to have done her no harm,' Dick said. 'She has found herself a very comfortable and profitable place in Lord Hunsdon's bed. Behold her jewels! Better than your wolf skin mitts, Kit.'

I grunted. Sometimes I found the conversation of my male companions offensive. To men they were tolerant, but they were more ready to pass judgement on women. Like me, this girl was an orphan, perhaps a Marrano, who had been forced to find a way to survive in a world of neglect and casual cruelty. Without my medical skill and my man's attire, I might have been forced into a similar life, though without the patronage of a pair of Countesses. I wondered what those noble ladies thought of their protégée's present occupation.

Will Shakespeare, leaning against the entrance to the tiring room, had said nothing, but his face spoke much. He was devouring Aemilia Bassano with his eyes, careless of propriety.

'Well,' I said, 'why are they here and when are we going for this dinner that I am promised?'

'As for the first,' Guy said, 'none of us know why they are here. They attended the play, though they had too much sense and too much dignity to sit amongst the cockscombs on the stage.'

The players all hated the preening young men who paid extra for stools on the stage. They drew attention to themselves, away from the players, interrupted the performance, and generally played the fool. Only Master Burbage was glad of the addition to the company's income.

'And as for the second?' I said. 'The dinner? I am hungry.' I exaggerated, for my meal at the Nuñez house had been substantial. They kept to the old ways at home, eating their main meal in the middle of the day, with but a light supper in the evening. But the rest of the world was moving toward a larger meal in the evening, including the players, who preferred not to eat heavily before performing in the early afternoon. It dulled their senses, so they said, though I believe it was partly due to nerves. I had been surprised as I had gradually realised that even the most seasoned players, like Guy, were high-strung and nervous before a performance.

'We'll eat once the gentlefolk go,' Christopher said, 'and once those sluggards finish dressing.' He jerked his head in the direction of the tiring house. Few of the young boys had appeared yet, but to do them justice, it took longer to divest themselves of their women's costumes. Christopher rolled up his hose and stuffed them into a pocket of his doublet, together with his needle, thread, and pincushion.

'Take care you do not stab yourself in a moment of inattention,' I said.

'You are right.' He laid his sewing materials on a ledge of the back scene, where they would no doubt lie forgotten in the dust until he next tore his hose.

Simon emerged, dragging a comb through his hair, and was followed by two of the youngsters, tussling in that way boys have, like puppies in a litter. They fell over Rikki, who yelped and showed his teeth, but did not bite.

'Have a care!' Guy cried.

In jumping away from Rikki, one of the boys had come near to treading on his lute. Guy got swiftly to his feet, cuffed both boys, and laid his lute carefully in its case. One of the boys, I saw, was Davy, former patient of mine and now an apprentice musician and acrobat under Guy. He had grown taller while I was away, though he remained very slight, a legacy of his harsh childhood.

'They are leaving,' Will said. He was still watching Aemilia. Then he shook himself and turned away. 'Hey, Simon,' he said, 'that is my comb!'

'Never fear,' Simon said, 'I've no nits.' He handed the comb to Will and grinned at me. 'Ready to entertain us, Kit?'

'I'll strive my best,' I said, 'though there is a tail end to my story that I did not know until this morning.'

Master Burbage was escorting the visitors from the playhouse with much bowing, as the last of the company joined us from the tiring house. He came back, wiping the sweat from his forehead with a large handkerchief.

'This heat is enough to drive a man mad, and no boon to civility when a man must dance attendance on a courtier.'

We began to move toward the street. Master Burbage handed the key over to the doorkeeper and we headed down towards Bishopsgate.

'I've spoken to the innkeeper at the Green Dragon, Father,' Cuthbert Burbage said. 'He is to keep space for us.'

'What was Lord Hunsdon's business,' Guy asked, 'that kept him after the play was done?'

Master Burbage ran his finger around inside his ruff to loosen it.

'Ah, well, he is a great lover of the playhouse, Guy, as you know. He thinks to become patron of one of the companies.'

'But all the good companies have patrons,' Cuthbert said, frowning. 'He is not thinking to create a new one, surely?'

The players looked at each other in alarm. There was enough competition already, what with Henslowe's men across in Southwark at the Rose, several boys' companies, and the irregular travelling troupes that appeared in London from time to time.

'Nay, I think not,' Master Burbage said. 'Where would he find his players? He was offering to replace Lord Strange as our patron, and was testing my opinion. Asking if we would come under his wing instead.'

This, too, was troubling news. It would not do to offend Lord Strange. He had been generous to the company. Besides, he also was a blood relation of the Queen.

'What did you answer him?' Guy was curious. 'It cannot have been a comfortable discussion.'

'I told him that Lord Strange, for all I knew, wished to remain our patron. That should he wish to withdraw, we would be most grateful to Lord Hunsdon.'

'And that was all?'

'In essence, aye. Dressed out in quite as fine words as Will would use.'

Will laughed. 'Indeed?'

'Perhaps not quite as fine. I had little time to ponder. I told him, with sugared words and much bowing, that I was most appreciative of his kindness.'

By the time we reached the Green Dragon in Bishopsgate the sun had begun its slow descent, relieving London a little from the fierce heat of the day, but the inn itself was stifling, as if the hot air remained trapped there, abundantly perfumed with the sweat of too many people, too crowded together. The innkeeper led Master Burbage toward a corner where several tables had been pushed together to accommodate our large party, but he shook his head.

'A man may not breathe in here. We will dine in the garden instead.'

A less distinguished patron than Master Burbage might have met with a surly refusal at this, but the innkeeper merely bowed and set three of his pot boys to moving tables, benches, and stools out into the garden which lay behind the inn, and we followed them. The Green Dragon was one of the great inns that lay along this major road into London from the northeast, boasting an excellent cook and an inn wife who took pride in her garden. Our tables were placed together under a shady arbour covered with climbing roses, just beyond the patch which provided herbs for the kitchen. Blowsy with the summer sun, the roses gave forth their scent in abundance, which mingled with those of lavender, rosemary, and thyme. Master Burbage had made a wise choice to retire to the garden.

The tables were soon loaded with dishes of every sort – roast beef and lamb, capons and duckling, parsnips, onions and leeks, all swimming in rich sauces. I realised suddenly that I had had more than enough to eat already that day and my appetite was not increased with the hot weather. My stomach had not yet quite recovered from the near starvation of my last weeks in Muscovy, so that I found the greasy abundance almost sickening. So as not to offend, I helped myself to a leg of capon, but only toyed with it.

Sitting opposite me was Master Wandesford, the bent little former cleric Master Burbage employed as a copyist. No one quite knew why he had abandoned his former profession. It was whispered that he had been unfrocked for some misdemeanour, but players are mostly a tolerant lot, never likely to enquire too closely into a fellow's past. It was Master Wandesford's task to take a play book, written by Will or Tom Kyd or Kit Marlowe, and copy out each player's part separately. It was an important task, for the players had to learn many parts, and learn them quickly. They performed a different play almost every day, though they would repeat a play after a week or two.

'Tell me,' I said, leaning forward across the table so that I could speak quietly to Master Wandesford. 'Who is that fellow at the far end of the table? The little foxy-haired fellow? I have never seen him before. Is he a new player?'

I did not really believe this to be true, for there is always something about your true player, a kind of confidence and ready tongue, even a swagger, which sets him apart from other men. This fellow was not merely small, like Master Wandesford, but somehow mean-looking. I had called his hair foxy from the ginger colour, but his face too was foxy – narrow and pointed, the eyes set too close together. He looked furtive. Those eyes never quite met yours, though the little I had heard of his speech sounded ingratiating.

Master Wandesford shrugged. 'He says that his name is John Stoker. Used to belong to Henslowe's company, he says, but more of a hanger-on than a player, I suspect. None of us ever saw him on the stage.'

'What is he doing here?'

'Trying to persuade Master Burbage to take him on as a player, but for the moment all he does is help maintain the playhouse, take the pennies at the door, move properties and costume hampers about, that sort. I'd not trust him, myself. He claims Henslowe owes him money. When he asked for it, Henslowe threw him out.'

'Hmph,' I said. 'Was it really Henslowe's players he belonged to? Not one of Henslowe's other businesses?'

Master Wandesford laughed. 'Aye, he'd be more at home touting for one of Henslowe's bawdy houses, or strangling injured dogs after a bear baiting.'

Stoker must somehow have sensed we were speaking about him, for he was too far away to have heard us. He gave us one quick speculative glance, then looked down at his plate again. I felt a shiver run up my spine. Wandesford was right. There was something definitely untrustworthy about the look of the man.

When everyone's hunger was satisfied and the ale jug had gone round several times, one of the pot boys brought a candle lantern out to light our table, for it had grown dusk. The light brought the insects of the night, who threw themselves against the horn windows of the lantern as if determined upon suicide. One beautiful large moth, silvery white with a dusting of brown like sprinkled cinnamon, returned again and again, before finally clinging to the lantern in a kind of hypnotised madness. I removed it once, carefully, and set it on a tendril of the rose bush behind me, but in a moment it was back again.

'Well, now, Kit,' Master Burbage said, stretching out his legs and nursing his tankard of ale, 'it is time to sing for your supper. Cuthbert and the other lads have told us of your adventures until they reached Wardhouse. What became of you afterwards, in that strange land?'

I had already given a formal account of my journey to the Governor of the Muscovy Company, and a rather more colourful one to Hector and Beatriz Nuñez, but I knew that amongst the players, who were not easily shocked, I could tell them everything, apart from those secret matters contained in Gregory's report. I must have talked for an hour, and for once I was the player, the others my audience. I found myself imitating the manners and speech of those I had encountered, recalling details I thought I had forgotten of my journeys by sleigh, my time in Moscow, and our last desperate ride through the forest. It was with difficulty that I spoke of little Tsarevich Dmitri, hardly able to keep my voice steady, and when I came to his death, I shook my head and had to stop speaking to steady myself. Guy, who was sitting beside me, refilled my tankard and patted me on the shoulder. Finally I reached the killing of Pyotr, and I shut my eyes, hearing again the thud of the crossbow bolt and Pyotr's last whispered words.

'So we came to Narva at last,' I finished briskly, 'where we were able to take ship back to London. I reached home three days ago.' Even as I spoke, the words seemed like a play or a story from a volume of old-fashioned romances. Sitting here in the garden of the inn, I felt that Muscovy and all that had happened there was taking on the aura of a dream.

On my other side, Will let out a sigh, as though he had been holding his breath.

For a moment they were every one of them silent, then they began to clap, as though we were indeed in a playhouse, and all my tale the words of a play.

'Bravo!' Master Burbage said. 'We shall make a play master of you yet, Kit.'

I shook my head. 'My story, sadly, is true. I could not make up a drama out of whole cloth.' I turned and smiled at Will.

Simon had been watching me closely all the while I had been speaking.

'But what is this new tail end to the story, Kit, which was unknown to you until this morning? You have left us aboard ship on the way home from Narva.'

I took a long drink of my ale. I had indeed let that news slip out before we left the playhouse. Now I was not certain that I wanted to announce my pitiful situation before the whole company, including the foxy faced John Stoker, but I saw no way to wriggle out of it now.

'Before we left London last year,' I said, 'the Governor of the Muscovy Company arranged for the nephew of his deputy, one Howard Wattis, to take over my duties at St Thomas's while I was away. He was to fill a position with the Archbishop of York this spring.'

Simon nodded. 'I remember. You were not happy about passing the work to an inexperienced student just down from Oxford, but an older doctor was to keep an eye on him till you returned to take up your duties.'

'Dr Colet. He died a few months ago, it seems, and Wattis has been on his own since then. The Archbishop no longer wants him.'

'No doubt he will find some other position,' Guy said comfortably, tipping his stool back and leaning against the side of the arbour.

'Indeed he has. The governors of the hospital have appointed him in my place. I am cast out.'

I tried very hard to keep my tone light, and not to sound too self-pitying, but I am not sure I succeeded.

Guy let his stool fall forward with a crash. Suddenly they all seemed to be talking at once.

'Cast out? But you were promised your position would be held for you! What are they thinking of? You are the best physician in the hospital!'

The voices blurred together and I felt my eyes prick at this warm tide of friendship and support.

'We must make them change their minds!' This was Dick, who looked ready to seize one of his player's mock swords and storm the hospital.

'Surely the governors will listen to reason.' Master Burbage's more measured tones.

'We could kidnap this Wattis, and carry him off!' Davy had sprung to his feet in his excitement, and seemed to want to set about it at once.

'Nay,' I said, shaking my head and smiling ruefully. 'There is nothing to be done. The governors have made an official appointment. To cancel it would humiliate them. They will not change their minds. I ask only that you keep your ears open for any position I might seek. Dr Nuñez is passing a few of his patients to me, but I fear it will not do more than keep Rikki and me in bread and small ale.'

Hearing his name, Rikki sat up under the table and laid his chin on my knee.

'And now that Sir Francis is gone, I no longer have my code-breaking work.'

With the players I maintained the fiction that all I had ever done in Sir Francis's service was code breaking, but they were not fools. Whatever they had suspected before, after sharing part of my journey to Muscovy with me, and hearing the full account tonight, they now knew otherwise. The man Stoker had said nothing, but I saw that he watched me out of the corner of those narrow eyes.

'You could join us as a musician,' Guy said, as I had known he would.

I smiled and patted his hand where it lay on the table between us.

'Nay, Guy,' I said. 'You know I have not the stomach to appear upon the public stage.'

'After what you have endured in Muscovy,' he said, 'the stage should hold few terrors for you.'

'But it does.'

I could not explain that, exposed on the bare boards of the playhouse, the cynosure of two thousand pairs of eyes, I was convinced my true identity would be revealed at last.

'Besides,' I added, 'I think these rich patients Dr Nuñez is bequeathing me would not care to see me in the playhouse. I shall have to maintain the dignity of a different profession from yours.'

'Aye, I know,' he said with a grimace, 'these grand folks believe us all to be rogues and vagabonds, though they are happy enough to sit in the Theatre and watch our performances.'

'That was not what I meant,' I said uncomfortably. 'I do not think you are rogues and vagabonds.'

'I know you do not.'

I looked around at them. 'I think you are doing something very worthy. Who would have thought, fifty years ago, that such fire and poetry would be spoken upon the public stage, which every poor man or woman in London can share for a penny? The world is changing. Who knows where it will take us, or where it will end?'

'Who indeed?' Will murmured softly. 'I thank you for that belief in what we do, Kit. All men are but players on the stage of life, and on the stage of the playhouse we try to put into words the lives of all men. Kings and emperors, true, but also the common man, *Everyman*, as the old play had it. I want to–' He broke off, and swigged the last of his ale.

I saw that his eyes glinted in the light from the lantern, and his hands were fiercely clenched about his tankard, however softly he spoke.

The following morning I decided I would visit St Bartholomew's hospital, to the west of the City, beside Smithfield. I had worked there as assistant to my father for five years and I knew they had thought well of me. If there were any places to fill, I thought my chances were good, though I would cost them more, now that I was a physician licensed by the Royal College. In my present need, I would have agreed to a lower salary, but I knew the College would not approve, for it would undermine the standing of other physicians.

I accepted Tom Read's offer to look after Rikki while I went to St Bartholomew's. There would have been changes and the old gatekeeper might no longer be there. He used to keep Rikki for me while I was working, as Tom had done at St Thomas's, although the Bart's doorkeeper had no dog of his own. I decided I must not pay for a wherry to take me up river, but it is a long walk from Southwark to Smithfield, though nothing to what I was used to in the past. However, in Muscovy I seemed always to have been on horseback or riding in a sleigh or a boat, so now before I had walked as far as Newgate my legs were aching with the unaccustomed exercise. Even though I had set out early, the sullen heat had begun to build up, so that I was sweating in my physician's gown by the time I reached Cheapside. I stopped at the Great Conduit. In weather like this I did not trust the water to drink, but I took off my physician's cap and plunged my head under the spout. I knew my hair, cut short again as soon as I had returned to London, would be dry before I arrived at the hospital.

The chestnut seller was not in his usual place near Newgate. Little wonder. No one would want hot food in the street today, and it would have been unbearable for him to stand over his brazier, even in the shadow of the grim prison. The whole building was silent. The poorest prisoners had not even scrambled to the grating to hold out their hands, pleading for food. The heat in the confined cells within must be a taste of Hell itself.

When I reached the great gatehouse of St Bartholomew's I stood for a moment to brace myself for the probable rejection I should encounter. Smithfield market had already been underway for some hours and the ground was littered with straw and dung. The lowing of cattle, the squawk of poultry, and the near human cries of sheep battered my ears, while my nose was assailed with the ammoniac stench of urine. When I had lived in Duck Lane, I must have grown so used to the noise and the smells that I hardly noticed them, but now I found them almost overpowering.

The gatehouse, built by old King Henry, was a substantial building and offered a few moments' shady respite. I paused, my hand on the cool, rough surface of the familiar brickwork. There was no sign of the gatekeeper. Probably he was dozing somewhere within his room, overcome by the heat. As I stepped out into the courtyard, I was relieved that the first person I saw crossing from the apothecaries' quarters to the main ward was Peter Lambert, the young apothecary who had been a close friend when I worked here.

'Peter!' As I hailed him, he stopped, turned on his heel, and hurried toward me, carefully carrying a flask of some medicament he must just have prepared.

'Why, Kit,' he said, managing a quick bow while still holding the flask cautiously in both hands. 'I heard that you were away in some foreign land.'

He looked truly pleased to see me.

I smiled gratefully. 'I was, in Muscovy, but I am back in London these three – nay, four – days now.'

'Muscovy? Isn't that where it snows all the time, and the rivers are frozen, and white bears eat men in their very homes?'

'Not quite,' I said. 'It snows a good deal in the winter, and the rivers freeze, but it is not so very unpleasant in summer. Unfortunately I never saw a white bear.'

'Fortunately, I should say!'

'Mayhap! How do you fare, Peter? I have not seen you these many months, not since before I went abroad. You must be married now.'

He smiled broadly and looked not a little pleased with himself. 'And I have a son, Kit. A great strapping lad, three months old.'

I had a strange sensation as Peter chattered on about the merits of this exceptional child. All the world seemed to have moved on and somehow left me behind. I remembered Peter as a scrawny boy when we had both come to Bart's. He was a servant then, until one of the apothecaries noticed his quick mind and

31

took him in hand. Now here he was, a married man and a father at one and twenty, while I was back where I had begun. Or not even there.

'Enough of my affairs,' Peter said. 'I must take this to the ward. There are several women with serious sunburn after working in the fields at the haysel. Are you come to visit us?'

I might as well discover what I could from Peter, before I ventured inside to confront the superintendent. Quickly I explained how I was now without a position, and had come to enquire whether one might be available at Bart's. Peter heard me out, exclaimed over the injustice of the governors of St Thomas's, but shook his head.

'Nay, Kit, there is nothing here. I would not waste your time. Dr Stevens – you remember old Dr Stevens? – well, he has left to live with his daughter in Middlesex. They have hired two new physicians to take over his work. That was but two weeks ago. And Dr Temperley, who took your father's place, he's still here, and his younger brother as his assistant. They'll not be taking on any more physicians, I'm thinking.'

'You are right,' I said, with a sinking heart. I had not truly expected anything else, but thought: *Had I but reached London two weeks earlier, I might have been one of the new physicians at St Bartholomew's.*

'If your salve is needed, Peter, I must not delay you.'

'Aye, I'd best go. Come and see us soon, come for dinner, Helen will be so glad, and you can meet my son.'

'Aye, that would be good,' I said, managing a smile and a bow as he turned away to the ward. But I would not go, I knew, not unless I had found work. I did not want to appear like some beggar, hoping for a free meal to fill my belly.

I stood a few moments longer in this place which had once been as much a home to me as the cottage in Duck Lane. As people crossed the courtyard I noticed a few familiar faces. Some of them bowed to me, and did not linger, for they were busy. I saw one man in a physician's gown, but he was a stranger.

I turned my back on St Bartholomew's and walked out into the noise and smells of Smithfield.

32

I could not accustom myself to being in London with no occupation, no work summoning me. It would be several days before Dr Nuñez could make the arrangements with some of his patients, to transfer their care to me. Then we would go together, to visit them, so that he might introduce me. I was still carrying the copy of Gregory's report in my satchel of medicines, where I had stored it weeks ago at the inn where we stayed just south of Moscow. I could not make up my mind what to do with it. Originally it had seemed quite simple. I would find Thomas Phelippes and either hand it over to him, or ask him where I should deliver it. I was uncertain what the Governor of the Muscovy Company intended to do with his copy.

But it seemed Phelippes now held some sort of clerical post at the Customs House, so perhaps he no longer dealt with the security of the state. I had also considered taking it instead to Lord Burghley. Two points argued against this. First, that might be where Governor Heyward intended to take his copy. In which case, I should look merely foolish, turning up with a second one, as if I expected a reward. And second, now I knew that Poley was working for the Cecils, I intended to stay well away from them.

In this state of indecision, I trudged back to my lodgings which, being high in the house, just below the garrets, had accumulated the heat of the rest of the house. I stripped off my gown and my heavy doublet and threw myself down on the bed, but I was restless, and soon sprang up again. I had a lightweight doublet which I donned over my shirt. I would fetch Rikki, then saddle up Hector and take him out for some exercise.

When I was raised up on horseback, the day did not feel so oppressive as it did down amongst those on foot, where tempers flared quickly. With Rikki keeping close beside us, I headed Hector out along Bishopsgate Street and through Bishopsgate itself. Like all the City's gates, it was beginning to crumble with age and neglect. How long since the City's walls and gates had been put in readiness for defence? Had the Spanish succeeded in landing their army on the south coast three years ago and marched to the capital as they had intended, it would have been impossible to hold even the heart of London against them. And now that the whole of London extended outside the walls, beyond this heart in the City itself, the invading army would have had no trouble in putting it to fire and sword.

Southwark was undefended. Westminster was undefended. And all along the north bank of the Thames, wherever the ground was not marshy or apt to flood, buildings had sprouted like mushrooms in a forest. I would swear London had grown even during the year I had been away. To the West, between the City and Westminster, the rich had been building their mansions for several generations. To the east, despite repeated regulations forbidding building, the shacks and hovels of the poor crowded together, housing the labourers in the shipyards and other industries which could not find space in the older parts of London.

Where I was headed, however, there were still open spaces. Past the great Dolphin Inn on the right and the Bedlam madhouse on the left, I continued north along Norton Folgate. Rikki paused at Hog Lane, expecting me to turn left for the Theatre, but I pressed on. After St Mary Spital the last houses dwindled away, except for the village of Shoreditch, with its handsome church of St Leonard. Here we were in true country at last, so I gave Hector his head and we galloped up the rising ground of Hackney Downs, his hooves thundering hollow on the dry earth. The breeze in my face was as refreshing as a splash of cold water.

On a little knoll there was a stand of trees, venerable oaks and chestnuts, interspersed with alder and rowan. I reined Hector in to a canter and then to a walk. As soon as we reached the trees, Rikki flopped down in the shade, panting.

'You are out of condition, my lad,' I said as I slid from Hector's back. 'You have been living the life of a lady's lapdog with Tom, your meals brought to you, only a yard or two to walk when you need to raise a leg.'

He looked at me enquiringly, so I tousled the rough hair on his head. I must take the scissors to him. Little wonder he was hot, with that thick coat. I removed Hector's bridle so he could graze and hung it on a branch. He was soon tearing at the juicier grass which lay out of the direct line of the sun, for much of the open turf was burnt yellow. He must be glad of the fresh fodder, for however well he was fed in the stable, it could not compare with grass growing on a country hillside.

I stretched out on the grass myself, just within the shade from the trees, but where I could look down on London below me. From here it appeared so tightly packed, the houses jostling each other cheek by jowl, it seemed there could be no room for the streets, no room for people to move about. Everywhere the spires of parish churches stabbed upwards, so that the city looked like a monstrous hedgehog crouched beside the Thames. Up here the air was clear, but a summer haze hung over the city, making it seem as insubstantial as a mirage.

Below this higher ground, between the Downs and the city, farmland stretched out to east and west. I could pick out the hay meadows, reduced to stubble now, where sheep and cattle had been turned out to graze. The sweet perfume of cut hay still filled the air, rising up to my perch like incense in a church. Surely the scent of hay is one of Nature's most blessed. It seems to hold the essence of summer. The fields of corn – wheat and barley and some oats – were already golden. They would be harvested soon, a month early at the least. This would be one year without famine. Weather was so unpredictable. Two or three years of bad harvests and the poor starved. Wasn't there some story in the Bible? About storing food for the lean years? Yet even in the good years there never seemed to be crops abundant enough to store in case of future need. London grew and grew, inexorably, with more and more mouths to feed, many incomers turned out of their country livings by landowners who saw more profit in sheep. Surely this must mean that the supply of food would be shrinking, even as the number of hungry townsmen was growing?

I pulled my satchel on to my lap and unbuckled it. On my way to fetch Hector I had bought a penny loaf, a lump of very hard cheese, and a handful of raisins. I had also begged a bone for Rikki from the butcher near St Thomas's, whose son I had once treated for eczema. Rikki fell upon the bone as if he was starving, although I knew very well that Tom would have fed him with kitchen scraps.

Remembering the butcher's son reminded me of Xenia, Godunov's daughter. The butcher had shown more sense, bringing his son to the hospital, than the grand folk who had Xenia in their care. I hoped she was still able to treat her own skin as I had taught her.

I shook myself. Muscovy belonged to the past. I must forget it, for there was nothing more I could do for those left behind there. I must confront the future. Hanging from my belt was the small knife I used for eating. I drew it out and scraped the mould from the piece of cheese. It was like scraping sandstone. The cheese would need to be chopped into small pieces or my teeth would make no impression on it. However, with my limited means now, I should need to become accustomed to poor fare. At least the bread was soft and fresh, and raisins are raisins, when all is said and done.

When I had finished my frugal meal, I lay back on the grass and looked up at the sky through the twigs which reached out over me. The leaves seemed limp from the heat and the lack of rain. Would that mean that the colours of autumn would come sooner? It has always puzzled me, that when you lie like this, staring up at the sky, the world seems to turn beneath you. Learned men had been arguing for years about the shape of the world and the nature of the universe. Men like Drake had proved for ever that the world was a round ball – you could sail east and return from the west. But the dispute was still fierce between laymen who swore that the sun was the centre of the universe, with our world moving around it, while churchmen fought a retreating action, maintaining that God had made this earth the centre of everything when he created the universe.

But, nay, it was too hot to ponder such arguments. I must think about my future.

Dr Nuñez had said my earnings from his patients would be barely half my previous salary from St Thomas's. Could I live on that? Before I gained my licence, I had lived on less, though not as little as half. I still had about two-thirds of the money from the Muscovy Company. I had an adequate supply of clothes, for I had no need to be fashionable, merely clean and professional. I must earn enough to feed Rikki and myself, and buy fuel for my fire when it grew really cold in winter. I could probably share a fire with Simon for part of the time, for the players were often on short rations in the winter when the playhouses were closed, unless they were able to use an inn as a playhouse, as they had done the winter before last.

My thoughts were straying. My father and I had always lived on tight rations, for we earned little enough. We had to eat, pay our maidservant, and keep warm in winter. Besides, we had carefully put aside money for the future, money which my father had gambled and lost on the Portuguese expedition. That was the fault of Ruy Lopez, fellow Marrano and physician to the Queen, who had persuaded him to invest in that misguided scheme. I knew Sara Lopez would help me, but she had rescued me before and I was loathe to go a-begging again.

Nay, I would rather eat mouldy cheese, and buy the overripe fruit and vegetables which the stallholders sold cheap at the end of the day. Somehow I would manage. I would have to.

Chapter Three

*T*he rest of that week was occupied in being introduced to Dr Nuñez's patients, who were now to become my responsibility. There were four families who lived in the large merchant houses along Cheapside, three of them goldsmiths, one a mercer. There was another mercer who had done well for himself, served as a Sheriff of the City, and built a house just off the north side of the Strand. Not quite rubbing shoulders with the great aristocratic mansions on the river side of the Strand, but certainly grand enough. There was the minor lord of a small manor out toward Windsor, but we would visit him later. That family was rarely ill, Dr Nuñez told me, which he attributed to the better quality of the air away from London. It would take us an entire day, riding there and back, and I believed he was reluctant to risk his own health while the heat lasted.

I had often wondered that the prosperous merchants, some of them the most powerful men in London, continued to live in Cheapside. In times past, these houses had held shops at the front, opening on to the street, with perhaps workshops behind, and the family's living quarters above. With the passing of the years, Cheapside, the street itself, had become one vast market of stalls and ramshackle booths, selling everything from buttons to poultry. Bleeding carcasses were brought here straight from the shambles near Smithfield, to lie amongst the flies and dust until, piece by piece, they were hacked up to be sold. The great merchants of Cheapside, who had prospered under the Queen, as London had prospered, mostly now did their business elsewhere, or through lesser men, and their houses had been enlarged and embellished, but the fact remained that they overlooked the grubby throng that was Cheapside.

I had never been inside one of these houses until I was taken there by Dr Nuñez, when I discovered that they were not as unpleasant as I had imagined.

'My dear Dr Nuñez,' Mistress Dolesby said, at the first house we visited, 'you must take a glass of wine with me in the arbour, you and young Dr Alvarez.'

She led us out of a grand door at the back of the house, which opened on to a terrace of turf, then down a flight of shallow steps into the garden.

'I am afraid that my poor garden is suffering with this intolerable heat,' she said, motioning at a maidservant to follow us with her tray. 'The gardeners do their best, watering twice a day, but it is scarcely enough.'

Gardeners? I thought. More than one? And as I looked about, I understood why, for the garden was vast. No need to look out toward Cheapside, when you had this refuge at the back of the house. There were large trees established many years, giving grateful shade, an ornamental knot garden planted with herbs (the enclosing low hedges must require constant pruning), a wide lawn laid out for bowls, and an orchard of fruit trees. Beyond the orchard a hedge discreetly concealed what I expected was the kitchen garden. Ruy Lopez had a large garden behind his house, but it was not as elegant as this. The orchard trees here were heavy with fruit, but I did not venture close enough to see whether they had been affected by the drought. Beside the orchard I could see the low brick wall surrounding a private well.

So the gardeners watered twice a day. I thought of the many London poor who could not even afford small ale and must risk their lives drinking tainted water. How much they would benefit from access to a well of pure water which was being lavished on plants, which would have benefited equally from river water.

'This way,' Mistress Dolesby said, tripping neatly across the end of the bowling lawn to an arbour the size of a small cottage.

Like the modest arbour at the Green Dragon, this was smothered in roses, which were flourishing this year, but it was also framed by two apricot trees in large glazed earthenware pots and a host of other flowering plants. Within the shady arbour was a marble table and some beautifully carved oak chairs which could not possibly live permanently outdoors. The servants, I supposed, must carry them in and out every day.

The maidservant set out delicate Venetian glasses and a jug filled with a golden wine. There were a dozen plates of tiny cakes and biscuits, ornamented with strawberries nestling in their leaves and with some variety of rare early apples carved into the shape of roses. My mouth began to water and I sat on my hands to stop myself reaching for the food. I had not eaten that day.

I made polite responses when I was addressed, but most of the conversation was between Mistress Dolesby and Dr Nuñez. With the heat and the wine and the food, not to mention a rather dull conversation, I was beginning to find difficulty in keeping my eyes open, until Mistress Dolesby's three children were brought out into the garden to be inspected. There were two little girls of eight and six, and a sturdy little boy of four. To be quite honest, he was more than sturdy. He was fat.

After Mistress Dolesby had praised her 'little angels' and Dr Nuñez had politely seconded her, I roused myself enough to examine them properly. All three had complexions the colour of uncooked pastry, the girls looked cross, the boy about as lively as a cow chewing the cud.

I ventured to speak. 'The children are too warmly dressed for this weather, Mistress,' I said, determined to be bold and establish my authority here. 'Have they nothing to wear in lightweight linen? And I suspect that they spend most of their time indoors, do they not?'

'Indeed.' She smiled complacently. 'The girls at their needlework, little Jonathan with his tutor.'

I shook my head firmly. 'Not in this weather. Their humours will become unbalanced.'

This woman would possess no knowledge of medicine and health beyond the most simplistic popular theories. I would use that as my reason.

'I must insist, for their health's sake,' I continued firmly, 'that while this intolerable weather continues, they should wear

40

cool garments only and spend most of the daylight hours out of doors in the fresh air, not cooped up indoors like hothouse plants. You have this beautiful garden – let them play out here.'

She looked at me in astonishment. 'But my girls will turn quite brown, like peasants!'

'Let them wear straw hats,' I said. 'I am sure the girls will have the good sense to stay out of the heat. It is shady here in the arbour, and there, under the trees. Even in the orchard. And they can keep a watch on their little brother. I am sure he needs to run about more.'

I was being as tactful as possible. I did not point out that the child was already developing a double chin, like a prosperous burgher in his middle years.

It was clear that I was not to be believed on my own account.

'What do you think, Dr Nuñez?' she said, casting a dubious look in my direction.

'My dear Mistress Dolesby,' he said, taking her hand to emphasise his point, 'Dr Alvarez is well known as especially gifted in the treatment of children. Perhaps you have not heard? He has just returned from Muscovy where he physicked not only the daughter of the most powerful man in the country, Boris Godunov, but the younger brother of the Tsar and heir to the throne, Prince Dmitri. You will be exceptionally fortunate, and the envy of all your friends, to be able to say that your children are in the care of a royal physician.'

He made no mention of Dmitri's murder, nor that I had left Muscovy fleeing for my life. However, this speech clearly impressed the lady and she looked at me with quite a different expression in her eyes.

'Very well,' she said, 'if that is Dr Alvarez's advice. Bet, take the children inside and dress them as the doctor suggests, then bring them out to play in the garden.'

Her tongue stumbled a little over the word 'play', as if it were a concept with which she was unfamiliar. However, the two little girls gave me such looks of intense gratitude that I could not forebear smiling back.

As it proved, our visits to the other households followed much the same pattern. We encountered only one of the husbands. On the afternoon when we visited one of the other goldsmith's households, Master Eastfield himself received us, his wife being prostrate with the heat. It seemed that word of my royal connections had now gone before me, for gossip flows through London like streams through a meadow.

'Heard you advise that the children should be out in the garden during this summer weather,' he said briskly. 'No time for idleness myself, but see no harm in it for the young. Still remember my time as a lad. Used to steal away from my tutor when I could and go fishing in the river, or rabbiting in Finsbury Fields.'

He laughed and rubbed his hands together. I found I liked him, despite the ostentation of his home and the array of rings on his fingers.

All this augured well for my acceptance amongst Dr Nuñez's patients. From my observations, however, they seemed on the whole to be strong and healthy, and so unlikely to provide me with much income, were I to think of them as a replacement for my hospital work. My only requirement as a physician on these first introductions was a visit to Mistress Eastfield, laid so low by the heat. As she was tightly laced into a bodice much too small for her buxom form, I prescribed a loose gown and supplied a lotion of witch-hazel to bathe her face and hands.

'No heavy wines while this heat lasts,' I said. 'Only small ale. And I will explain to your cook how to make a cooling drink from berries. You will find it refreshing and wholesome.'

The idea of wholesome fare seemed to puzzle her somewhat, for to these merchant families, rising in importance and sometimes marrying into the gentry, food and drink was a weapon of social prestige. However, when I called on her the following day, she was quite recovered and truly grateful.

'I have suffered with such terrible headaches, Dr Alvarez,' she said, 'ever since this heat began. Today is the first time I have been free of them.'

I provided her with tonic of feverfew, to be taken as soon as she felt the first sign of another such headache. It is but an old wives' remedy, but very efficacious. I named the fee recommended by Dr Nuñez, which seemed exorbitant to me for so little physicking, but she paid it happily, instructing her steward to remunerate me in coin at once. This was a relief, for I feared I might need to send in a bill and wait a long time for payment. The money would add to my small hoard which I counted over every night, wondering how long it would last.

When I mentioned to Dr Nuñez that I had been paid at once, he smiled.

'Not all of my patients are so obliging, Kit, but I know you are in no position to wait for payment. I have selected those I know will not be dilatory.'

'But . . . you are keeping for yourself the neglectful?'

'I have a comfortable cushion of coin in my business interests,' he said. 'They all pay in the end. I would not continue to physic any who failed to pay their just accounts.'

'Don your best doublet and hose,' Simon said, catching me on the stairs of our lodgings that afternoon. 'You are bid to dinner at the Green Dragon.'

I had been sitting, idle and gloomy, in my room since returning from Dr Nuñez, until Rikki demanded a walk. Now I was plodding back upstairs, wondering how I could occupy myself for the rest of the day.

'Again?' I said in astonishment. 'I have recounted all my adventures. There is no more to tell. Master Burbage has no need to pay me for entertainment in kind.'

'It is not Master Burbage who invites you,' he said, his eyes gleaming. 'It is the Lord Chamberlain, Lord Hunsdon himself.'

'Do no be foolish, Simon. Lord Hunsdon does not know me, has never heard of me. Why should he invite me to dine?'

I protested loudly, though one corner of my mind considered that he *might* have heard of me. My work for Sir Francis was not unknown to some of the high officials of the Court. Besides, he might have interests in the Muscovy Company.

'Well, he has not exactly invited you personally,' Simon admitted, 'but he has invited the entire company, and Master Burbage told me to include you.'

'That was kind of him,' I said, a little stiffly.

I could recognise charity when I saw it. I had only once been a temporary member of the company, when their performance was used as cover for me. It had enabled me to come close to an assassin bent on making an attempt on the Queen's life, an attempt which Phelippes knew was to take place during the Twelfth Night Revels. Still, it was kind of Master Burbage, to ensure me another good meal. I must make better use of it this time.

'Hurry,' Simon said impatiently, following me into my room.

I peeled off my physician's gown, which became more intolerable every day that the heat continued.

'I am wearing my best doublet and hose,' I objected. 'I have been visiting one of my new patients.'

'Very well. Come, then. You need not bring that battered old satchel.'

I suppose my medicine satchel did look somewhat battered, for I had owned it ever since I had begun working with my father and it had seen some rough usage, especially in the last year.

'I am sorry if it embarrasses you,' I said with a grim smile, 'but I go nowhere without it. You know that.'

'Oh, very well. But try to keep it out of sight.'

'What about Rikki?' I had taken him with me to see Dr Nuñez earlier and since we had returned from his walk he was pushing his empty dish along the floor in a rather pointed manner.

'You will need to leave him behind. He won't mind staying here.'

'I suppose not.' I broke up some stale bread into Rikki's dish and added the last of some meat broth which was to have been my frugal supper. He fell on it eagerly. I feared he was missing the ample meals he enjoyed during my year away, supplied by Tom Read from the hospital kitchens.

44

Leaving Rikki in my room, we clattered down the stairs and were soon hurrying across the Bridge, heading north for Bishopsgate Street.

'Why is Lord Hunsdon entertaining the players to dinner?' I asked. 'Is he still hoping to persuade Master Burbage to leave the patronage of Lord Strange?'

Simon shrugged. 'Who can say? Master Burbage would not wish to offend Lord Strange. Perhaps Lord Hunsdon has not taken his measure yet.'

When we reached the Green Dragon, we saw that far more sumptuous preparations had been made for this dinner. An awning had been erected in the garden and a large table laid out with starched white table linen. The glasses were as fine as those at Mistress Dolesby's house, and I wondered whether the inn owned them, bringing them out for very distinguished guests, or whether they had been obliged to borrow them. Instead of benches and stools, cushioned chairs had been arranged around the table. Bowls of scented herbs and rose petals were placed amongst the fine dishes, which included finger bowls of cool water garnished with mint and lemon slices for the guests to rinse greasy fingers. I realised that Simon was right. My rubbed and stained satchel was grossly out of place, so I hid it down at the side of the arbour.

Most of the players were already here, clustered in a nervous group in the garden, although Master Burbage remained at the door of the inn to greet the Lord Chamberlain. I saw the new man, Stoker, lurking furtively at the back of the group. It seemed he was hardly welcome amongst them. As I joined the players I greeted Master Wandesford, who was wiping his face with a large silk handkerchief, looking rather drawn. He staggered and put out a hand against a stunted apple tree to steady himself. I noticed that the pupils of his eyes were much enlarged.

'Are you quite well?' I said.

He was having difficulty breathing and seemed to be sweating more even than the heat of the day warranted. He shook his head.

'This heat disagrees with me. My stomach has troubled me all this week past and I am in no mood for a vast meal, but

45

Master Burbage felt we should be here, everyone, to show courtesy to Lord Hunsdon. I have felt dizzy and drowsy too. And my sight has been blurred, so that I have had difficulty copying the players' parts. I hope I may not disgrace you all by falling asleep at table.'

His speech was somewhat slurred, unusual in a man who drank little, and he ran his tongue over dry, cracked lips.

'It may be the weather,' I said sympathetically, 'or it may be that you have eaten something tainted by the heat. If you wish, I will visit you tomorrow and we will see what can be done to relieve you.'

He gave me a grateful, but shaky, smile. 'That would be a kindness, Kit. I have had odd pains and flutterings in my chest as well, which has worried me, I must confess.'

At this point we were interrupted by the entrance of Lord Hunsdon, accompanied by Master Burbage and followed by Aemilia Bassano and two gentleman servants who fussed over the table and the inn's arrangements.

Before long we were seated, Lord Hunsdon at the centre of the long table, next to Master Burbage, the rest of us arranged on both sides. I took a place near the end, feeling that it was not for me to sit too near the great man. To my surprise, instead of taking the other chair next to her patron, Mistress Bassano sat almost opposite me, next to Will and opposite Simon.

Perhaps noticing my look of surprise, she laughed. 'I have enough of the conversation of great lords every day. I am far more interested in this company of players and what you have to say for yourselves.'

That was enough to freeze tongues temporarily, but we soon relaxed after Guy, sitting on her other side, had teased her a little about her family and talked of a new motet he had bought. They were soon engrossed in talk of music, drawing the rest of us in, for although Guy was the principal musician, all of the players could play an instrument or two, when needed, just as they could perform dances as complex as any at Court.

I saw Will once again eyeing Mistress Bassano thoughtfully, but despite his occasional wildness and his fondness for dalliance, I hoped he knew better than to try to seduce the Lord Chamberlain's mistress.

From the start, I liked and admired Aemilia Bassano for her independence and her scorn of gossip. Somehow – I am not sure how – we had moved on from music to the part women must play in society.

'A woman,' she said, pointing an admonitory finger at me, 'has an intellect as good as any man. She can be as fine a scholar – observe the Queen, one of the greatest scholars of our age and a gifted linguist. We can compose or paint or write as well as any man, did the men not stand in our way and mock us.'

I saw that Simon was watching us with amusement, as we sat around over the Golden Dragon's sumptuous fare, eating forgotten in the enthusiasm of our discussion.

'Ah,' said he, 'but Kit's former tutor, Dr Harriot, would swear that no woman can understand mathematics or astronomy.'

Aemilia opened her mouth to protest, but I forestalled her.

'I agree with you Mistress Bassano. And I do not agree with Dr Harriot, on this point at least.'

She was clearly surprised at this answer.

'You believe women can be scholars and writers?'

'Why not?'

'It is good to hear that from the lips of a man. Someday,' she said quietly, 'I shall publish a book of my own, of my poems.' She gave me a shrewd and somewhat disconcerting glance.

'I should be glad to read it,' I said. I wondered what she would think, were I to reveal my secret to her. She would probably urge me to continue to practise as a physician, even openly as a woman.

Will was watching us with that look of his, keen as a hunting hawk. Sometimes his eyelids would fall heavily over his eyes, shielding his expression, then that bright glance would dart forth again, sudden as a rapier. I also found that disturbing, as if I were being stripped naked.

'It would make an excellent subject for a play,' he said, 'an academy of learned women, who perhaps have forsworn the company of men.'

Aemilia looked at him somewhat belligerently. 'I suppose you would write a comedy of it, and make us a mockery for the groundlings.'

He smiled thoughtfully. 'I would never make a mockery of you, mistress. And, true, it would be a comedy, in that a comedy begins when something is awry in the world and ends when a balance is restored. From chaos to order. Indeed, it would be a world in chaos if love were denied, but love and learned women can surely live together, can they not?'

I saw Aemilia blush at that, and thought again that Will must be careful.

'And Kit,' he said, 'I might bring in a few Muscovites, in your honour.'

I laughed. 'I'll wager you cannot manage it. An academy of learned women, *and* Muscovites? I think that would stretch credulity too far.'

Afterwards, I would ponder long and hard on what Aemilia had said. Spending time in her company as I came to know her better in later months, I longed to have her freedom and her assurance that she had the right to be both a woman and a person of talent and learning. To my discomfort, I even envied her beautiful clothes. Would I ever have the courage to cast aside my male disguise and live again as a woman? I would have to sacrifice much, but could I find the kind of freedom she had? One thing was certain. I was known to too many dangerous men in London. If I were to carve out a new future as a woman, I would have to leave.

Our discussion of the position of women moved on to discussion of the company's new plays, several of which had been written by Will. I caught the admiration in Aemilia's eyes as she spoke of his gift for poetry and sensed that Will was responding with more than usual warmth.

The inn's maidservants, more smartly dressed than usual, cleared away the broken meats and greasy dishes. Then the innkeeper himself appeared, lit on his way by two pot boys carrying flambeaux, which streamed out behind them in the dark like the tails of comets. The innkeeper bore on high a vast platter, on which stood a castle all made of sugar, which glittered in the light of the flames like hoar frost under a winter sun. We all gasped in admiration. The castle appeared to stand on a rocky crag, and affixed to the side of it was a flat disc of sugar paste, delicately painted with Lord Hunsdon's arms. We burst into spontaneous applause.

'Aemilia my love,' Lord Hunsdon called down the table to her, 'the honour of breaching my fortress falls to you. Come, and do your duty.'

She rose, shaking out her skirts, and went obediently to his side. So, I thought, she has not so much freedom after all. Not as much freedom as I, if the truth be told. When the man who owns her calls, she must obey.

'It seems a shame to spoil it,' she said. 'Someone has expended much time and artistry to make this.' She smiled across the table at the innkeeper. 'Was it made here at the Green Dragon?'

'Nay, my lady.' The innkeeper looked confused, uncertain how to address her. 'We have no such skills here. It was made by a confectioner in Petty France. One of those Huguenot refugees from Paris.'

'Then please convey our thanks and admiration to him – or her. Is it a man or a woman who has such talent?'

'It is a woman.' He looked even more uncomfortable. 'I understand she was trained in the royal household in Paris before the family fled to England.'

'I thought I detected a woman's delicate handiwork.' She flashed a smile down toward our end of the table before she began carefully to demolish the exquisite edifice, passing portions to a maidservant who carried them to the guests in turn.

The maid had just reached Guy, with a plate containing a small sugar turret, when there was a curious sound from the far end of the table, a groan which ended in a sharp cry. Everyone stopped speaking and looked in that direction, but the end of the table, being beyond the light of the flambeaux, was in deep shadow.

'What's amiss?' Master Burbage called sharply.

'I'm not sure, Father.' It was Cuthbert. 'I think Master Wandesford has been taken ill.'

There was another cry, then a crash and a tinkle of broken glass. One of the precious Venetian goblets, I thought.

'Kit!' Cuthbert's voice was urgent. 'I think you are needed.'

I sprang from my chair and retrieved my satchel before running to the far end of the table.

'Light!' I said, 'bring those torches nearer so that we can see what is amiss.'

As the pot boys hurried after me, the scene became clear. Master Wandesford was slumped in his chair, the upper part of his body sprawled across the table. One arm, thrashing about, had smashed two glasses and the fragments glinted in the light from the flames. A stinking pool of vomit lay amongst the plates of sugar confectionery and his neighbours had drawn away from him in disgust. He was convulsing and moaning.

I grabbed one of the damask table napkins and lifted his face from the pool of vomit so that I could wipe his mouth and nose clear. His breathing was laboured and shallow. When I felt the pulse in his neck, I detected a racing heartbeat.

He was trying to speak, so I leaned over, my ear as close to his mouth as possible. His lips, I saw, were turning blue.

'In. My. Glass,' he said. 'Tasted it . . . before. Sweet but nasty.'

'Which is Master Wandesford's glass?' I demanded of Cuthbert.

He pointed to one which had escaped breakage. There was perhaps half an inch of wine left in it. I sniffed it, then set it down again.

'Get me a clean glass,' I told the maid. 'Anything, not this fine glassware. Anything, as long as it is clean.'

She ran off.

Simon had appeared at my side. 'Keep his head out of the vomit,' I said, 'while I mix a vomitive. He has brought some of it up, but–' I let me voice trail away.

Working as quickly as I could, I added the familiar ingredients to the pewter cup the girl handed me – *eupatorium cannabium*, *sambucus nigra* and *viola tricolor*, all purgative and emetic, together with *salvia officinalis* to ease his throat. Then I stirred in fresh wine. I helped myself without a word to the jug that stood between Lord Hunsdon and Master Burbage. This, at least, should be safe.

'Now, you must drink this,' I told Master Wandesford. 'It will not be pleasant, but we must empty your stomach of anything that is left there.'

He tried valiantly to swallow, but I knew from the blue tint under his staring eyes and around his lips that I was losing him. Simon met my glance over the man's head. I knew that he was thinking, as I was, of the day we had met and I had treated the man Poley with this same vomitive.

'You said you had tasted it before,' I said. 'In the wine, was it?' I took the cup away from Wandesford's mouth. He had managed barely a sip of the mixture, for the muscles of his throat were knotted. He could not swallow. In the light from the flambeaux, I could see that the pupils of his eyes were hugely dilated.

He moved his head slightly in an attempt to nod. 'In the wine,' he whispered. Then he was gone.

I let Simon take the weight of Wandesford's body, while I picked up his glass and sniffed the contents again. Then, gingerly, I dipped the tip of my finger in the contents, and touched it to my tongue. There was a tingling sensation, even from that tiny drop, and a curious sickly sweetness. I turned aside and spat the saliva from my mouth on to the grass, but the taste lingered.

Wandesford said he had tasted it before. Then why had he not avoided it? For this time the dose must have been stronger, to prove fatal. Someone had been slipping it to him, during the week he had been feeling ill. Stomach cramps, drowsiness, staggering, palpitations, and enlarged pupils.

Most of the players had gathered around, though some kept their distance, looking queasy.

Master Burbage pressed forward and, to my surprise, I saw that Lord Hunsdon was beside him. I had thought he would withdraw from such an unpleasant scene.

'Is he–?' Master Burbage cleared his throat. 'Is he dead?'

'Aye,' I said briefly.

51

'Poor fellow. He has not been well these several days past, but we did not realise it was serious. Was it his heart, do you suppose?'

Here was a dilemma. I was not sure I wanted to announce what I had discovered to the whole company, including the young boys and our distinguished host.

'He was certainly suffering from palpitations of the heart.' I chose my words carefully.

Master Burbage turned to the innkeeper, who was looking shocked. I realised he must fear something in the dinner might have killed Wandesford, and was glad I had kept my tongue behind my teeth.

'Have you an outbuilding where we may lay the poor soul,' Master Burbage said, 'until I can arrange for him to be taken to his parish church, St Botolph's?'

'Indeed, indeed!' The innkeeper could not hasten fast enough to assist. 'There is a shed next to the one where we keep the ale barrels, quite clean. Come, lads, light the way.'

As I packed my satchel, Guy and Christopher lifted Wandesford's body between them and followed the pot boys into a courtyard beside the inn. I found an empty phial in my satchel and carefully poured the remains of Wandesford's wine into it. Looking up as I corked it and sealed it with wax, I saw Simon and Will watching me. Everyone else had drifted away, whispering amongst themselves. Master Burbage, Lord Hunsdon, Aemilia Bassano, and their two menservants were walking back into the inn.

'So,' said Simon. 'Not heart failure, then?'

I looked from him to Will. I could trust them to hold their tongues.

'*Atropa belladonna*,' I said. 'Deadly nightshade. Master Wandesford was poisoned.'

Chapter Four

An hour or so later, Simon, Will, and I were sitting in Simon's room, Rikki sprawled on the floor at my feet. Simon had flung open the window to let out the stale air, although the air that drifted in from outside was hardly fresher, carrying with it, for some reason, a strong scent of onions. We could hear raucous laughter and badly played hurdy-gurdy music coming from the whorehouse just along the road. Bessie Travis, who kept the house, had recently been given the hurdy-gurdy in lieu of cash payment by one of her clients and was determined to learn how to play it. All her neighbours were suffering.

'How do you know Wandesford was poisoned?' Will asked. 'Could it not have been a simple heart attack?'

Simon paused in pouring out ale for us and raised his eyebrows questioningly. He had been with me all those years ago when I had immediately and correctly diagnosed that Robert Poley, at the time an inmate of the Marshalsea prison, was suffering from food poisoning, having eaten bad oysters.

'I know of an attempt to use *belladonna* to poison the Earl of Leicester,' I said, 'though fortunately it was unsuccessful. However, I have seen a death from *belladonna* before.'

It was an unpleasant memory.

'When I worked with my father at St Bartholomew's,' I said, 'a little boy was brought into the hospital. He would have been about five or six, I suppose. He had all the same symptoms – staggering, grossly enlarged pupils, slurred speech, raised heart beat, difficulty breathing. He kept crying out that snakes were crawling up his legs. Then he went into violent convulsions. We fought hard to save him, but we failed.'

I turned away from them. I could still see that child, the terrible fear on his face.

'His right hand was tightly clenched on something. After he died, my father managed to prise his fingers apart and found several *belladonna* berries. He had already said that he had suspected that was the cause. This confirmed it. He had seen a few cases of the poisoning before, in Portugal. Deadly nightshade grows everywhere in Europe, and every part of it is poisonous. The root is the most virulent, but not something you might consume by accident. Even a single leaf can kill an adult. The berries are particularly dangerous, because to a child they look like blackcurrants. They even have a sweetish taste.'

I looked down at the finger I had dipped in the poisoned wine. As soon as we reached Simon's room I had washed it thoroughly, but it still felt tainted.

'My father had me touch a tiny fragment of a crushed berry to my tongue, so that I would recognise it. The taste is unmistakeable. It is there. In that.'

I gestured toward the phial containing the dregs of Wandesford's wine, where it stood on the table between us. We all looked at it.

'But the rest of us drank the wine with no harm,' Simon said.

I nodded.

'So somehow the *belladonna* was slipped into Wandesford's glass alone, sometime during the meal.' Will looked at me.

I nodded again.

'Which part of the plant would it have been?'

'Probably neither root nor leaf,' I said. 'They would have left fragments in the wine, and there are none. It must have been juice from the berries. There will be berries on the plants now, at this time of year. They are probably growing all over London, wherever there is waste ground.'

'It was dark, down at that end of the table,' Simon said, 'so it would have been fairly easy to slip something into his glass. Who else was sitting there?'

We racked our brains.

'I think all the boys were there,' Will said slowly. 'Master Burbage wanted them well away from Lord Hunsdon, lest they got up to mischief.'

'Aye, you are right,' I said. 'And Cuthbert was there too, because he was the first to notice that Master Wandesford was ill. He called me to come to him.'

'He must have been sitting next to Wandesford,' Simon said.

I closed my eyes and tried to visualise who had been sitting there.

'Nay,' I said, 'Cuthbert was not next to him, he was nearer to his father. There was an empty chair between him and Master Wandesford. The trouble is, by the time I reached them, the glasses were smashed and Wandesford had vomited. People had drawn back, out of the way.'

I shook my head, trying to remember. 'Certainly Cuthbert was there, and several of the lads, and that new man, Stoker, and Christopher. And the doorkeeper.'

'Pillings,' Simon said.

'Aye, Pillings.'

'You do not suppose,' Will said slowly, 'that one of the lads, or several of them, did it for a prank? Not realising how serious it would be? I saw Wandesford box Davy's ears the other day, for turning cartwheels near his table and knocking ink all over the parts he had just copied.'

I felt a moment's panic, for I was responsible for finding Davy his place in the company. Then I shook my head.

'I do not think so. This was not the first time that Wandesford had been given *belladonna*. If the boys were playing a prank, it would surely only have been tonight.'

They both stared at me.

'What do you mean?' Simon asked.

'I spoke to Master Wandesford briefly before the meal,' I said, 'and he was already showing signs of the effects of the poison. He told me he had been suffering all week. Then just before he died, he said more.'

'He spoke before he died!' Will exclaimed. 'I thought he was past speech.'

'He was, very nearly. He was losing control of the muscles of his throat and mouth. But he managed to say that he had tasted it before, whatever was in the wine. He must have meant the taste of the *belladonna*. As I said, it is very distinctive, but unless you recognised it, you would not immediately think it was poison.'

'What you mean,' Simon said slowly, 'is that someone has been trying to poison him over several days.'

'That is what I suspect. Whoever did it must have used small quantities earlier, perhaps thinking that a larger quantity would be detected from the taste, however he administered it, in food or drink. It is so lethal, he must have used very small quantities indeed, or Wandesford would have been dead before now. Then tonight the–' I hesitated. 'The killer increased the dose, and it was fatal.'

'It *must* have been added to his glass during the meal,' Will said.

'It must. Probably not until it was getting quite dark. I'm sure that would not have been the first glass Wandesford drank. Another symptom is a very dry mouth. I noticed that his lips were dry and cracked. He would have been thirsty.'

'Why is it called *belladonna*?' Simon said. 'It seems an inappropriate name, "beautiful woman", for something so deadly.'

I smiled bitterly. 'Fashionable women put drops of the tincture into their eyes because it enlarges the pupils. I have to say, if they look anything like Wandesford's eyes, it must give them the appearance of a toad.'

They both laughed, though uncomfortably.

'It is not entirely an evil herb,' I said. 'It has certain valuable uses outside the body, but never, ever, to be taken internally.'

'What I do not understand,' Will said, 'is why anyone should want to hurt poor Wandesford, let alone to kill him. He has always seemed a harmless old fellow to me. You have known him longer than I, Simon. Had he any enemies?'

Simon shrugged. 'None that I ever heard of. He was already with the company when I joined as a boy actor, straight from Paul's school. All I know is that he was once a clergyman. Why he ceased to be one, I do not know. There have been whispers that he did not choose to leave but was unfrocked for some misdeed. That's nothing but rumour. I cannot imagine that he did anything very terrible, a quiet little man as he was. Like you, I have always thought him harmless. Guy might know more, he was already in the company when Wandesford joined.'

'If the reason for killing him does not lie in the past, it must lie in the present,' Will said. 'But what could he possibly have done to make someone want to kill him?'

'There, I cannot help you,' I said. 'I am quite certain *what* killed him and *how* it was administered, and we are sure *when*, but *why* or *who* I have no idea. I barely knew the man.'

They both looked baffled.

'I will talk to Guy in the morning,' Simon said. 'He probably knew Wandesford better than most of us. They have both been with the company a long time, back when Cuthbert and Dick and Christopher and I were still boys. And I doubt Master Burbage ever knew him well.'

'Aye, that's a good plan,' Will said. 'I might have a word with his landlady, to see if she knows anything about his life outside the playhouse. His lodgings are not far from my new place.'

'Did he have a life outside the playhouse?' Simon got up to fetch us more ale. I shook my head, but Will held out his tankard. 'I always felt he was alone, with no one – no family, no friends but for Burbage's company.'

'What I do not know,' I said, 'is whether there will be a coroner's inquest. What is the law, do you know? I believe there is usually an inquest after someone dies in a brawl or is stabbed, but what happens if someone dies suddenly like this, while dining at an inn?'

'I do not know,' Will said. 'But what I *do* know,' he added shrewdly, 'is that Master Burbage and Lord Hunsdon will want this whole affair brushed aside. They'll want to avoid any scandal. A heart attack, that is what they will say.'

I looked at them wretchedly. 'That is all very well, but I am a licensed physician and I was there. I cannot let it pass. The man was poisoned. This was murder.'

Unfortunately I could do nothing to help Simon and Will the following morning, for Dr Nuñez sent a message to say he had decided that this was the day we should ride out to the one remaining patient he was making over to me, the wealthy mercer who had turned minor gentleman and had built himself a small manor house near Windsor.

At any other time I would have welcomed the diversion, but I felt I should be helping the others in trying to discover more about Master Wandesford and who might have had a reason to kill him. However, my new patients would be important for me, so I collected Hector, then rode round to Mark Lane, where Dr Nuñez was just mounting his own horse, a steady old grey cob. We headed along Thames Street, making for Ludgate and the Strand.

'We have not ridden together since our time in Portugal, Kit,' he said.

I shuddered. That last ride from Lisbon to Cascais had been terrible, reining back the horses to keep pace with the sick and dying foot soldiers who struggled to make the journey back to the ships.

'Do you still think of Portugal as home, sir?' I asked. The Nuñez family had come to England long before my father and I had done, but I remembered that when we had been sailing there he had spoken of it as "home".'

He took some time answering. Finally, he shook his head.

'Nay, for many years I yearned to go back. I built my business here, and I have prospered, but I still hoped that one day I would return. After the Spanish invaded our country, I clung to the belief that they would be driven out, and of course that was the object of the expedition.'

'For some it was.'

'Aye, for some.' He sighed. 'After we returned to England, Beatriz told me quite firmly that she never wanted to go back, once she had heard all the details of our disaster. At first I could not quite give up hope . . . but now? Now I see that I was mistaken. I was foolish ever to suppose that I could recapture the Portugal of my childhood. The world has changed. The vicious blight which is the Inquisition has fallen over the country. The leaders of our people who might have made a stand against Spain were executed because of our clumsy invasion, as you well know. Nay, now my home is England, and I am English in spirit. My children and grandchildren will be English. They are even starting to call themselves "Nones" instead of "Nuñez".'

We began riding north and west from Westminster, taking the country road that led to Windsor, as he turned in his saddle.

'And what of you, Kit? Do you feel any ties to Portugal? Or do you think of yourself as English?'

'For myself, I am English,' I said slowly. 'Aye. That is how I think of myself now. Nearly half my life has been here. And I have no love of Portugal. But I have one link still with the country.'

I thought I had never told him this, but saw no reason why I should not now. There was no one I trusted more, and he had been endlessly kind to me. Why should I keep it a secret from him? There could be no harm in telling him. I trusted Simon. Of course I did. But I was not sure that I trusted myself with him. Not since he had kissed me when we parted in the harbour at Wardhouse. It had not felt like the kiss merely of a friend. If I started to tell him about this hidden part of my life, I might accidentally reveal too much.

'I have a younger sister still in Portugal,' I said.

He looked at me in astonishment.

'I thought that you and your father were all that were left of your family.'

I shook my head. 'My younger sister and brother were with my grandparents when my parents and I were arrested. They were to have come to England with us, but were taken ill, and my brother died. Isabel was too ill to travel.'

I looked past him at the road ahead. On either side, the country folk were already out harvesting the grain crops, fully six weeks early. They were right to hasten and gather the crops in, for there was a feeling in the air, a kind of hush, that foreshadowed a break at long last in this unrelenting heat wave. The heavy air carried the sweet scent of the cut stems and even here on the dusty road we could hear the rhythmic swish of the scythes through the wheat, like the sound of a heavy silk gown trailing down a wide staircase. The women following behind the reapers were singing as they built the stooks, their movements like a complex dance known since childhood – a stoop to gather an armful of wheat, a tap to level the bottom of the stems, a quick twist of straw to bundle them firmly together, then the careful placement of each bundle in its rightful place in the stook. Six bundles, two and two, leaning their grainy heads together, one bundle at each end, to support the group.

After a long pause, as the horses plodded on at the steady pace that Dr Nuñez favoured, I sighed, and continued.

'Do you remember that I went away for a few days, while the expedition stayed at Peniche?'

He nodded.

'I went looking for Isabel. I expected to find her at my grandparents' house, but when I arrived there, I learned that both of them were dead and my sister living at a farm on the estate. One of the farmers claimed she was his wife, but I don't believe they were married. She had two children, and another on the way.'

Dr Nuñez looked shocked. 'But . . . how old was she? You were nineteen that summer. She is younger?'

'She was seventeen then. She cannot have been more than thirteen when she bore the first child. I tried to persuade her to come away with me, but the man terrifies her, treats her like a slave, and she would not leave the children.'

I twisted round in my saddle to look at him. 'Some day,' I said fiercely, 'someday I will rescue her from him. I do not know how, but I will do it.'

He was clearly both astonished and worried by my revelations. 'You must be careful, Kit! If you return to Portugal, you will be in great danger.'

'Oh, I know,' I said drearily. 'It was a wild scheme, back then. And how would she have survived that march to Lisbon, pregnant, and perhaps with the children too? I should have had all their deaths on my head. Nay, I must find some other way, but I swear, some day I will make the attempt once more.'

Then he frowned, and said slowly, 'Kit, I had forgotten. Did you not tell me before of a sister?'

I was confused, then a dreamlike memory returned. Sitting on the ship's deck, on our death journey back from Portugal.

'On the ship?'

'That was it. I think we have both tried to close our minds to everything that happened then.'

We rode on for some while in silence. I had never spoken my half-formed intention to return and rescue Isabel out loud before, but it had been growing in me. Somehow, telling Dr Nuñez about Isabel relieved the burden of that terrible memory a little. Spoken out, it seemed no longer the nightmare which still visited me from time to time, but a reality I could confront. When the children were a little older, when I was able to construct a feasible scheme, not an ill thought out gamble, then I would find Isabel and bring her to England.

Clearly I had worried Dr Nuñez by my sudden declaration, and he began arguing against it.

'Never fear,' I said ruefully. 'It will need time and money to devise a means, and for now I have neither.'

Then I sought to divert him from the subject by telling him about the death of Master Wandesford the previous evening.

'Because it was Lord Hunsdon who gave the dinner, my friends believe that he and Master Burbage will wish to imply it was a natural death, from a heart attack. They will not want the Lord Chamberlain to be associated with a scandal.'

He nodded. 'Very likely.'

'But I am certain Master Wandesford was poisoned, and indeed had been given poison for some days before the dinner.'

I described Wandesford's symptoms, and the adulterated wine left in his glass.

'Aye, it certainly sounds like *belladonna*,' he said. 'The man could not have taken it himself, by mistake?'

'Gathered the berries? Squeezed the juice from them? Carried it to the inn? Then added it to his wine?'

I gave a sceptical grimace.

'Unlikely, I agree,' he said. 'However, I have heard of a few cases where people have taken small doses of *belladonna* because it gave them vivid hallucinations, but I believe they are almost invariably devilish visions and very frightening. It takes a strange mind to wish to indulge in such a thing. A witches' coven, perhaps . . .'

I remembered the snakes the little boy thought he had seen.

'Master Wandesford was no such person,' I said firmly. 'He was a quiet, shy, decent man. Nay, he would never have taken *belladonna* deliberately.'

I paused. I still did not know the answer to a question that was worrying me. 'Do you know whether there is likely to be a coroner's inquest?'

He pursed his lips. 'Difficult to say. As you suspect, powerful men may wish to divert any attention from the episode, but if it was known to be a deliberate poisoning, then I think there would need to be an inquest.'

'You say "if it was known". I know, and Simon Hetherington and Will Shakespeare know. Possibly Cuthbert Burbage overheard me last night. I have not spoken to Master Burbage, he was too occupied with Lord Hunsdon at the time. Do you think I should tell him?'

'Aye, I do. He employed the man. He has an interest in his death, even if he also wishes to oblige Lord Hunsdon. Or of course you could go directly to the coroner yourself.'

'I would not like to do that behind Master Burbage's back.'

'Aye, better not. Take your evidence to him, and see what he says.'

'And if he does not wish to pursue it?'

'Then it will be on your conscience.' He smiled grimly. 'Either to go to the coroner against his wishes, and the wishes of the Lord Chamberlain, or to suppress the knowledge that the man was murdered.'

I groaned. 'Not a pleasant choice.'

'Nay. But personally I have no doubts about where your conscience will lead you. Have a care, though. Great lords can be dangerous enemies.'

We rode on in silence. Dr Nuñez had simply articulated what I knew to be the truth of the matter, which had changed nothing.

'There,' he said at last, pointing ahead where a pleasant small manor house built of warm brick stood atop a low hill about half a mile away and slightly off to the right. I could make out a stand of newly-planted young trees, and an area of brown earth where something was to be constructed, perhaps a terrace, a place where the owner could sit of an evening with a glass of wine and survey his small kingdom. I wondered whether it was possible to see Windsor Castle from there.

The former mercer, Thomas Buckford, proved affable and courteous, taking us on a tour of his newly acquired demesne. Thatchers were roofing the recently completed stables (although the house was roofed with Flemish tiles). Everywhere about the grounds gardeners were at work, laying out formal beds, and planting more trees, including an orchard.

It was pleasant to walk about outdoors, for up here on the hill there was a whisper of a breeze, but I could see that Dr Nuñez was growing tired, so I was glad when Master Buckford led us inside to meet his wife, who had a cheery homely face, though she affected rather elegant clothes, and their six children, so close in age that I thought they must have arrived at yearly intervals.

The whole family was ruddy with health, no doubt partly owing to the country air here, well away from the insalubrious fumes and fogs of London. I doubted I would have much medical business here. However, it had been a delight to escape those same fumes and fogs myself today, for the continuing heat and the growing threat of thunder were making London almost intolerable.

Our ride home in the early afternoon was peaceful. As we passed them again, I noticed that the harvesters had moved on to the next field. We chatted about everyday matters; no more mention of that terrible journey to Portugal. Dr Nuñez also told me all the details of a tiresome legal case he was pursuing through the courts, in an attempt to recoup a debt owing to him these many months.

'I shall end by paying out more to my lawyer than I shall recover – if I ever do recover the monies owing to me.'

'Is it then worth the effort and the worry?' I asked.

'Aye, it is. One must take a stand against those who default on their debts, otherwise no man would ever pay his due and every merchant would flounder. This was payment for a shipment of spices and silk – half the cargo of one of my smaller ships. The fellow had the goods from me near a year ago, he has had plenty of time to pay. He will have sold everything now, so will have no lack of cash in hand. There is no excuse not to pay me, only greed. My ships and my crews are risked on the high seas to fetch these precious commodities. Are they to be risked merely for his convenience? Of course the lawyers will try to draw out the case, for the longer it takes, the more they will be paid.'

He was still complaining about lawyers and their practices when we reached Mark Lane.

'Come within, Kit,' he said. 'you will be the better for a cold drink.'

I shook my head. 'I thank you, but after I have stabled Hector, I think I will go and confront Master Burbage with my discoveries about the death of Wandesford.'

He smiled, as he always did, when I mentioned my horse by name, for he too bore the name Hector.

'Very well. That is the right thing to do. It will place the first burden of choice on Master Burbage's shoulders. It will be interesting to see which way he turns.'

'Aye,' I said, without too much conviction. 'It will indeed.'

After stabling Hector at the Walsingham house in Seething Lane, I made my way to the Theatre, having collected Rikki from the stable lad Harry. It was too early for the players to have finished their performance, so I followed a country lane which led west and then north into Finsbury Fields, skirting the drying green where the weavers stretched their finished cloth on tenter hooks, and continued on well beyond the archery butts. These were always in use, as the male citizens of London practised their shooting skills, and indeed regular practice at the butts was laid down by law for every male between the ages of seven and sixty, despite the fact that gunnery was becoming more and more the weapon of war. A good archer could fire a dozen arrows while a musket man was reloading after his first shot, so archery was still of considerable importance. I had managed to avoid the requirement to practise, for certain professions, like that of physician, were exempt, although sometimes I thought it might be a useful skill to acquire.

I made sure we were well past the butts before I let Rikki run free. Accidents can happen when arrows are flying about, and there are those who will take deliberate aim at a dog. Here at the northern edge of the Fields, past the windmills, there was the beginning of a wood, where I had once come with the players to gather Christmas greenery. Today it was a relief to walk under the shade of the trees. Already they looked tired from lack of rain, although from time to time the branches seemed to shiver, as a gust of wind passed through them, more like a dying gasp than a true breeze.

However, Rikki was enjoying himself, pursuing new scents amongst the undergrowth and last year's leaf fall. It was not often that I was able to bring him right out of the city. Clearly he relished the freedom here under the wood, but when I reckoned, by the angle of the sun, that the play would be finished for the day, I buckled on his lead and made my way back to Hog Lane and the playhouse.

The last of the playgoers were just drifting away, and I waved to Katarina, one of the former beggar children who now sold oranges here, as she headed south with the crowd, no doubt hoping to make more sales as she went. I found Simon and Will with Guy and the other players in the tiring house, sharing a jug of ale after a hot performance, but before I could ask whether they had discovered any clue as to why anyone should want to kill Master Wandesford, there came an angry bellow from the back of the tiring house where a number of small rooms provided a store for costumes, an office for Master Burbage, and a room where the play books were kept.

Guy glanced toward the source of the noise and gave a wicked grin.

'I feared as much,' he said. 'Our new copyist does not meet with Master Burbage's approval.'

'You have a new copyist already?' I said, perching on one of the chairs that did duty as a throne when required. 'With poor Master Wandesford not yet in his grave?'

'The work cannot stop, Kit,' Guy said. 'We all grieve for the poor old fellow, but players cannot rest, not during the summer when the playhouse is open. And parts must be learned. We have new pieces by both Will and Tom Kyd, all to be copied. Wandesford had made a start on Will's play when Davy knocked over the ink. He had barely started again before he died.'

'Then Master Burbage was fortunate to find a new copyist so soon,' I said, with a touch of irony.

They all grinned at each other.

'There was no need for him to go searching,' Simon said, 'for – behold! – we were nursing an expert penman here amongst us and never knew.'

'What do you mean?' I knew they were teasing, and I was too worried about the matter of the *belladonna* to join in their fun.

'You will soon see,' Will said.

At that moment Master Burbage came stamping out from the room where the play books were kept, waving a bundle of paper at us. The foxy faced Stoker stumbled behind him, looking annoyed.

'Here!' Burbage shouted, thrusting the papers under Simon's nose. 'Read this for me.'

Simon took the papers from him. I could see that they were crumpled and bore several large ink blots, but I was too far away to read the writing. Simon frowned, then grinned to himself.

'Befred awk lown,' he said, 'htur cum twa shuldl?'

Guy snorted and covered his mouth with his hand, but Will started up indignantly.

'Where is my script?' he demanded.

'Fear not,' Master Burbage said, 'that – the saints be praised – is still safe on the table. There are one or two blots–'

Before he could finish, Will had rushed away and came back holding the precious sheets tenderly against his chest.

'I do not believe I could write it again. It would never be the same.' He turned on Stoker. 'You fool! You strident coxcomb! You whoremaster!'

'Now, Will,' Burbage said. 'No call to be abusive.'

'If you let that . . . that slayer of poetry near my work again, I shall take it to Henslowe.' Will was breathing heavily, his nostrils flared. I had never seen him angry before.

'Fear not, Will,' Simon said as well, passing the creased bundle of papers over to him. 'I think you need have no worries on that score.'

Will grabbed the papers and frowned down at them, then his anger dissolved into laughter. I leaned over his shoulder to look. The top sheet was covered with wildly leaping writing which wandered up and down the page like the footsteps of a drunken ant. Few of the letters could be made out, while those that could conveyed about as much sense as the bit Simon had read out. There were half a dozen large blots, as though the drunken ant had stopped for a drink during his wanderings.

Cuthbert took the papers from Will.

'You fool!' He turned on the hapless Stoker. 'Why did you claim to have excellent penmanship? You can barely write. Now you have wasted us an entire day, when we might have set about finding a copyist who at least knew his alphabet. We are to perform this next week, and we must have the parts copied.'

He shook the papers in Stoker's face, and the man cowered away. I did not like him, but I began to feel a little sorry for him.

'Perhaps I could help,' I said. 'I have nothing to occupy my time nowadays. I write a clear hand, secretary hand. It will save you a little time. If Will would trust me with his script?'

I looked at him enquiringly, and he nodded.

'Aye, if you promise not to write like a b'yer lady apothecary.'

'I give you my word.'

Will took me to the room where the play books were kept, which also served as the copy room.

'I sometimes write in here myself,' he said. 'There is a window you can open if it grows too hot.' He pointed to a small window between the shelves. 'But be sure always to close the shutters and bolt them. We even have a lock on the door here, for our play books are our most precious possessions. Costumes can be replaced. Our play books cannot.'

He cleared away a mess of screwed up paper and broken quills from the table.

'Master Burbage will not be pleased at this waste,' he said. 'We use the cheapest paper, but even so it is a great expense. Here are some uncut quills and I'll refill the ink pot. Has Stoker been drinking it?'

While he poured the ink, I sharpened a handful of quills.

'Were you able to see Wandesford's landlady?' I asked quietly, not wanting my voice to carry out into the tiring house.

'Nay, she was not there when I called. I will try again this evening. Will you join us to dine? Master Burbage will owe you something for this.'

He pointed to where I was laying out his script and the fresh paper.

'Perhaps,' I said. 'Now, explain to me what I should do. Shall I copy the longest part first? That will need the most time to learn.'

'Aye, that's the way. Head the paper with the name of the character. Then you should head each speech with the last sentence of the person speaking before, so that your character knows when to speak. Like this. Start with Talbot's part.'

He ran his finger along the lines, which were set out neatly, though in places the writing itself became a little careless and rushed.

'Sometimes the words come so fast, I have to write them quickly, before I lose them.' He smiled apologetically. 'If there is anything you cannot read, come and ask me, don't waste time trying to guess. We will be on stage, rehearsing tomorrow's piece.'

'It seems clear enough,' I said, turning back my sleeves so that they should not be stained by ink. 'When I have finished this first part, which should I do then?'

'This one. And then this.' He pointed to the head of his script, where he had listed the names of the *dramatis personae*, as he called them. I noticed how very ink-stained his fingers were, the ink ingrained into the creases of his knuckles. He also had a lump on the side of the end joint of the middle finger on his right hand. I had seen it before on scholars and clerics, a writer's lump, as it is called. I realised Wandesford had had one too, testimony to the long hours spent writing. Stoker had none.

'Why do you suppose Stoker put himself forward as a copyist?' I said, as I dipped my first quill in the ink, and tried it out on one of the torn scraps of paper. 'The man is barely literate.'

Will shrugged. 'He seems desperate for work. He can read well enough. He has acted as prompt a few times, when no one else was free.'

'Well, not all those who can read can also write well.'

'That is very true. It was curious, though. He was always hanging about Wandesford when he was working. Perhaps he thought that by watching he could learn to write correctly. He must have had some education.'

'But not enough,' I agreed.

'Indeed. I will leave you to your labours. This is a great kindness, Kit.'

'Not at all. Better than sitting in my lodgings, chewing my thumbs.'

He left me then, closing the door behind him. At first I was aware of the murmur of voices from the stage, but I soon became absorbed in the play. It was a great temptation to read it through, but I must concentrate on one man's speeches only, which I found tantalising.

It began to grow warm in the copy room, so I opened the window and almost at once a large blue butterfly flew in, taking up a position on the window sill, where he appeared to be watching my progress with interest. My studies with my father from an early age had taught me to write quickly and neatly, for he would not tolerate careless handwriting. By the time the players had finished their rehearsal I had copied out the three longest parts, as Will had suggested, and done two more, which I judged to be the next in importance. I was just starting on a sixth when he reappeared.

'Excellent!' he said, taking up my finished work. 'You have been very quick, yet your writing is perfectly clear.' He made as if to thump me on the shoulder, until he saw that I was still holding an inky quill, keeping it well away from his script.

'Come, Master Burbage says you have not only earned yourself dinner, but some chinks as well. Set that aside.'

I laid down my quill carefully and flexed my fingers. I saw that the blue butterfly had gone, but I had been too absorbed in my work to notice. I stood up and closed the window, then bolted the shutters over it. It was a heavy iron bolt, not wood. The players clearly took great precautions to protect their play books.

Master Burbage loomed up behind Will, beaming at me.

'Kit has copied out the five longest parts,' Will said, 'and begun on the sixth.'

'We are more grateful than I can say, Kit.' Burbage gave one of his flourishing theatrical bows. 'But set that aside now and come to the inn. Our new copyist, when we find one, can finish the work.'

'But if you are to perform next week . . .' I said. 'I could finish this. There is not so much left yet to copy. If Will trusts me with his script, and you can provide the paper, I will take it home and copy the remaining parts there. I should be able to complete it by midday tomorrow.'

Will looked anxious for a moment, then assured me that he would trust me with his precious play book.

'We do not usually allow them to leave the playhouse,' he said, 'but for one night, and if you guard it with your life . . . ?'

'I promise,' I said, 'your infant shall be safe with me.'

Master Burbage, while pretending reluctance to trouble me, was clearly relieved to be spared this immediate problem. I overrode his polite objections and stowed the play book and a

70

supply of paper in my satchel, realising as I did so that Gregory's report still lingered there.

Will watched keenly as I buckled my satchel.

'I will truly guard it with my life,' I said. 'It's very good.'

He suddenly looked shy, and younger than his years. 'I thank you, Kit. The other players seem to like my scribblings. Let us hope the groundlings do as well. But I know I can do better than this.'

'Come along, come along.' Master Burbage hurried us across the tiring room and on to the stage. 'I could eat a horse. Or at least a foal.'

'Where are we going?' Guy asked. 'Not, I think, to the Green Dragon?'

Master Burbage looked worried for a moment, but quickly hid it with his usual banter. 'Nay, we shall go to the Cross Keys. It is further to go, but the walk will sharpen our appetites.'

We went down through Bishopsgate, then turned right and headed for Gracechurch Street and the Cross Keys. None of us had any desire to return to the Green Dragon.

After eating well, but rather quietly at the Cross Keys, where the players were well known and made warmly welcome, Simon and I, with Rikki at our heels, walked back to Southwark together. I could feel the bulge of a purse from Master Burbage in a pocket of my doublet. It was small, and I had been too polite to count the coins it contained, but it would probably feed Rikki and me for a few days.

'Were you able to learn anything that might bear on Master Wandesford's death?' I said.

Simon shook his head. 'I wasn't able to speak to Guy on his own all day, and I thought it wiser not to question him in front of others.'

'Aye, probably for the best. Will could not see the landlady either.'

'I know. We must simply try again tomorrow.'

On these long summer evenings, the gates on the Bridge stayed open late, so we could save the cost of a wherry. In any case, wherry trips were unpleasant at the moment. The river was so shrunken that passengers must make their way many yards across the mud before reaching a boat, and again after disembarking. The wherrymen had laid down walkways of loose planks of wood, but it was still very disagreeable.

We stopped part way across the Bridge, as we often did, where there was a break between the houses and we could look up and down the river. Downstream, the Customs House stood massively above the legal quays.

'It seems Thomas Phelippes is now working there as a clerk,' I said, leaning my arms on the low parapet.

'Not working in intelligence any longer?'

'It seems not.'

'Could you not find code-breaking work somewhere? With the Cecils, perhaps?'

I made a face. 'It seems Poley is now working for them.'

'I see.'

We crossed to the other side of the Bridge and looked upriver.

'How low the Thames is,' Simon said. 'I have never seen it so low, even when the tide is out, like this.'

I grabbed his sleeve. 'Look! Down there – almost beneath us!'

We both craned over the edge of the parapet. A gaggle of young men in the blue tunics of apprentices, were below us, actually in the river! Shouting and laughing – they were the worse for drink – they were wading across from shore to shore.

'The water is barely up to their knees,' I said, watching in astonishment as one of the lads staggered and almost fell, but was propped up by his companions.

'Idiots!' Simon said, but I could see that he half wanted to join them.

'This must be the deepest point,' I said. 'If they can wade past here, they'll reach Southwark.'

One of the apprentices had seen us.

'Come and join us!' he shouted. 'We're on our way to sshee the Wincheshter geeshe, Wincheshter–' He flourished his arms about and nearly fell over.

We both laughed and shook our heads.

72

'Best make haste,' Simon said, 'or we'll meet them outside Bess's bawdy house, covered in mud, and I've no mind to join them.'

'Nor I.'

But I shook my head in wonderment. What a portent! What a marvel! The Thames so low, men could walk across it! Would it disappear for ever?

Chapter Five

*T*he next morning early, I sat down to copy the remaining parts from Will's manuscript as soon as I had broken my fast with a frugal crust of rather stale bread, shared with Rikki, and half a mug of small ale, not shared. I was not really hungry, however, since the meal at the Cross Keys yesterday evening had been ample. The cook, who knew Rikki from past encounters, had even provided him with a bowl of kitchen scraps. As I wrote, I found myself drawing together all the elements of the play, which I had only grasped in part the previous day. It dealt with the early struggles between the houses of York and Lancaster for the crown of England, struggles that had taken place in the last century. Previously I had taken little interest in those bloody and fruitless wars, for had not the house of Tudor usurped them both? Will's play, however, brought living people before my eyes, and I was looking forward to seeing it acted upon the stage. It showed very clearly how a nation under a weak ruler will begin to fall apart. Before the clock on St Mary Overy struck ten I had completed the task, packed all the papers into my satchel, and headed for the City.

One aspect of the play puzzled me. Almost to the end, Will had portrayed Joan, the Maid of France sympathetically. She was devout, inspired, chaste, courageous. She bolstered the courage of the mostly pusillanimous Frenchmen. Then suddenly, near the end of the play, Will had her conjuring devils. When she is condemned to be burned, she starts pleading that she is pregnant, because of course a pregnant woman may not be executed, since it would also mean the murder of an innocent unborn child. Why this abrupt change in her character? I supposed that he had inserted these scenes to feed the violent Francophobic temperament of the groundlings, but I was disappointed. I felt somehow betrayed. Joan had lived as a woman in a man's world and acquitted herself admirably. Perhaps the final scene could be played as a young girl suddenly finding herself deserted by her heavenly voices and absolutely terrified. She had probably been put to the torture, and I knew what that meant.

I had lain awake much of the night, fretting about the best course of action I should take over Master Wandesford's death. As I had told Dr Nuñez, I had gone to the playhouse the previous day intending both to discover what Simon and Will had learned and to tell Master Burbage of my conviction that Wandesford had been poisoned. There had never been an opportunity to speak privately to Master Burbage, and I was convinced that it would be wiser to do so out of the hearing of others. For all I knew, the killer might be amongst the players. Indeed, it seemed that was the inevitable conclusion. The only other people present at the dinner were the inn servants, Lord Hunsdon, Aemilia Bassano, and Hunsdon's two attendants.

Even if I were not overheard by the killer, someone else might overhear and then gossip about what I planned to reveal to Master Burbage. Until he decided what to do, any careless gossip could only cause trouble. I knew that he always arrived at the playhouse long before the players, so that he could deal with his accounts and various business matters in peace, for he had interests in other ventures besides the two playhouses, the Theatre and the Curtain. I would catch him now before the rest of the company (who were late risers) arrived at the Theatre.

It proved that I had made the right decision. After the doorkeeper admitted me to the Theatre, I found Master Burbage at work alone in his small office behind the tiring house. I had been afraid Cuthbert might also be there. Unlike his younger brother Richard, Burbage's elder son was only interested in the business affairs of the company, although he could take small parts of a few lines when needed. However, this morning Cuthbert was not assisting his father with the accounts. On the whole, Master Burbage was looking well content as he turned over the pages of his ledger. In the past I had known him pale with anxiety when bad weather or epidemics closed the playhouses. This year, matters were looking more fortunate.

'I have completed the copying out of the roles,' I said, laying down the individual parts, fanlike, on his desk. 'And here is Will's original play book.'

'I will lock it away,' he said, taking it from me and carrying it off to the store.

'Take a seat, Kit,' he said when he returned.

He poured us both ale and pushed a plate of fruit buns toward me, still warm from the bake house. I saw that his papers were already liberally sprinkled with crumbs. I took one gladly, for the walk across London had given me an appetite. He picked up my sheaf of papers and quickly scanned them, then smiled.

'This is excellent,' he said. 'We can read through after the performance this afternoon and start rehearsing the day after tomorrow. You have saved us considerable time and worry.'

He drew up a heavy purse attached to his belt and counted out a small pile of coins which he pushed across the desk to me.

'I am afraid that I am not able to pay a copyist a great deal of money, but I hope you will accept this.'

I was in no position to be proud and refuse, so I thanked him and slipped the coins into my own purse.

Burbage drank deeply of his ale and sighed with pleasure. 'Ah, that is good. This heat is very trying, but it has served us well.' He tapped his account book with the feathered tip of his quill. 'We have had larger audiences this year than I ever remember. London has developed a great love for the playhouse, it is quite the favourite entertainment nowadays, surpassing even bear baiting and cock fighting.'

He took another gulp of his ale.

'I saw your expression of surprise just now, when I was in a hurry to lock away Will's play book, but our books are a commodity almost above price. Our whole business rests on them. I am grateful that we have play makers like Will and Tom Kyd who can write fast and feed the hungry maw of London, ever demanding something new.'

'It astonishes me that the players can learn so many parts so quickly,' I said. 'Surely, once they are memorised, you do not need the play books?'

'Perhaps not, though new players join us from time to time and must learn fresh parts. Nay, the real reason we guard them is that we must ensure no other players steal them.'

'Would they do that?' I was amazed.

He laughed at my innocence.

'Of course they would. Not every company has a Shakespeare or a Marlowe, scribbling away for them. And like us they must supply fresh entertainment for the groundlings or they will starve for want of an audience. Theft of our plays has happened in the past, and I intend to ensure that it does not happen here in future.'

'Very wise,' I said, though it was a crime I had not suspected before.

He looked down again at my copies of the players' parts.

'You have an excellent clear hand, and have written these out very quickly. Now that you no longer work at St Thomas's, could I interest you in becoming our copyist? I know that it would be a very inferior position for someone of your standing, but perhaps until you find another post . . . ?' He looked at me quizzically.

It *was* an inferior position. I was, after all, an experienced physician, licensed by the Royal College to practise. Working as a minor clerk to a company of players would be considerably below my station. On the other hand, I must eat and pay my rent.

'I shall still have some medical work,' I said hesitantly. 'Dr Nuñez has arranged for me to take over some of his families. All of them with some position in society. If they summon me, I must go.'

'I understand that,' he said. 'However, the copying may done whenever you are not occupied with patients. As long as it is done as soon as it is needed. You may work here, in the book room. I will provide paper, ink, and quills. As I said, I cannot afford to pay much. Let us say, a shilling a play?'

I could not accept so little. I shook my head.

He smiled. I guessed he expected me to negotiate, he was a shrewd businessman, after all.

'I think five shillings would be nearer the mark,' I said. 'I spent a good while on that.' I nodded toward the stack of paper.

'Four and sixpence,' he said, 'and dinner at my expense every night except Sundays, during the season when the playhouse is open.'

'Done,' I said, and we shook hands on it.

Clearly he thought our business was finished, but I must screw up my courage to speak about the death of Wandesford.

'Master Burbage,' I said, 'the night before last at the inn, Master Wandesford's death–'

'Ah, a sad business.' He shook his head. 'Poor fellow! And just when the Lord Chamberlain was entertaining us, and his lady present . . . I have arranged for the funeral in two days' time, at St Botolph's. You will be very welcome, if you would care to come. I realise you did not know him well. I fear few of us did. He kept very much to himself.'

In two days' time! There was not a moment to waste. I began again, clearing my throat.

'Master Burbage, I believe you think he died of a heart attack.'

'Aye. Well, was not that what you said?'

'I said merely that his heart had stopped. Which indeed it had, but not from a heart attack. Indeed, not from natural causes.'

He looked at me in alarm. 'Not from natural causes? But you said nothing at the time.'

'I thought it unwise, with Lord Hunsdon and Mistress Bassano there. Besides, the person who killed him was almost certainly there as well.'

He turned quite pale and poured himself more ale, with a hand that shook.

'I think you had better explain yourself, Kit.'

'He died from poisoning by *atropa belladonna*, or to give it its common name, deadly nightshade.'

I went on to explain the symptoms I had observed in Wandesford both before the meal and as he lay dying, my tasting of the dregs of wine left in his glass, and my own earlier experience of such a poisoning. Out of my satchel, I drew the phial containing the wine and placed it on the table in front of him.

For a long time he said nothing, though he picked up the phial and turned it in his hands, as if it might give him some guidance.

Finally I broke the silence. 'I am not sure of this, but I believe when a death is due to natural causes, there is no need for a coroner's inquest, but if there is a suspicion of foul play, then it must be reported to the coroner and an inquest held, in the presence of the deceased. Is that not correct?'

I ran a finger round the neck of my shirt. It was not only the hot weather that was making me sweat.

'In this heat, it will be vital to hold the inquest quickly,' I said, 'before the condition of the body becomes intolerable. I understand the inquest must be *super visum corporis*, that is, in sight of the body. Where is Master Wandesford's body now?'

'In the crypt of St Botolph's. It is relatively cool there, but you are right, if there is to be an inquest, it cannot be delayed.'

'Then should we report to the coroner?'

'Kit, this is not something you or I can decide. Lord Hunsdon was the highest ranking person present. He believed the death was caused by a heart attack and there an end to it. We cannot go to the coroner without consulting him.'

This did not come as altogether a surprise. I was handing over responsibility to Master Burbage, and he would hand it over to Lord Hunsdon.

'What do you think will be his view of the matter?' I said.

'He will not be pleased,' Burbage said bluntly. 'He wanted the whole matter kept quiet, to avoid scandal. A cousin of the Queen, entertaining a company of players to dinner at a public inn, together with his mistress? And one of the company dying at the very table where he was seated? That would have been scandal enough, but there would have been no need for an inquest if it had been due to natural causes.'

He raked his fingers through his thinning hair.

'But this – poison by *belladonna*! What you are saying is murder.'

'Aye,' I said grimly. 'It is murder.'

He set the phial down on the table. 'You would be prepared to give evidence at an inquest? That in your opinion it was murder?'

I swallowed with difficulty, but then I nodded. I was always loathe to draw attention to myself, but it could not be avoided.

'It is my duty,' I said quietly. 'My duty as a physician. And my duty to the dead.'

'I fear it may make you unpopular with Lord Hunsdon, and he is a powerful man, first cousin to the Queen.'

I nodded again. I did not need to be continually reminded of Lord Hunsdon's close link to the Queen. There were many who said his lordship might be even more closely related to Her Majesty. At the time of his birth, his mother, Mary Boleyn, was married to William Carey, but she was also King Henry's mistress. It was possible that Henry Carey, Lord Hunsdon, was the Queen's illegitimate half brother. No one, of course, mentioned this in company.

Master Burbage heaved a sigh, then rose to his feet.

'There is nothing for it. We must put the case before Lord Hunsdon and seek his guidance. It will be for him to decide whether the coroner should be informed.'

I said nothing, but I was troubled. If Lord Hunsdon decided against notifying the coroner, would he be breaking the law? And if so, should I defy him and report the killing myself? It was an unpleasant prospect.

The phial was still on the table. As I reached out to pick it up, Burbage said, 'You may leave that here.'

Nevertheless, I did pick it up and returned it to my satchel. 'Perhaps not,' I said. 'The killer was certainly present at the meal. If he saw me pour Wandesford's wine into the phial, he will be anxious to destroy it. And it is evidence, which the coroner will wish to see.'

'You do not really believe the killer was one of my company?' There was a note of pleading in Burbage's voice.

'I think we cannot be too careful.'

Master Burbage left word with the doorkeeper Pillings that Cuthbert was to oversee the preparations for the afternoon's performance and hand out the parts from Will's play that I had copied for the players to learn, then we walked as briskly as we could bear through the stifling crowds of the City, down Bishopsgate Street, past the Green Dragon, then along Gracechurch Street and Fish Street, until we reached Old Swan Stairs. As with all the other wherry stations on both sides of the river, the boats could only be reached by walking out over the glistening mud, stinking of dead fish and sewage. Boards had been laid, but they were slippery and treacherous. More than once I thought I should fall.

Master Burbage signalled to the nearest wherry. 'Somerset Place,' he said.

'Aye, maister,' the wherry man said in a resigned tone of voice. It was a fair way to row from Old Swan Stairs to the mansion on the Strand.

'Does Lord Hunsdon own Somerset Place?' I asked as we sat down on the seat in the stern of the wherry.

'I believe it is rightly the property of the Crown.' Burbage removed the cap he had donned on leaving the playhouse and used it to fan himself. 'After the Earl of Somerset was executed, it was seized for the Crown, but I have never heard that Her Majesty has used it since she came to the throne, though she lived there when her sister was queen. Perhaps that is an unpleasant memory for her. I believe she has granted it as a residence to her cousin.'

The river was so low, even in the centre, that from time to time the wherry lodged on mud banks, so that the wherryman was forced to push us off with an oar. Moreover, he was so exhausted with the heat and he rowed so slowly that I thought we should never make any headway against the current, even as sluggish as it was. It began to seem that we would have taken less time had we walked all the way from Shoreditch to the Strand.

At last, however, the imposing Arundel House appeared on our right, standing behind its fine sweep of gardens which stretched down to the Thames. Just beyond it upriver lay the sprawling shape of Somerset Place. Here, too, formal gardens were laid out between the mansion and the shore, but there was scaffolding erected up one side of the building itself.

Master Burbage pulled a face. 'The Earl began building that more than forty years ago, and it is *still* not finished. It is a scandal!'

I recalled that before he became the great playhouse owner that he was today, Master Burbage had been a builder. Indeed, he had built both the Theatre and the Curtain.

'It is a very handsome building, though,' I said.

Somerset Place was three stories high, very elegant and modern, with large windows and a colonnaded portico. My father had once pointed it out to me as an example of the Italianate style, the first in London. It was, understandably, somewhat marred by the present excrescence of scaffolding. Even from this distance, out on the river, the scaffold boards look old, warped, and weathered. I wondered whether they had remained there since the Earl of Somerset died, leaving his great project unfinished.

Our exit from the wherry involved the same nervous traverse across boards, though these were less slippery, having been subjected to little traffic from the public. We climbed the steps to the water gate and were admitted to the mansion's grounds by a liveried servant.

Once we were within the walled precinct of the gardens, sounds from the outside world of city and river were cut off. As we were conducted along a cool path between pleached lime trees, we were enveloped in the languid perfume of roses, growing in profusion within their geometric beds and climbing up ornamental pergolas, while my gown brushed against a low border of lavender beside the path, releasing its sweet but slightly astringent scent, and disturbing a cloud of bees. The air was full of them, flying purposefully along their invisible aerial highroads, back and forth from the abundance of flowers which filled the immaculate garden across to a row of hives, dripping with their sticky gold, which stood under the shelter of the brick wall surrounding the property. One zipped past my face with a hum like an arrow in flight, so close I could feel the tremor in the air.

We emerged from the garden on to a low terrace which lay all along this southern face of the building. At its centre, the façade was pierced by an elaborate archway leading to the central quadrangle, around which the house was built. Although we were conducted swiftly toward an outside stairway leading to the first floor, I had time to notice the decorative terracotta plaques adorning the walls of this inner courtyard, one above every third window. I had no time to study them closely, but I thought they depicted the gods and goddesses of classical mythology.

Another servant in Hunsdon's livery awaited us at the top of the steps. He led us through a doorway and along a corridor laid with expensive turkey carpets, so that I was anxious, lest my shoes leave muddy footprints all the way. At the end of the corridor he showed us into a small chamber, saying that Lord Hunsdon would see us presently.

At first even Master Burbage hesitated to sit down on the chairs which had been padded in the new fashion, layers of horsehair covered with French damask, but after we had waited about an hour, he yielded to temptation. I went to stand by the window, looking out over the garden to the river, which was almost empty of boats. Until the tide came in, nothing larger than a wherry would be able to navigate it. The farmers who sent produce by barge down from Oxfordshire, and all the counties in between, must be cursing the shrinking of the river. And the London shopkeepers who depended on them would be cursing too, finding themselves unable to supply their customers. Were it not for the small farmers between Southwark and Lambeth, and those along the road to Hackney Downs, London would have started to go hungry, an ironic state of affairs in a year of abundant harvests.

Finally I sat down myself on the seat built into the window embrasure.

'How long do you suppose he intends to keep us waiting?' I said softly.

Master Burbage shrugged. 'Great men, Kit, great men.'

'It is uncivil, great man or not,' I muttered, but hardly loud enough for him to hear.

At last there came the sound of footsteps along the corridor, though they were muffled by the carpet. They were too light and swift to be Lord Hunsdon, nor were they the dignified tread of an upper servant. The door opened and Aemilia Bassano swept in.

Maria Nagaya, mother of the young Tsarevich, whom I had met in Muscovy, had been exceptionally beautiful in a remote, imperial way. Aemilia Bassano possessed beauty of quite a different kind. She was dressed today in a grass green gown of some very light material. Not silk, but perhaps a very fine linen or Italian cotton, with a thread almost as fine as a human hair. The split over-skirt showed the under-skirt of pure white, delicately embroidered with pale yellow flowers and leaves of the same green as the gown. Her sleeves were of an unfashionable cut, loose and trailing, like something out of an old tapestry, and they looked marvellously cool. Her ruff was narrow and simple, and her only jewellery a gold cross set with pearls. Caged in the heavy folds of my physician's gown, I envied her.

Burbage and I both sprang to our feet.

'Master Burbage,' she cried, 'and Dr Alvarez! Why have they put you in here? How long have you been waiting?'

Burbage murmured something about it being of no consequence, but she shook her head impatiently.

'It is monstrously rude. You should have been conducted to my lord at once. Follow me.'

With that she swept us out, along the corridor, past the door to the stairs, to the other end of the south wing, and flung open a door.

'Henry, my love, here are two gentlemen come to see you and left kicking their heels in that miserable little chamber.' She waved her hand back in the direction we had come. 'I have only just heard of it. They have been kept waiting for more than an hour.'

Lord Hunsdon rose from behind a desk and bowed politely. We returned it, rather more deeply, and I retreated behind Burbage.

'Burbage, my dear man,' his lordship said, 'how may I be of service? I must apologise for the negligence of my servants.

They shall be reprimanded. Aemilia, ring for some refreshment for our guests.'

Burbage made a deprecating gesture, 'My lord, there is no need. This should not take long, although it is a serious matter.'

Lord Hunsdon emerged from behind his desk and motioned us to chairs, while Aemilia strolled over to the window, as if to admire the same prospect as I had seen from the other room, but I was certain that she was listening attentively. Lord Hunsdon paid no more attention to her than to a pretty ornament adorning the room. Perhaps he was one of those men who believe women cannot comprehend the serious affairs of the sterner sex.

'It concerns the death the night before last at the Green Dragon,' Burbage began awkwardly.

His lordship shook his head, but did not appear deeply concerned. 'Alas, a sad affair. Your copyist, I understand? Not one of the players.'

'That is correct. Our copyist, Master Wandesford.' Burbage hesitated, as if unsure how to continue.

'It comes to us all, in the end, Death's sickle may cut us down without warning in the midst of life. A heart attack, I believe?'

Burbage cleared his throat. 'That was what I believed at the time. It seems that was not the case.'

He glanced sideways at me. I suddenly realised that Lord Hunsdon had no idea who I was, and so, equally, could have no idea why I was there. Aemilia had talked to me throughout the meal, and so might have told him, but I doubted whether I was of sufficient importance to have been mentioned. He might have seen me rush to attend to Wandesford, but it had been dark at the far end of the table and Master Burbage had hurried him away almost at once. It seemed Burbage now realised that he needed to explain my presence.

'This is Dr Alvarez, my lord, a licensed physician of the Royal College. As a friend of the company, he was present at the dinner in the Green Dragon.'

I stood up and bowed. Lord Hunsdon inclined his head.

'Dr Alvarez observed a number of things about Master Wandesford's appearance – um – symptoms of . . . signs which suggested that the man did not die of natural causes.'

Lord Hunsdon had been sitting relaxed in his chair, but now he leaned forward, his hands on his knees and fixed me with a sharp look. I realised that he was not, after all, quite so unconcerned about the sudden death as he had tried to appear.

'Perhaps, doctor, you had better tell me what you think you saw.'

I did not care for the implications of that condescending 'you think', but it would do no good to allow it to annoy me. Clearly and dispassionately, I described the symptoms Wandesford had shown before the dinner, the violent signs of poison before he died, my own experience of *belladonna* poisoning, and my testing of the wine left in the glass. I took out the phial and held it up. He looked at it, but made no move to take it.

He said nothing for a time, then gave a brisk nod. 'Your deduction seems valid. I have no such medical training myself, but I will take your word for it that the man appears to have died from *belladonna* poisoning, however administered.'

He turned to Burbage. 'But why have you come to me?'

Burbage shifted uncomfortably in his chair.

'It is a matter, my lord, of the coroner. In a case of suspected foul play, one is required by law to inform the coroner. Dr Alvarez is convinced there was foul play.'

'The man might have taken it himself.'

They both looked at me, as though they expected me to have the answer.

'Very unlikely,' I said. 'Indeed, I believe, impossible. I'm no lawyer, but even if he had taken it himself, would that not still count as an unlawful killing, wilful self-murder? And require a coroner's inquest?'

His lordship nodded. I noticed that Aemilia had turned a little away from the window and looked from one to the other of us. She was regarding me speculatively.

Lord Hunsdon tapped his teeth with his thumbnail.

'You will understand, my lord,' Burbage said, 'that we would not wish you to be caused any distress or inconvenience over this matter . . .'

'The truth is, Burbage, if there is a coroner's inquest, it must come out that I was present. There is no way it can be concealed.'

Master Burbage looked even more uncomfortable, but could clearly find nothing to say.

Lord Hunsdon fixed me again with that sharp stare. 'You are quite sure of your facts, young sir?'

I meet his eyes firmly. I would not be patronised. 'I am quite prepared to testify on oath that in my opinion. Master Wandesford was poisoned with *belladonna.*'

His lordship sighed, then he got up and rubbed his hands briskly together. 'Very well, then there is nothing for it. We must abide by the law. Burbage, you had better report the matter to the coroner at once.'

It took us a considerable time to return to the playhouse. There were, of course, no wherries at the water gate of Somerset Place, and while a passing wherry could have been hailed with a cry of 'Eastward Ho!', there were also no wherries passing along the river as the sun rose to the zenith and the very mud at our feet dried and cracked until it took on the appearance of shards of terracotta.

Lord Hunsdon's private barge was moored just off shore, but neither of us wished to trouble him further, so in the end we scrambled along the shore to Strand Lane which led up to the Strand itself.

'I think it is too hot to walk,' Master Burbage said.

'I agree.' I was beginning to feel faint beneath the unrelenting sun, but was reluctant to remove my gown until we were well away from Somerset Place. 'If we go through Temple Bar and down Middle Temple Lane, we should be able to pick up a wherry at Temple Stairs.'

This was what we did, although it meant trudging along a street thick with dust, kicked up by passing feet in a choking cloud, then another precarious walk over boards, during which

Master Burbage accidentally stepped off the side and sank one foot up to the ankle in the mud. The curses he showered down on the weather, the Thames, and the careless placement of the boards were enough to burn the ears of a more sensitive companion, but I have spent time in the company of soldiers. I have heard worse.

By the time we eventually reached the Theatre, the afternoon performance was already underway. While we were being rowed down the Thames, we had discussed how best to proceed. Master Burbage would report to the coroner at the Guildhall as quickly as possible, for he would most likely wish to hold the inquest the very next day, in view of the probable deterioration of the body. I would go to St Botolph's to warn the rector that the body would need to be removed for the inquest.

'It will probably be held at the Green Dragon,' Burbage said. 'I have only once attended an inquest, and I know that coroners prefer to hold their enquiries as near as possible to where the incident occurred.'

'It seems somewhat unpleasant,' I said. 'Were I the innkeeper, I should not like an inquest involving a dead body to be held on the premises where I serve food and drink. It will surely harm his business.'

'His business will be harmed anyway,' Burbage said grimly, 'once word gets out that a man died of poison at the Green Dragon, however innocent the inn may be of any involvement.'

'I am sorry for it,' I said, feeling somewhat guilty. The innkeeper was a cheerful, obliging soul, and I did not like to think of him taking harm for something which was no fault of his. 'But will word get out?'

'You do not know how these matters are arranged, Kit?'

I shook my head.

'The jurors will be made up of respectable men from the neighbourhood, so they will soon be apprised of all the details. And any citizen may attend the inquest. Londoners are ghouls when it comes to hangings. They are no different when it is an enquiry into murder. The room will be packed with as many people as can force their way in.'

88

'Poor Master Wandesford,' I said. 'He would have hated to end like this.'

At the playhouse, we stopped just long enough to explain to Cuthbert what had been decided with Lord Hunsdon, then went to carry out our separate errands. Master Burbage accompanied me, retracing our steps as far as St Botolph's, which lies just past the madhouse, then he continued on into the City to find the coroner.

The rector of St Botolph's was setting out fresh candles in the church, ready for evensong, and I quickly explained that the coroner's men would be coming to fetch Master Wandesford's body for the inquest, and why an inquest must be held.

'It is likely to be tomorrow,' I said. 'To avoid any more delay.'

He looked distressed. 'Poisoned! That anyone could do such a thing, to a gentle soul like Master Wandesford! He was a good man. It seems so disrespectful of the dead, to be laid out on public view. Is it really necessary?'

'I believe it is the law.'

He shook his head. 'Not a humane law, then.'

'It is important that justice should be done. Master Wandesford was murdered. The murderer must be caught. He might attack someone else.'

At the word 'murdered', he shuddered. 'The poor man is already in his coffin, ready for the funeral the day after tomorrow. Master Burbage has paid for a coffin, so that he should not be buried like a pauper, merely in a winding sheet.'

'Perhaps they will simply take him in his coffin,' I said. The conversation was becoming macabre. Everything about this business was. 'Is it fastened down?'

'Not yet.'

'Then I am sure they will carry him in his coffin. He may be viewed, then covered again.'

I left the rector on his knees at the altar, praying, I supposed, for Master Wandesford's soul. As soon as I was outside the church I dragged off my gown. It had been necessary to wear it when visiting Lord Hunsdon, for I wished to be taken seriously, and I had kept it on to go to St Botolph's, out of respect for the dead copyist and the living rector, but I could dispense with it now. I loosened my small ruff and untied the strings of my shirt at the neck. In the street, labourers were going about stripped of their shirts, their pale English skin reddened under the sun.

Before I returned to the Theatre, I decided I would stay the pangs of hunger that had begun to assail me. Hours had passed since my skimpy breakfast, and, although I would be enjoying a dinner which was to be part of my wages for copying, that would not be for some hours yet, after the read through of Will's play.

In this weather, it was wise to exercise caution in choosing what and where to eat. There was an ordinary just inside the city gate where Simon and I had often eaten. The food was plain, no fancy sugar confections there, but it was as clean as one could expect in such a place. Even so, I would avoid meat and fish, either of which might have turned putrid. I choose a bowl of pease pudding, some bread, and a little hard cheese, washed down with small ale, for my throat was as dry as the desert.

By the time I had walked back to the playhouse, the performance was over and the players were relaxing briefly before starting their read-through. When Will saw me, he beckoned me over to join him where he sat playing a desultory game of cards with Simon and Guy.

'We have heard the outcome of your visit to Lord Hunsdon,' Simon said. He glanced aside at Guy. I wondered whether he had yet told Guy the details of my discoveries about Wandesford's death.

I pulled up a stool to the costume hamper they were using as a table. 'I am sure Guy can help. Have you asked him about Master Wandesford's friends, and any possible enemies?'

'He has,' Guy said, laying down his cards and resigning from the game. 'I am afraid I can be of little help. Wandesford was a solitary fellow. In all the years we have both belonged to Master Burbage's company, I never really came to know him. He never mentioned any family, or spoke of his life before he came to London. I am not even sure how we came by the notion that he had once been a clergyman. When he first came, he had something of the north in his speech. Possibly Yorkshire. I cannot rightly remember after so many years.'

Simon and Will played out the last of their cards, and Will scooped up his winnings – four silver pennies, an apple and a sweet pasty.

'From the north,' Simon said thoughtfully. 'Possibly Yorkshire. Perhaps a former clergyman. No family. You do not suppose he could have been a Catholic priest?'

We looked at each other wildly. If he had been a Catholic priest, a violent death was not unlikely. In Walsingham's day, he would have been arrested and questioned.

'Nay.' I shook my head. It was a tempting speculation, but unlikely. 'Catholic priests who come to subvert the Queen's peace do not remain quietly copying out play books for – how long did you say he was with the company, Guy?'

'It must be fifteen years.'

'Fifteen years,' I said. 'Nay. That is not their way. They come swiftly over, mostly from Rheims, and move about the country, never staying in one place for long. Their excuse is merely to minister to those of the old faith, but they support the Pope's excommunication of Her Majesty, and they are agents of Spanish and French plots to invade England. Certainly they may take on many disguises – I knew one who pretended to be a flamboyant mercenary captain – but I am sure Master Wandesford was not one of them. Besides, the rector of St Botolph's spoke warmly of him.'

'Might he not be mistaken?' Will said.

'Not in matters of faith, I think.'

He nodded.

'Were you able to speak to Wandesford's landlady?' I asked.

'Aye, on my way home last night. She said he was very quiet, never any trouble, never had any visitors. But she was upset – someone had been in the house while she was out, and she was sure Master Wandesford's room had been searched.'

I felt a tiny quiver of excitement. This was almost like the old days in Walsingham's service. 'Why did she think that?'

'She showed me his room. Always very tidy, she said, not a thing out of place.'

I nodded. That seemed in keeping with the man's character.

'It was pulled about. Nothing badly damaged, as far as I could see, but papers scattered everywhere, an inkpot overturned. His few books dropped open and careless on the floor, as though someone had riffled through their pages. And one curious thing. The goodwife said there were usually crushed sheets where he had blotted or spoiled his writing. Every one of them was gone.'

Chapter Six

*T*he inquest was called for seven o' the clock the next morning, to be held in the main parlour of the Green Dragon inn, situate in Bishopsgate Street. So we were told by one of the city officials, who arrived at the Theatre on Master Burbage's heels, just as the players had begun the read through of Will's new play. I had been looking forward to this, but was sorely disappointed, for the players were so disturbed at the thought of an inquest that they hardly gave their attention to the reading.

Apart from Simon, Guy, and Will, this was the first moment that the players realised Master Wandesford had been murdered. Unless, of course, the killer was there amongst the crowd of agitated men and boys, some of them distressed, some – mostly the boys – excited. All who had been present at the meal given by Lord Hunsdon were to appear at the inquest. There was a written summons for me, requiring me to provide evidence as to the unlawful killing of the deceased. A similar written summons was handed to Cuthbert Burbage, as the person sitting nearest to the victim, who had first called attention to the man's sudden illness.

'Except,' I said to Simon later, 'that someone else was sitting between them. Could it have been the killer?'

'Surely Cuthbert will remember who sat next to him.'

'If he does, there is a good chance that was the killer.'

'Unless the killer was sitting on Wandesford's other side,' Simon said.

'Or opposite.' I closed my eyes, trying to visualise the scene at the table. I opened them again. 'People were milling about when I got there. But I think it would have been possible to reach across the table and drop something in his glass. The table was not very wide.'

We were sitting in my room at our lodgings that evening, unable to forget what was to happen the following morning. We had eaten a subdued supper at the Cross Keys before returning to Southwark, but we were too restless to retire, even though we must rise at dawn, something Simon was not used to. I would be obliged to leave Rikki with Tom again. I could not continue to make a habit of it, and this was troubling me too.

'Does it worry you,' Simon said, 'being required to give evidence as to the cause of death? It was you who started this hare running. Without your discovery of poisoning, there would have been no inquest.'

'I know that.' I spoke somewhat sharply, but I was worried. Indeed, I was afraid, but I was not prepared to admit it. The whole case for murder rested on my testimony. But I was an unemployed physician, cast out by St Thomas's hospital. Might the coroner and jury think that I was up to mischief, calling attention to myself for some personal reason? But attention was the very last thing I wanted. I suspected that Lord Hunsdon had not altogether believed my assertion that Wandesford had been poisoned. He would be obliged to attend the inquest, something he surely would not relish. The inconvenience and the scandal could all be laid at my door.

I began to pace about the room.

'I do have the wine from Wandesford's glass in the phial, still sealed with wax. You and Will saw me seal it. The coroner could call for someone else to examine it.'

'Who?'

'An apothecary or another physician would do. They should be able to recognise *belladonna*. It is not an obscure poison.'

'Perhaps you should suggest that to the coroner. You could send him a message.'

'At this time of night?'

'Write it now,' Simon said, 'then give it to the Atkins lad in the morning. If he runs straight to the Guildhall he should be able to deliver it before the coroner leaves for the Green Dragon.'

'Aye,' I said. 'That's a useful suggestion. I will explain that I have some of the wine from Wandesford's glass and would like a second person to sample it, in order to confirm my suspicions.'

Simon returned to his room to catch what sleep he could, while I wrote and sealed a message for the coroner. I had barely closed my eyes before it was time to rise again. I dressed carefully, after brushing my robe and rubbing my shoes with a cloth to rid them of dust. Probably a waste of effort, for the streets between Southwark and the Green Dragon would be thick with dust and they would soon be soiled again. My hair needed cutting, but I combed it, then tucked it under my physician's cap. I picked up my satchel and checked yet again that the phial was still inside, then whistled to Rikki.

On my way downstairs, I banged on Simon's door.

'I am taking Rikki to Tom Dean,' I called. 'I will meet you at the Bridge gate, but if you are not there, I shall go on ahead. I must not fail to be at the inn on time.'

Simon answered with a grunt, but I was already halfway down the stairs, calling to young Jos Atkins to take my message to the Guildhall.

When I returned to the Bridge from the hospital, Simon was just running toward me, so I waited and we crossed the river together.

'My head is pounding,' I said. 'I suppose it is lack of sleep.'

'Or the weather,' he said.

He was right. A brassy glaze lay over the sky and the air seemed almost too thick to breathe. The weeks of heat had built up in layers, so the very ground failed to cool during the night, but instead hoarded the heat like a baker's oven when the fire is first raked out. The streets of the city burned through the soles of our shoes. Jagged black lines, like flashes of lightning, flickered across my sight, and my skull felt ready to burst.

We reached the Green Dragon, whose very sign was peeling in the sun, as if the dragon's scales were lifting in menace, having taken on a life of their own. Already a crowd was gathering outside and we had to push our way to the door, muttering 'coroner's witnesses' by way of apology. Beside the door, a gaunt woman thrust out her basket at us.

'Nosegays, to sweeten the air, my fine sirs! Sweet nosegays for the gentlemen!'

Simon looked startled, but I nodded.

'How much?'

'A ha'penny each, my master.'

I shook my head and made to go on.

'Too much.'

'A poor body has to live, master,' she whined, with a hint of menace in her tone. 'Sweet nosegays, picked fresh this morning out beyond Finsbury Fields.'

This was clearly a lie, for the flowers were already beginning to wither, and they were the sort of wild flowers that could be found in odd corners of the city. She had not walked far to gather them, nor picked them this morning. However, I knew what the atmosphere would be like by midday, with the crowd and the corpse, confined in one room.

'I'll give you a farthing for two,' I said, holding the coin out to her.

She snatched it from me and thrust two small bunches into my hand. I handed one to Simon as the woman pushed her basket under the nose of a fat man I recognised as a local baker.

'What do we want with these?' Simon asked.

'They won't help much, but you'll be glad of it, nevertheless. Poor Master Wandesford has been lying unburied these three days.'

'Oh,' he said, understanding.

Inside it was already hotter than in the street outside. The innkeeper was standing at the door to the parlour, his face reddened by the heat and a look of despair in his eyes. When he caught sight of me, he glowered.

'This is all your doing,' he snapped. 'All this talk of poison. I'll have you know this is a decent house and we have never had any trouble. Never.'

'I promise you,' I said, 'I do not believe that the poison had anything to do with you, and I shall make that quite clear to the coroner.'

'That is all very well,' he began, but he could not finish, for Simon and I were shoved into the room by the press of men coming up behind.

'Give way, there!' It was a large stout man I recognised as a butcher with a business just round the corner from the inn. 'We are the Coroner's Jurors.' He spoke with a swaggering exaggeration, and I suppose to be chosen to sit on a coroner's jury was an event to excite a man who spent his life hacking apart fly-blown carcasses.

'Give way yourself,' Simon said crossly. 'I am a coroner's witness, and Dr Alvarez here is the expert with knowledge of the method of killing, so look to your manners, sirrah!'

The butcher made a snorting noise. He did not apologise, but he stopped pushing. Even so, we were propelled forward by the sheer bulk of people crowding into the room. A harassed sergeant from the coroner's office in the Guildhall marshalled the sixteen jurors on to two rows of benches on one side of the room, and directed us, together with the remaining witnesses, to benches facing them. Between the two groups, a large chair had been placed for the coroner, with the official banner hung on the wall behind, displaying the royal arms and those of the City of London, while in front a table was set out with writing materials and a large and beautiful nosegay of roses, lavender, and healthful herbs.

I recognised at least half of the jurors by sight – as well as the butcher, two local bakers, a cordwainer, a clerk, a fishmonger, a carpenter, and the farrier who shoed the Walsingham horses. Once all the witnesses and jurors were seated, the public were allowed to enter, which they did with much shoving and ramming of elbows, until every available space was crammed with people, except for a cleared area in front of the coroner's table, occupied by a pair of trestles. I was surprised to see a fair sprinkling of women amongst the men in the crowd, decent, respectable looking goodwives, and not of the poorest class either.

Just when it seemed not another person could squeeze through the door, a second coroner's sergeant cleared a passage through the press for one more person, who joined us on the witnesses' benches. He smiled and bowed at me before sitting down.

'Do you know him?' Simon whispered. There was no need for him to whisper, for the crowd of newcomers were all talking at full pitch.

'It is Master Winger,' I said, 'the senior apothecary at St Bartholomew's.'

I was relieved. There were many apothecaries in London, and not all were honest men, but I had known Master Winger for years and I was certain he could be trusted to support my analysis of the wine. His daughter Helen was married to Peter Lambert, and he was newly a grandfather.

'Should Master Wandesford's body not be here?' It was Guy, crowded up against my other side. 'I thought the inquest must be held *super visum corporis*.'

'I expect that is why the trestles are there,' I said.

'Ah.'

As if they had heard us, the sergeants now began thrusting a wide path through the crowd of gaping onlookers, as four stout men staggered in, carrying a simple coffin of cheap unpolished wood. The crowd which had grumbled at being pushed aside now avidly surged forward, trying for a glimpse of the body, although the lid was still on the coffin. I felt suddenly sick. Not at the thought of seeing the body, for I had seen many, but at the morbid curiosity of these people. Poor, quiet Master Wandesford. I was filled with disgust. Had I dared, I would have sprung to my feet and left this wretched, unseemly gathering.

The coffin bearers paused in front of the trestles. Sweat was running down their faces, and even where I was sitting I could smell that sweat. The sergeant who had escorted us to our seats made a final adjustment to the position of the trestles, then nodded at the bearers, who laid the coffin down with relief and straightened up, some flexing their fingers, others wiping their faces on their sleeves. The sergeant leaned over the coffin and lifted off the lid, setting it on the floor beneath the trestles. The crowd leaned forward. The jurors maintained their dignity, but one and all they stiffened expectantly.

The stench from the body rose like a sickly miasma into the room, mingling with the stink of hot, unwashed bodies, crowded together in too small a space. The only window had been opened, yet there was no hope that it could mitigate the foulness of the air. I raised the bunch of wilting flowers to my nose, but their meagre scent was no match for the stink. On either side, Simon and Guy were pressed up against me so tightly I could feel the heat of their bodies.

There was a door in the wall behind the coroner's chair, leading, as I knew, to a smaller parlour, where a private dinner might be accommodated. The two sergeants now approached it and stood on either side. The buzz of talk from the crowd, which had faded as the coffin was brought in, now rose in pitch and excitement. There must have been some signal from beyond the door, for one of the sergeants threw it open and then drew back. Witnesses and jurors were motioned to stand. The coroner entered.

He was a tall man, dressed in long black robes, lawyer's robes, not very different from my own physician's gown, though the yoke and sleeves are distinctive, indicating the different professions. However, whereas my gown was of rough woollen cloth, irritating in the heat, the coroner's gown whispered silk as he moved gravely to his chair, bowed to the company and took his seat. We all resumed our own seats.

I tapped Simon's arm and whispered, 'I know him.'

He raised an interrogative eyebrow.

'Sir Rowland Heyward. Last year as Governor of the Muscovy Company he sent me on my mission, then I reported to him when I returned. And I've remembered seeing him once before, at a meeting of the governors of St Bartholomew's.'

Guy leaned forward. 'He stepped in as Lord Mayor when John Allot died before finishing his term of office. I've heard the Lord Mayor may act as coroner *ex officio*.'

So that was why he was here.

One of the coroner's sergeants frowned at us. It would be difficult to silence the public, but the jurors and witnesses were expected to behave in a seemly manner.

Before the business of the court could begin, there was a stir by the door. One of the inn servants was pushing his way through, carrying a cushioned chair before him like a battering ram, which he place at the end of our row of benches, then bowed deeply and stepped aside. There were several gasps and a rise in the level of noise as the newcomer was recognised. Lord Hunsdon, resplendent in a velvet doublet of dark green, slashed with copper coloured satin, gave the merest hint of a bow to the coroner and took his seat, ignoring the rest of us and staring straight ahead. Normally sober in his dress, he was clearly making a point with the wealth displayed on his person, in clothes, rings, and his very bearing. No one could doubt that this was the highest ranking individual in the coroner's court. It was clearly intended to intimidate, though I did not think that Sir Rowland himself was intimidated.

It was only then that I realised one person was missing. All those who had been present at the dinner in the garden of the Green Dragon had been ordered by the coroner to attend. The whole of Master Burbage's company and I were here, as were the inn servants, Lord Hunsdon and his two attendants, who now followed him in and took up a position standing behind his chair, for there was no more room on the benches. There was no sign, however, of Mistress Aemilia Bassano.

I wondered whether Sir Rowland knew that she had been present at the dinner, but considered that the testimony of a woman had no value in the present case. Or had Lord Hunsdon used his considerable influence to suppress the fact that she had been there, and so protect his reputation? Perhaps he even cared for her reputation, but since he openly flaunted her as his mistress I was inclined to doubt it.

With a certain inward irony, I thought that, had all those present realised that the case for murder had been raised by a woman, moreover a woman masquerading as a man, this whole performance would not be taking place. For it did seem like a performance, those of us participating in the inquest were the players, the citizens of London were the audience. To the less sensitive of that audience, who had not known the man whose body lay before them, it must have seemed much like a play, staged for their benefit.

I closed my eyes briefly. The pain in my head was getting worse, but I must not let it overwhelm me.

The inquest began. Unnoticed by me, a man with inky fingers had slipped in after Sir Rowland and seated himself behind a small table at the coroner's elbow. He had paper, ink, and quills, so I realised he must be the clerk of the court, here to write down the proceedings. He dipped his pen in the ink and waited with it poised over the paper.

One by one, each juror was called forward by an official and handed a Bible on which he must swear to speak only the truth. He was then required to state his name, occupation and address, all carefully entered in his official record by the clerk of the court. This took some time, and the audience grew restless, the room hotter.

Once the jurors were sworn in, they were led to the coffin and required to take note of the deceased person over whom this inquest was taking place, to determine the cause of death. They made a fine show of manly courage as they studied the body, but both of the bakers looked decidedly green, while a small man, unknown to me, pressed a handkerchief to his mouth and rolled his eyes, with the air of someone like to vomit at any moment. As they return to their places, he retreated to the back and fixed his eyes firmly on the ceiling, swallowing repeatedly.

The jurors dealt with, it was the turn of the witnesses, starting with Lord Hunsdon, who spoke with some arrogance, as if he hardly expected to have to account for himself or state his name. The official, though polite in his manner, made no distinction for his birth and position. In previous encounters I had found his lordship pleasant enough and by no means as lofty as many men of lesser rank, but I had some sympathy for him in his present situation. He had entertained the players to dinner merely because of his interest in the playhouses, and now found himself caught up in this disreputable affair, which almost certainly had nothing whatsoever to do with him.

After Lord Hunsdon, Master Burbage and then the rest of us who were witnesses swore and gave our particulars. Finally the preliminaries were over and Sir Rowland spoke for the first time.

'Who is present in this court to identify the deceased?' he asked, looking towards us.

Master Burbage and Guy rose to their feet.

'We are, your honour,' Master Burbage said.

They both approached the coffin and looked down. Master Burbage had his back to me, but I saw a spasm of pain cross Guy's face.

'Do you recognise the deceased? If so, name him.'

'His name is Oliver Wandesford,' Master Burbage said, 'late copyist to Lord Strange's Men, of which I am the governor.'

'I also confirm that this is Oliver Wandesford,' Guy said.

'And how long have you known the deceased?'

'Fifteen years.'

'Fifteen years.'

'There is no doubt in your mind that this is Oliver Wandesford?'

'None.'

They were waved back to their seats.

The coroner now asked Lord Hunsdon to give an account of how and why the dinner in the garden of the Green Dragon had taken place three nights before, which he did with remarkable brevity.

'And are all those who attended the dinner now present?'

'They are.'

Hunsdon spoke without hesitation or so much as a flicker of an eyelid. I suppose courtiers must learn to lie smoothly from a very early age. Next the innkeeper was required to give an account of all the victuals served, where they had come from, who had prepared them, and how they had been served.

He had barely finished his very long-winded and defensive account of the excellence of the food provided by the Green Dragon when there was a disturbance in the audience. The coroner frowned and signalled to the sergeants to investigate. It soon became clear that two people had fainted from the heat and the close atmosphere, which made it so difficult to breathe. One was a young boy. Barely up to an adult's elbow, he must have suffered more than the rest from the stifling air. The other was a pregnant woman, not far off her time. I half rose to go to their assistance, but Guy pulled me back down.

'You cannot leave until the proceedings are closed,' he whispered. 'They will find another physician.'

The woman and the boy were bundled unceremoniously out of the inn, and we were unable to see what became of them. Once quiet – or relative quiet – had been restored, each of the witnesses, including me, was told to give an account of the dinner. For the moment I was not being singled out. The evidence was mostly repetitive and seemed to go on for hours. Our audience, clearly eager for excitement, grew restless, and bored, and noisy. Several times the sergeants reprimanded them. They even went to far as to turn a few of the noisier offenders out into the street.

Cuthbert was questioned in particular about how he had seen Master Wandesford taken ill, vomiting and collapsing on to the table.

Once we were all seated and the clerk had finished scribbling his notes, Sir Rowland spoke again.

'This inquest has been called because there has been an allegation of foul play in the demise of the deceased. Who has made this allegation?'

Feeling more sick than ever, I rose to my feet.

'I do, your worship.'

One of the sergeants waved me over to stand in front of the coroner's chair. Brought face to face with me, he seemed for the first time to recognise me. I saw him give a slight start. Perhaps some official had handled my request for an apothecary, not Sir Rowland himself. He must have heard me sworn in, but it had been a tedious business, so perhaps he had allowed his attention to wander. His lips twitched in the shadow of a smile, which I took for a good sign. After my mission for the Muscovy Company, I thought he respected me. I began to feel a little less nervous.

'Dr Alvarez,' he said, 'I understand that when you attended the deceased, having been called to him by Master Cuthbert Burbage, you made certain observations which caused you to suspect that he had been poisoned.'

'That is so,' I said. 'However, I had noticed certain signs earlier in the evening, before we sat down at table.'

He raised his eyebrows and leaned forward, resting his chin on his clasped hands.

'Are you saying that the deceased had already been poisoned *before* he arrived at the inn?'

'Not fatally poisoned, nay. By the symptoms he exhibited, I would say that he had previously been given a very small dose, one that had not proved fatal, but which had begun to work upon his body, causing trembling, slurred speech, sweats, and enlarged pupils of the eyes. He complained of dizziness, pains, and blurred vision. When he walked, he was unsteady on his feet.'

'You are sure he had not simply taken too much drink?'

There was a snigger from the crowd, quickly reprimanded by one of the sergeants.

'Nay, your worship, the symptoms were not those of excess drink. The effect on the eyes of *belladonna* poisoning is quite unmistakable.'

'And is it your belief that this previous dose, if such it was, overcame him during the meal?'

'Nay. He received a further and fatal dose in a glass of wine.'

I reached into my satchel and drew out the phial. There was a gasp of delighted excitement from behind me. At last matters were becoming interesting. 'There was still a little of the wine in his glass,' I explained. 'I took the precaution of emptying it into this phial. Before sealing it with wax, I tasted a drop. The wine had been poisoned with *belladonna*. Two of the witnesses here saw me place the wine in the phial and seal it, Master Hetherington and Master Shakespeare.'

Simon and Will stood up and affirmed that they had seen this done.

I then described Master Wandesford's final throes.

'Before he died,' I said, 'he indicated that he recognised the taste in the wine, and that he had been given it before. He died before he could tell me when it had been given him or by whom. I therefore assume that it was not administered by the inn or its people, but by someone who had given it to him on an earlier occasion.'

'Are you able to name this person?'

I shook my head. 'I am not. The person who placed the poison in the glass must have been nearby, but it was quite dark where Master Wandesford was sitting and by the time I reached him from the other end of the table, people were moving about.'

'Master Cuthbert Burbage has already told us that he cannot recall who was sitting where at that end of the table.' The coroner looked over at the benches where the guests at the dinner were now sitting. All looked uneasy. It seemed certain that whoever had added the *belladonna* to Wandesford's wine must be there amongst them.

'I understand you have asked for another opinion on the contents of this phial.' Sir Rowland held out his hand and I set the tiny bottle down on the table in front of him. Such a small thing, to determine the cause of a man's death.

'Master Winger,' the coroner said, 'please examine this sample and give us your opinion.'

The apothecary came to the table and picked up the bottle. I moved to one side so as not to block the light. He took a small penknife from a sheath on his belt and cut away the wax which secured the cork. He smelled the contents, then tipped a drop on to his forefinger and touched it to his tongue.

The coroner looked at him enquiringly, but Master Winger did not speak until he had spat into his handkerchief, replaced the cork, and set the phial down on the table again.

'*Belladonna*,' he said, 'without a doubt.'

'The phial might have been tampered with, and the poison added after the dinner,' the coroner said coolly.

I felt my stomach clench in horror. Was he accusing me of fabricating the evidence?

Master Winger shook his head. 'I have known Dr Alvarez for many years and can state that he is a man of honour and a physician of impeccable reputation. I would take my oath on this being a sample of the wine drunk by the deceased.'

Sir Rowland nodded. 'You may both resume your seats.'

I collapsed on to the bench, my legs shaking. I had not foreseen that the coroner would cast that kind of doubt over my evidence.

Sensing my alarm, Guy muttered, 'He had to ask that, don't you see? Otherwise one of the jurors might have raised the question.'

Perhaps he was right, but my head was truly swimming now.

Cuthbert was questioned again, but could only remember a few of those who had been sitting near him.

'I apologise, your honour,' he said. He was looking worried and distressed. 'I had spent most of the dinner conversing with Lord Hunsdon, on my left, with my back turned toward that end of the table. As Dr Alvarez has said, it was quite dark. Apart from scolding some of the boys who were making a noise, I hardly spoke to anyone to my right. It was only when Master Wandesford fell forward and the glasses were smashed that I realised anything was untoward.'

'Very well. You may sit down.'

The coroner turned to his clerk, who passed up the notes he had been taking. While he was reading through them I heard the clock from one of the nearby churches strike twice. On the one hand it seemed impossible that so many hours had passed, but on the other we seemed to have been sitting in this hellish room for ever. I could feel a rivulet of sweat running down my backbone, and the strands of hair which had escaped from my cap were clinging unpleasantly to my temples. The heat pressing in from all those crowded around me aggravated the rising heat of my own body. The bench was too narrow, and without a back, so that my spine was cramped and aching, while my feet had swollen so that my shoes pinched. But all of this was as nothing, compared to the charnel house stench of the room. Even the eager observers had begun to find the atmosphere too much to endure. Perhaps a quarter of them had slipped away, as I observed to Guy.

'Probably not gone far,' he said. 'They'll be refreshing themselves at the nearest ale house and come back for the verdict. They won't want to miss the climax of this free entertainment.'

The open window was almost exactly opposite us, facing west, so that as the sun moved round it fell more directly on us. When I looked up, I thought my vision, distorted by my headache, was conjuring up black blotches around the window frame. Then I realised that the blotches had a life of their own, and were made up of clusters of flies. Lured away from other enticing smells in the neighbourhood, the fishmongers' and butchers' stalls, the town middens and uncleared gutters, the flies were drawn to the object of the inquest. Singly, in two and threes, in whole colonies, they swarmed about the coffin in such numbers I could hear the buzz of their wings even over the chatter in the court. It was intolerable.

With great daring, I rose from my seat and approached the coroner's chair, and bowed.

'Sir Rowland,' I said softly, 'I am sorry to presume, but might the lid of the coffin be replaced? There are a great many flies, and the miasma which rises from the dead can be of great harm to the living, especially if it is spread by flies.'

He looked startled at being approached, but after a moment's thought he nodded and turned to one of his sergeants.

'Dr Alvarez is right. We should not endanger the health of those present. The jurors and the witnesses have viewed the deceased. The lid of the coffin may be replaced.'

As I returned to my bench, I could not avoid a glance into the coffin. It was hard to equate the object crawling with flies to the neat person of Master Wandesford. It was the ultimate degradation. Whose hand had been raised against this harmless old man and brought him to such a humiliating end? Nothing that had been said so far during the inquest had brought us any nearer to an answer. Would the authorities in London make any attempt to find the murderer? Or was the victim of such little importance that no search would be made?

As I took my seat, Guy smiled at me. 'That was well done. Poor fellow. It is only decent to cover him up.'

'Decent, and an attempt to avoid the spread of sickness,' I said, 'though it may already be too late for that.'

The coroner had laid down his papers and the sergeants once again attempted to silence the talking in the room.

'Dr Alvarez,' Sir Rowland said, 'I have a further question.'

I stood up again and stepped forward. Had I called too much attention to myself with my request? But it seemed the coroner had a genuine question concerning the case.

'Your worship?' I said.

'I have been told that on occasion, some persons will take *belladonna* to induce visions. In your opinion, could that be the case here? So that the death might be either a form of *felo de se* or of accidental death, due to consuming too large a dose?'

It was the same point Dr Nuñez had raised when I had discussed Wandesford's death with him, and once again I argued against self administration on the basis of what I knew of the deceased's character. Also questioned, on the grounds that they had known him longest, Guy and Master Burbage supported my argument. We were all three questioned as to whether we had any knowledge or suspicion of any individual who might wish the deceased harm. All three of us stated that we had no such knowledge or suspicion, and were permitted to resume our seats.

The coroner now turned to the jurors.

'Gentlemen,' he said, 'you have heard the evidence of how the deceased met his death during a dinner in the garden of this inn. The witnesses are agreed that he collapsed while sitting at table and died very shortly thereafter. You must now withdraw and consider your verdict as to the cause of death. I will summarise for you. First, do you find the deceased to be Oliver Wandesford, copyist, late of the parish of St Botolph's? Second, did the deceased die of natural causes? Third, if you do not believe he died of natural causes, what do you conclude caused his death? Do you accept the opinion given by the physician Dr Alvarez and the apothecary Master Winger that his wine contained *belladonna* and that this was the cause of death? Fourth, do you judge the poison to have been added to the wine by the deceased himself or by some other person, with malice aforethought? Finally, can you name this person?'

Some of the jurors looked worried at this barrage of questions to be answered, others nodded wisely, as if passing such judgements was a regular feature of their lives.

'You will be taken to a private room,' the coroner continued, 'and the door will be locked. No food or drink will be provided. When you have come to an agreement as to your answers to these questions, you should knock on the door and you will be returned to this court of inquiry, where we shall hear your verdict.'

I saw that all the jurors had gaped in disbelief at the news that they would be given no food or drink. It was now early afternoon and none of us had taken anything since early morning. They must all be as hungry and thirsty as I was. I suppose it was a certain way to ensure that they would reach their verdict quickly.

The coroner stood, and we did likewise. He withdrew to the small parlour as the jurors were ushered by the sergeants out of the main door and across to a room opposite, which I believe was the private parlour of the innkeeper's family. The audience began to slip away after them, no doubt in search of an ale house or ordinary, to take some refreshment while they could.

Simon leaned across Guy and me to speak to Master Burbage.

'Must we also remain here, without food or drink? I am like to faint away if they take too long over their deliberations.'

'I believe we must remain here,' Master Burbage said, 'but I see no reason why we should not ask the innkeeper to provide some refreshment.'

The innkeeper was only too willing, having already lost a day's trade to the holding of the inquest. It was not long before he had pot boys scurrying in with jugs of ale, followed by his wife and maidservants with bread, cold meats, cheese, and fresh salad greens.

'I would avoid the meat,' I warned, but not everyone heeded me. The rest of the food I believed would be safe enough.

Lord Hunsdon did not join us, but demanded a private room and withdrew to it with his two attendants. He was probably in breach of some law and should have remained with the rest of the witnesses, but I think no one had the courage to reprimand him.

The ale was cool and did something to slake my thirst. The room, too, became less oppressive, now that everyone but the witnesses had departed. We walked about, shaking the stiffness out of our limbs from so long sitting, and enjoying the release from being packed together like herrings in a barrel.

I piled chunks of bread with cheese, onions and lettuce, and walked as far as the door while I munched it. I had realised how thirsty I was, but only now became fully aware of my hunger.

'You may not leave the court,' one of the sergeants said officiously, barring my way to the door.

'I do not intend to.' I was fairly brusque, for I was hot and tired, and my head was no better. 'However, we all need air. Have you opened the door to the street? There will be no breeze, but a little of this foul air might disperse before everyone returns.'

He inclined his head, and ordered one of the pot boys to open the street door and wedge it in position. I could feel a faint, very faint, movement of air, which might disperse some of the miasma.

Gradually all the witnesses wandered back to the benches and the inn servants cleared away the traces of our scrappy meal. From across the corridor beyond the door came the sound of loud knocking.

'God be praised!' Will said. 'I hope that means the jurors have come to some decision.'

A few minutes later, the jurors were once more escorted to their benches, closely followed by Lord Hunsdon, who hitched his chair a little further away from us, as if to make clear the fact that he was not part of our disreputable company, rogues and vagabonds as all players are known to be. I now found myself sitting next to Master Winger.

'I thank you for supporting my diagnosis,' I said.

'There was no mistaking it. Definitely *belladonna*, and the symptoms you described are certainly those of *belladonna* poisoning. Do you remember that case of the boy who had eaten the berries?'

'Aye,' I said grimly, 'who could forget it? That was what made it easy for me to identify the symptoms.'

Our discussion was interrupted by one of the sergeants calling upon us to rise. The previous crowd had pushed back into the room, having acquired some new faces, all looking eagerly at the jurors. The coroner and his clerk returned from the small parlour, where I had no doubt they had been regaled with rather better fare than we had.

We all sat down. The coroner turned to the jurors.

'Who speaks for you?' he asked.

The fat butcher stood up, oily with importance. 'I do, your worship.'

'How do you find on the first count? Do you find the deceased to be Oliver Wandesford, copyist, late of the parish of St Botolph's?'

'We do.'

'Second, did the deceased perish from natural causes?'

'Nay, your worship. We do not believe he died from natural causes.'

The clerk made a note.

'Third, what do you believe was the cause of death?'

'We believe the evidence that the death was caused by *belladonna* added to the deceased's wine during the dinner.'

The coroner nodded. I supposed he must appear neutral and leave the verdict to the jurors, but I thought he had probably already made up his own mind.

'Fourth, do you believe this was a case of *felo de se*, the diseased having caused his own death, or do you believe the poison was administered by a third party, with malice aforethought?'

The butcher cleared his throat. He was hoarse, and growing hoarser. He must be longing for something to drink.

'On the evidence of those who knew him, your honour, we do not believe the deceased added the poison himself. We believe it was given to him by someone else.'

Once again the coroner nodded. The clerk was writing briskly.

'Finally, do you find yourselves able to name the perpetrator of this deed?'

'Nay, your worship, we do not.'

'Very well. You may resume your place.'

Throughout this interrogation, the room had fallen totally silent. Now, as Sir Rowland rose to his feet, I could hear the silken rustle of his gown.

'The verdict of this court, therefore, is that the deceased, Oliver Wandesford, was murdered by person or persons unknown.'

Chapter Seven

*T*he day after the inquest Simon came to my room, barely able to contain his laughter.

'There has been a development with the inquest,' he said.

I could not see how anything related to the inquest could be amusing him, so I waited.

He pulled one of my chairs away from the table and sat on it back to front, resting his chin on the back rail.

'It seems the coroner has ruled that, since this was an unlawful killing, there must be a *deodand*.'

'A what?'

'A *deodand*. It is apparently the law that a fine equivalent to the value of the murder weapon must be paid to the Crown.'

'But there was no murder weapon. Or at least, only the berries of *belladonna*, which have no monetary value.'

'You and I might think that, but not the Crown. The glass in which the poison was administered is deemed to be the murder weapon.'

'But–'

'Aye, it seems absurd, but there you are. That's the law for you.'

'Who is supposed to pay the fine?'

'Normally, it would be the murderer, but as no one knows who the murderer was, the innkeeper, who supplied the glass, is deemed liable.'

I began to laugh. It was indeed funny, but . . . 'Poor man,' I said. 'They were very fine Venetian goblets. Two were smashed as Wandesford lay dying, and now he must pay for a third. What do you suppose they are worth?'

'As you say, fine Venetian glass. Master Burbage reckons not less than three shillings each. A fortune.'

'The Green Dragon will never want to set eyes on us again,' I said.

I saw very little of the players during the following week. I was not even able to attend the performance of Will's new play concerning the struggles between Lancaster and York, which I had so laboriously copied out. The Dolesby family summoned me, and continued to summon me every day. This was a taste of what was involved in the care of rich private patients. For the poor at St Bartholomew's or St Thomas's, the physician is almost a god, someone with healing in his hands, who may end your pain or save your life. He is looked up to and respected. For the rich private patient, the physician is but a servant, of no higher position than the tailor or shoemaker or groom. He may be a professional man, but the patient is paying for his services, and expects to be able to summon him at will.

Mistress Dolesby declared herself to be monstrously ill, but I soon discovered that she was suffering from no more than a summer cold. I suspect that she was one of those people who enjoy fancying themselves to be ill, for it adds drama to their dull lives. Then the children developed the same cold, but rather worse, with sore throats and headaches. At first Mistress Dolesby would not allow that anyone could be as ill as she was – a characteristic of these hypochondriacs – but when the youngest, four-year-old Jonathan, developed a fever, she became frantic. Twice I was summoned in the middle of the night, Master Dolesby having sent a servant over the river by wherry to fetch me. Dr Nuñez had warned me of some of the perils of private practice, but I had not quite believed that it was as tiresome as he suggested.

Dosed with febrifuge herbs, given plenty of boiled barley water to drink, and a light diet to eat, the children soon recovered, at which point their mother experienced a relapse, no doubt occasioned by the unpleasant experience of not remaining the centre of attention. I am perhaps being cynical, but having been accustomed to the real and serious illnesses of my hospital patients, I had difficulty in taking her histrionics quite seriously. However, I was prepared to make sympathetic noises and to prescribe some harmless potions, such as a soothing drink tinted with beetroot juice to make it more dramatic for her. At the end of a week I was tired of the Dolesby family and fortunately a visit from her sister, who lived near Lincoln, gave the lady of the house something else to think about. The children had recovered fully and the lady herself was now occupied in setting her sister right on such matters as the latest fashions at Court.

On the first day when my presence was not demanded in Goldsmiths' Row, I allowed myself the unaccustomed luxury of rising late from my bed in the morning. The compensation for my frequent visits to Cheapside was additional coins in my purse, so while giving Rikki his morning walk I called in at a decent butcher who kept a clean shop next past the whorehouse and bought half a dozen slices of bacon. Rikki and I had just finished breaking our fast in a most satisfactory manner when Simon pounded on my door, this being the late hour at which the players were accustomed to rise.

'Have you inherited a fortune from a rich benefactor?' he said, coming in and sniffing like a deer hound on the trail of a promising quarry. He headed toward my fire, which was now dying out.

'I have earned it,' I said, 'after a week of Mistress Dolesby.'

He broke a piece off my loaf and used it to soak up the savoury juices from the pan on my hearth.

'Alas, we poor players feed on nothing but the rich physician's leavings.'

'You have just eaten the last of Rikki's breakfast,' I said. 'And this rich physician dined on nothing but scraps in the goldsmith's kitchen last night, like a scullion, while the poor players must have eaten well at an inn.' I was still feeling aggrieved at my treatment in the Dolesby household.

'Aye, you have several dinners owing you from Master Burbage,' he said. 'I have a message for you. Your skills as a copyist are required, if you can be spared from the merchants of Cheapside. Our play book of Tom Kyd's *Spanish Tragedy* has all but fallen to pieces. Master Burbage would be grateful if you could make a new book of it before it is lost altogether, and then copy out the separate players' parts.'

'Aye, I can come with you now. But why do you not take your plays to the printer, so they may not be lost for ever?'

He stared at me as if I had taken leave of my senses.

'*Print them!* Why then every fool of a would-be player could stumble through our plays and demand that an audience pay for the joy of it! We should give away our livelihood! Surely you understand that, Kit? Without our play books we are nothing but poor mumbling shadows, aping the substance of life.'

'You are beginning to sound like Will,' I said. 'Too much poetising in your cups, I fear.'

We set off for Shoreditch, bickering amiably as we went. Recently I had begun to think that I had imagined more to that farewell kiss at Wardhouse than was ever meant. If Simon had truly guessed that I was a girl, he had shown no further sign of it.

'How went your second performance of Will's new play?' I asked. 'Perhaps I shall have the chance to watch it one of these fine days.

'It went well,' he said, tossing a coin to a fruit seller on the Bridge and helping himself to an apple. 'I enjoy playing the treacherous French dauphin, a part to tear a cat in. I'll never make a comic like Guy, but it's good to play a villain from time to time, especially one who is not entirely a blaggard. Will's clever that way.'

He took a bite of his apple.

'First fruits. They must be picking Kentish apples early this year. Want a bite?'

I took a bite and handed the apple back. It was fresh and juicy, unlike the final withered specimens from last year, which had been the only apples generally available this summer until now.

'We must perform while we can,' he said. 'Pillings says a break in the weather is coming, and he's a weatherwise fellow.'

'It needs no Pillings to tell me that,' I retorted. 'Look at those clouds.' I pointed up river, to the west. 'Those are thunder clouds building.'

'Then you'd best come to the Theatre the day after tomorrow, if you want to see Will's new play before we are rained out.'

'The Dolesbys permitting, I shall come,' I promised.

Only a few of the company had arrived at the playhouse before us. Guy was putting Davy through his acrobatic moves in the open space where the groundlings stood during a performance, while Christopher was sitting on the edge of the stage, kicking his heels.

'Well met, Simon!' he called. 'We need to practice our sword play from Act Three. We finished too quickly last time. Our customers expect more thrills for their pennies.'

'I will fetch a foil,' Simon said.

He headed for the room where the costumes and properties were kept, while I sought out Master Burbage in his office.

'Ah, Kit,' he said, 'you come very timely.'

He held out to me a bundle of paper, tied together with a bit of frayed ribbon. The edges were ragged and the top page looked as though several dripping ale cups had rested upon it at some time.

'This has not been well treated,' I said severely. 'I thought these play books were your life blood.'

'They are, indeed they are, but Tom Kyd is a careless fellow. Last time he took this away to make some changes I had asked for, it came back in that state. He had even lost six sheets from the middle of the second act. Fortunately he managed to find them again, mixed in with some epic poem he was trying to write.'

His tone was scornful. Clearly he had no great opinion of the higher aspirations of poets. He wanted his play makers to be practical fellows, with an eye to writing what would please an audience. Will had once admitted to me that he often wrote short poems, but kept them well out of Master Burbage's sight.

'For fear,' he said, 'that he will suspect I am frittering away precious hours, when I might be making him a new play. But there you are, one cannot for ever be writing in five acts.'

'Is this now the final version of *The Spanish Tragedy*?' I asked. 'Or will Master Kyd want to make more changes?'

'Not if I can stop him,' Master Burbage said grimly. 'He will make no more changes except what I demand, and he will make them here, under my eye.' He thumped his desk to make his point. 'I'll not risk him carrying it off to his lodgings again. Besides, he shares lodgings with Marlowe now, and Marlowe is writing for Henslowe. Kyd's work for me might find its way into the Rose playhouse.'

I could never quite understand the relationship between the two great playhouse managers, Burbage and Henslowe. Sometimes they were the best of friends, lending players to each other, bemoaning their lot over a jug of wine, and cursing the censorship of Sir Edmund Tilney, Master of the Revels. At other times they were bitter rivals, not speaking to each other, doing their best to poach each other's audiences.

'When I have copied this out again, must it be signed off by Sir Edmund once more?' I said. 'Or since it was passed already–?'

Master Burbage waved a hand in the air, as if he was swatting flies. 'If we have any worries on that score, we will simply leave the original final page attached, with Sir Edmund's signature. Now, there is plenty of paper in the book room. If you require anything else, ask Stoker to fetch it. He can make himself useful, if he wishes to remain with the company.'

'He is not earning his keep?' I said, gathering up the loose bundle of manuscript. I was little interested in Stoker, and liked him less.

Burbage shrugged. 'He is useful when we need to move properties and costumes, but he is no use for anything else.'

'He hardly proved himself a competent copyist.'

'He is even worse as a player. I have used him once or twice to bulk out a crowd, but even then he is as animated as a bedpost.'

Stoker was hanging about the door to the book room, offering to fetch anything I required, but I told him somewhat curtly that I required nothing. I thought that I caught a venomous look in his eyes, but it was no more than a flash, then his eyelids dropped modestly. It was understandable, I suppose, that he should resent me, employed in the post he had hoped to occupy himself.

I opened the window shutters to throw some light on my work, and left the door of the room wide, for it was small and stuffy, hardly more than a cupboard. Once I had trimmed several quills, I began my copying, accompanied by the clash of rapiers from where Simon and Christopher were practising their swordplay on stage. Kyd's writing was vile, even worse than Will's hasty scrawl, so I made slow progress at first. After a few minutes I looked up to see that Stoker had sidled up behind me and was peering over my shoulder. He was reading the manuscript, for I could hear him faintly speaking the lines, though with poor understanding or expression. Master Burbage's mention of the bedpost seemed apt.

'Do you want something, Stoker?' I said. 'Only I find it unpleasant to have someone reading over my shoulder.'

'I could help you, he said, employing that ingratiating manner which I had noticed before. 'If I read the lines out to you, then you could work more quickly.'

'I think not,' I said. 'I need to see how the lines are laid out on the page.' I wished the man would go away. I could even feel his hot breath on the back of my neck, and he was not overly clean.

At last, by speaking quite rudely, I managed to rid myself of him. I was not sure whether he was still attempting to lay some claim to the copyist's work, or whether he was merely a frustrated player. Whatever the reason, I was thankful when at last he took himself off.

Perhaps he did still hope to become a player, for while I continued at my work all through the afternoon, the stage was occupied by a performance of another of Will's plays, the one with all the foolery about twins and mistaken identity. The audience loved it. Even from where I sat I could hear the laughter and applause, which distracted me, I must confess, from my copying. I noticed, moreover, that Stoker stayed just within the tiring room, where he could not be seen by the audience or the players. All the while, he mouthed the lines along with whichever player was speaking. He seemed to be memorising all their parts. A futile exercise, it seemed to me, for clearly Master Burbage would never employ him as a player.

After the performance, there was a short rehearsal of *Friar Bungay*, a limping old comedy the players despised, but which Master Burbage insisted on mounting regularly, since it was perennially popular with the less cultured of his customers. While the weather held, he was filling the Theatre as often as he could.

Over dinner that evening – in the Black Bull this time, for a change of scene – I asked whether there had been anything further in the matter of Master Wandesford's death, since the day of the inquest.

'We have had the coroner's sergeants round at the playhouse several times,' Guy said, 'asking more questions, trying to discover whether his death benefitted anyone. It seems as inexplicable as ever. He had made a will, but he had few goods – his clothes, a few books. No money was found in his room.'

'But Will said he thought someone had searched his room,' I said.

'I cannot be certain,' Will said, 'but his landlady thought his belongings were thrown about when they were usually neat, and his working papers had gone. Perhaps the intruder thought they were valuable. He may have taken any coin lying around.'

'If Master Wandesford made a will, what could he bequeath?' I said.

'His possessions are to be sold, by his directions,' Guy said. 'His clothes are worth little, but the books will fetch something. However, there are no named beneficiaries. The money from the sale of his goods is to be given to an almshouse in some small town in Yorkshire. His birthplace, perhaps. It seems I was right in my guess that he came from those parts.'

'So no single person would benefit from his death,' I said slowly. 'It is hardly likely that the paupers from a Yorkshire almshouse travelled to London to poison him. The whole case becomes stranger by the day.'

'Perhaps it was a mistake,' Christopher suggested. 'Someone took Master Wandesford for another man.'

Will shook his head. 'That will not do. As Kit has shown, the final dose of poison was given to him during the dinner. Everyone there knew him.'

'Except the servants,' Christopher said. 'And Lord Hunsdon and his mistress.'

'But they could not have administered the earlier dose,' I said. 'He had certainly ingested some *belladonna* before that evening.'

Everyone around the table was looking uncomfortable, for the inescapable conclusion was that the killer must be sitting amongst us. I wished that I had not started the subject. I turned to Master Burbage.

'I am sorry I was not able to attend the funeral, but I was called away to a patient.'

'Far more attended than we had expected,' he said. 'Most of the players of London must have been there.'

'One of our own,' Guy said. 'Not a player himself, but still one of our own. And though a quiet, self-effacing man, he was well liked and respected. Without his work, hidden and unseen, we could not have brought our plays to the stage.'

It was a fitting tribute, although I thought that Wandesford's name would soon vanish into the dust.

The Dolesby family must be in good health, or else the sister from Lincolnshire was keeping them occupied, for I was no longer receiving a daily summons and was able to continue my copying work at the Theatre. I was glad of it, for it meant a small but steady income and one good meal a day, with scraps for Rikki, who had developed a look of hungry patience which went down well with the players. They could recognise a good performance when they saw one. And as well, I enjoyed the companionship, a welcome change from moping alone in my lodgings, thinking how my skills and training were being wasted. From time to time I had heard gossip from Tom Read about the discontent at St Thomas's with the work of my successor, who was reckoned a poor physician and an arrogant fellow. I was not tempted to find any pleasure in this, for I grieved for my Southwark patients.

At the playhouse I felt myself amongst friends, and although I was there to perform lowly clerical tasks, I also found that I was learning more about this world which was so different from my own. A curious variety of men and boys washed up at the playhouse. Some came because they cared passionately about the work, like Simon and Will. Some were born into it, like Master Burbage's two sons, Cuthbert and Dick, although their two interests were very different. Some found in the playhouse an outlet for talents learned elsewhere, like Guy with his music and comic turns and young Davy, discovered as a toddler in a ditch and exploited by travelling vagabonds. Some, like a number of the boys, had been found a place here because their families could not buy them an apprenticeship but they could pass well enough in women's parts until their voices broke. I was not quite sure about Christopher Haigh. He worked hard enough, but I felt that if something better offered, he would be away.

I began to know more of the players better. There was Geoffrey de Claine. He must have been no more than thirty, but once he was on stage he became a quavering old dotard. And Thomas Hulin, who played the older, more difficult women's parts, too demanding for the young boys. He could be anything from a mighty queen to a scheming hag, but needed to shave several times a day, being dark and whiskery.

Until I started to spend so much time with them, I had not realised how hard the players worked. They must memorise the words and actions of anything from a dozen to twenty new plays mounted in each summer season, a feat I could barely comprehend.

'But you must learn all your potions and poultices,' Dick Burbage said one day, when I had commented on this. 'You must remember hundreds of different illnesses and how to treat each one, and all the learned writings of the past, handed down to you.'

'That is different,' I said, though I admit I was at a loss to explain why.

'It is a matter of what engages you.' Guy had been listening to us. 'Dick cares about the parts he plays, so learning the words is far less arduous for him than it would be for you, Kit. Whereas you have a passion for curing the sick. Learning how best to do so calls for all your mind and effort. Besides, I expect you started your studies very young, did you not?'

'At about the age of seven,' I admitted, 'studying with my father.'

'There you have it. It is like Davy's acrobatics. He was trained to it as a small child. I could not take one of the older boys, of twelve or thirteen let us say, and persuade his body to perform the sort of contortions which cause Davy no difficulty at all.'

I conceded that there was some truth in what Guy said. Yet the hard work of the players did not end with learning so many parts. Day after day they must perform upon a public stage. An audience might be bored or hostile or simply very small, but still the players must take their parts with the same delight as when they had an enthusiastic crowd filling all the tiers of seats and the pit before the stage. I saw that before each performance they were lit up with a kind of sick excitement, so that they seemed larger, more vivid than in their everyday world, and this enlarged character they took on seemed to grow while they were on stage. After a performance they looked either drained and exhausted or else febrile with a sort of left-over ferment. Burbage very wisely, I realised, allowed them a calming break before starting the rehearsal which generally followed in the later afternoon.

Two days after I returned to my copying work, I was able, at last, to watch a performance of Will's play about the early troubles in the reign of the sixth King Henry. I had found it very complicated when I was copying out the parts, and I am not sure I had all the details clear in my mind after watching it on stage. So much political manoeuvring, alliances made and broken – not just between the English and the French, but amongst the English nobles during the early reign of a young and weak king. One thing Will did make clear, amongst all these shifts of power –

civil war is inevitable when the monarch is weak. No wonder that the last century had been a time of so much fear and bloodshed.

Dick Burbage played the role of the English hero, Talbot, betrayed to his death by the internecine strife of York and Somerset, each determined to control the young Henry VI. Simon was suitably devious and untrustworthy as the French dauphin, ready to betray not only peace treaties but his own supporters. The most dramatic of those supporters was the young French farm girl, Joan La Poucelle.

The part would once had fallen to Simon when he was younger. Recently he had been training two of the boys to take the leading women's roles: Henry Condell, whose voice was near breaking, and a lad called John Spencer. Spencer was very talented and was given the part. Joan the Holy Maid, revered in France, though betrayed by Frenchmen, and reviled in England, became through his performance the poignant human sacrifice to the vicious quarrels of great men, although Will had retained the English view that she was a witch, which had troubled me when I copied the part. Young Spencer portrayed with considerable skill Joan's abject terror in her last scene. It left me very thoughtful. Such is the end of women who dare to break into the world of men, even – or perhaps especially – women who surpass the men amongst whom they live. Involuntarily, as the players took their bows, my mind turned to Aemilia Bassano. I wondered whether she had seen the play.

The weather continued unbearably hot and windless, while the thunder clouds also continued to pile up on the western horizon, but with the lack of wind they drifted no nearer. Despite the profitable time in the playhouse, with the Theatre full almost every day, I sensed that the players would have welcomed a good rain storm to send the audiences away for a few days. They were becoming very tired. Tempers were growing short and a number of squabbles broke out over quite trivial matters.

Once I had finished making a fair copy of *The Spanish Tragedy*, Master Burbage set me to work producing better copies of some of their older plays, which also existed in somewhat tattered form. Becoming so familiar with the texts, I began to understand a little – though not a great deal – about the play maker's craft. These old plays were very simple, the same characters appearing again and again – the young lovers, the wicked villain who tries to part them, the foolish old man (often the girl's father), the clever servant, who might also be a comic (so a part for Guy). They reminded me of nothing so much as the puppet plays I had watched at Bartholomew Fair. The language too was usually crude and limping.

When I compared this old stuff with Will's new plays, I understood that he was creating something quite different. The language was beautiful. But it was more than that. The people he created seemed to live and breathe in the very ink on the page, before they were even performed on the stage. They had all the complexities of the people you might meet in your real life. As Simon had said, even the supposed villains were not simply evil, they were complicated, troubled people. I did not like Kit Marlowe. Although I had seen some of his plays, I had disliked their violence, and in particular their fascination with evil, but I began to understand that he, like Will, was fashioning something the like of which had never been seen or heard before. Even Tom Kyd was touched with this new spirit of creation, as I realised when I copied his latest play. And I now understood why the Master of the Revels kept such a close watch on any play to be performed in the public playhouse. There was a latent power here that could prove more dangerous than a troop of armed men. A play, I now understood, could start a rebellion.

I was copying one of the old and rather dull plays in a desultory fashion one afternoon while a rehearsal for the next day's performance was taking place on stage. The snatches that reached my ears sounded desultory too. The players were hot and tired. Then there was a loud shout from somewhere beyond the stage which brought the rehearsal to an abrupt stop and nearly caused me to drop a large blob of ink on to my almost completed page. I managed to flick it back into the inkwell and stood up, flexing my cramped fingers. I laid down my quill and crossed the tiring room to the door leading out on to the stage.

Master Philip Henslowe, owner of the Rose playhouse, a bear pit, a pawnbroker's business, and several bawdy houses, stood below the stage, his face red with exertion, and breathless, as if he had run all the way from the Rose in Southwark – although I did not really believe he had. He must have been twenty years younger than Master Burbage, but he already possessed the stately figure of middle age.

'Lying there like a dead man!' he said. 'We have carried him inside, but he is still insensible.'

I joined the players on stage.

'What's amiss?' I said to Will.

'I am not sure. One of his company has been attacked. This afternoon. In the full light of day, near the Rose.'

Master Burbage sent one of the boys to bring a jug of ale from his office and he sat down on the edge of the stage with Henslowe. The rest of us crowded nearer, to hear what was afoot, some on the stage, some in the pit, some seated on the steps leading up to the stage.

Master Henslowe drank deeply of his ale, then ran his fingers through his hair, lifting the strands, damp with sweat, that clung to his forehead.

'My copyist, Walter Holles, had gone to his lodgings to fetch the parts he had been writing out, from the manuscript of a new play by Kit Marlowe.'

He glanced at Master Burbage out of the corner of his eyes. I knew there was some rivalry between them as to who should gain possession of the best new plays.

'His lodgings are just round behind the Rose. He should have taken no more than a quarter of an hour. When he hadn't returned in twice that time, I sent one of the boys to look for him. Holles likes a drink or two, and in this weather . . . Well, there he was, not more than two hundred yards from the playhouse, lying on the cobbles in a pool of blood, a great gash in the side of his head. He had been struck down and robbed.'

'Your copyist, you say?' Master Burbage spoke carefully.

'Aye. And the satchel that he carried his papers in was gone as well. Edward Alleyn went to his lodgings to see if it was there. It was not. Nor was Marlowe's new play.'

'Stolen!' Cuthbert exclaimed.

'Aye, stolen. And I recalled that your man who was poisoned, Wandesford, he was your copyist too, was he not?'

'He was.'

Furtive glances were exchanged between us. Another copyist? I had not realised I had undertaken a dangerous trade.

'The coroner's sergeants, and the city constables,' Master Henslowe said, 'are they any nearer discovering who poisoned poor Wandesford?'

Master Burbage shook his head. 'We have heard nothing, but I am sure, if they had discovered anything, we would be told.'

'And you cannot account for it yourselves?' Master Henslowe looked round at us. 'Was anything stolen? Any new play he was copying?'

At that, Master Burbage looked at Will.

'We cannot be sure,' Will said reluctantly. 'Some papers may have been stolen from his lodgings, but nothing of importance, it seems. Why kill a man for that? There must have been some other reason. Your man Holles – was he carrying coin? God knows, there are enough rogues in London will hit a man over the head for sixpence. Surely you will find Kit Marlowe's play cast aside in the satchel, but the chinks gone.'

I saw that he had gone very pale. Surely he could not believe that the plays themselves could be the cause of this violence?

'I merely find it very strange,' Master Henslowe said, 'that the copyists of the two leading companies of players should be attacked within days of each other.'

'Aye.' Master Burbage poured him more ale. 'It does seem strange. We have not had a play stolen, but then I keep our play books safely locked away.'

'And so do I, usually. However, I was in a hurry for the parts from the new play and Holles had taken the play book home to copy overnight.'

I had heard that Henslowe was something of a hard master. If so, it seemed that both he and Walter Holles had paid for it.

'There is no other copy?' Will asked. I could see he was grieving for the loss of the play.

'None.' Henslowe looked grim. He turned to Burbage. So have you found a new copyist?'

'For this time, Dr Alvarez is helping us,' Master Burbage said, nodding toward me.

Master Henslowe turned and looked at me attentively for the first time. 'Dr Alvarez? I thought you were a physician at St Thomas's?'

'I was,' I said quietly. I disliked having to account for myself in public, but I could hardly help it in the present circumstances. 'While I was absent in Muscovy, my temporary replacement at the hospital was given a permanent appointment. At the moment I am attending private patients only.'

'Well, Burbage,' Henslowe said, 'it seems you have found yourself a very grand copyist. He'd best look to himself when walking the streets. That satchel might hold a play book.'

He pointed to my physician's satchel.

'I assure you it does not,' I said, stung. 'Nothing but the instruments of my profession.'

'Aye, but will any footpad stop to ask you politely?'

It occurred to me that my satchel also still contained Gregory Rocksley's report on the dealings Boris Godunov had had with the Spanish. I had best rid myself of it, lest it, too, should be stolen and fall into the wrong hands.

'Returning to the matter of Wandesford and Holles,' Guy said, 'it may be no more than coincidence. Wandesford was poisoned while dining during the evening, at an inn in the City. Holles was knocked over the head during the day, walking along a street in Southwark. Apart from their trade, there seems nothing to link the attacks. In the case of Wandesford, nothing of value seems to have been stolen. In the case of Holles, his satchel was stolen, but that may mean no more than a thief seizing an unforeseen opportunity.'

'Aye, perhaps you are right,' Master Henslowe said reluctantly. 'My first thought was the similarity of the victims, but the methods, the times, the places, all are different. London is a violent town and no one can guess how many other attacks have taken place in the time between these two. I am sorry to have troubled you. I acted in haste.'

'You have not troubled us, Philip.' Master Burbage was at his most affable. 'If we are told anything further about Oliver Wandesford's death, I will inform you at once.'

As they shook hands on it, I picked up my satchel.

'Would you like me to see to Master Holles?' I asked Henslowe. 'Blows to the head can be serious. Or have you already called in a physician?'

For the first time Master Henslowe looked embarrassed, and it was quite clear that he was considerably more worried about his lost play than his injured copyist.

'I left the lads caring for him,' he said, 'but I would be glad if you were to take a look at the fellow. But he has a hard head, does Holles. Can drink any man under the table.'

I forbore to say that having a strong head for drink had nothing whatsoever to do with the resistance of a man's skull to a violent blow.

'I will put away my papers, then come over to Southwark with you.'

It took me no more than a few minutes to tidy away my work, lock the door, and hand the key to Cuthbert Burbage, before setting out with Master Henslowe for Southwark. I was glad to be going to a patient with a genuine need, the first since my return to London. Although I was happy to assist the players for the moment, medicine was my real love.

'I think we had best walk,' Master Henslowe said, setting a fast pace for all his bulk. 'I caught a wherry on the way over, but the walk across the mud at either end is so slow and trying, the saving of time by wherry in the centre of the river hardly compensates.'

I agreed. 'I shall be glad when the promised rain comes at last.'

'Aye, well, it will mean the playhouses will be empty.'

I could imagine him mourning the loss of every penny.

We made polite but meaningless conversation as we pushed through the crowds on the Bridge, bursting out at the far end like a cork out of a bottle. Master Henslowe's playhouse, the Rose, was not far beyond my lodgings, set a little back from the river. When we arrived, it was to find a group of worried players

129

gathered in the Rose's tiring house about a couch (clearly playhouse scenery) on which the copyist had been laid. The gash in his head was still bleeding freely on to a rolled up lump of canvas which had been placed under his head.

'Any sign of life?' Master Henslowe asked abruptly.

'He is still breathing, but he has not woken.'

I recognised the speaker as Edward Alleyn, betrothed to Henslowe's step daughter, for I had seen him on the stage. Like Dick Burbage he favoured the big dramatic roles, such as Marlowe's Tamburlaine. He appeared to be in charge here, the leading player. As we approached the injured man, the other players melted away. I set down my satchel and began taking out what I needed.

'Can you send for some boiled water?' I said to Master Alleyn. 'Boiled, mind. Not just any well water.'

'I'll see to it myself,' Alleyn said. 'Do I not know you?'

'Dr Alvarez,' Master Henslowe said. 'Late of St Thomas's.'

'Aye, that's it.' Alleyn did not enlarge on this, but went off to a small room like those at the back of the Theatre, where it appeared the players of this company were accustomed to cook for themselves. It seemed that some of them were making a supper, but cleared a space for Alleyn to boil a pot of water on a brazier there.

When he brought it, I added cleansing herbs and bathed the split in Holles's scalp, which was as long and almost as wide as my index finger. The blood continued to well up, but only thinly, as I took my suturing needle and stitched the wound together. The man winced, but did not wake. Alleyn turned pale and looked away, but Henslowe seemed not to mind. For a man accustomed to the slaughter of animals in a bear pit, I suppose a little raw flesh is no great worry.

Once I had finished the stitching, I spread a salve composed mainly of woundwort over the place.

'I will not bandage it for the present,' I said. 'With the weather so hot that will cause sweating, which will slow the healing, or even cause the flesh to rot. Best if it is open to the air, but it must be kept clean.'

Master Henslowe nodded. 'Can you warn the others, Ned? I am going to the parish constables now to see whether that satchel has been recovered.'

Alleyn nodded, then turned to me with an apologetic smile. 'He is concerned for Holles, but now that he has seen him cared for, he is wild to recover Kit Marlowe's play. We were to perform it next week.'

I looked up from packing my satchel. 'What do you think? Do you believe Master Holles was attacked by common pickpockets? Or did someone indeed intend to steal the play?'

He shrugged. 'Who can say? But new plays are valuable. And a new play by Will or Kit is nigh priceless.'

'Words on paper?' I said in a lightly disparaging tone, intending to provoke him.

He smiled. 'Aye, words on paper. Nothing more valuable than that. But look on a play as a commodity, as Master Henslowe would. You pay a play maker to write a play, let us say ten pounds. That is an investment. You expect to make a return on that investment. In the first year you will perform that play perhaps twenty or thirty times. Already it has earned back your investment and begun to make a profit. The word spreads. "Master Henslowe has a fine new play." The company is then summoned to perform that play at some great nobleman's house, or even at Court. Greater financial profits. In the second year it is no longer new, but if it is a notable play – and the plays by Kit and Will are notable – some will return to see it a second time, or even a third. And it will go on earning until every citizen in London, and every foreign ambassador, has seen it.'

I buckled the straps of my satchel. 'Go on.'

'Now there are at present only two great companies of players in London. Lord Strange's Men, managed by Master Burbage, and the Admiral's Men, managed by Master Henslowe. But we are not the only players. There are the boys' companies. There are at least half a dozen other men's companies, whose patrons are lesser nobles, men who are vying for positions at court and in the government. Not all of them sponsor players through love of the playhouse. They see it as a way to gain fame and popular support for themselves, to make their mark.'

'Aye.' I nodded. 'I can see that.' I could, though I had never before considered the ownership of a players' company as a weapon in the fight for advancement.

'Now the problem for these companies is this.' Ned Alleyn was clearly enjoying himself lecturing me. 'They do not have play makers. Oh, they may have some fellow who can cobble together an old story in broken rhyme and call it a play, but these are poor, sickly things. And they are losing their audiences. There is no money coming in. They cannot pay the rent for their playhouses or inn courtyards. Their players are penniless and starving. *They need plays*!'

He had assumed the stirring tones he employed on stage. I looked at him dubiously.

'Do you truly believe such people would steal plays? And kill for it?'

He shrugged and laughed. 'Perhaps I am making a Spanish tragedy out of pure coincidence and speculation. Nay, it is probably no such thing. And in any case, no one stole a play when Oliver Wandesford was killed, did they? I expect Master Henslowe will return with the satchel and Marlowe's play, and the whole idea will prove to be moonshine.'

'Look,' I said, 'I believe Master Holles is coming to himself.'

Indeed the man on the couch was stirring. He groaned and reached a shaking hand toward the gash in his head.

'Careful!' I warned, catching hold of his hand to stop him. 'You have received a nasty blow and I have had to stitch it. You must not touch it.'

His eye lids flickered and opened, and he looked up at me in confusion.

'I am a physician,' I said. 'You are in the tiring house at the Rose and quite safe. You were attacked in the street and struck on the head.'

'Aye, Walter,' Alleyn said. 'All's well now.'

The man groaned and struggled to sit up, but I pushed him gently back.

'Lie still for a little. Tell me, do you feel dizzy? Nauseous?'

He started to shake his head, but thought the better of it. 'Nay. But I have a headache to end all headaches.'

'A good night's sleep and it will not be so painful in the morning. Only small ale and light food tonight and tomorrow, else your stomach may not like it.'

I turned to Alleyn. 'See to that, will you? A blow to the head affects the whole body.'

'Aye. I will keep my eye on him.' He turned to the man, who was stirring restlessly and groping about him. 'What ails you, Walter?'

'My satchel! Where is my satchel? I remember me now, I was bringing Master Marlowe's new play back to Master Henslowe. He sent me to fetch it. I was up most of the night, copying the parts.'

'I'm afraid the thieves took it,' Alleyn said, not quite able to hide the concern in his voice.

'Oh, Lord!' Holles gave a louder groan than ever and closed his eyes. 'Henslowe will flay me alive. But it was he ordered me to take the play book home with me. I could have finished it today, working here, but nay, he must have me stay up all night.' His voice took on an aggrieved note. 'I was that tired, I forgot to bring it with me this morning, otherwise none of this would have happened.'

'No one is blaming you, Walter.'

Privately, I suspected Master Henslowe might well blame the hapless Walter.

'I must away,' I said, 'for I'm to sup with Burbage's men tonight. I will call tomorrow to look at that gash, Master Holles. Remember, keep it clean and do not touch it. And only light food.'

'Aye, doctor,' he said, 'and I thank you. You've done me a kindness and I've done naught but moan.'

'You've a right to moan, after a blow like that,' I said, giving his shoulder a pat.

As I took my leave of them, Master Henslowe arrived, the outcome of his visit to the parish constables writ large on his face.

'Well?' said Alleyn, raising his eyebrows.

Henslowe shook his head. 'Never a sign of the satchel. I fear it is lost.'

Chapter Eight

*W*e were all somewhat subdued at supper that evening. We had returned to the Cross Keys, where the players had once held a winter season and were well known, so the innkeeper and his wife made us very welcome, but word of the attack on Walter Holles had started all kinds of speculation amongst the players.

'He will recover,' I said, reassuringly. 'It was a nasty blow and almost certainly he will be left with a scar here.' I indicated the area just above my right ear. 'He recalls little about the attack, but from the position of the wound I would say that he was attacked from behind and struck with something heavy and hard.'

'A sword?' Master Burbage asked.

I shook my head. 'Nay, it was not a clean cut. I should say something more like a club, which split the scalp, rather than cutting it.'

Christopher shuddered, and pushed away his plate. He was a fine mock swordsman on stage, but I think he would not have lasted long in a real sword fight.

'And could the motive have been to steal the play?' Master Burbage had also stopped eating and shot a sharp glance at me.

I shrugged. 'Who can say? Ned Alleyn argued the case for one of the nondescript companies of players stealing from the two great companies, but after he had expounded it, he agreed it was just as likely the rogues thought the satchel might contain money.'

'You said "rogues".' Guy turned to me. 'There was more than one?'

'I meant nothing by it. Holles did not see his attackers. It might have been just one man.'

'It seems to me,' Geoffrey de Claine said, in the elderly judicial voice he used on stage for men of substance, 'that the attack on Holles can have nothing to do with the killing of Master Wandesford. They were both copyists, but what does that signify? You might as well say, if a fishmonger is attacked by his apprentice one day in Billingsgate and a week later another falls in the Fleet and is drowned, that these matters must be connected because the two men were fishmongers. I do not believe it.'

Having delivered himself of this, he sat back and drained the last of his beer.

'Geoffrey is almost certainly in the right,' Master Burbage said. 'The attack on Holles is regrettable, but let us not confuse it with the murder of Oliver Wandesford, which remains as much of a mystery as ever. I begin to think that it will never be solved.'

There was a general murmur of agreement, and our conversation turned to other things.

Later I walked back to Southwark with Simon and Will (who had found yet another lodging, on our side of the river). The sun was setting in a spectacular blaze of orange and purple, behind the heaped clouds which seemed to have gained the solidity of mountains.

'Ominous,' Will said. 'The ancient Romans would have seen that as forecasting disaster.'

'Not only the Romans,' Simon said. 'There are any number of astrologers here in London who will say the same.'

'And do you believe our fates are written, unchangeable, in the stars?' Will cocked his head at Simon.

Simon shrugged. 'How can we know?'

'Kit?'

'I do not believe it,' I said fiercely. 'If we cannot choose how we will conduct our lives, how can we count ourselves human? No better than the beasts. Do you favour the Puritans, Will, with their belief in the Elect?'

Will leaned down and rubbed Rikki in his favourite place behind his ears.

'Nay, the Puritans would happily burn me and my licentious scribblings. So, without free will, to sin or no, we would be no better than the beasts, you say? No better than your faithful hound, do you mean? Who stays beside you, closer than a shadow?'

I smiled. He had trapped me neatly.

'Ah, well, Rikki is an exceptional beast. He saved my life at a time when we were scarcely acquainted. Nowadays, I think he understands me better than most men. Churchmen would condemn me for saying it, but I believe there is good and evil amongst animals too, probably more good and less evil than you will find amongst us two-legged creatures. So does Rikki choose his path through life? He certainly chose to attach himself to me. Was that his free will, or something fixed in the stars?'

Arguing ourselves around the debate from every angle, we reached Southwark, where Simon and I parted company with Will.

'What do you truly believe, Kit? Simon asked, as we climbed the stairs at our lodgings.

'Whether our fate is dictated by our stars?' I said.

'Nay, about Wandesford and Holles.'

'I cannot believe there is any connection. Ned Alleyn waxed very eloquent, but more as if he were giving a performance at the Rose than if he was persuaded by his own arguments. The cases are so very different. I expect that satchel will be found, with Marlowe's play still in it, or else it has been tossed into the Thames and is even now subsiding into the mud.'

'Let us hope not,' Simon said seriously. 'I know you do not care for Marlowe, but I would rather that play were stolen and performed by some rogue company of players than it should sink into oblivion.'

I smiled wryly. 'You have the right of it. Even I would not wish to see one of the great Master Marlowe's plays lost for ever. Give you good night.'

A few days later, as I was walking along Gracechurch Street, I met Thomas Phelippes, whom I had not seen since the death of Walsingham. He greeted me with surprising joviality and drew me in to an inn, where he insisted upon treating me to a meal and wine.

Having in the past been Phelippes's young assistant, I had not expected this eagerness to please me, although we had in time become close friends during my final years in Walsingham's employ. Perhaps his manner had something to do with my apparel. The weather had taken a strange twist. Although thunderclouds still threatened from the west, a sudden wind had blown in from the north, bringing with it unseasonable cold, so that, as well as my physician's gown and cap, I wore a cloak lined with rabbit skin which I had purchased – secondhand but in good condition – with some of my earnings from my new patients. I suppose I must have seemed to Phelippes much changed from the young lad who had first been brought in to assist him five years before.

'Now, Kit,' he said, when we were well fed and sitting over the last of our wine, with our legs stretched out to the unaccustomed fire. I had shed my cloak and felt pleasantly entertained, with no fear that I would be unable to withstand any proposal he might make. He took off his spectacles and polished them on his sleeve. Without them his eyes looked vulnerable. Until that moment we had spoken of general matters, London gossip. I could tell from the change in his tone that we were coming to the reason for his treating me. I decided to take some control of the conversation.

'And how are you yourself, Thomas?' I asked, boldly. 'Are you employed?'

He smiled a little at my manner. Before, I would not have called him Thomas. He put his spectacles on again, and at once became the sharp-eyed code-breaker and merciless intelligencer.

'Indeed, indeed, I am employed. Francis Bacon is drawing together many of us who used to work for Walsingham. When his brother Anthony returns from France he will have charge of the new service. Both brothers have long been friends of mine.'

This was not quite what I had heard, that Phelippes was a clerk in the Customs House. Although I remembered that someone had spoken about the Bacon brothers.

'Francis and Anthony Bacon?'

I knew of them, certainly, but they held minor government appointments. They had neither the money nor the position to organise a service like Walsingham's.

'They are, of course,' he said, 'in the service of a greater man.'

'Of course.'

He leaned forward confidentially. 'My Lord of Essex.'

I felt myself recoil physically. This was unexpected. The brothers were Burghley's nephews, first cousins to his son Sir Robert Cecil. How could they ally themselves with the Cecils' greatest enemy, when Lord Burghley himself was setting up an intelligence network? Here was more of this dangerous rivalry, whose repercussions might bring about unforeseen trouble.

'My Lord of Essex imagines himself the new Walsingham?' I asked, heavy with sarcasm.

He smiled enigmatically. 'Perhaps not that. My Lord is, of course, the greatest nobleman in the kingdom, and of ancient lineage. Walsingham, though a dedicated servant of Her Majesty, was not.'

So soon consigned to the midden of history, I thought. Phelippes did not speak of Walsingham in such terms as these in the past. Nor was Essex of ancient lineage. His father had been the first of his family to hold the title. A few generations back the Devereux were minor squires, or even yeomen, farming their acres in the rural wilderness of Herefordshire on the borders of even more benighted Wales.

'I am glad,' I said politely, 'that you have found employment.' I wondered whether it was he who had taken Walsingham's secret papers and given them to Essex. But this I doubted. He had seemed as shocked as I had, when we discovered the theft in Walsingham's office.

'You say there are others from Walsingham's service with you in Essex House?'

'Nay, not Essex House. I have an office in the Customs House. It is convenient in many ways. Aye, some of our friends are there – Arthur Gregory, Standen, Rolston, others you may or may not know.'

'Robert Poley?' I asked cautiously. I had no wish to reveal what I had heard about Poley.

'Poley is now employed by Sir Thomas Heneage, the Queen's Vice-Chamberlain, but I believe that they work with Burghley.'

Clearly Essex himself was working against Burghley, without question, I thought. So Poley and Phelippes were now in the employment of the rival factions. Each of them intent on setting up their own intelligence service. In such a contest, a wise man would put his money on the Cecils, for Lord Burghley had initiated the intelligence service many years ago, before handing it over to Walsingham. But Essex! What did Essex understand of the subtleties, the long drawn out projections of intelligence work? Vividly before my mind flashed the image of Essex leaping into the deep water at Peniche, causing the death of so many of his men. This contest over an intelligence service would land him in just such deep water. I wanted none of it. I gathered up my cloak and prepared to leave. Phelippes remained where he was, smiling benignly up at me.

'It may be that I will be able to offer you employment, Kit, once Anthony Bacon has returned to London.'

I flung my cloak round my shoulders and put on my square cap. Standing over him, I knew I looked what I aspired to be: a respectable physician of good standing, with wealthy clients who valued my skills. I shook my head.

'Nay, I think not, Thomas. I am not a boy any longer. And I have earnings enough to satisfy me.' This was an exaggeration, but despite my shortage of the chinks I would not work for Essex.

'Caring for the filthy paupers at St Thomas's?' he said, with sudden and uncharacteristic venom.

Did he know that I no longer worked there? I was not prepared to enlighten him.

'They are all God's creatures,' I said piously. 'I am glad to do what I can to care for them. My list of private patients might surprise you.'

He shrugged. 'We shall see. It would be a pity to waste your remarkable talent for deciphering and forgery. Good day to you, Kit.'

'God speed, Thomas. I thank you for an excellent dinner.'

As I walked up Gracechurch Street toward Bishopsgate, I realised that the encounter had shaken me. Despite his assumed air of confidence, I could detect an underlying unease in Phelippes. That remark about the paupers of Southwark was quite unlike him. He was not a sentimental man, but he had always shown compassion toward the poor. I could not believe that he liked working for Essex any more than I would do. Why had the Cecils not recruited him immediately after Walsingham's death? He was England's most talented intelligencer, subtle, experienced, gifted with a remarkable flair both for code breaking and for understanding the methods of foreign agents.

Walsingham's stolen papers must lie behind this. Phelippes had stood beside me at Walsingham's funeral. And it was during the funeral that the burglary at Seething Lane had taken place. The most likely culprit was Robert Poley, who would happily sell his own child (if he had any), should it prove to his advantage. Of course he would take them to the Cecils, Walsingham's natural heirs, and would have sold them either for coin, or for employment, or both. By doing so, he would have cut Phelippes neatly out of the post which should have been his, in charge of the new organisation.

As for Essex heading a rival organisation, it was laughable. He would want some spectacular victory quickly, or he would tire of it. Phelippes would find himself dragged down or tarnished with the brush of failure. Thoughtfully I tapped my satchel and heard the rustle of paper inside. I would certainly not pass Gregory's report to Phelippes now.

Very early the following morning I received a summons from Master Buckford, the owner of the small manor out near Windsor. The note he sent with a servant was couched in more polite terms than the brusque orders I had received from the Dolesbys, so I was the more ready to comply with it. Moreover, it gave me an opportunity to exercise Hector, who had been confined and drooping in his stall at the Walsingham house for many days now. For myself, I welcomed the chance to escape from the foetid air of London, out into the countryside.

141

Hector was as pleased as I was to leave London behind, and Rikki trotted beside us as we left the scattered fringes of Westminster behind and headed up river towards Windsor. I gave Hector his head once we were clear of the houses, so that we arrived at the Buckfords' manor in a much shorter time than when I had made the careful journey with Dr Nuñez. On reaching the manor, I handed over Hector and Rikki to a groom and knocked at the door, which was opened so quickly by the master of the house that I thought he must have been on the watch for me.

'I thank you for coming so promptly, Dr Alvarez,' he said. 'It is our young boy, Andrew. He has been very pale and quiet these last two days, and now he will neither eat nor drink.'

While he spoke he was leading me to a little parlour at the back of the house, where we found his lady holding a child of about five on her lap. His eyes were closed and he lay as limp as a bundle of cloth. I could see that the mother had been weeping. I did not care for the look of the boy, but I assumed a cheerful tone, as one must do with anxious parents, else they will tend to make a sick child worse.

'Can you lay Andrew down here, mistress?' I said, indicating a low table. I would have preferred to have physicked him in his bed chamber, but I was concerned that any loss of time might prove fatal.

I began to remove the child's shirt and breeches. I would judge he was not long out of skirts, but his loose breeches were drawn in tightly with a belt. It must be causing him pain. 'When did he last eat, and what did he eat?'

'It is two days since he ate a meal,' Mistress Buckford said. She was standing too close, clasping her hands tightly together and blocking the light. 'He ate what we all ate. Beef. Chicken. A galantine of ham. A sugar confection afterwards.'

'A little too rich for such a young child in this exceptionally hot weather,' I said, striving to keep my voice level, but feeling some anger. The rich can kill their children with affluence as easily as the poor may be forced to see their children starve.

'Has he had any vomiting? Loosening of the bowels?'

The lady looked shocked, as if she did not expect such words to be spoken in her hearing. She covered her mouth and did not answer, but the father did.

'Aye, he has vomited several times. As for his bowels . . .' He strode across the room and threw open the door. 'Send Eva here at once,' he shouted.

It seemed that while his wife had gone a little too far in assuming the manners of the gentry, the father was but a step away from his life as a London tradesman.

A woman ran in, a plump, motherly woman, who had also been crying.

'Best ask Eva, doctor,' Master Buckford said. 'She is the children's nurse.'

By now I had all of the child's clothes off and I could see that his belly was hollowed in, like a victim of starvation. Clearly he had retained no nourishment for some time. Children can waste away so quickly.

Questioned, the nurse agreed that the boy had vomited repeatedly and his bowels had been loose for the last two days.

'Any blood?' I asked. She was a sensible woman, though she was clearly distressed.

'Nay, master, God be praised. It is not the bloody flux, I'm thinking.'

'It is not, but he is weakening fast. Have you any barley water in the kitchen?'

'Aye, there will be some, that I'm sure.'

'Fresh?'

'If not, I'll make some, 'twon't take but a few minutes.'

She hurried off. I turned to Mistress Buckford. 'Andrew will be best wearing nothing but a loose night shift with a light blanket for a cover, nothing constricting. Can you fetch those?'

She nodded and followed the nurse out of the room.

'How serious is it, doctor?' Master Buckford said, as soon as the door had closed behind her.

'It would be serious it if were left untreated,' I said. 'You son has eaten tainted meat and his body had rejected it. And that has weakened him considerably, all the vomiting and the diarrhoea. Sometimes these continue long after the offending matter has been expelled, and we need to help the body regain its balance, before the wasting is too great a trial for his bodily strength. He has lost too much fluid, so that his body is drying out.'

I saw that Andrew, who had seemed almost comatose before, was now listening to us, his eyes open, but full of misery.

'We will soon have you better,' I said, smiling at him. 'I am going to give you a very pleasant drink and soon you will be well again.'

'I'm thirsty,' he whispered, 'but I don't want to puke any more. I thought I was turning inside out.' He gave me a shaky grin.

'You're a brave fellow,' I said.

His mother returned and dressed him in the loose garments which would not constrict his stomach. She was followed by the nurse with a jug of barley water and a pretty blue glazed cup.

'I've brought your favourite cup, Master Andrew,' she said.

I saw that his mother looked puzzled. It seemed she was unaware that he had a favourite cup.

'Now, Andrew,' I said, 'you are going to help me make up the medicine.' I poured some of the barley water into the cup and took a phial of oil of peppermint from my satchel.

'Smell this.'

He sniffed the neck of the phial cautiously. Already the distraction was bringing a little life back into his weakened form.

'I know that smell,' he said. 'My aunt makes comfits that smell like that.'

'I expect she does. I told you this would be good. There. I've added just enough. It is oil of peppermint. Will you stir it for me?' I handed him one of the spoons I always carried.

As he stirred, I returned the phial to my satchel and took out another.

'This is meadowsweet. I am sure you know meadowsweet.'

'Little white flowers?'

'That's it. These have been dried and powdered. I'll add a pinch, and you must stir again.

He was taking a great interest now, stirring vigorously and watching the fragments of meadowsweet whirl in the cup.

144

'One last ingredient,' I said. 'Do you like raspberries?'

'Aye, I do!' His face glowed. 'Shall we add raspberries?'

'Not the fruits, I am afraid, but the leaves are very good for you as well. This is an infusion of the leaves, and we'll add a spoonful of that.'

'What's an infusion?'

'You soak the leaves in boiling water to draw out the goodness, then strain it, because we don't want bits of leaf floating about, do we?'

'I suppose not.'

'And because you have been such a good assistant, we'll add some syrup of raspberries, to make it even tastier. There. We shall make an apothecary of you yet!'

The syrup of raspberries had no great medicinal value, but it turned the concoction a most pleasing rose pink and would make the flavour very acceptable to a child.

'Now!' I said, like a conjuror about to perform some clever trick, 'let us see whether you can drink that down to the last drop.'

He seized the cup and drank it thirstily. His mouth must have been parched and acid, poor lamb, from all the vomiting.

'That was good,' he said with a sigh. 'I mixed it well, didn't I?'

'I could not have done it better myself. I am going to make up a whole jugful for you. and you may have a cup four times a day. Apart from that, you may drink as much plain barley water as you want. No solid food for the next three days.'

I looked at the parents and the nurse, not sure which of them I should be addressing.

'No solid food,' I repeated. 'Possets of oatmeal, cream and honey from tomorrow. In two days' time, he make take a very small amount of fine bread, but if it causes distress to his stomach, leave it for another two days. Make sure he drinks as much as possible. He should soon recover now, but if you are worried, send for me again.'

The nurse was nodding, and I reckoned she could be relied upon to see that the patient was given the diet I prescribed.

I stood up.

'And no more great meals of heavy meats, they are too strong for a young child, especially in hot weather.' I did not think the meat could have been seriously tainted, or the rest of the family would also have been ill, but even slightly tainted meat can affect a child.

I thanked Andrew again for his assistance, and asked Eva to take me to the stillroom, where I made up enough of the potion to serve for three or four days. As I was leaving, Master Buckford hurried out to the stableyard to see me on my way.

He shook me by the hand, then pressed a heavy purse into it, and I saw that, although he had remained calm before, there were tears now in his eyes.

'I thought we had lost him,' he said. 'At first it seemed only one of those childish upsets. As you saw on your last visit, we have a large family, we have had our share of children's ailments. But last night he turned so much worse. He seemed to waste away.'

'Children can go down very quickly,' I said. 'You were right to send for me. He should fare well now, but do not wait to send again, if you need me.'

The groom had brought Hector and gave me a leg up. It was only then that I became aware of a change in the light. There was an unnatural greenish yellow cast to the sky.

'Thunderstorm approaching, I fear,' Master Buckford said. 'You may have a wet ride of it, back to London.'

At that, as if to underline his words, there was a sudden flash of lightning, setting Hector to dancing about in alarm.

'I'd best be off,' I said, touching my cap, and turning Hector's head to the gate. It promised to be an unpleasant journey.

At first the storm only threatened in the distance, with occasional flashes of lightning, followed by the far-off growl of thunder. They say that if you count steadily between the flash of the lightning and the sound of the thunder, that will tell you how far away the storm is, in miles. I know not whether it is true, or nothing but some old wives' tale, but I found myself counting after each flash, as best I could, for Hector was nervous and skittish and difficult to handle. By that reckoning, the storm was

146

at first around ten miles away, and I was heading away from it. Either it kept pace with me or my counting was not accurate, for I was unable to put any more distance between us, although I urged Hector to a steady canter.

He was more than willing. Indeed, I needed to keep a tight rein on him, or he would have broken into a gallop, which he could never have maintained for the twenty-five miles or so we needed to go. I had never before known him afraid of anything, but it was clear that the lightning frightened him. Every time it lit up that ominous sky, he shied and tried to bolt, so that my arms began to ache, holding him in check. Rikki ran valiantly beside us, but I could see that he too was frightened. He jumped nervously to the side, every time the lightning flashed or the thunder cracked. I could hardly avoid flinching myself, and I expect the animals could sense my own nervousness.

The rain still had not reached us when I reckoned we had covered about half the distance, but the clouds had come racing after us, rolling over the sky and blotting out the sun, so that it already felt like evening. The air turned cold. A wind whistled through the trees on either side of the road, setting their limbs tossing like the arms of drowning men. Then the rain began. At first it fell in single huge drops, heavy as sixpences, then, after a gasp in the wind, the full storm was upon us, rain cascading down like a waterfall, beating the dry ground so that the scent of wet earth rose around us, like the scent of an unglazed pottery jar when you fill it with cold water. Soon I could barely see ahead and had to slow Hector down, for fear of missing the sight of a fallen branch or a pit in the roadway.

In minutes I was soaked right through, so that my sodden clothes squelched against the leather of the saddle, while the reins were slippery in my hands and difficult to hold. I looked around for Rikki. One moment he was there, a miserable bundle of wet fur, and limping. The next, I could not see him.

'Rikki!' I called, 'Rikki!'

But the lashing of the wind in the trees and the hammering of the rain on the ground, hardened from weeks of drought, sent the words back into my mouth. I spotted a fallen tree at the side of the road which would provide me with height enough to remount Hector, and reined him to a stop.

'Rikki!' I shouted again as I slid down. 'Come here, Rikki!'

I thought I had lost him. I looped Hector's reins over a branch and began to feel my way back along the road, although I was nearly blinded, for I was now facing into the wind and the rain was flung into my face as though by a malicious hand. There was hail mixed with the rain, which stung like thrown pebbles.

At last I found him, hobbling anxiously toward me on three legs, his right fore paw held off the ground. I knelt on the muddy ground and put my arms around him.

'What have you done to yourself, you poor old fellow?'

He licked my chin apologetically, but I was too blinded by the storm to see what was amiss. Instead I carried him back to where I had left Hector and lifted him up to lie across the horse's withers. His wet fur had soaked the breast of my doublet even more, so that I shivered with cold. The fallen tree was barely high enough for me to use as a mounting block, Hector being such a tall horse, but I managed to scramble awkwardly into the saddle. I had ridden like this with Rikki before, but on that occasion horse and dog were not both slippery with wet. I used a strap from one of my saddle bags to fasten Rikki to my own belt. It was far from secure, but it was the best I could do. As I set off again, I knew that I would need to keep Hector at a slower pace, or I should never be able to hold on to Rikki.

If the journey was wretched before, it now took on a sense of nightmare. Because the downpour was as dense as a fog, I could barely make out the road and twice I found myself following a side turn. Forced to retrace my steps, I began to fear I had missed the London road altogether. Not another soul did I see for what seemed like hours. It had been around mid day when I left the Buckfords' manor, but the dark and the blinding storm meant that it could be any time from mid afternoon to evening. I could barely see, except when an intense burst of lightning lit up a scene of chaos for a moment – a road already turning into a stream and strewn with the debris of broken branches. Once, moments after the lightning had struck so close that Hector reared in panic, I heard the unmistakable crack and groan and rushed tearing of a falling tree. As it hit the road behind me, I could feel the earth and air shaking.

At last I reached the outlying cottages on the skirts of Westminster. There were candles lit in windows, but I had still no clear idea what time it might be. Having pursued me all the way from Windsor, the storm now pulled away ahead of me, driving eastwards down river toward the estuary and the open sea. It continued to rain, but half-heartedly now, so that I had no difficulty picking my way through Westminster and along the Strand, toward the City. At the doors of some of the great houses, servants with sacks over their shoulders against the rain were sweeping water away from the entrances of their masters' homes. The Strand itself was a river, the water lapping almost to Hector's hocks, and every time we met a side road leading down from the higher ground to the left, it felt like crossing a rushing stream or a waterfall.

It was no better after we had passed under Newgate into the City. All the streets here were awash, shutters ripped off and scattered, roof thatch and tiles strewn under foot. It seemed to be growing even colder, and by the time I turned into Seething Lane, Rikki and I were both shivering uncontrollably. Hector had been kept warm by staying on the move, but I knew that as soon as he stopped he would begin to be chilled.

When at last I reached the stableyard I hooked one arm around Rikki and slid to the ground, but my legs would not hold me and I collapsed on to the cobbles in a lake at least three inches deep, but I was already so wet I could not get any wetter.

'Dr Alvarez!' It was Harry, and another stable lad called Arthur, running out from the tack room where the lads had snug quarters of their own. 'Where have you been in this b'yer lady storm?'

I stayed where I was, not feeling much inclined to climb to my feet. Rikki appeared to be of the same mind.

'Riding back from Windsor,' I said. 'Can you see to Hector?' The poor horse stood with drooping head, the white areas of his coat almost as dark with the rain as the black ones. Water dripped from his mane and tail.

'Aye, I'll take him,' Arthur said. 'Happen he'll be glad of something warm to eat. This has gone from summer to winter in an hour.'

'Warm bran mash, aye,' I said. 'He'll be glad of it.'

'You cannot sit there all day,' Harry said reasonably, reaching out a hand to heave me to my feet. 'What's amiss with Rikki?'

'Hurt his paw somehow. Wait, Arthur, while I get my satchel from the saddle bag.'

As Arthur led the horse away, Harry and I made for the tack room. I was carrying Rikki, although my arms were aching from the long ride holding Hector in check.

'You'd best get them wet clothes off,' Harry said. 'We'll have something here you can borrow, if you don't mind a whiff of horse.'

He must have been surprised when I refused, but I assured him that I would soon dry out, and took a stand as close as was safe to the brazier where the lads cooked for themselves. They were regularly fed from the kitchen, but they preserved their independence by preparing fried collops and spiced wine whenever they felt the pangs of hunger. Working with horses can make you ravenous. While I began to steam gently, I examined Rikki's paw. There was a deep cut across the pads which had bled, although a scab was now beginning to form.

'Poor lad,' I said. 'He must have trodden on something sharp. A stone or the splintered end of a broken branch. It was wild out there. Can you pass me my satchel, Harry?'

Rikki yelped once as I cleaned and salved his paw, but tolerated it. I bound it with a small bandage, though I knew it would soon come off, or be worried away. As I was finishing, Arthur came in to heat some bran mash on the brazier.

'He's fine, is Hector,' he said. 'I rubbed him dry and put on a blanket, for it's turned cold as a virgin's heart out there. He's jumpy, mind.'

'He didn't care for the lightning,' I said.

Harry grinned. 'Nor didn't we!'

'It got so dark and I don't know how long I was on the road,' I said. 'What time is it?'

'I heard St Katherine Colmans chime six not long back,' Harry said. 'Mebbe half an hour ago. Are you off home now?'

I considered. I had dry clothes at home, but I had to walk there first, with no fire in my room until I had one lit and burning through. The players were dining at the Green Dragon tonight, out of concern for the inn's lost trade, for which Master Burbage felt obscurely responsible. It was not far to the inn and they would have lit fires to chase away the cold and wet. I could dry out there, and eat a hot meal.

'Nay,' I said, 'I'm for the Green Dragon and supper with the players.'

'That were a strange business,' Arthur said, 'what happened to Master Wandesford. Do they know who done it?'

I shook my head. 'Not yet. Though I am sure the coroner's sergeants will solve the matter before long.'

I was not as confident as I sounded, but could not stay and speculate if I wanted to reach the inn for supper. Rikki seemed prepared to follow me, still limping but determined, so we set off through the last spatterings at the tail end of the storm.

The players were already at the Green Dragon when I arrived – looking a miserable spectacle, no doubt. I was hauled away to the fire, and Rikki with me. The innkeeper had a pot of spiced wine heating on the hearth and the first tankard was pressed into my cold hands. I cupped my fingers gratefully around its warmth and sipped the wine while it was still almost too hot to drink. Rikki must have felt as cold as I did, for he crawled so close to the fire I feared he would singe his fur. Both of us gave off clouds of steam.

While the innkeeper and his pot boys were carrying in our supper, an explanation was demanded of me – why had I arrived looking as though I had just been fished out of the Thames? When they learned I had ridden all the way back from Windsor in that storm, I was told I was both a fool and a hero – quite which I am not sure – and I was pressed by Master Burbage into the chair nearest the fire. I was heartily grateful for that meal, for I realised that I had eaten nothing all day, and had I returned to my lodgings I would have had nothing but a bit of cheese and some stale bread. And I think there might have been an egg. As it was, the Green Dragon provided braised beef cooked with onions, carrots, cabbage and garlic, excellent for keeping out the cold, with fresh rolls to mop up the juices, and honeyed frumenty to follow, studded with almonds and raisins.

By the time we were sitting over the last of the spiced wine I could feel that my back was nearly dry, but I still seemed to be sitting on a heap of wet washing, my padded breeches having acted like a sponge. After I had sneezed several times, I decided I must head back to my lodgings before I developed more than a mild cold.

'Aye,' Will said, 'those of us living over the river had best be moving. With the river so low that the wherries could hardly move, they have been keeping the Bridge gates open later than usual, but the rain may have filled the river and we shall need to take a wherry.'

'The heavens fairly opened,' Guy said, 'but I doubt the river will have recovered yet. It will take a few days, with the water flowing down from upstream, to make up for all the water we have lost these last weeks.'

Guy had known London all his life and was probably right, but once I had made a move, Simon and Will were ready to leave with me. To spare Rikki's injured paw, I thought I would carry him, but he was a big dog, and heavy, so the other two took it in turns with me. Rikki seemed puzzled at first, but then settled into his privileged position like a young prince.

Just past the entrance to Gracechurch Street we nearly collided with two men who came running out of an alleyway on our left. Both had hoods pulled over their heads and dodged away from us, heading back up toward Bishopsgate Street. Instinctively my hand went to my sword and Will half drew his dagger, though Simon, who was carrying Rikki, could have done nothing to protect himself.

'Footpads!' Will cried, whirling round.

'Leave them!' I warned. 'They are not after us, we are too many for them.'

It was then we heard a groan from the direction of the alleyway.

'Someone is hurt,' Simon said.

We all three turned and took a few cautious steps into the alley. It could be a trap, to lure us away from the street – where there were lanterns hung before most doors – into a dark corner where we could be attacked. Hardly had we ventured more than a couple of yards when Will stumbled against something on the ground.

'There's a man here, hurt,' he said.

Simon set Rikki on the ground and fumbled in his purse for a strike-a-light, but when we moved aside so that light from the street shone far enough in for us to make out the figure at our feet, Will said, 'It's Stoker!'

I knelt down on the muddy ground. 'He wasn't at supper, was he?'

'Nay,' Simon said. 'Come to think of it, I don't think he was. He's usually skulking somewhere in the background, but he wasn't there tonight. How badly is he hurt?'

After that first moan, the man had made no further sound. I ran my hand over his chest and it came away sticky.

'Blood,' I said. 'He's been stabbed. Stoker? Can you hear me?'

I saw his eyes turn toward me. There was a gasp of breath. Then the eyes were still, glinting with reflected light from the street. I pressed my fingers to the pulse in his neck. Then I stood up.

'He is dead,' I said.

Chapter Nine

The three of us never reached home that night. After our gruesome discovery, Simon and I stayed with Stoker's body, while Will went in search of a constable. He seemed to take a very long time about it, and I grew more and more aware of my sodden clothes. Both Simon and I were nervous, for it was far from pleasant, standing guard over a body at the mouth of a dark alleyway which led into a huddle of disreputable buildings, furtively crowded together as if they were watching us. The heavy rain had driven everyone indoors, so that even Gracechurch Street, a busy thoroughfare by day, was deserted.

'I wonder,' said Simon, 'should we seek help from one of the respectable houses in Gracechurch Street? I am starting to think that Will may have met those same two cutthroats we saw running away. They might have been lurking, waiting for him.'

It was true that Will had headed in the same direction, hoping to find a parish constable around Leadenhall.

I shook my head. 'Who would open a door to us at this time of night? We might be thieves or cutthroats ourselves. Would you open your door? Even if they did, they'd as like draw a sword or a musket on us as offer the hand of friendship. We'd best wait. We've heard no sound of an attack on Will, and it is quiet enough tonight.'

Indeed, the usual noise of London was missing. Now and then a dog barked in the distance, and there was still the gurgle of water running off roofs and down the kennels of the street, but otherwise it was uncannily quiet. But why was Will taking so long?

154

It was more than an hour by the chiming of church clocks before he returned, dragging with him two very reluctant constables, each carrying a candle lantern.

'I was afraid I might not find you again,' he said grimly. 'I have been all round the parish until I found these two snug in an ale house, instead of keeping the peace as they should.'

'No blame to us, maister,' one of them said, going on the attack, a big hulking fellow, who might be a blacksmith when he was not serving his term as a parish constable. 'Silent as the grave, the City's been since the storm. No need for us to freeze off our arses and wear out good shoe leather, when there's no one abroad but you.' He glared round at us. 'Who's to say you a'nt the killers?'

'Any man with two brains in his pan would know that!' I said angrily, for I was very cold and very tired. 'If we were the killers, would we come hunting for the two laziest constables in London? Or stayed freezing here, where those two killers might pay another visit? Use your head, man! Take charge of the body and let us be on the way to our beds.'

'Not so fast.' The other man was less impressive physically, but his narrow weasel face displayed more intelligence.

'Your mate here says he knows the man.'

'We all do,' Simon said, in a conciliatory tone. 'His name is John Stoker and he is employed doing rough jobs with Lord Strange's Men.'

'Players, eh?' The man said, narrowing his eyes. 'Rogues, the lot of you.'

'Watch your tongue!' Will said.

'I am a physician,' I said, deciding we would be arrested ourselves if we were not careful. 'Dr Alvarez. I have ascertained that the man is dead. It is difficult to judge in the dark, but he appears to have been stabbed in the chest and perished quickly, for two hooded men ran up the street just as we arrived. Master Stoker made only incoherent noises before he died. Do you not think you should move his body to somewhere more seemly?'

'St Peter's Cornhill is the nearest church,' Simon said.

'Aye,' weasel face conceded. 'I'll go knock up the churchwarden. I know where he lives.' He turned to the other man. 'You stay here and keep a watch.' He gave us a meaningful look before striding away up Gracechurch Street.

I leaned back against the wall of the nearest house, for I felt I could not continue to stand upright without support.

'Someone is awake.' Simon nodded toward a house on the opposite side of the street, where light had appeared around the edge of the shutters. As we watched, the shutters were thrown open and we could see shadowy forms moving against the candle light. A man – I think it was – leaned out and peered across at us.

'It's a pity they were not watching earlier,' Will said. 'They might have got a better look at those men than we did.'

There was another long wait before the constable returned with the churchwarden and we all made our way to St Peter's, the two constables carrying Stoker's body between them. The churchwarden unlocked the church door, then led us into a side chapel.

'You could put it here, I suppose,' he said dubiously, pointing to the dusty floor.

'That is not suitable,' I said firmly. I had never liked Stoker, but I would not allow him to be treated like some filthy piece of rubbish found in the gutter. 'Put him there.' I pointed to a flat tomb which stood at the back of the chapel.

'But that is the tomb of a benefactor, from two centuries back,' the churchwarden objected.

'Then he is in no position to complain,' I said.

Reluctantly he agreed, and Stoker was laid out on the stone slab.

'Bring those lanterns nearer,' I said, leaning over to examine Stoker more closely, now that there was more light to see by.

There was a rip in the front of his doublet, a little to the left of centre. A narrow wound to the flesh below the torn fabric. Blood around the wound, but not a great deal. Death had been swift.

'A narrow dagger,' I said. 'Not a sword. And the killer knew his business. He went straight for the heart.'

156

The churchwarden shuddered. 'To think that such evil walks the streets, and barely a stone's throw from this holy place.'

None of us answered. If the man was unaware of the evil that walked all the streets of London, he must be living in the land of Cockaigne.

Just then, from over our heads, the church clock struck three.

'We'll be about our duties,' weasel face said. 'This must be reported, but it can wait till morning.'

With that, the two men took themselves off. 'Back to the ale house, no doubt,' Will said. 'But what shall we do? We shall never be able to cross the Bridge now.'

The churchwarden looked uncomfortable. As clearly as if he had spoken, I could see that he was thinking that in pure Christian charity, he should offer us a roof over our heads for the rest of the night, but he did not like the look of us.

'We had best find an inn that will take us in,' Simon said. 'If any will open their doors to us.'

'Not the Green Dragon,' I said. 'They have had troubles enough.'

'The Cross Keys,' Will said. 'We are known there. Even if the cook will give us a chair by the kitchen fire it will serve.'

'Aye.' Simon and I both agreed.

'Master churchwarden,' I said (for I still did not know his name), 'might you lend us a lantern? The moon and stars are still blotted out with storm clouds, and we need to find our way through the dark streets.'

He was only too glad to find us a lantern and be rid of us. As we walked away, Will now carrying Rikki, who had fallen asleep in the church porch, we could hear him locking the church door.

In the morning, stiff and crumpled from our few hours on benches in the kitchen of the Cross Keys, we made our way to the Theatre, anxious to inform Master Burbage of the night's events before some official, alerted by the parish constables, arrived with a garbled account of our involvement in Stoker's death.

157

As usual, Master Burbage was already at work early in his office. I found myself a seat on a stool in the corner and left it to Simon and Will to tell him what had happened after we had left the others the previous evening. They were his own men, and also colleagues, after a fashion, of the dead man. When called upon, I described what I could of the fatal stabbing, from my brief view of it.

'This becomes more and more disturbing,' Master Burbage said. 'Two of our men murdered and one of Henslowe's attacked and robbed. Has someone started a war on the players' companies? The City authorities have never liked us.'

None of us answered.

'And all to do with the copying of play books,' Will said at last. 'Wandesford and Holles both copyists. Stoker sought to be a copyist. Kit Marlowe's play stolen.'

'Nay,' said Master Burbage, 'surely not. You fear for your plays, Will, but they are safe enough. I take greater care than Philip Henslowe.'

'Will may have good reason,' I said. 'Stoker took a mighty interest in the texts of the plays. All the while I have been at work copying, Stoker has been hanging about, wanting to read the lines out to me, or peering over my shoulder, until I told him to go away.' I gave a somewhat forced laugh. 'I hope I may not be the next victim.'

'You would recognise *belladonna* and not drink it by mistake,' Simon said. 'And you are a more than adequate swordsman.'

'I thank you for that,' I said, a little stung at his 'more than adequate'. 'There are, however, other methods.'

'You know,' Will said thoughtfully, 'I have often wondered what Stoker was doing here. He claimed to have been with Henslowe's company. Has anyone ever asked Master Henslowe if that is true? And he was given very menial work with us. Why did he stay? And why was he so anxious to become a copyist, when it was evident that his writing was poor?'

'He could read fluently,' I said. 'He kept muttering the lines in my ear, driving me to distraction.'

Will nodded. 'I noticed that he was always mouthing our speeches too, when we were rehearsing or during a performance. Was he memorising the parts?'

'I wondered that myself,' I said. 'I thought he hoped to impress Master Burbage and persuade him to employ him as an actor.'

Burbage shook his head. 'Never. I believe you remember my comparison? As animated as a bed post?'

'And so was his reading,' I said.

'I wonder whether those constables will report this death to the coroner,' Master Burbage said. 'Or whether it falls to me, as the employer both of the victim and of those who found him. The coroner may begin to think it very curious, that murder dogs our steps.'

'I wonder–' Simon said.

'Aye?' Master Burbage looked at him. 'What do you wonder?'

'When Will looked in Master Wandesford's room after he was killed, it seemed that someone had searched it. I wonder whether anyone has searched Stoker's room.'

Will jumped to his feet. 'You have the right of it, Simon. We should go and look at once, before those bumbling constables go ferreting about and turn all to chaos.'

Master Burbage frowned. 'The coroner may not like it.'

'Damn the coroner!' Will said. 'How is he to know?' He turned to Simon and me. 'Will you come?'

'I will,' Simon said eagerly.

I was more doubtful. We might be breaking some law. But in the end, curiosity won me over. 'May I leave Rikki with you, Master Burbage?'

'Aye, leave him here. You do not want him to leave bloody paw prints all over the man's room.'

'Where did he lodge?' Will asked.

Burbage pulled a paper toward him. 'I have it here. Cockspur Lane. Sign of the blue dove. Not Cockspur Street. Cockspur Lane.'

'I know Cockspur Lane,' Simon said. 'Off Wormwood Street. We will find it easily enough.'

In the event, it was not as easy as he expected. The lane was narrow and dirty, the signs indicating the names of the buildings mostly so covered with filth they could hardly be made out, or else they were missing altogether. Eventually we found what we took to be the blue dove – the sign fallen down and propped against the base of the house wall. The creature it portrayed was a sort of bluish grey and looked more like a Barbary parrot than a dove, but we could find no other sign which resembled any kind of bird.

Will hammered on the door.

The house was completely silent, with a sort of watching silence, although it was long past the hour when every citizen should be at work. The shutters had perished or been torn away from one of the ground floor windows, so I tried to peer inside. In this poor district the windows were still made of oiled paper. What with that, and with the dirt inside and out, I could make out little, but I thought I could just distinguish a furtive movement.

'There is someone there,' I told Will. 'Keep knocking.'

He knocked until his knuckles were sore, then began kicking the door. His boots were stout and the door was a poor thing, so that it buckled under this assault.

'Take care you do not break it down,' Simon warned, 'or we shall find ourselves in trouble.'

Eventually I suppose the person I had dimly seen inside must have realised that we were not going to leave. There was the scrape of bolts being drawn back, then the door opened a crack, just enough to allow the view of half a face, which might have been man or woman. A labyrinth of dirt-filled wrinkles turned a human visage into something resembling an explorer's map. One bloodshot eye glared at us balefully out of this visage, and half of a gap-toothed mouth demanded, 'What do you want?'

The voice was deep and husky, but I guessed it was a woman's although I was still not quite sure.

'We have come from Master Burbage,' Simon said politely, recoiling slightly from the stench of the creature's breath. 'John Stoker's master. We are here to examine his room.'

'Whyfor would you be doing that? Master Stoker is not here. I can't let you in.'

'Master Stoker is dead,' Will said. Somehow he had managed to insert his shoulder and the toe of his boot into the crack in the door. 'We have come to collect his possessions.'

'Dead!' This was a shriek of genuine horror. Perhaps the man had friends after all. A moment later I was undeceived.

'Dead! He owes me three weeks' rent, the bastard! Got himself killed, has he? No wonder, the company he keeps. Three weeks' rent! You'll leave his goods here, I'll take them in payment for the rent.'

'You'll do such thing,' Will said. 'The coroner will want to see them. Now, out of the way, goodwife. We have no wish to harm you.'

By dint of pushing, Will and Simon managed to force the door open and we slipped through. Will had guessed right, the creature was a woman, perhaps not as ancient as I had first supposed, but poverty, drink, and an ill temper had aged her beyond her years.

'Where is his room?' Will demanded of the creature.

Though it was clearly a woman, from the draggled skirts, her head was almost as bald as a man's, sprouting a few sparse hairs. She gave off a powerful stink of strong beer and unwashed body.

'First floor back,' she said, glaring at him malevolently. She jerked her head toward a set of rickety stairs.

They were hardly even stairs, we realised as we climbed them. Starting life as a ladder, they had been hammered to a cross beam in the ceiling, with risers of rough planks nailed between the treads to create a makeshift staircase that shook under our feet. As we emerged into the upper floor, we had to stoop to avoid colliding with the roof beams, for this was no more than a sloping attic, partitioned with thin boards into three separate sections. Stoker's room was cramped and mean, holding no more than a trestle bed, a couple of joint stools, and a board laid across two broken barrels to form a sort of table. A few clothes lay tumbled on one of the stools, the bedclothes were dragged half on to the floor as though the occupant had just arisen, and the only window was covered by nothing but a flimsy shutter, which Simon opened to give us more light.

Seeing the poverty and misery of Stoker's lodging, I felt a twist of pity and wished I had been kinder to him. Too late, as such regrets often are.

Simon was poking about on the makeshift table, where a rotting apple core weighed down some sheets of paper.

'Will,' he said, 'look at this.'

Will took the papers from him and tilted them toward the light.

'I knew it!' The words burst from him in an explosion of angry breath. 'The writing is foul, but this is the opening scene of my Henry play. There are blunders, and the lines start and end in the wrong places, but there is no mistaking it. What skulduggery was he about? Was he planning to sell my play?'

The two players look at each other in consternation. Master Burbage, it seemed, was wrong, and Will was right. All these troubles seemed to point to the theft of plays.

'But,' I said, 'surely Stoker could not pass it off as his own work? And in any case, what you have there cannot be the entire play.'

Will thumbed through the pages. 'The beginning of Act One and part of Act Two. He seems to have been memorising it and then coming back here and writing it down.' He glanced up at me. 'Some people would not question too closely whether or not he had written it. They would pay for it and keep quiet.'

'You mean Ned Alleyn was right?' I said. 'Guessing that it might be some rogue company of players who have no plays of their own to bring in an audience?'

'It is as good an idea as any,' Simon said, 'though whether this theft of Stoker's is related to the attack on Holles, who can say? And as for his death, that may be no more than a stabbing during a robbery.'

I gestured at the poverty of the room. 'Would a man like this possess anything worth stealing?'

'Unless he had copied other plays,' Will said slowly. He peered at the sheets in his hand again. 'Or . . . These are poorly written, even for Stoker. There are blots of ink and some beer stains on some of the sheets. I wonder whether these are rejected sheets. I finished my Henry play some time ago. What if he had already made a better copy, and that was what was stolen from him?'

Although it was clear that Stoker had been up to no good, I thought Will was too obsessed with the theft of his own work. It was more likely that Stoker, in death, was just another victim of London's dangerous streets.

'Besides,' I said, what can any of this have to do with Master Wandesford's murder, which came first of all?'

'Wandesford's room had been searched,' Simon said. 'Perhaps Will is right and a play had been stolen from there.'

I shook my head. 'You are forgetting. Wandesford always did his copying in the playhouse. The papers Will saw in his room were his own private affairs.'

'His landlady said that his rough papers were missing.'

'But do we know they were anything to do with the playhouse?'

'Perhaps not,' Will admitted gloomily. 'In any case, we had better keep these papers for the coroner, in case they throw any light on Stoker's death.'

We decided to leave Stoker's poor garments where they were. If the coroner wanted them, he could send a servant to fetch them, but Will was determined not to let the fragments of his play fall into anyone else's hands but his own. As Simon turned to close the shutter again, he moved out of the beam of light, so that it fell suddenly across the bed and the wall behind it. For the first time I noticed that there was a shelf above the bed, containing a few objects.

'We should look at what we have here,' I said, leaning across the bed in order to see better.

'There is a razor and a pot of ink,' I said. 'A piece of mouldy cheese, with mouse droppings near it.'

Then, at the very back, there was a glint of light on a small glass bottle.

'What is this?'

I lifted it down and held it up toward the window. A murky liquid, somewhere between grey and purple in colour, slightly viscous when I shook it. I drew out the cork and sniffed it. Then I sat down suddenly on the unmade bed.

'What is, Kit?' I suppose what Simon read in my face must have alarmed him.

I held it at arm's length, as if it might bite me.

'It is the crushed juice of berries,' I said. '*Belladonna.*'

Walking back to the Theatre we were too subdued to talk. All that we had decided was that we must first tell Master Burbage what we had found, and then someone (we hoped Master Burbage) would need to inform the coroner of our discoveries.

'You are quite sure this is *belladonna*, Kit?' Master Burbage said. He was troubled, yet at the same time relieved.

'Quite sure,' I said.

Rikki was pressed up against my knee, where I sat on a stool in Burbage's office. Simon was leaning on the doorframe. I could not quite read his expression. Will was pacing back and forth, running his fingers through his hair until Master Burbage ordered him to sit down. He collapsed on a bench, knocking off a pile of papers, but none of us bothered to pick them up.

'It would not seem too far fetched, then,' Burbage went on, 'to assume that it was Stoker who dosed Oliver Wandesford with *belladonna* and brought about his death.'

I nodded. 'It seems likely that he was the murderer,' I agreed.

'But *why*?' Simon said. 'As far as we know, the two of them had never met before Stoker joined us a few weeks ago. And even after that, they can have had little to do with each other. Master Wandesford spent most of his time shut away in the book room, at work on his copying. Stoker was fetching and carrying, or running errands.'

'How closely did any of you observe him?' I asked. 'As I told you before, he was always hanging about me when I was copying. Perhaps it was the same with Master Wandesford. Stoker was an insignificant fellow. You hardly noticed where he was or what he was doing, unless he was bothering you. Why, I think we had hardly noticed that he did not dine with us last night, not until we found him dying in the street, and then Simon remembered that he had not been at dinner.'

164

'Are you saying,' Master Burbage looked at me keenly, 'that he bothered Oliver Wandesford while he was copying, and they had some sort of quarrel? A quarrel so serious it could lead to murder?'

'Nay.' I shook my head. 'Had there been a quarrel that serious, someone would surely have noticed it. I only meant that they might have come to know each other better than you suppose.'

'You have to realise,' Will said, 'that it is all to do with the plays, the copying and theft of plays.'

'Will,' Master Burbage said kindly, 'try not to see everything as connected to your plays.'

'But I think,' Simon said slowly, 'that Will may be right. There are just too many threads linking all these events together and to the plays.'

'I agree,' I said. 'Do you not remember, poor Master Wandesford was barely cold before Stoker was trying to take his place as your copyist?'

They all looked at me soberly, then Master Burbage voiced what they were all clearly thinking.

'Are you suggesting, Kit, that Stoker would *murder* Wandesford simply to step into his shoes as copyist?'

'It seems far fetched,' I agreed. 'But desperate men do desperate deeds. It was clear from his lodgings that Stoker was penniless. Perhaps he only meant to make Master Wandesford ill, so that he might take his place and earn his wages.'

Will shook his head. 'You are forgetting that, having failed to secure the position as copyist, he was memorising the plays and writing them out at home. Which meant, incidentally, that he would have to buy paper. Where did he get the chinks for that?'

'And writing them out at home would earn him no wages,' Simon said firmly, 'unless . . .'

'Unless someone was paying him,' Will finished.

'Aye.'

'But the murder of Stoker,' I said, 'that can have nothing to do with whatever scheme he may have been caught up in, for the copying of plays. He was merely stabbed in the street, the kind of killing that happens nearly every day in London.'

165

'What I do not understand,' Simon said, 'is why he was out there anyway, instead of with us. As you say, Kit, the fellow was poor. He must have been glad of one good meal a day. I have never noticed him miss another. Why was he in an alley off Gracechurch Street, just after that thunderstorm, instead of eating a welcome hot meal at the Green Dragon?'

Master Burbage shook his head. 'We shall probably never know. I doubt whether the coroner will be able to find the killers. There appear to have been no witnesses and none of you could identify the hooded men you saw running away. It is quite another matter when a stabbing occurs in a fight by day, with people all around. In this case it is unlikely the cutthroats will be found.'

He stood up with a sigh.

'I suppose I must go again to the coroner's office. It will do our reputation no good, being linked to two murders.'

'You can never be sure,' Simon said wryly. 'It might make the citizens of London all the more anxious to spend their pennies to come and gawp at us – the notorious company of players, Lord Strange's Men. Two murders already! Who will be next?'

'I do not find that even a little amusing, Simon.' Burbage held out his hand to me. 'Best let me take that *belladonna* juice to the coroner, Kit. And, Will, I'll need to hand over those pages you found.'

'How secure is the coroner's office?' Will asked. 'They might fall into the wrong hands.'

'What good would these few pages do anyone?' Burbage asked. 'Give me the pages, Will. Your Henry play book is safely locked away.'

Reluctantly, Will handed them over and Master Burbage set off for the Guildhall.

'I suppose the coroner will rule that it is likely Master Wandesford was killed by Stoker,' I said. 'I do not see what other conclusion he can come to.'

The following day, the whole sorry business of an inquest took place again, although fortunately the cooler weather after the thunder storm meant that the atmosphere was not so oppressive.

This time I did not feel as conspicuous, since I had not instigated the whole investigation of the death. Simon, Will, and the two parish constables were also witnesses to the finding of Stoker's body, and there was no ambiguity over the cause of his death, although there was little hope that the two hooded men would ever be found. The stabbing would probably go down in the court records as yet another unsolved killing in the streets of London.

However, there was no escaping mention of the items found in Stoker's room. As we had expected, we were reprimanded by the coroner for having interfered with the investigation of his own sergeants, but the fact that the papers and the bottle had been handed over at once to the coroner's office went some way to pardoning us.

Will put forward his idea that some scheme was afoot to steal plays from Burbage's and Henslowe's companies. Sir Rowland listened politely, but shook his head.

'You have produced no evidence linking these papers found in the deceased's lodgings with either his death or that of the other member of your company. It appears to me purely incidental and of no relevance to the inquiry before this court.'

He turned to me.

'However, Dr Alvarez, your discovery of *belladonna* in the deceased's possession would appear to have a connection with that other death. As you suggested in the previous case, I have had the contents of the bottle examined by an apothecary, who agrees that it is the concentrated liquid from the crushed berries of the *belladonna* plant. It is not the purpose of this inquest to rule on whether or not this was the poison used in the murder of Oliver Wandesford. Nevertheless, that seems a reasonable conclusion, and it will be entered in the record.'

He cleared his throat.

'We have a further point to consider here. The three of you who have given evidence of finding the *belladonna* at the deceased's lodging are also the three who have alleged that you found his body in the street. Now we must consider the possibility that, having discovered what appeared to be proof that this new member of your company murdered an old and valued friend, you took it upon yourselves to avenge that death by killing the deceased.'

He sat back, amidst a gasp from most of those in the court. I felt paralysed by shock. I had feared we would face trouble for searching Stoker's room, but I had never suspected that it might be twisted in this way. I looked wildly round at Simon and Will, who seemed stunned.

'Your honour.' Master Burbage sprang to his feet. 'You must consider the order of events. The three witnesses came to me shortly after discovering the body. It was *after* that, several hours *after* the man was dead and carried to the church by the parish constables, that they visited his lodgings. They had some difficulty gaining entrance, as I am sure you will be able to ascertain from the woman of the house. It was only then that they discovered the *belladonna*, long after Stoker was dead.'

He sat down again and wiped his face with a large handkerchief. I suppose in a moment of panic he saw his play maker, his (temporary) copyist, and one of his promising young players hauled away to the gallows.

Sir Rowland inclined his head in acknowledgement of this nervous speech. I thought I saw a gleam of amusement in his eye. Surely he must be fully aware of the order of events? Perhaps he meant merely to have a little entertainment for himself, frightening us with his suggestion of a revenge killing.

As before, the new panel of jurors was sent away to debate their verdict, having been told that they need not consider the possibility that we had killed Stoker ourselves. It took them less than ten minutes to decide, for this was a simple case, a stabbing in the street, an everyday London occurrence, the killers unknown.

Nevertheless, I was relieved to escape from the court, although this time the proceedings had taken less than half a day. Even if the suggestion that we had been responsible for the killing was meant as no more than a diversion, it had been a shock.

'So, you have escaped the halter this time, Will!'

We were hailed in the street and I saw that amongst the crowd leaving the inquest was Ned Alleyn.

'Let me stand the three of you a sup of ale. You all went as white as bleached linen when he started accusing you of murder.'

He began to steer us toward an ale house across the street.

'Not there,' Will said. 'It will be overrun by all the gawpers from the inquest. There's a decent house in Cornhill. Most people won't walk that far. I think we need to discuss this matter of stolen plays, Ned.'

'Aye. He soon silenced you about that, did he not? But these rich City men, they only understand the commodities they trade in. They do not understand the value of the words on paper, save for their contracts and bills of sale.'

We made our way to Cornhill, Will and Ned leading the way and talking playhouse gossip, Simon and I following a little behind.

'What do you think of Will's idea, Kit?' he asked. 'Could it be possible?'

I hesitated before answering. 'It is quite outside my experience in Walsingham's service,' I said, 'this matter of the financial value of plays, but I am beginning to understand it. What I did learn from Sir Francis, aye, and from Thomas Phelippes too, is that words on paper may have more value than Sir Rowland's Russian furs, or be more dangerous than the gunpowder stored in the Tower. Men have been robbed and killed for words on paper. It was words on paper that brought the Scottish queen finally to her death. Those were words of state importance, words concerned with war and treason, but in a smaller way, I can see that Will may be right. Perhaps Stoker's death was not a random street stabbing, but is somehow linked to this matter of the play books.'

Once we were settled in a discreet tavern in Cornhill, Will explained to Ned Alleyn just what we had discovered and conjectured about Wandesford and Stoker, then asserted again his conviction that there was some plan afoot to steal plays from the companies of Lord Strange's Men and the Admiral's Men.

'Just as you yourself told Kit,' he concluded. 'And as far as we know, you have not recovered Marlowe's play that was stolen from your man Holles.'

'Nay, we have not.' Ned was leaning forward, listening keenly. 'I was merely guessing when I talked to Kit, but since our play is still missing, and with all that you have told me now, I am more than ready to believe that someone is after our plays. Someone who was paying Stoker, and attacked Holles, or sent someone else to do so. Whether the murder of Stoker is also connected is not clear, I think.'

'Nay, it is not,' Simon agreed.

Up until now I had listened quietly, but now I put a question.

'This play of Marlowe's that was stolen – what was its subject?'

Ned gave me a sideways glance and smiled ruefully. 'I do not think Marlowe would want me to say.'

'Why?' Will asked scornfully. 'Does he fear I would steal his ideas? I have no need to do that.'

'You know how jealous Marlowe is,' Ned said, 'and how quickly he can fly into a rage. It has landed him in trouble before now, and I value my life too much to want to find myself spitted on the end of his rapier like a roasting pig. Why do you ask, Kit? What can it matter?'

'It was only a thought I had,' I said slowly, 'while Simon and I were speaking of the value – and sometimes the danger – of words on paper. I think there is no secret about your play, Will?'

'Nay.' Will shot a sharp look at Ned. 'I am not afraid to speak of it. It is my Henry play that Stoker was copying. Set in the early years of the sixth Henry, last century. It has already been performed several times. Thousands of the citizens of London have seen it.'

'And it has been highly praised,' Simon pointed out.

'Why should that be dangerous, Kit?' Ned asked.

'Probably it is not. Truly, it was only the smallest seed of an idea.'

'Could you not ask Marlowe?' Simon suggested. 'If he says you nay, there is no harm done. If he is willing for you to share the subject with us, then Kit can tell us what this seed of an idea might be.'

170

We agreed that Ned would speak to Marlowe that evening at the Rose, seeking permission to tell us the subject of his stolen play. In the meantime I was reluctant to enlarge any further on the vague idea that was taking shape at the back of my mind.

Chapter Ten

I was growing accustomed to the players' habit of late rising in the morning, so the next day it was with some irritation that I heard our landlady, Goodwife Atkins, toiling up the stairs as I was spreading my morning bread with some honey Tom Read had given me a few days before, culled from the hospital's bee skeps.

'There be a lad here with a message for you, Dr Alvarez,' she said, breathing heavily and pressing a hand to her chest, as if that would strengthen her lungs. 'Seems you're needed.'

My irritation grew. No doubt Mistress Dolesby's sister had returned to Lincolnshire by now, where her husband held a substantial manor. Equally beyond doubt my troublesome patient had amused herself in directing her sister's purchases of the latest fashions in gowns and piccadills – those large lacework collars some of the courtiers had taken to wearing instead of ruffs – and now must have found herself in need of diversion in the form of a medical consultation. With a sigh I collected my satchel, bade Rikki to stay where he was, and followed Goodwife Atkins downstairs.

To my surprise, I recognised the messenger. It was one of the lads who ran errands at St Thomas's.

'Why, Eddi,' I said, 'what do you here?'

'You're needed, urgent, doctor. Goodwife Appledean says, Will you come at once?'

'But, Eddi, I no longer work at St Thomas's.'

'I knows that, maister, and so does Goodwife Appledean. She says she'll make all right with Superintendent Ailmer.'

This was mystifying, but Goodwife Appledean would not have sent for me without real need. Perhaps my successor, Howard Wattis, was taken ill, or was absent. If a patient needed me, I would go, and the rights and wrongs of my interference in Wattis's lordship could be resolved later. I followed Eddi at a run along the river to the hospital.

Parting from Eddi, I made my way up the stairs and along the familiar corridors to the Whittington lying-in ward, where an agitated group of midwives clustered around a bed at the far end. Something troubled me about the ward that I could not quite place as I laid my cap and satchel on a stool. Then I recognised it. The air was not quite fresh. There was no stink of poverty here, but a smell lingered of old food blended with the underlying metallic tang of blood. Blood is always present in a lying-in ward, but I had demanded regular scrubbing of the floors with soap and the changing of bed linen several times a day if it was needed. All the linen and the women's shifts were rinsed in lavender water, and we kept bowls of lavender, hyssop, and other healing herbs in the ward. I had always insisted, too, that, whenever the weather permitted, the windows should be kept ajar. This last had been the cause of a lengthy battle with Goodwife Appledean (who had been trained to keep her labouring women sealed tight and airless), but I had finally triumphed.

It seemed all my work had been undone. Had the midwives reverted to their questionable old practices? Or was this evidence of Wattis's regime?

'Sophy,' I said to one of the younger midwives, 'we will have the windows open, if you please. It is a beautiful day, washed clean by the storm. The women will benefit from some fresh air.'

'Aye, Dr Alvarez.' She smiled at me and hurried away to do as I bid.

'Oh, doctor!' Goodwife Appledean surged toward me, hands outstretched. 'I was not sure whether you would come. I've sent word to Superintendent Ailmer, though I have not had a minute to speak to him myself. I am sure he will not object, for I said that I was sure only you could save her.'

She was urging me across the floor as she spoke, so I caught up my satchel and followed her. The woman on the bed was young, perhaps no more than sixteen or seventeen, and of very delicate build. Her hair, dark with sweat, clung to her face, the bed was pooled in blood, and she seemed at the point of exhaustion beyond which the human frame cannot endure.

'What is the problem?' I said, as I peeled off my heavy physician's gown and then my doublet. This was clearly a time where there was no case for the trappings of dignity.

'It is a breech birth, doctor. The babe is large and wedged, immovable. And I think there is another, smaller one, trapped behind. I am not sure if either of them is still alive, and I do not think the mother can last much longer.'

I began to roll up my sleeves.

'Where is Dr Wattis?' I asked bluntly. 'By rights this is his case and I should not be here.'

A mixture of anger and disgust coloured her voice. 'He went home early yesterday, saying there was nothing he could do for her. That if it was God's will she should die, he would not interfere. He has not come in this morning, although Superintendent Ailmer sent for him. Often he does not come in.'

'He was prepared to let her die, without making any attempt–?' I was so angry I could not finish.

'His attempts would have been fatal in any case,' she said bitterly. 'The last time we had a breech birth, he cut the woman, killing the baby in the process, and wounding the mother so badly that she bled to death in a few hours. I tell you the truth, doctor, I do not want him near my women.'

There was nothing to be said to this.

'I need plenty of boiling water to steep healing herbs,' I said, 'and a flask of oil of olives, with a bowl.'

I looked around. 'Where are the washing basins with soap?'

'Dr Wattis did away with them, saying they were an unnecessary expense and he intended to show how to save the hospital money.' She lowered her voice and muttered to herself, 'He can show us little of any other skills.'

Sophy, having opened the windows, had anticipated my demand for soap and water, and came in carrying a basin she had fetched from elsewhere in the hospital, with a towel over her arm. It is a mystery to me that physicians who are scrupulous about washing their hands before meals will treat one patient after another without dreaming of cleaning themselves.

By the time I had washed, Goodwife Appledean had found me a flask of oil of olives, with which I oiled my hands. English midwives will use butter or beef grease, but I was trained in the Portuguese way by my father and have always found that olive oil serves much better as a lubricant to bring a stubborn baby into the world. The mother was so exhausted I feared she could do little to help me, although her body was convulsed by regular contractions. At first, though, I wanted her to lie quiet.

As Goodwife Appledean had deduced, the baby was presenting the wrong way up and by now it was too late to try to turn it. I would have to deliver it feet first. The following half hour was a struggle. A struggle between me, the recalcitrant geometry of a breech birth, and an infant who seemed determined not to leave the womb, but at last I won and the baby slid reluctantly into my hands. To add to my difficulties, he was near to strangling himself on the cord, but Goodwife Appledean was quick with twine and knife, freeing him from the last link with his failing mother.

There was indeed another baby, but this one so small and facing head down, that she slipped into the world almost before I could hand her brother to Sophy, to be washed and wrapped in a soft blanket. Where the boy was exceptionally large, the girl was very small, so small I feared she had a poor chance of survival, but she let out a hearty yell at the shock of confronting this doubtable world.

'Small,' I said to Goodwife Appledean with a smile, 'but I think this one is a fighter.'

While the midwives tended to the babes, I turned my attention to the mother. She lay flaccid and exhausted, too weak even to sit up and hold the children who had cost her so dear.

'We will move her to another bed,' I said to Goodwife Appledean. 'This one is so drenched and soiled I am not sure the mattress can be saved. Help me to lift her to that empty bed.'

Between us we carried the girl, who weighed no more than a child, to a neighbouring bed, where two of the midwives stripped her of her soiled night shift, washed her, and slipped a clean one over her head, before laying her down. Seeing that her eyes were open, I took her hand in both of mine.

'How do you find yourself now?' I said.

'Sore.' She attempted a smile, which was a brave effort after all that she had endured. It seemed she had been in labour for more than thirty hours.

'I have applied a healing salve, for I am afraid that vast son of yours caused your skin to tear, but it should heal cleanly.'

'It is a boy, then?'

'Aye.' It seemed she had been barely conscious during the final stages of that battle. 'Aye, a fine big boy and a dainty slip of a girl, though she has a mighty pair of lungs on her.'

'A girl as well?' She was astonished. It seemed she had not suspected she was carrying twins. Silent tears began to run down her face, though whether of joy or sorrow, I could not tell. It is not uncommon after giving birth. The women who came to this charitable ward at St Thomas's sometimes had tragic histories.

'You will be busy with the pair of them,' I said. 'Now, I want you to drink all of the beef broth I have sent for. Every drop, mind. And then you may sleep as long as you wish, until it is time to feed the pair of them. The women here will care for you. They are all good, skilful women.'

'But where have you come from?' Her brow creased in a frown. 'I have not seen you before, only that other physician, the one who keeps his distance and speaks Latin like a churchman.'

'Oh, I used to be the physician here, in charge of this ward, so Goodwife Appledean sent for me when she needed my help. I must leave now. Drink your broth and sleep.'

I stood up, feeling suddenly exhausted. I had forgotten how tiring these battles with the angel of death could be. Sophy came with the broth and helped the girl to sit up, as I walked to where I had left my discarded doublet and robe. While I was donning them, Goodwife Appledean returned from supervising the stripping of the soiled bed.

'I am mighty grateful to you, Dr Alvarez,' she said. 'I did my best, but I could not shift that great lad. We would have lost them, all three, if you had not come.'

'I was glad of it,' I said, truthfully. 'I have missed you all. There is surely no better branch of a physician's skill than bringing new life into the world.' I looked around the ward, and lowered my voice. 'Can you not bring back our practices of washing and clean linen? I see some of the women have soiled bed clothes. The floor needs scrubbing. And can you restore our pots of fresh herbs to sweeten the air?'

'I'd do all happily, doctor, if *that man* did not prevent.' She was letting her annoyance get in the way of her natural courtesy. Her contempt for Dr Wattis was clear.

'Do you think it would help if I spoke to Superintendent Ailmer?' I said.

'I cannot see that it would do any harm.' She looked at me hopefully. 'He sent word he would like to see you before you leave.'

'Ah,' I said. 'He is displeased.'

'Nay, I do not think so.'

'I will just look in on the children before I go,' I said. 'Though I suppose none there will know me.' I could not conceal the note of regret in my voice. I had last visited the children's ward in the spring of the previous year.

'You will find a few of our regulars.'

I returned her smile. There were some very large, very poor families in Southwark. Hunger was a regular visitor to their homes, which meant that our regulars would appear from time to time, suffering from malnutrition, and weakened so that they caught every sickness passing through the area. Scurvy, too, was rife amongst them, owing to a poor diet. We would keep them in the children's ward and feed them up, until they were strong enough to move to the hospital's almshouse, home to the destitute who were not sick. Then eventually they would go home. It was a constant cycle which kept most of them alive and relieved their families of part of their burden for a while. A few of these children even made a permanent move to Christ's Hospital, if they were deemed to deserve a place there. And those were often the lucky ones, given bed and board, and education, and a trade.

The regulars in the children's ward did remember me, at which I was absurdly pleased, and I stayed for a while, talking to them about their families and meeting some new children. In this ward too I saw signs of neglect, but the sisters here were usually the young ones, who lacked Goodwife Appledean's authority. It was unlikely they would be able to resist Dr Wattis's economy measures, even had they wanted to. I knew one of them, but the other girl was unknown to me and looked quite slovenly in her dress.

When I made my way at last to Superintendent Ailmer's office on the ground floor, I was feeling dispirited at what I had seen in the two wards which had once been my responsibility and my pride. I hinted as much to him.

'It is not a happy situation, Dr Alvarez,' he said gloomily, 'that I will admit to you freely.' He passed his hand over his face and I noticed that he was looking older and more tired. Worry about money was one of his greatest burdens. 'Dr Wattis was appointed, as you know, through his family's influence with our governors, and I had no part in the matter. There have been . . . difficulties since he has been with us, especially since the death of old Dr Colet, who kept a careful eye on him. But what can I do?'

He raised his hands in despair.

'Goodwife Appledean would like to return to the practices I introduced in the lying-in ward,' I said. 'She cannot do so without your support. With your support, however, I believe it would be possible.'

'Practices?' He was puzzled.

I explained about the washing of the women's shifts and bed linen, the scrubbing of the floor, fresh air, lavender and other herbs.

'It appears that Dr Wattis wishes to save St Thomas's money by cutting down on washing, but all my training has taught me that patients recover much more quickly if their surroundings are clean. And fresh air costs nothing, while the herbs that sweeten the air cost only pennies. Many can be gathered free from the hospital's own herb garden. These things would indeed be an economy for the hospital, for the swifter the cure, the less it will cost.'

'I had no idea that Dr Wattis had embarked on so misguided a regime,' he said. 'I will certainly give Goodwife Appledean my support. I will also ensure that Mistress Maynard knows of this.'

I nodded. Mistress Maynard was in charge of all the nursing sisters. Dr Wattis would find her a formidable opponent.

Gathering up my satchel, I stood to take my leave. 'I hope you have no objection to Goodwife Appledean summoning me,' I said. He had mentioned no objection, but I thought it wise to hear it from him, in case Howard Wattis should make trouble later.

'Certainly not, Dr Alvarez,' he said, with a sad smile. 'I understand that you saved lives which would otherwise have been lost. The midwives did right to summon you.' He sighed. 'I should be glad to have you back with us.'

As I left St Thomas's, I was torn by conflicting feelings. In the lying-in ward that morning I had felt at home, doing the work I was trained for, the work I loved. Yet St Thomas's was closed to me, and I left it feeling myself a stranger and an outsider.

Some of the players were meeting at midday in an ordinary near Bishopsgate, where they would eat a light meal before the afternoon's performance, so I decided to join them, to learn whether there had been any further news after Stoker's inquest. He was to be buried the following morning and despite the general assumption that it was he who had killed Wandesford, intentionally or not, most of the company would attend the funeral. Master Burbage had declared that there would be no performance the next afternoon, after the funeral, as a mark of respect for the two slain members of Lord Strange's Men. Ned Alleyn had promised to join the players at the ordinary today, if he had been able to speak to Marlowe about the subject of his stolen play.

When I arrived, I found half a dozen of the players already eating at a table in the garden behind the ordinary. There were no well kept shrubs and flowers here, no rose clad arbour, as we had enjoyed at the Green Dragon, but it was a popular place where the food was plain and cheap, but good, and the cobbled garden was hardly more than a yard behind the kitchen, into which, during the summer, as many tables and benches as possible were crammed.

Guy moved up along one of the benches, allowing me to squeeze in beside him, and I was followed in not only by Ned Alleyn but by Kit Marlowe as well. The table was loaded with jugs of ale, platters of cheese and cold bacon, and baskets of bread, which was baked by the woman of the house herself, who had a good hand with dough. I helped myself to food and drink, and was careful to ignore Marlowe when he deliberately leaned across me to take the ale jug, then set it down out of my reach. I was used to his ill manners and insults toward me. At one time I would have retaliated, but I realised that he took pleasure in baiting me and it would annoy him much more to be ignored.

Once we had all satisfied our initial hunger, Marlowe leaned back, grinned at Guy, and said, 'I realise I take my life in my hands, joining Burbage's men at table, for who knows what poison may be slipped into my cup through jealousy?'

'Ah,' said Guy, 'but you know that you are safe enough, Marlowe. We only poison our fellow diners at night. Here it is bright sunshine, and no one could tamper with your drink without being seen. Best stay away from us after dark.'

Marlowe gave a laugh which sounded hollow in my ears. 'At any rate,' he said, 'I shall expect to be excused my share of the reckoning, since I come at your request, to give you information you are seeking.'

'Your play,' Will said, leaning forward, 'the one that was stolen, What was it about?'

Marlowe grinned again. 'Alas, poor Will, still trying to emulate my success? Why should I tell you?'

Will flushed angrily, but before he could answer, Guy intervened smoothly.

'We have been discussing this whole matter of the attacks on plays and copyists with Ned. It seems to make no sense, and perhaps it is just a random series of incidents, but one idea we raised was that the kind of play being stolen might make some sense of it.'

Marlowe toyed with his cup, refilled it, and hesitated maddeningly.

'Very well,' he said at last, 'it was a play of the second Edward, how Mortimer conspired against him, overthrew him, and finally had him murdered. A fine, bloodthirsty subject to please our fine bloodthirsty London citizens.'

'Pity,' Will said. He had regained his composure. 'I was thinking of just such a play about Edward, but no doubt it is better suited to your morbid tastes. I know you are jealous of the success my Henry play has achieved.'

'Let us not quarrel,' Guy said. 'We are all victims here.'

'And you believe that someone has been trying the steal your Henry play, Will?' Alleyn said.

'Aye,' Will said. 'They may have failed. We think our man Stoker was involved, him that was stabbed in the street. No doubt you know that Ned was at the inquest, Marlowe. So he will have told you everything that was said there. The fellow seems to have been memorising my play from glimpses of the book and listening while we performed, then writing down what he remembered when he returned to his lodgings. Either he was being paid to do it, or he hoped to sell the play.'

'And before that,' Simon said, 'it was Stoker who gave our copyist *belladonna*, perhaps merely intending to make him ill, and so gain access to Will's play book.'

'It may be that the two thefts are connected,' Marlowe said, 'or it may be no more than chance. I cannot see that the *subjects* of the plays could have any importance, they are simply the two latest plays from the two important players' companies. I can understand that thieves would be eager to steal any play of mine. Even Will is beginning to gain a little fame.'

I felt Ned kick Marlowe under the table, but the fellow merely smirked.

'Guy,' I said, turning my back on Marlowe, 'explain to me exactly why the Master of the Revels insists on reading every play before he will grant it a licence for performance.'

Guy looked at me in surprise, for he knew I was perfectly aware of the reasons.

'He is looking for anything which might be deemed insulting to Her Majesty or the Court, but above all he will censor anything which hints at treason, heresy, or rebellion.'

'Even the Jew boy must know that,' Marlowe sneered.

I ignored him. 'Now, consider this, Ned, and you too, Guy. Marlowe's play concerns the overthrow and murder of an anointed king. Will's play concerns the struggles for power in the early years of another anointed king, who was eventually defeated by rebellion and suffered the usurpation of the crown. Does that suggest anything to you?'

Guy gaped at me. Ned sat up sharply.

'Are you suggesting,' Guy said incredulously, 'that the Master of the Revels is behind this? That he has had them seized?'

'I am not.' I smiled at him. 'Sir Edmund Tylney had already seen and licensed both plays. Will's has already been performed several times, the other one was about to be performed. Sir Edmund could have put a stop to them at any time.'

'But–' Ned said.

'Who else might want these plays, not to ban them, but to use them?' All my training under Walsingham was driving my reasoning now. 'Someone who could use them – perhaps by exaggerating certain themes or inserting new speeches – to proclaim treasonable ideas, with a certain veneer of subtlety, in public. Under the guise of history to stir up trouble amongst the populace.'

They all stared at me in consternation.

'But who?' Guy murmured at last.

I shook my head. 'That I cannot say. Had Sir Francis still been alive, he might have known the answer, but now?' I shrugged. 'Who can say? Some traitor, an ally of Spain? Another covert plot, sponsored by the Pope and the Catholic church? It just seems to me that, since both plays deal with treason and rebellion against the monarch, it is not a coincidence that these are the plays which might be of interest to someone who is working for the overthrow of the Queen.'

I looked round at the them, I had their attention now. Even Marlowe seemed taken aback. 'It would not,' I said with authority, 'be the first such conspiracy.'

It was clear that they were all thinking hard, turning over my suggestion in their minds, but before we could discuss the matter further, we were interrupted. While we had been eating, some of the other tables in the yard had been occupied – a family with four children at one, a group of journeymen (carpenters by the sawdust in the folds of their clothing), a pair of lovers whispering together in a corner – but now a rowdy group of youths came bursting out of the door from the parlour of the ordinary. They had that indefinable look about them of the sons of wealthy fathers, sons who have no need to work and who have abundant time on their hands to drink and make mischief. This group had certainly managed to consume more drink than the time of day warranted.

As they roamed past our table, jostling us deliberately and knocking off Ned's hat, so that he just managed to save it from the ale jug, one of them stopped and pointed at Will.

'Hey, you there! Player, aren't you? Fellow who writes the drivel you rogues expect us to pay good money to hear?'

These were the sort of idle youths who would pay extra to sit on the stage and torment the players with their silly comments and posturing. Will looked irritated, but managed to keep his tongue behind his teeth. Master Burbage would not like it if he offended a wealthy customer.

Marlowe answered for him, united, for once, against an assault from without the players' profession.

'That is Will Shakespeare, and he does not write drivel.'

A compliment indeed!

'Well, but he's a thief.' The fellow's words were slurred.

Will half rose. 'What do you mean? I'm no thief!'

The other youths had gathered around and they snickered.

The first man, who was clearly intent on causing trouble, waggled his finger under Will's nose. 'Came to see your play yesterday. Already seen it somewhere else. *The Lamentable*

History of the Sixth Henry. (Except that he said *Hishtry of the Shixt Henry.*)

Ned jumped to his feet and seized the man by his arm. 'Where do you claim you saw this play? This lamentable history?'

'Leggo my arm!' The man struggled to pull free and his friends looked as though they would enjoy a fight. Several of them laid their hands on their daggers. Marlowe sprang up next to Ned and his dagger was half drawn. He was notorious for getting into trouble. I could see there would be a fight, and blood spilt, any minute now.

'Just tell me where,' Ned said quietly. 'That's all I want to know.' He let go of the man's arm.

Released, the fellow staggered back and collided with the man behind him, who shoved him away so that he nearly lost his balance.

'A'right, a'right. No harm meant. It was over at the Blue Boar at Queene Hythe. New players. No shtage, jus' inn yard. But fine rollicking play.'

He had some difficulty with 'rollicking'.

He glared at Will. 'Made more sense than yours. Too many people in yours. Couldn't keep 'em straight. Fine rol . . . fine play at the Blue Boar.' He nodded wisely. 'Shouldn't steal other people's plays.' He wagged his finger at Will again. 'Sh'write your own.'

His friends, having sheathed their daggers, must have decided they had had enough of this exchange, for they took him by the arms and led him off to a table at the far end of the yard, leaving us staring at each other.

Will, Ned, and Marlowe sat down again.

'It would be very interesting,' Guy said, 'to attend a performance of this play at the Blue Boar.'

Ned nodded. 'I will find out when it is to be performed. If it is possible, as many of us should attend as we can muster.'

'If we find that this other play is a version of Will's,' I said, 'we should report it to the coroner. It may throw light on the two murders.'

'But,' Simon said, 'the murder of Stoker cannot be part of this. If someone was paying Stoker to steal plays, why kill him?'

'Unless,' Guy said slowly, 'Stoker became greedy and demanded more money for his services. Perhaps he wanted more for Will's play than these people, whoever they are, were prepared to pay.'

'Or perhaps they were finished with his services and wanted to silence him,' I said. I thought of others I knew of, who had been disposed of, once they had served their purpose, the hirelings of more powerful, unscrupulous men. 'What I would really like to know is – who is behind this? Someone must have hired the Blue Boar and paid the players, as well as the men who attacked Holles and Stoker. Someone with money. Someone who had a reason. The players are running a risk. If they do not have a licence from a noble patron, they are liable to be arrested.'

'We all know that, Jew boy,' Marlowe said.

It seemed that the temporary truce was over.

Suddenly noticing that it was growing late, Simon and the other players from Burbage's company hurried to pay the reckoning and set off back to the Theatre in time for the afternoon performance.

'I am not due to perform today,' Ned Alleyn said. 'I shall go in search of the Blue Boar at Queene Hythe, to see what I can learn there. I'll send you word. Kit, will you come?'

For a moment I thought he was addressing me, then realised that he meant Kit Marlowe.

Marlowe shrugged. 'I have better things to do with my time. You may send me word as well. You know my lodgings.'

It suited Marlowe, I thought, to pretend contempt for our ideas. Had he originated them himself, his attitude might have been different. Underneath it all, however, I suspected he was as worried as the rest of us. Above all, he must be concerned about the loss of the sole copy of his play about Edward II. Will, at least, still had the original play book of his Henry play, even if Stoker had managed to steal it in some form.

It was difficult to know what to make of Stoker's role in the matter. Certainly he was engaged in illicit copying of Will's play, but had he been hired by someone to carry out the theft? Had he already handed over his copy before he was killed? If what the drunken louts said was true, some version of Will's play was being performed illegally. But had Stoker's murder been somehow connected to the theft, or was it no more than a chance killing?

After we had parted outside the ordinary, I walked part of the way toward the river with Ned, until he turned off to the right and headed for Queene Hythe, while I hurried back to Southwark to rescue Rikki, who had been shut in my room ever since I had been summoned to St Thomas's.

Back at my lodgings, I found Goodwife Atkins washing the windows in an uncharacteristic fit of cleanliness.

'Message for you, Dr Alvarez,' she said. 'That lad came again to say that Goodwife Appledean – is it? – sent word that your three patients are doing well. The mother much recovered and the babes feeding. Also, the other doctor has not returned.'

'Thank you,' I said. 'That is good news indeed.' I did not specify, even to myself, how much of it was good news.

That evening I joined the players for a meal at the Cross Keys, Master Burbage feeling that he had done his duty by the Green Dragon for the time being. I took a seat between Guy and Simon.

'Any word from Ned Alleyn?' I asked Simon quietly. I was not sure whether our meeting with Ned and Marlowe at midday, and the remarks of the drunken youth, had been mentioned to the other players.

'Aye,' he said. 'He sent a lad with a message just as we finished this afternoon.' He gave a nod toward Master Burbage. 'We thought it best to tell Master Burbage everything we learned today.'

'And what did Ned say?'

'There is to be a performance tomorrow at the Blue Boar of this *Lamentable History of the Sixth Henry*. We have discussed it with Master Burbage. As there is to be no performance tomorrow, Guy, Will, Cuthbert, and I will attend. Do you want to come?'

'I could not bear to miss it! After copying the original play I must know it almost as well as Will.'

'Indeed you must.'

'It might be wise not to arrive all of us together,' I suggested. I knew the players too well. They would be likely to attract attention, for they simply could not help themselves. Poor agents they would have made for Sir Francis, where the most important quality was anonymity.

'Probably best if Guy goes with Will,' I said. 'He may needed to be restrained, if he is sure they are speaking his stolen lines.'

Simon laughed. 'You have the right of it. I will mention it to Guy. Shall you come to the funeral in the morning?'

'Aye, there have been too many funerals lately, but I will come, though I never liked Stoker.'

'I cannot think of any who did.'

'Poor fellow,' I said wryly. 'It is a sad epitaph.'

The funeral the next morning was a dismal affair. I think we were all glad when it was over and Stoker sent to meet his maker. No one would ever know whether he had intended to kill Wandesford; that was a secret he took with him to the grave. Perhaps we would never know, either, why he had been killed in that dark alley when he should have been dining with us at the Green Dragon.

Simon, Cuthbert, and I made our way to Queene Hythe, leaving Guy and Will to follow on behind. It took us some time to find the Blue Boar, none of us knowing the area well. Nick Burden, I thought, would have known it. The older agent I had often worked with knew every alleyway and hidden court in London, I believe, and was especially familiar with the river front in the rougher parts of the City. The Blue Boar turned out to be a large inn of the usual type favoured by players who possessed no playhouse. A penny admitted us to an almost circular inn yard, with the galleries leading to the bed chambers surrounding it in three rising tiers. For another penny we gained admittance to the first gallery, where we reckoned to have a better view of the players, and a third penny each secured a shabby joint stool, otherwise we should have been obliged to stand. In no way could this makeshift playhouse compete with the Theatre, the Curtain, or the Rose, but it began to fill up quickly, mostly with apprentices and young journeymen, many of them in company with a girl. The Blue Boar had one principal advantage over the three playhouses. It did not entail the long walk to Shoreditch or Southwark. It was in the heart of the City, a convenient location for young men slipping away from their masters' premises for an afternoon of illicit entertainment.

As we settled ourselves on our stools, with our elbows on the gallery rail, I saw Will and Guy come in and find places a little way to our right. I had already seen Ned Alleyn settled further away on our left. To my surprise, I noticed that Marlowe was with him. Perhaps he was more anxious about this rogue company than he was prepared to admit. So far we had failed to discover any name for this group of players. They had hung a flag from the lintel above the entrance to the yard, but it bore no name or coat-of-arms belonging to a patron. It was nothing but a bit of shoddy blue and white striped cloth, such as you see forming the canopy over any street stall in Cheapside – a butcher, costermonger, or petty toy maker.

While we waited for the players to begin, Cuthbert passed us a bag of hazelnuts he had bought in the street as we walked to Queene Hythe. We sat cracking them with our teeth and spitting the shells on to the floor of the gallery, though Simon launched a few on to the unsuspecting heads of the groundlings below us.

The fellow at the ordinary who had told us about this company had said there was no stage, but it seemed the players had since been at work, for there was now a raised platform at the far end of the yard, directly opposite us. It was perhaps three or four feet high and about twenty feet wide and fifteen deep, not providing the players with much room, but far better than trying to perform on the surface of the yard, where most of the groundlings would have been unable to see them and might have started hurling abuse as well as more solid missiles.

Cuthbert drew a small notebook from his pocket and began to jot something down in it, pausing from time to time to lean over the balcony or to turn and scan the tiers of galleries.

'What are you doing?' I asked.

'Calculating just how much the takings are for this one performance,' he said grimly. 'If they are performing Will's play, we may have a case in court for damages.'

'Do you really think so?'

'It is worth considering.'

I wondered whether any court would care enough about the financial loss to a company of players, but Cuthbert's father was a shrewd man of business, and nothing upset the business community of London more than financial loss.

There was a stir in the crowd below us. I turned from Cuthbert to see that a man had stepped up on to the platform, entering from a door behind it, which must lead to the inn's parlour or tap room. He was not richly costumed like Burbage's players, but wore everyday tunic and hose. As he began to speak, I realised that this was some sort of Prologue. Perhaps this was not Will's play after all, in which case we could simply sit back and pick holes in some jobbing writer's poor efforts. The man began to speak:

> *And who shall say, that this man should be king?*
> *Does blood alone make royalty of him?*
> *What foreign notion this, that sacred oil,*
> *Dabbed on one Adam's son, lifts him above*
> *All other men? Nay, men of England, heed!*
> *Where monarchs fail, 'tis nobler sure*
> *To cut them out, like fatal cankers*
> *Weakening the body of our English state!*

With this the man bowed and withdrew. Simon, Cuthbert, and I looked at each other in alarm. This was not Will's play, but if this limping Prologue was anything to judge by, this play was hinting at treason. I glanced along the row of stools at Will. He was grinning at Guy and leaning back, relaxed. If it was not his play, he would enjoy mocking it later.

Now a crowd of players made their way on to the platform. Perhaps there were no more than ten of them, but they were crowded together. Some stood awkwardly, as though they had no idea what to do with their hands and feet. Prologue was a professional player. He knew how to fill that large space by projecting his voice. But three or four of these new men had clearly no experience as players. The costumes varied considerably in quality, from workaday clothes to a few which had certainly at some time belonged to a person of wealth. Their mysterious patron? Two of the better dressed players stepped forward to the front of the platform, adopting sorrowing looks, and one began to speak.

> *Hung be the skies with black, yield day to night!*
> *Comets, promising change of times and states,*
> *Wave crystal tresses in the sky,*
> *And with them scourge the twice rotating stars,*
> *That have consented unto Henry's death!*
> *King Henry the Fifth, too famous for long life!*
> *England has lost a king of so much worth.*

I found I was holding my breath. I felt sick. It was almost correct, but originally Will's words had been:

> *Hung be the heavens with black, yield day to night!*
> *Comets, importing change of times and states,*
> *Brandish your crystal tresses in the sky,*
> *And with them scourge the bad revolting stars,*
> *That have consented unto Henry's death!*
> *King Henry the Fifth, too famous to live long!*
> *England ne'er lost a king of so much worth.*

I gripped Simon's arm, but leaned across Cuthbert to see what Will was doing. He had gone very red in the face and was trying to stand, but Guy had grabbed him by the back of his doublet and was pulling him back down on to his stool. I looked in the opposite direction, to where Ned and Marlowe were sitting. Ned was looking at us interrogatively. Simon and I both nodded vigorously.

Aye, I thought, this is Will's play, stolen and garbled, but recognisably Will's play. Yet that Prologue was never even a garbled part of his play. Who were these players? They belonged to no licensed company, yet there was money behind this. And someone intending black mischief was behind that Prologue.

190

Chapter Eleven

*T*he performance we watched at the Blue Boar was a much shorter version of Will's play. To tell the truth, Will's Henry play was very complex, as he endeavoured to do justice to the manoeuvrings of the great nobles in the early part of Henry VI's reign. This made it difficult to follow. The version we were now seeing cut out much of the complexity, making it simpler, but less satisfactory. The groundlings seemed to be enjoying themselves, although they were a rowdy crowd, talking, buying nuts, arguing. There was an outburst of shouting soon after the start of the performance, when a stout journeyman found that his purse strings had been cut. The thief was caught by his friends, the purse retrieved, and the scoundrel soundly beaten, sent away with a bleeding nose and an eye half closed from a well-aimed blow. All the while the players attempted to carry on as if nothing was happening.

Moved by patriotic fervour, a member of the audience threw a half sucked orange at Joan La Poucelle, catching the deep-voiced 'boy' actor squarely in the face. La Poucelle faltered and strode to the edge of the platform, looking as though he intended to tackle his assailant, but it was impossible to tell who had thrown the fruit. The players resumed, and there were no more disturbances until we neared the end of the truncated play.

At this point, the script departed entirely from Will's. The various nobles put their heads together and began gleefully to plan the overthrow of the king, turning to the audience and inviting them to join the rebellion against the Crown, which they justified in the name of 'freedom'. I began to feel very uneasy.

Sir Francis would have put a stop to this. The Master of the Revels would be up in arms if he knew what was happening here. Simply by sitting in the audience we were, in a sense, participating in an incentive to commit treason. When the player portraying Henry VI came on stage near the end, wearing a crown made of paper, clearly intended to humiliate him, a barrage of missiles greeted him.

'This is too well organised to be spontaneous,' I said to Simon and Cuthbert, having to raise my voice to make myself heard over the noise that had broken out below, and even in the better seats.

'You think so?' Cuthbert said.

'I am certain. Look, they are throwing things from the galleries. Your tupenny and thrupenny customer does not usually come armed with rotten fruit.'

'I think we should leave,' Cuthbert said.

'I agree.' Simon was already standing up. 'Look, Guy and Will are going already.'

Our neighbours complained as we stepped over their legs to reach the stairs, but fortunately no one attempted to stop us. In the street outside we caught up with Guy and Will. Not surprisingly, Ned and Marlowe were just behind us. Without a word we turned and made our way quickly out of the riverside area and walked back to the ordinary where we had eaten the previous day.

Once we were seated with cups of ale in front of us, Cuthbert turned to Will.

'Well? Kit here says that parts of it *are* your play.'

Will was white with anger.

'Massacred!' he said, through clenched teeth. 'Their additions were the work of some grubby, damned street rhymer. But where they used parts of my work, it was flawed and broken . . .' He stopped, as if the horror was too much to contemplate, and drained his cup.

'Aye, that is what Kit says.' Cuthbert took out his notebook. 'And I reckon they made at least ten pounds fifteen shillings and sixpence.'

At that we all laughed, a relief from the brooding tension.

'True enough, Cuthbert,' Guy said, 'let us reckon our losses. But what are we to do about the stolen plays? That is,' he turned to Marlowe, 'if your play is also in the hands of these rogues.'

Marlowe shrugged. 'We have no proof. But I'm willing to wager a sovereign to a groat that they are behind it. We have heard of no other unlicensed companies at large in London.'

'Kit,' Guy said, turning to me, 'I know this is not the sort of crime Sir Francis would have pursued, but you have more experience of such things than the rest of us. What do you think?'

I saw Marlowe stiffen and realised that the others had forgotten – or perhaps had never known – that he too had worked for Walsingham, though only on an occasional and irregular basis. I waited a moment for him to speak, but he kept his tongue behind his teeth. It might be that he did not wish to broadcast his work for the service.

'You say that it is not the sort of crime Sir Francis would have pursued,' I said, 'but I am not so sure. There is more afoot here than the theft of plays. I've said already that I thought the subjects of the plays might be of importance. After what we have just witnessed, I am convinced of it. They used Will's play as the scaffolding for their performance, but the Prologue and the invitation to join in rebellion with which they finished were their real purpose. At least that is how it seems to me. And staging it in a rough area of the City, yet close to where many of the apprentices work, meant that they were trying to sow the seeds of rebellion amongst the class of young men who are always ready to cry "Clubs!" and join in any trouble. There was enough in what we have seen today to have made Sir Francis take note.'

'I think you probably have the right of it,' Guy said, 'but what are we to do? We cannot pursue these scoundrels ourselves, and Sir Francis is no longer here to take action.'

'The Master of the Revels should be informed,' Cuthbert said. 'He has the authority to stop the performance and fine or imprison the players.'

The others nodded.

I hesitated. I was an outsider here, for this was the business of the players, both Burbage's men and Henslowe's men, but I was not sure the Master of the Revels was the right man to take charge.

'We should not forget what else is concerned in this matter,' I said. 'Two murders and a violent attack. They are not the business of the Master of the Revels, but of the coroner. If we were doubtful of the connection before, we should not be so any more. It seems certain Stoker poisoned Wandesford with *belladonna* in order to gain access to the play books. What we have seen today proves that he gave or sold a garbled version of Will's Henry play to these players, which they altered still further by adding their subversive parts. More and more I am coming to believe Stoker's killing was not a random affair. I think either he had served his purpose and was killed to silence him, or he had fallen out with those who employed him.'

'Perhaps they did not employ him,' Simon said thoughtfully. 'Perhaps he was one of these conspirators himself, in favour of a rebellion against the Crown.'

I nodded. 'That is quite possible. He was also very poor. Perhaps they wanted him to steal the play for no reward, but he demanded money. That would not surprise me.'

'I expect we shall never know,' Guy said. 'In any case, I believe Kit is right. We should take what we know to Sir Rowland, since it must have relevance for his enquiry into the death of Stoker, and seems likely to have a bearing on why Stoker killed Wandesford.'

I looked across the table directly at Marlowe who, unusually for him, had offered no opinion on what action we should take. Normally I avoided speaking to him or even looking at him, having grown wary of his verbal assaults on me. But now I needed to know something.

'So far,' I said, 'we have no proof that these same men have your play of Edward II. The subject of Will's play was well known, since it had been performed a number of times and hundreds of people – even several thousand – had already seen it. However, your play has not yet been performed. You were even reluctant to tell us what its subject was. These men could not have deliberately stolen it unless they *knew* that it would serve their turn, which we can now see is to stir up treachery. How could they have known? Who, besides you, and Ned, and presumably Master Henslowe, knew that you had written about the overthrow and murder of a king?'

I heard Ned catch his breath. It was odd, really, that this had not occurred to any of the others.

Marlowe looked at me in surprise and almost, I fancied, with a little respect. He replied civilly enough.

'Those you mention, certainly. Our copyist, Holles, of course. A few of the other players, though our plan was to make it known only when we announced the first performance. They are unlikely to have discussed it with someone outside the company.'

'Master Henslowe may have mentioned it to our patron,' Ned said, 'though I cannot imagine the Lord Admiral would have spoken of it to anyone else.'

'He might,' Guy said. 'The murder of King Edward II was a scandalous affair, a blemish on the history of this country. Would the Lord Admiral have approved of its being enacted in public, or disapproved?'

'He does not take a close interest in our affairs,' Ned said, 'not like Lord Hunsdon, who is so anxious for a company of his own. But if Master Henslowe did mention it to him, and if he did disapprove, I am certain he would have made his feelings known.'

'So we are no nearer an answer,' Simon said. 'A few people knew. Someone might have mentioned Edward II casually, over a jug of beer, meaning no harm. Nay, until we know for sure these fellows have Marlowe's play, we cannot be certain it was they who attacked Holles.'

'Nevertheless,' Guy said, 'I believe we should tell the coroner what we do know. It will be for him to decide whether to take the matter further. Who is to go to him?'

'I believe you should go, Guy,' Ned said. 'You are the senior man here. The two murder victims investigated by the coroner were your men. The play we know to have been stolen is by your play maker.'

'Very well,' Guy said, 'if that is what you wish. I think Kit should come with me. His service with Walsingham means he is better informed about such matters than I am. Besides, Sir Rowland knows him from his service to the Muscovy Company.'

'If you wish,' I said reluctantly.

This whole affair was thrusting me too much to the fore, something I have always tried to avoid. Too much attention paid to me might one day reveal my hidden identity.

Guy and I were unable to see Sir Rowland that afternoon, since he was occupied with his many business affairs, but we were told by his secretary that we could be seen, briefly, at eight o' the clock the following morning.

'And I mean briefly,' the man said. 'He has an important meeting at the half hour and he insists on punctuality, for himself and everyone with whom he has dealings.'

He looked at us down a long nose, which I thought uncalled for. Guy was respectably and soberly dressed, while I wore my physician's gown and cap. Now that the weather had turned cooler it was more bearable.

Therefore, promptly just before the City clocks began to strike eight the next morning, we presented ourselves again at the Guildhall. Sir Rowland, I thought, must spend much of his day rushing from one office to another – the Muscovy Company, the Lord Mayor's office, the governors' office at St Bartholomew's, and the offices of his own mercantile company. I wondered whether he had any family, and whether they ever saw him.

Just as we were being admitted through the door, a horseman drew rein behind us and dismounted, handing the horse over to a groom.

'Dr Alvarez, Master Bingham,' Sir Rowland said warmly, 'come in. I understand you have information which may relate to the two inquests on the men from Lord Strange's Company.'

'That is so, Sir Rowland,' Guy said, as we followed him into a room which was large and comfortable, but by no means as lavish as the one where he had received me at Muscovy House. Sir Rowland turned over an hour glass. Clearly the secretary had been speaking no more than the truth.

I left it to Guy to explain why we were there, describing the performance we had attended at the Blue Boar the previous day, merely assenting when my opinion was asked. When he finished, Sir Rowland looked from one to the other of us.

'A great deal of this is surmise,' he said bluntly.

I nodded. 'Perhaps, individually. But taken together, it seems to make a whole.' I reached into my satchel and drew out some sheets I had written the night before.

'I have here the first few speeches from Master Shakespeare's play and – as near as I can remember them – the way those speeches were delivered at the Blue Boar. You will see that they are quite close, but with the small differences that might arise from someone, such as Stoker, trying to write down what he had overheard. Also, as far as memory will serve, I have written out the provocative Prologue these men have added to the play, and the gist of what was said in the final scene. I am afraid we were all somewhat disturbed by then and I cannot recall the exact words.'

I handed him the papers, which he scanned quickly.

'Aye, this certainly seems to show that they have stolen your play, but I am not sure that it is definite proof that the man Stoker was involved.'

I thought he was being over cautious, but Guy patiently explained again everything that linked Stoker with the rogue players.

'There is not a great deal I can do,' Sir Rowland said frankly, pressing down the papers I had given him with the palms of his hands. 'I am prepared to report this illicit company, performing an unlicensed play, to the Master of the Revels. For if the play is as much changed as you suggest, then it does not possess a license. He can close them down and fine them. If they can be shown not to have a noble patron, then they can be whipped out of town as vagrants.'

Guy winced at this, and I wondered briefly whether he had ever been whipped as a vagrant, but now was not the time to ask. I was impatient with Sir Rowland and longed for Walsingham, who would have seen at once that closing down the rogue company and dispersing its members would not be the solution. It took a particular cast of mind, I knew, to be able to delay action in order to take a longer view.

'Sir Rowland,' I said, 'although we are concerned at the theft of our play and the possible theft of a play by Christopher Marlowe of the Admiral's Men, simply punishing these men is not the most important issue here. There must be more at stake to justify two murders, as well as a vicious attack which might have led to a third death. I think perhaps we have not explained clearly enough what was afoot at the Blue Boar yesterday.'

'Go on,' he said, though he glanced at the sand running through his hourglass. It was not far off the halfway mark.

'It was not mere bombast,' I said, 'the call to rebellion. It was seriously meant, and seriously understood by the people in the audience, the most of them young men. Some, I am sure, were already privy to what was to happen, and had come armed with rotten fruit for the mock "stoning" of the player king at the end.'

'Throwing rotten fruit?' He was dubious. 'Does this not happen in every playhouse? I confess I rarely have time to attend.'

'Not in our playhouse,' Guy muttered.

'It was symbolic,' I said. 'They did not intend to hurt the player who took the part of King Henry, for he is one of this conspiracy. Aye, I believe it is a conspiracy.'

I was speaking more quickly, my eyes on that fast flowing sand. 'Should it not be reported? Perhaps to Lord Burghley?'

Lacking Sir Francis, I could not think who else to name.

There was a tap on the door and the secretary entered. Sir Rowland stood up.

'Gentlemen, I am afraid I have another meeting. For the moment we will not inform the Master of the Revels or Lord Burghley, but leave these players unhindered. That will give you the opportunity to find more evidence, first, that this matter is in any way connected to my enquiries into the two deaths, and second, whether there is a serious threat of treason. Come to me at once if you discover anything further.'

He bowed, and we were hurried away by the secretary, passing, on the way out, a group of wealthy merchants who regarded us in some astonishment.

'Well,' Guy said ruefully, 'that was hardly worth leaving our beds for, so early in the morning.'

'Early?' I said. 'The rest of the world has put in half a morning's work already. Not everyone is such a slug-abed as you players.'

He punched me on the shoulder as we began to make our way to the Theatre. Master Burbage at least would be awake and would want to know the outcome of our meeting with the coroner.

'I do not believe it was entirely fruitless,' I said as we hurried through the streets. 'He saw sense in not sending in the Master of the Revels to close everything down. He has given us time to find out more. If you look at the lie of the land from his viewpoint, our tale must seem very odd, especially to a man who did not sit in the Blue Boar as we did, witnessing that clear incitement to treason. To a great merchant, dealing in vast piles of coin for goods passing to and from England, the value of a mere play must seem like a purse full of pennies. What is Will paid for a play?'

Guy lifted his cap and scratched his head. 'Near seven pounds, I think, now that he has begun to make a name for himself.'

It sounded like a great deal of money, although I knew that Master Burbage sometimes spent as much as ten pounds on one of the magnificent costumes that adorned his stage monarchs, and which he sometimes enjoyed borrowing for himself. If Will continued to write his plays rapidly, he would soon be a rich man.

'Aye, well, I suppose seven pounds seems little enough to a man who must meet all the Lord Mayor's expenses out of his own pocket,' I said, 'but I think toward the end of our meeting Sir Rowland began to believe there might be some real danger of conspiracy. We shall just need to find more proof. I wish we might discover what has happened to Marlowe's play.'

I also wished, though I did not voice it aloud, that I could share all this with Phelippes or Nick Berden. They would help to ferret out who was behind whatever was afoot at the Blue Boar. It was clear to me, now that Wandesford's death could be attributed to Stoker – and no one had cared much for Stoker or his death –

that the players were solely concerned about the theft of the plays. They nodded politely when I spoke of treason, but they did not really fear it. I was very fond of my friends of the playhouse, but at times like this they seemed as naïve as children.

Master Burbage seemed unsurprised that the coroner had not taken us very seriously, though he was glad that nothing was to be done yet about approaching the Master of the Revels.

'We must keep our ears open for any word of what this company at the Blue Boar means to do next. Do they plan to perform their Henry play every day? Or do they not perform every day? Let us all find out what we can.'

This was all very laudable, but too vague and hardly practical. I spent some time during the rest of that day making a fresh copy of some old version in English of a Roman play which seemed hardly worth the keeping, but my mind kept wandering back to thoughts of Phelippes and Berden. The lad Harry at the Walsingham stables had told me that Berden now ran a poultry business, but he had not mentioned where it was located. Chances were that, like others in the same trade, his premises would be in the appropriately named Poultry.

The next morning I set out to find him.

I decided that I would search through the area where the poulterers were mostly located, and only if I failed to find him would I ask Harry if he knew the address. In the event, he proved not too difficult to find. Berden's was a fine clean shop, round the corner from Bucklesbury, just past St Benet Sherehog.

'The maister be back in his office, my maister,' an apprentice told me, pausing as he plucked a goose while carefully stowing the feathers in a sack. He jerked his head toward a door at the back of the shop.

To my tap on the door, a familiar voice called out to me to enter.

'Why, Kit!' Nick surged to his feet, scattering papers as he did so. 'I have not seen you this year and more. Last I heard, you were away in the frozen north. Come, in, come in!'

'It is good to see you, Nick.' I found myself beaming as he seized me by both hands and pumped them up and down.

'I swear, you have grown taller. Do you still have that dog we rescued in the Low Countries?'

'I do. And as I remember it, he rescued us, as much as we rescued him.' I looked around. 'This tradesman's life seems to suit you. You have grown somewhat larger about the waist, I see.'

'Indeed, I fear I have.' He patted his stomach. 'Too much sitting about, trying to make my accounts balance. Not enough chasing of villains.'

'Now that,' I said, 'is exactly what I have come to see you about.'

'Caught up in more nefarious deeds, are you?' He gave me a shrewd look. 'Not working for Phelippes?'

'Thomas Phelippes has tried to recruit me, but he is now in the employ of Lord Essex, so I declined.'

'Hmm. I recall that you do not care for his lordship.'

'I do not.'

'So who are the villains you want to talk to me about?'

Briefly, I gave him an account of the whole affair, from the death of Oliver Wandesford, the killing of John Stoker, the stolen play by Marlowe, down to our visit to the Blue Boar and what had happened there. It was a relief to set it all out for someone who would immediately seize the salient points and recognise, as I had done, just how dangerous the events at the Blue Boar might prove to be. The players were keen to discuss everything endlessly, and grew quite excited about it all, but I had the uneasy feeling at the back of my mind that it was not truly real to them. It was as though they were caught up in the drama as they might be in one of their plays. To Nick, as to me, there were here the certain signs, all too real, of some nasty conspiracy.

'So,' Nick said, tilting back his stool until he could prop his shoulders against the wall behind, 'there is clearly something afoot. Do you think it is another plot against the Queen?'

'That is how it seems. All the suggestions in their version of Will's play were that the monarch should be overthrown.' I frowned. 'But what I find so curious is the blatant *openness* of it. Whenever we have dealt with conspiracies in the past, the perpetrators have been at pains to conceal everything from view until the last minute. Do you not find it strange?'

'Aye, 'tis odd. Either they are very bold, or very stupid.'

'Exactly what I think. And I need your help.'

'Now that is a great temptation.' He gathered up his scattered papers, tapped them into a neat pile and laid them on the table, held down with a smooth stone. 'I tell you truly, Kit, it may be a great honour to be poulterer to the Court, but it is expensive. The Court does not pay its bills. It may be that my grandsons – if the Lord bless me with any – will be paid, but I fear I shall never see the money in my life time.'

I made a sympathetic noise, while trying to hide my smile. It seemed this quiet life as a tradesman was not as agreeable as Nick had hoped.

'And do you still keep your friends amongst the–' I was not quite sure how to phrase it tactfully. I could hardly say *ruffians of London's streets*.

'Amongst the men who used to work for you?'

'Aye, I do.' He gave me a shrewd look. He knew exactly what had been on the tip of my tongue. 'I was born amongst such men, Kit, until I was whisked off to Westminster choir and school.'

'I never knew that,' I said.

He smiled complacently. 'Sang like an angel, I did. At seven years old I was put to the choir. An angel at singing and a devil's imp at everything else, though I learned enough of books and arithmetic, aye, and even Latin, to make my way in the world. But I did not forget where I came from.'

I nodded. It accounted for much I had not understood before about Nick.

'Now, how do you want me to help you?'

I felt a sudden surge of hopefulness. Berden was a formidable ally.

'We need to discover two things.' I leaned forward, my elbows on my knees and my chin propped on my fists. 'First, was Marlowe's play also stolen by these men? Was Stoker killed by them, and why? But, most important, who is behind this staging of plays framed to incite rebellion?'

'That is three things.'

'I suppose it is, and the killing of Stoker is probably the least important, being over and done with, though the truth about how it happened will strengthen the coroner's hand. The first and the last points are the most vital. Do they have Marlowe's play about the murder of a king, do they plan to use it, and who is the chief conspirator?'

'You are sure there is someone other than the men in this unlicensed company?'

'If you had seen them, you would agree. They are indifferent actors, poor jobbing players, probably scraped together from some vagabond wandering troupe. They do not even have boys to play the women's parts. La Poucelle – you know, her they call "Joan of Arc" – was played by a man at least thirty, with a baritone voice and the stubble of a beard. The one most like a professional player was the one who spoke the Prologue and then was the most vociferous of the nobles at the end, calling for the overthrow of the king, but even he did not impress me as a leader. Difficult to put my finger on it, but if you had been there, you would agree.'

He nodded. 'I trust your instincts. So . . . there is somebody else, not a player, who has devised this plan of using plays to stir up, at the very least, trouble. At the most, it may be a serious attempt to incite rebellion, though I agree that it is a curious way to go about it.'

He clasped his hands behind his head and tilted his stool back still further, until I feared it might tip over.

'It must be someone with money,' I said bluntly. 'The men must be paid, the Blue Boar hired, the costumes (though poor) bought.'

'Therefore, either a wealthy merchant or a noble.'

'No wealthy merchant would want to stir up trouble. Too damaging to trade.' I grinned. 'No one to buy his geese and capons.'

He laughed. 'Nay, we wealthy merchants prefer the status quo, and peace for our commerce. Hence, it must be a nobleman.'

'Or,' I paused, 'could it be another Catholic conspiracy, financed from abroad, with the Pope's blessing?'

'It doesn't *feel* like a Catholic plot to me,' he said. 'This feels home-grown.'

'I agree,' I said. 'I doubt any Catholic agent, coming from abroad, would understand enough of how our playhouses work, and the powerful influence they can have. That is why the Common Council is always looking for an excuse to shut them down, and why the Master of the Revels is so strict about giving out licences.'

'There is another point.' He let his stool fall forward on to its front legs, and I felt the vibration of the floor through my shoes. He had certainly put on weight.

'Which point do you mean?'

He wagged an admonitory finger at me. 'What agent from abroad would understand the significance to Englishmen of Edward II and Henry VI?'

'Aye,' I said slowly. 'You have the right of it. Therefore, let us agree that this is not the work of foreign Catholic agents of the King of Spain, nor is it the work of discontented London merchants, annoyed that the Court never pays its bills. That leaves us with the English nobility. But who?'

We were both silent, turning over what we knew of English nobles who might wish to overthrow the Queen.

'In the early days of the reign of the House of Tudor,' Nick said slowly, 'there were a number of uprisings and attempts to thwart their rule. Henry VII silenced most of them, including remaining descendents of the House of Plantagenet who might have a claim to the throne. Henry VIII despatched any who were left.'

I nodded. One did not speak of such things in public, but Nick and I trusted each other.

'However, there is one possible claimant to the throne still living, though he is part of the Tudor dynasty, not a Plantagenet.'

I racked my brains, trying to think who he meant. Lord Hunsdon was a cousin of the Queen, but that was through the Boleyns, not the Tudors. I shook my head.

'Lord Strange,' he said. 'Or at least his mother, the Countess of Derby, Margaret Stanley, née Clifford. By Henry VIII's will, she is next in line after his children, should they die childless. Two have already done so, and Her Majesty is past child-bearing. The Countess of Derby is Henry VIII's great-niece, granddaughter of Mary Tudor. She must be nearly of an age with the Queen.'

'Of course,' I said, 'I had forgotten the Stanleys. But surely she would not–'

'Nay. But there have been rumours before this of Catholic plots to put Lord Strange on the throne. Some believe him to be a Catholic, though it has never be openly proved. That fellow Parsons, whom we arrested over the affair of the Scots queen, thought Lord Strange could not be relied on as a Catholic, though others have felt differently.'

I shook my head. 'I do not believe Lord Strange could be behind this, or even people putting him forward. He has always been generous to Burbage's company. I cannot think he would countenance the murder of two of them. And he has great admiration of Will's work, being something of a poet himself. He would not agree to the theft of Will's play and its use in some plot. He is . . .' I strove to explain my conviction. 'He is too admirable a man to behave in such a way. Nay, I think it must be another.'

'Perhaps you are right. Let us not place him high on our list, then.'

He began turning his stone paper weight over and over in his hands. 'Our problem, Kit, is that we are no longer in touch with the political threads running through England today. If Sir Francis were but with us still!'

'Something I wish almost daily.'

'What do you want me to do?'

I smiled at him. Always straight to the point, Nick.

'It has helped just to talk it through with you, but if you could send some of your men to ask around, listen to the word on the streets. I know they have been clever in the past at rooting out secrets in those riverside taverns. The Blue Boar is a few steps better than that, but it is located in the same part of the City. Perhaps they can discover whether these men dealt with Stoker, and killed him. Were they the footpads who struck down Henslowe's copyist and stole Marlowe's play? And if they can discover who is behind it all, we shall know whether it is just mischief-making or a serious threat of treason.'

He nodded. 'They can certainly try. I expect my lads can soon discover just what these rogues have been up to. Whether they can identify the man lurking in the shadows behind them may be more difficult.'

'Aye, but it is worth the try.'

I stood up. 'Thank you, Nick. It is good to be working with you again, even if we have no Sir Francis to lead us. You can reach me at my same lodgings in Southwark.'

He stood as well and gave me an odd look.

'Are you free of your duties at St Thomas's today, Kit? I would have thought that your patients would need you.'

I found myself flushing. It should not embarrass me to admit what was not my fault, but it did.

'When I returned from Muscovy, I learned my post at the hospital had been given to another, the man who took my place while I was away.'

'That's hard,' he said, 'and not what you were promised. So have you no work?'

'I have taken over a few of Dr Nuñez's private patients, but it does not provide me with a living. In order to pay my rent and buy food, I have been working for Master Burbage as a copyist, ever since Master Wandesford died. That is how I came to be entangled in all this matter of the stolen plays.'

He shook his head. 'One of Sir Francis's best code-breakers and forgers, come to this! Are you quite sure you do not want to join Thomas Phelippes?'

'I should not mind joining Phelippes, were he not answerable to the Earl of Essex, though how long that may last, I am not sure. Essex takes up one thing after another to enhance his fame, but commanding an intelligence service is surely too quiet and slow for a man of his tastes. Hardly spectacular enough.'

'Aye, you probably have the right of it. Is not Lord Burghley taking up intelligence work again, with his son? He began it all, years gone by. In fact, I had an approach from Sir Robert Cecil myself, but I said I had retired from such work.'

'Poley is working for the Cecils,' I said.

'Is he indeed?' Nick raised his eyebrows. 'I am surprised they trust him. I have always suspected he took money from our enemies. Sir Francis could never prove he was a double agent, but he thought him dangerous and unreliable. I often wonder whether it was Poley who stole our files.'

'And I too.' I shook Nick's hand. 'It has been good to see you again. And I am glad that the poultry business has not altogether blunted your taste for intelligence work.'

He laughed. 'Not altogether. As soon as my men learn anything, I will send you word.'

As I walked away down Bucklersbury, I was feeling more cheerful than I had been since this whole matter had started with the death of poor Wandesford. One matter Nick and I had not discussed was how his men were to be paid. In the past, Walsingham's budget had covered such things. Perhaps Nick would pay them in eggs or capons.

For the next few days, I did not see the players, for there was an outbreak of chest colds amongst the children who lived in Goldsmiths Row. It was too early for the usual winter chest infections, since we were only just coming to the end of summer, However, these families all knew one another, so once one child was affected it spread through the rest like fire through dry tinder. It was not serious, but unpleasant, depriving the children of rest and leaving them feeling weak and sorry for themselves. I was busy dispensing soothing syrups and chest rubs of warming herbs. For some reason it did not affect their parents, for which I was heartily thankful. It meant that Mistress Dolesby was not able to place herself at the centre of attention and concern.

On the morning of the fourth day after I had called on Nick Berden, I received a note from him, short and to the point, as always.

> *The players will be performing a new play tomorrow, Thursday,* The Lamentable Overthrow and Death of Edward II. *I would judge it to be your Marlowe's play. They show little imagination in their choice of titles. No word yet of the man we seek.*
> *NB*

Hardly 'my' Marlowe, I thought, but this was vital news. None of my patients required my services today, the children all being over the worst, so Rikki and I set off at once for the Theatre. Master Burbage was there, and also Guy, putting Davy through his paces in some new acrobatic tricks they were perfecting. I had thumped on Simon's door as I passed, but heard only a grunt in answer.

I had not yet told the players of my visit to Nick, not wanting to raise their hopes unnecessarily, but I now explained to Burbage and Guy that Nick was having enquiries made, and I showed them his note.

'It must be Marlowe's play,' Burbage said, his eyes lighting up. 'This is excellent. The coroner will surely now accept that everything points to this group of thieving rascals being behind everything that has happened.'

'We still have no proof that they killed Stoker,' I said. 'We must decide how best to proceed.'

'First, we will inform Sir Rowland,' Master Burbage said. 'I shall go myself, at once. Although before I leave I shall write a message to Philip Henslowe, and Davy can take it to the Rose. Do you suppose Marlowe could provide the coroner with at least some of the lines from his play? We need to convince him that it is indeed Marlowe's play these fellows have in their hands.'

'Marlowe says it was the sole copy that was stolen,' Guy said, 'but perhaps he may have some rough papers, or can remember some of the lines he composed well enough to write out a passage for the coroner.'

I could see that they were all afire to catch the thieves who had stolen their plays, but I was worried that if the men were arrested and driven out of London, we should never know who was attempting to use the playhouse to incite rebellion. When Burbage went into his office to write his note to Henslowe, I followed him.

'Master Burbage,' I said, 'there is more at stake here than the stolen plays.'

'Aye, I am well aware of it,' he said. 'Two men have been murdered. Two men employed by me. I am not likely to forget it.'

'Do you truly believe that murder would have been done, merely to steal plays? I know they are of great value to whichever company owns them, but – worth two lives?'

'What are you saying, Kit?'

Before I could answer, we were joined by Will, who must have been told the latest news by Guy, for he had the light of battle in his eye.

Before he could speak, I answered Burbage. 'I am saying that we should not lose sight of what really lies behind these thefts. It is not simple financial gain. This group of players at the Blue Boar have not set themselves up as a permanent company. They must know that, sooner or later, the Master of the Revels will hear about them and close them down, so they probably intend to disappear before that happens. They are not even performing every day, as any legitimate company would do, while the weather holds. Cuthbert calculated how much they earned the day we were there, but unless they perform every day, they will starve. Someone is paying them.'

'Who?' Will said.

'I discussed it with Nick Berden. He was one of Sir Francis's most experienced and skilful men. We think this . . . let us call it a conspiracy . . . this conspiracy originates here in England. It has not originated abroad. It has none of the marks of a Spanish Catholic conspiracy. We think some great man – or perhaps more than one man – intends to stir up treason against the Queen. Someone like the late Duke of Norfolk. He was home bred, and bred a home grown rebellion, with the intention of marrying the Scots queen and seizing power for himself.'

'And lost his head for it,' Will said.

'He did. Who might be trying now to stir up the trouble-making youth of London? We do not know. But we need to proceed cautiously, so that these players may be questioned and their employer unmasked before real danger erupts in London.'

'What you say makes good sense, Kit,' Master Burbage said. 'I think you should come with me to see Sir Rowland. If we can, we will persuade him to come with us to the performance at the Blue Boar tomorrow. If he is convinced of the danger, then he has the power, either as the coroner or as the Lord Mayor, to have the men held for questioning. The Master of the Revels would simply have them driven out of town.'

'That is what I fear,' I said. 'If that happened, then we should lose all chance of tracing the instigator. I will gladly come with you to see Sir Rowland.'

'I shall come as well,' Will said grimly. 'I do not care for having my work distorted and travestied to serve the purposes of evil men.'

'Very well,' Burbage said. 'Let us take our case to Sir Rowland.'

Chapter Twelve

*T*o my surprise, we were able to see Sir Rowland at once, despite his secretary's attempts to prevent us. Our arrival at his office coincided with that of Sir Rowland himself, so he brushed his secretary aside and ushered us in ahead of him. I noticed Will darting glances about, taking note of everything. I believed he did this all the time, storing away impressions of people and places to serve as the raw warp and weft from which he wove his plays. One of these days, I was sure he would use those lazy parish constables, a perfect type for Guy to make mock of.

Will and I hung a little back, before anyone had even taken a seat, leaving Master Burbage to explain why we were here. He was accustomed to dealing with London merchants and knew better than to waste any precious minutes. As he paused, Sir Rowland waved us to chairs.

'Nicholas Berden, eh? I recall that he was one of Sir Francis's best men. Certainly one of the best for ferreting out information in London.'

He looked at me, and there was a smile in his eyes. 'So he is selling poultry, is he?'

'And not finding it a very fulfilling life,' I said, returning the smile. I began to hope that Sir Rowland was finally prepared to take us seriously.

'Well,' he said, 'this certainly does appear to make it quite clear that this same group of players is behind the thefts of both plays, though we still cannot be sure that they also killed John Stoker.' He fingered his beard, gazing at the ceiling. 'You say their play of Edward II is to be given tomorrow afternoon. I might be able to free myself so that I may attend with you. Walker!' he called, and jingled a small bell on his desk.

The secretary appeared so quickly that I suspected he had been listening outside the door.

'Sir Rowland?'

'Walker, I need to rearrange any meetings I have tomorrow afternoon. And I shall want a full complement of sergeants to attend me.'

'Certainly, Sir Rowland.' The secretary gave us an unpleasant look.

'And they are to wear their ordinary clothes, not livery. I do not want them to draw attention to themselves.'

'I will instruct them, Sir Rowland. Where are they to attend?'

'At the Blue Boar inn, Queene Hythe.'

The secretary's mouth fell open and he seemed temporarily deprived of speech.

'Off you go then, Walker.'

When the secretary had closed the door behind him, Sir Rowland rubbed his hands together.

'We will attend this performance, and if I am satisfied that there is sufficient reason to investigate further, I will have my sergeants arrest these players and bring them here for questioning. My own interest, of course, is in any light which may be thrown on my inquests into the deaths of your two men.' He nodded toward Master Burbage.

'However,' he said, directing his gaze toward me, 'if Dr Alvarez is right in his assumption that there is more to this than the theft of two plays, if indeed there is a political motive, an incitement to treason, then I shall hand the men over to Lord Burghley, so that he may question them as to who may be behind it.'

This was all that could be hoped for. Everything, however, depended on convincing Sir Rowland that these players were directly connected to the death of Stoker, which might not be easy. Our brief meeting soon over, we were dismissed. Will and I had hardly opened our mouths, except to explain the layout of the

212

Blue Boar and the best points at which to place Sir Rowland's sergeants in order to effect the arrests, if he gave them the signal. Knowing these rambling London inns, extended and enlarged over the years, I thought it likely that some of the players might escape even so.

Master Burbage and Will returned to the Theatre, Will looking more cheerful now that there was a prospect of closing down the bastardised version of his Henry play. I hoped that the performances already given at the Blue Boar would not have damaged his reputation amongst the London audiences. I turned in the opposite direction, for I felt it needful to tell Nick Berden exactly what had been decided by Sir Rowland. He might also have learned more from his men since he had sent me the note.

Nick listened carefully as I outlined Sir Rowland's plan.

'I do not know how many sergeants he may be able to muster,' I said. 'I did not ask, for fear of overstepping the mark. However, he seems to think he will be able to cover all the exits and have enough men to arrest and hold the players.'

'I hope he may be right,' Nick said. 'I had a look at the place after you were here, and it is a regular coney warren. Like all these old inns, it will have a maze of cellars underground, and no doubt there will be trap doors for delivering barrels. Still, we may expect him to be able to seize most of them.'

'*If* he is convinced,' I said.

'Aye, if he is convinced. I have learned a little about who they are – a travelling troupe from the Welsh borders, over Shropshire and Herefordshire way. They were drummed out of town at Shrewsbury, Leominster, and Hereford, suspected of theft from local houses, though nothing could be proved against them. They disappeared for a few weeks, then turned up here, where they have been spending more money than their intermittent performances would seem to warrant.'

I nodded. 'So someone is paying them.'

'Indeed. Someone is paying them, and generously, by all accounts. And just before you arrived, one of my men was here. Do you remember Tom Lewen, who was injured that time we were on the watch for the Italian puppeteers? You physicked him.'

'Aye, I remember him.' And remembered how bravely he had endured my stitching of his wound.

'Well, Lewen has heard a rumour of who might be handing out the chinks, a Sir Thomas Oxley. Have you heard of him?'

I shook my head. 'The name means nothing to me.'

'He is a gentleman of the Earl of Essex's household.'

Having lit this smoking barrel of political gunpowder, Nick sat back, clearly pleased by the expression on my face.

'But how could that be?' I said. 'Whatever his faults, Essex is devoted to the Queen. As I have heard, he came to Court a penniless young heir to a country title, and it is the Queen who has raised him up. Though,' I added, 'if the tales be true of her flirtation with him, it does appear unseemly.'

I knew I sounded prim, but the Queen was old enough to be Essex's mother, if not his granddam.

'All of that is true,' Nick said. 'Certainly Essex has been dependent on Her Majesty for his rise to power, though it may be that he grows a little too high and mighty of late. It may also be that Oxley does not act with Essex's knowledge but is a traitor within his household. One thing to consider, though – where are the Devereaux ancestral estates?'

'Herefordshire,' I said slowly.

'Indeed.'

We looked at each other, then Nick smiled. 'How Sir Francis would have loved this conundrum!'

'Aye,' I said, with a fond smile. 'He would.'

I considered the implications of this extraordinary news.

'Will you tell Sir Rowland about Oxley?'

'At the moment it is no more than rumour. Let him question these fellows first, and if the name does not come up in their answers, then I will tell him.'

I got up to leave. 'Will you attend the performance tomorrow?'

'Try to keep me away!'

Early the following afternoon, all those I thought of as 'our' forces made their way in twos and threes to the Blue Boar. I went with Simon and Guy, although we walked part of the way with Ned and Marlowe.

'I have written out some passages from *Edward II*,' Marlowe told Guy, indicating a sheaf of papers in his hand. 'I will hand them to Sir Rowland before the performance, so that he may compare them with what these rogues dare to parrot upon their stage. I did not attend either of the inquests, but Ned will point him out to me.'

'Good,' Guy said. 'The more evidence we can provide that links these men to the death of Stoker, the readier Sir Rowland will be to act.'

They parted from us then, for it was essential that we should not be seen arriving at the Blue Boar in a large group together, lest we alarm the rogue players too soon. Guy, Simon, and I climbed up to the first gallery as we had done before. It would provide a clear view of the stage but we were also near enough to the stairs to make a swift exit if that should prove advisable. I noticed that Sir Rowland was seated quite close to us, with others of Burbage's and Henslowe's men scattered through the audience. I could not identify Sir Rowland's sergeants, but I assumed they must be there. I spotted Nick Berden down amongst the groundlings, and recognised several of his men, including Tom Lewen.

And so the second performance we attended at the Blue Boar began. I thought at first that I imagined an uneasy feeling in this makeshift playhouse, arising from my own keyed up sense that more dramatic events were about to take place off the stage than on it. Then I realised that I was not imagining it. For a start, the crowd of groundlings below us in the yard seemed different, though I did not realise at first what it was that was different about them. Then I noticed that, whereas before many of the men had girls on their arms, now there was scarcely a woman to be seen. And whereas before the crowd had been restless and noisy, now they were quiet and intent. Was it merely that the play held their attention more? I thought not, although the play was powerful – as all Marlowe's plays were – while also being dark and unpleasant. Again, as all Marlowe's plays were.

The man who had played Henry VI before now took the part of Edward II, portraying him as even weaker and more contemptible than Henry. The one accomplished player amongst them, he who had spoken the Prologue before, today was Mortimer, traitor and slayer of the anointed king.

I stole a sideways glance along the row of stools at Sir Rowland and saw that he was studying some papers in his hand, which must be the passages Marlowe had written out for him. Not having a copy of the original, Simon, Guy, and I could only speculate on whether we were hearing Marlowe's words, but they had the ring of authenticity. Perhaps it was easier for the players, having the full script of this play, instead of Stoker's unreliable memories of the Henry play, to perform it without making changes, at least if it suited their purposes in its original form. I knew the terrible story, but I did not know how Marlowe had written it.

It became clear that Marlowe was fascinated by the illicit love between Edward and his male favourites, giving them sensuous and luxuriant lines to speak. Later I read in the script what had struck me as I listened to the words spoken at the Blue Boar:

> *I must have wanton poets, pleasant wits,*
> *Musicians, that with touching of a string*
> *May draw the pliant king which way I please:*
> *Music and poetry is his delight;*
> *Therefore I'll have Italian masks by night,*
> *Sweet speeches, comedies, and pleasing shows;*
> *And in the day, when he shall walk abroad,*
> *Like sylvan nymphs my pages shall be clad;*
> *My men, like satyrs grazing on the lawns,*
> *Shall with their goat-feet dance the antic hay;*
> *Sometime a lovely boy in Dian's shape,*
> *With hair that gilds the water as it glides*
> *Crownets of pearl about his naked arms,*
> *And in his sportful hands an olive-tree,*
> *To hide those parts which men delight to see,*
> *Shall bathe him in a spring; and there, hard by,*
> *One like Actæon, peeping through the grove,*

Shall by the angry goddess be transform'd,
And running in the likeness of an hart,
By yelping hounds pull'd down, shall seem to die:
Such things as these best please his majesty.

There was no doubt that Marlowe was a gifted poet, although in passages like this his words were almost too lush, like a surfeit of rich food, so that after a time, one's gorge rose. The suggestions of illicit lust were all too apparent. I remembered a conversation I had once had with Simon, when I had mentioned the rumour that Marlowe preferred boys to women.

And of course, cleverly, these sickly sweet speeches formed a shocking contrast with the actions that followed. The Lucifer figure, or 'Lightborn', was terrifying, he who was the murderer of the king on the orders of Mortimer, and even the rough men in the yard gasped at the violence enacted on stage. Then Mortimer entered, crowing over the death of the king. Coming to the edge of the stage he held out his hands to the audience and invited us to join him in rejoicing at the rightful killing of an unworthy monarch.

And so the play ended.

Guy turned and whispered fiercely to us, 'That is not Marlowe's ending! He told me that he includes the execution of Mortimer and the crowning of Edward III. They have chosen to end the play quite differently.'

'They have chosen to end it as it suits their purpose,' I said. 'The question is, will Sir Rowland now act?'

'The question is,' Simon said, 'how are those fellows down there going to act?'

He pointed down to the yard, where the groundlings, instead of drifting away as they would normally do at the end of a performance, were gathering together in tight groups, each about some sort of leader. Some were drawing out clubs or knives which had been hidden in loose shirt sleeves. I found myself sweating with alarm. This looked like the mustering of an army, about to go forth and do battle. Sir Rowland had come prepared to arrest the players. He could not possibly contain the whole of this dangerous crowd.

'The Lord help us!' Guy cried. 'The rebellion is starting now. We had better leave at once, if we want to avoid a knife in the ribs.'

Around us other people were also scrambling to their feet. It seemed that the organised traitors were all down in the yard, while the occupants of the galleries were innocent playgoers. Sir Rowland had seen what was happening, for he was standing up and leaning over the balcony railing. He was jostled by people pushing past, trying to reach the stairs. Up here there was shouting and growing panic, while below it was ominously quiet, except for a hum of low voices, like a swarm of bees. Where was Nick?

Sir Rowland was gripping the railing hard with one hand, to stop himself being toppled head first over the edge of the balcony by the press of the crowd. With the other hand he raised something to his mouth. There was the shrill blast of a whistle, such as the Watch and the parish constables use. This must be the signal to Sir Rowland's men, but would they know what to do? They had come to arrest a few shabby players, not to contain a dangerous riot.

A pale wave of turned-up faces below.

The whistle had given pause to the ruffians in the yard. Another blast of a whistle from somewhere near the stage. Then another from somewhere beneath us, which must be by the entrance to the yard from the street. Suddenly I saw Nick. He also had a whistle. He blew a series of short notes, some sort of signal to his men.

'Come *on*, Kit.' Simon was pushing me hard in the back, urging me to follow Guy who was fighting his way through the crowd to the stairs.

I lost sight of Guy, then stumbled over someone fallen on the floor. Panic had made people indifferent to others and men were climbing over the prone body of an elderly woman. I stooped down and got my hands under her armpits.

'Help me, Simon!' I gasped. 'She's heavy.'

Between us we managed to heave her to her feet. She was a stout, respectable body, though her hat was half dragged off her grey hair and there were dirty footprints on her clothes, where

218

escaping playgoers had simply trampled over her. She seemed half dazed and hardly able to walk, so Simon and I seized an arm each and bundled her down the stairs between us.

At the bottom of the stairs men with pikes were blocking the exit from the inn yard – some of Sir Rowland's men I hoped – but there was room for those of us coming down the stairs to push through the archway and into the street outside. Guy was waiting for us, his face creased in anxiety.

'How do you feel now, mistress?' I said, trying to brush the worst of the dust off her skirts. 'Can you walk? Have you far to go?'

She felt for her hat and pulled it back into place. The colour was coming back into her cheeks.

'Only to Cheapside.' Her voice was shaking, and she clutched at my arm. 'What is happening?'

'Rogues bent on making trouble, but they'll be stopped,' Guy said soothingly. 'Come with us, mistress. We'll see you safely to Cheapside.'

Some of the crowd outside the Blue Boar were waiting, watching avidly to see what would happen next, although most, like us, were eager to get away. Even as we began to make our way to Thames Street, more men approached us at a run, from the Watch and the local constables, summoned by more blowing of whistles. There came a crash of splintering wood from inside the inn. I hoped no one had fallen from one of the galleries.

'Should we not stay and help?' I whispered to Simon.

The woman had now taken Guy's arm and was walking ahead of us.

'No need,' he said. 'I think Sir Rowland has it in hand. And did you say Nick Berden was there?'

'Aye, and some of his men. He will help contain the trouble, though whether the players manage to slip away in the confusion is anyone's guess.'

I stopped and called ahead. 'Guy, I am going back. In all that crush, some may be injured.'

He looked over his shoulder. 'Have a care, then, Kit. Wait until Sir Rowland has the trouble under control.'

As Guy continued along Thames Street with the woman, I turned back toward the inn.

'I suppose I had better come with you,' Simon said, 'to keep you out of mischief.'

A few minutes later, back at the inn, we were met by a scene of chaos. Somehow Sir Rowland, the Watch, and the constables had managed to prevent the rioters from spilling out on to the street, but there was a fight going on in the yard of the Blue Boar. A few men were already under arrest and sitting sullenly in the dirty roadway, nursing their bruises. None had injuries that required my attention, though from the noise within, there would be worse to come. After about half an hour, it was over. Most of the rioters from the inn yard were led away by the Watch, to be shut up in the Poultry Compter, as the nearest prison. A few young boys were sent home to their mothers, as being no real danger to anyone. There were bloody noses and blackened eyes aplenty amongst them all, but nothing that needed serious physicking.

However, knives had been drawn. Within the yard of the inn there were four dead and half a dozen with serious knife wounds, so I had been right to return. I was on my knees tending to them when Nick hailed me. He had a bruise on his left temple and a small cut on his chin, but he was grinning happily.

'That was an unexpected fight,' I said.

'Nay, not unexpected at all,' he said. 'My lads had word that today was the day, so we came along, to join in the fun.'

He squatted down beside me as I stitched up a gash in the arm of one of the rioters, who swore at me as I did so.

'Haven't lost your touch with the needle, I see.'

'Shall I sew up your chin?' I grinned at him.

'Never fear. This will heal very happily by itself.' He looked around at the damage to the inn's doors and railings. 'The innkeeper will spend more on repairs than ever he was paid for the use of this place.'

'Were the players arrested?' I asked, as we stood up.

'Aye.' He jerked his head toward the pile of broken timber which had once formed the temporary stage. Sir Rowland was there, in conversation with one of the sergeants I recognised from

Wandesford's inquest. More of his men surrounded a group of players, who looked excessively sorry for themselves. This was not how their triumph on the London stage was meant to end. I could pick out most of them from the rags of their costumes which they still wore, although I could not see the one I thought of as the leading player.

'I think there is one missing,' I said. 'Him who played Mortimer.'

'Aye, you have the right of it. My lads chased him through the cellars, but he escaped somehow. Still, Sir Rowland has done well to capture most of them.'

He lowered his voice. 'There were some shocking things said and done in that play, were there not? I pride myself on a strong stomach, but that Gaveston, and then the murder of the king . . .'

'That is Marlowe for you,' I said. 'His mind is ever fixed on the darkest side of the human condition.'

Simon had gone off to help where he could, but he reappeared now.

'There's a lad here was pushed over the balcony,' he said. 'You'd best look at him, Kit. There is something amiss with his shoulder.'

'Then he is lucky it is no worse,' I said, picking up my satchel. 'He could have broken his head or his back.'

'I think the fellow he landed on suffered worse,' Simon said. 'He is one of the dead.'

The boy with the damaged shoulder was not one of the rioters. He had been sitting on the second gallery with his father, but in the place furthest from the top of the stairs. When the rush to leave had begun he had been shoved aside, hard against the gallery railing, which must have been rotten at that point. Under the impact the wood had given way, so that he fell in a cascade of broken timber into the yard below. It had been his good luck that one of the men in the yard had broken his fall, at the cost of his own life, for one of the timbers had broken his neck.

Seated on a stool, the boy was weeping softly, though he tried not to show it, while his father stood over him looking helplessly around.

'Now this is painful, I know,' I said, when I had felt the shoulder carefully, 'but there is nothing broken here. It is dislocated.'

The lad looked at me blankly.

'The joint of your shoulder has been knocked out of place,' I said. 'I can put it back. It will hurt while I do it, but afterwards it will only be a little sore. Do you understand?'

He nodded, and wiped his eyes and nose with the back of his good hand. I got Simon and Nick to hold him steady while I pulled the arm out sharply until the shoulder clicked back into place. The boy gave one loud yell of pain.

'That is it,' I said. 'Now I am just going to strap it, so it is held in place while everything heals, and I'll fix a sling to take the weight of your arm. Soon you will be quite fit again.'

When I had finished, I turned to the father. 'Let him rest for a few days, and don't let him use that arm if possible. He should have no further trouble.'

The man fumbled in a worn purse for a coin, but I shook my head.

'Get you away home and let his mother fuss over him.'

By now the inn yard was almost clear, except for the bodies of the dead. Sir Rowland's men were escorting the sorry group of players, trailing their shabby finery, out through the archway. Some of Nick's men were assisting them. Tom Lewen tilted his cap at me as he joined them.

'Well,' Nick said, 'that has been a more entertaining afternoon than sitting over my accounts, trying to puzzle out why I am always three shillings and seven pence farthing either richer or poorer than I should be!'

'Always the same amount?' Simon asked.

'Always the same amount.'

I laughed. I had forgotten that these two knew each other.

'Come back with me,' Nick said, 'and help me drink a jug of excellent beer. I will allow Kit to dab some of his marvellous salve on my chin the while.'

So that was what we did.

The following day, Sir Rowland sent word that he would like to see Master Burbage, Guy, Will, Simon, and me in his office at midday, if that would be convenient.

'It will be convenient if he does not detain us too long,' Master Burbage grumbled. 'I have two playhouses to run, and I am building a new house for one of the Shoreditch aldermen up on Hackney Downs. I have been neglecting business at the Curtain of late, and we have not so many weeks of good weather left to us.'

The rest of us, however, were keen to learn whatever Sir Rowland might have been able to discover thus far from the players. Indeed, I was sure that Master Burbage was just as keen, but he wished to emphasise quite how busy he was. Cuthbert was left in charge of preparations for the afternoon's performance. Guy would need to hurry back, for he was on stage in the first act, though Will and Simon had only small parts in acts three and four.

When we arrived at Sir Rowland's office, we found Master Henslowe, Ned Alleyn, Marlowe, and the copyist Holles already there. On Sir Rowland's desk there was a shabby satchel not unlike my own.

After we were all seated, a little like a small inquest jury of our own, Sir Rowland steepled his hands beneath his chin and nodded at the satchel.

'Master Holles has identified this as his satchel which was stolen from him after he was attacked in Southwark several weeks ago. It still contains a few miscellaneous personal papers of his.'

'What of my play?' Marlowe demanded.

Sir Rowland frowned. 'In good time, Master Marlowe. At first the players we arrested claimed they knew nothing of the satchel, then they claimed that it belonged to one of them. They swore that play of Edward II had been written by one of their company, the very fellow who, unfortunately, managed to avoid capture by us.'

Marlowe sprang to his feet, clenching his fists. He looked as though he might be about to attack Sir Rowland, but Master Henslowe grabbed his arm and dragged him down again. I thought him exceptionally ill mannered, but I caught Will giving him a sympathetic look.

'However,' Sir Rowland continued, as though he had not noticed Marlowe, 'when my sergeants searched the rooms at the Blue Boar occupied by these rogues, they found this.'

He opened a drawer and drew out a thick wad of paper, which looked, to my eye, about the right size for the script of a five-act play. It was dirty and dog eared. Sir Rowland laid it on his desk and peered at it, as if seeing it for the first time. He cleared his throat.

'*The Troublesome Reign and Lamentable Death of Edward the Second, King of England, with the Tragical Fall of Proud Mortimer.*'

He looked across at Marlowe. 'Would that be your play that was stolen, Master Marlowe?'

'It would,' Marlowe said, looking relieved, 'I shall be glad to have it back.'

He stood up and reached out for the manuscript, but Sir Rowland laid his hands on it. 'All in good time. Please keep your seat, Master Marlowe.'

Glowering, Marlowe sat down again.

'Now, Master Shakespeare, we also found this.'

He laid another manuscript on the desk. This was even more untidy, consisting of uneven sizes of paper, frayed at the edges.

'Who might be able to identify the hand?'

Master Burbage stood up and joined Sir Rowland at the desk. He turned over the sheets slowly, then finally sighed.

'This is undoubtedly the hand of John Stoker. It is an ill formed hand, almost illiterate. I am surprised these fellows were able to read it. There is no doubt in my mind that Stoker wrote this. Poor Will, how he has massacred your work!'

'Very good,' Sir Rowland said. 'We have established that this is Master Marlowe's play, stolen from Master Holles in the satchel which he has identified as his. We have also established that this is a garbled version of Master Shakespeare's play, written by the deceased John Stoker, most likely from imperfect memory.'

'Have these men admitted that they got the play from Stoker?' Guy asked.

'Oh indeed, they have admitted it.'

'Have they admitted that they killed him?' I dared to ask.

'That too they have admitted,' he said grimly.

I had a good idea under what conditions the admission had been made.

'What I think none of us understand,' Guy said slowly, 'is *why* they should kill Stoker. That is why we have half believed all along that he was simply the victim of an ordinary street stabbing. If he was working for them, why should they kill him? They might have wanted him to steal more plays.'

They did not, I thought. *That was not their intention at all.* But I kept my tongue behind my teeth. I was curious to see how Sir Rowland would answer. He did not do so directly at first.

'After these players were brought back here late yesterday afternoon,' he said, 'they were put to the question. Then again this morning, they were once again put to the question.'

I saw Master Burbage flinch, and Sir Rowland must have noticed it as well, for he smiled reassuringly. 'These are not very brave men. They are nothing but tupenny ha'penny rascals who thought their fortunes had been made when they were approached to put on these performances, just a few, and to be paid handsomely for it. They have lived comfortably at the Blue Boar for several weeks, I find, their every whim catered for, and paid for. They were simply carrying out instructions. When they were shown the instruments by which they might be persuaded to answer our questions, they could not answer them quickly enough.'

This I found somewhat puzzling. Sir Rowland's office was attached to the Guildhall, and I did not believe the Guildhall kept the kind of instruments he was referring to, which were certainly to be found in the Tower, some also, perhaps, at the larger prisons. I suppose there may have been smaller, more portable instruments of the torturer's art which might have been waved before the terrified players. It was an unpleasant thought, but no doubt they deserved the fright. The deaths and injuries which would have resulted had the riot not been stopped would have affected dozens of innocent citizens of London.

'So what answers did they give?' Master Henslowe asked.

'They prevaricated at first, naturally, but one by one they admitted that Stoker had been placed in Master Burbage's company in order to gain access to Master Shakespeare's play. It was known that the play books of Lord Strange's Men are very well guarded, so only someone within the company could gain access to them. Stoker was very frustrated, being unable to get hold of the play book, and he was being pressed by the leader of the players, the man we failed to capture.'

He picked up Stoker's version of Will's play and leafed through it. 'They swore that the poisoning of your copyist, the deceased Oliver Wandesford, was solely the plan of Stoker, and that it was only intended to make him ill.'

He sniffed. 'Myself, I find that hard to credit. However, once Stoker was able to produce some sort of version of the Henry play, he started to demand more money. Originally he was promised five pounds, a remarkably generous sum in my opinion. After Master Wandesford died and the inquest was held, he began to panic. He demanded twenty pounds, claiming that he would need to leave London and make a new life for himself well away from the city, for he feared that if he stayed here, he would eventually be found guilty and hanged. Which, of course, would have happened.'

I doubted he would have been caught, but it was no longer relevant.

'When Stoker met the two players in the alley off Gracechurch Street, he had his copy of the play with him, but would not part with it unless he was given twenty pounds. The players, of course, had no such sum. There was a struggle, in the course of which Stoker was accidentally stabbed, and the players ran off with the play, the men seen by you.' He nodded toward Will, Simon, and me.

'Accidentally stabbed!' Marlowe scoffed. 'I think not. An accidental slash, perhaps, but not a blow deep enough to kill a man. I do not believe it.'

Sir Rowland shrugged. 'That will be for the jury to decide, when the inquest on John Stoker is resumed.'

'They found it easier to steal Marlowe's play,' Master Burbage said, with an ill-concealed air of complacency. 'You had best take care to lock up your play books in future, Philip, and make sure the world knows it.'

Master Henslowe bowed. 'It is already done, James.'

'The matter of Stoker now seems much clearer,' I said, 'although the final verdict awaits, as you say, Sir Rowland, the resumed inquest. But who is behind this whole conspiracy? You have said that these players were hired. Who was paying them?'

Berden had told me of the rumour that it was Sir Thomas Oxley, but I kept that to myself for the moment.

Sir Rowland bowed to me. 'You are quite right to remind us of the most important aspect of this case, Dr Alvarez. The men claimed at first that only their leader, a man called Richard Upton, dealt with their "patron", as they called him, but in the end they named him, although they persisted in the claim that only Richard Upton had dealt with him directly.'

'And the name?' I prompted.

'A gentleman by the name of Sir Thomas Oxley, a man of the country gentry, whose estates lie near the Welsh borders. He has been in the household of the Earl of Essex for some years. I have men out searching for him now.'

So Nick Berden had been right about the name.

'But why should he wish to do such a thing?' I said. 'To stir up rebellion against the Crown, here in the heart of London? My lord of Essex is the Queen's favourite, none are closer to her.'

Sir Rowland shrugged. 'That we shall hope to learn when we find him. Now, I believe that is all for the present. I think I may let you gentlemen have these manuscripts, though I may require them to be brought to the resumed inquest.'

Will and Marlowe retrieved their papers, though I thought Will would have little use for Stoker's travesty of his play save to light fires with it. Holles picked up his satchel. We were all preparing to leave when Sir Rowland made one final remark.

'It is curious that this fellow Oxley should be in my lord Essex's household. As we were escorting the players away from the Blue Boar, who should ride up, accompanied by a group of armed followers, but my lord of Essex himself, come, he said, to put down the rebellion. I assured him that there had been no rebellion, nothing more than a fight in the yard of an inn, and all was now quiet.'

He smiled.

'My lord seemed quite disappointed.'

Chapter Thirteen

*A*s we were leaving his office, Sir Rowland tapped Will on the shoulder.

'In future, young man, have a care what you write in your plays. I do not accuse you of deliberately fomenting trouble, but you have seen what danger can result when a play about a dangerous political issue is used as a weapon by unscrupulous men.'

Will's eyes smouldered. I believe he did not care to be given lessons on what he should or should not write. I thought he would burst out with some protest, but I saw the exact moment when he swallowed his anger and chose the wiser course of silence.

Sir Rowland turned to Marlowe.

'And as for you, sir, you seem over fond of dwelling on the practices of Sodom and Gomorrah. Watch your language in future. We do not want such filthy habits paraded before our London audiences dressed up in flowery verse.'

Like Will, Marlowe looked ready to burst with indignation at thus being instructed, but Master Henslowe and Ned Alleyn hurried him away before he could speak. Master Holles paused only long enough to wish us good day before following them. Once the door had closed behind Sir Rowland, the rest of us exchanged glances but did not speak until we had left the building and were out of the hearing of the secretary.

'I shall write what I please!' The words, held back till now, burst from Will in a passionate cry.

Master Burbage stopped and faced him. 'On the contrary, Will, you will do as you are told. Sir Rowland is merely giving you good advice. After what happened at the Blue Boar, the Master of the Revels and all his spies will be watching for the slightest step out of line. Anything that smacks of treason, and you will find yourself fined, pilloried, banned, or even in the Tower.'

'I do not write treason,' Will said grimly.

'Perhaps not intentionally, but others may twist your meaning. Or perhaps some in the audience may take it that way.' He took Will by the arm. 'Come along, now. We have a performance this afternoon. Let us think about a cheerful comedy for your next play. Everyone loves a comedy.'

They headed off toward Bishopsgate. Simon, Guy, and I followed.

'Poor Will,' Simon said.

'Aye, I said, 'it is hardly fair. Will only wrote a play using the known history of King Henry VI's times. In his original version there was no call to rebellion. It seems hard that he should suffer for what others have done with his work.'

'It will pass,' Guy said mildly. 'You children cannot take a long view over the way these struggles have worked themselves out in the past, between government authorities and the players' companies. They fear us. They fear our power to awaken men's minds. They refuse to see that such an awakening may lead to good as well as evil. But by little and little we are winning the war. We cannot expect to win every skirmish.'

I expect Simon, like me, did not care to be called a child at the age of one and twenty, but I suppose Guy could give us twenty years.

While the others returned to the Theatre, I thought I would call on Nick Berden again, since Master Burbage had no copying work for me at present, so I parted company with them.

'And how are your injuries, Nick?' I asked.

We were sitting in the small area behind his shop, which he called a garden, but had little of the garden about it. There were outbuildings where he housed the poultry bought in from farms outside London, some of the geese having walked all the way from the fenlands of East Anglia. Here he would fatten them up before selling them on to private customers, or at Smithfield, or at one of the smaller markets that were beginning to be established in and around the city. He also had one shed where he kept laying hens, sending out his women servants with baskets of fresh eggs every day to sell on the streets. One corner of this back area had been kept free of livestock, however, and here we sat, enjoying the late summer sun.

'My injuries do very well, I thank you, Kit,' he said, bowing in mock solemnity. 'The bruise on my temple is displaying all the colours of the rainbow, but it will fade.' He tilted back his head to look at the sky, which was a very pale blue, veiled with thin cloud, almost imperceptible. He sighed. 'I fear autumn will soon be here, and winter not far behind. Some are saying that such a hot, dry summer foretells a bitter winter.'

'Some say quite the opposite,' I countered, 'but I am not here to discuss the weather. I wondered whether you or your men have heard any more about the business at the Blue Boar.'

'Not a great deal. Word is, that Sir Thomas Oxley is fled abroad, to the United Provinces, where we spent those entertaining few weeks.'

'I am not surprised he is fled, though I *am* surprised that the authorities failed to stop him.'

'It seems he was already on his way out of the country before yesterday's play was even performed. No doubt he reckoned that his hired accomplices owed him no loyalty and would betray him as soon as they were apprehended. Which they were bound to be. They have a history of being apprehended for this and that.'

'They do,' I agreed. 'It seems to be quite a way of life with them.'

I drew up one leg and rested the heel on the edge of my stool, clasping my arms around my knee. The buildings shut out most of the noise from the street, so that I could now distinctly hear the hum of bees. I had not noticed before that Nick had a bee skep nestling close up against the side of his hen house. It is surprising how many people keep bees in London. You would imagine that there would be nowhere for them to forage.

'The whole affair seems very strange to me,' I said. 'Why should this fellow Oxley have gone to all this trouble and expense in order to instigate a riot? Could he have believed that it would blossom into a full blown rebellion against the Queen? Clearly he cared nothing if lives were lost. Not only Wandesford and Stoker died, but those who perished at the Blue Boar. Is the man a Catholic, acting as an agent for Spain? I would expect any scheme from that quarter to involve more than a crowd of London bully boys armed with clubs and knives. Where are the soldiers? Where are the swords and muskets?'

'I agree,' Nick said. 'There is no evidence that he is a Catholic. Did he expect to initiate a rising amongst the citizens? If so, he misread the feelings of Londoners toward Her Majesty. We may grumble about taxes, but the Queen is loved, despite her failure to name an heir and the uncertainty that causes about the future. It is under Elizabeth that the nation of England is grown great. She is not called Gloriana for nothing.'

'I suppose there is no word of the leading actor, who managed to evade capture by Sir Rowland's men?'

'I blame myself for that,' Nick said. 'We pursued him into the cellars below the inn. It was clear he knew them well and had probably planned in advance to use them as an escape route. It was a regular maze, so we managed to lose him. Afterwards we found two open hatches into the street. He could have climbed out through either of them.'

'It was hardly your fault,' I said. 'None of us were anticipating that the riot had been planned to start immediately following the play, whatever whisper your men may have heard. We thought the performance of Marlowe's *Edward II* was part of a longer term scheme, and went to the Blue Boar thinking it was a matter of simply arresting the players. No one expected we would have to deal with hundreds of rioters at the inn itself. And there were all the harmless playgoers caught up amongst them. It was a miracle more were not killed, either in the fighting or trampled to death by those trying to escape it.'

'True enough. However, I have one more fragment of news. I have learned that the leading player is named Richard Upton, and from all that I can discover, he has gone to ground in London, so we may root him out yet.'

'Sir Rowland had also extracted his name from the other players,' I said. 'You should tell him what you have learned of the fellow's whereabouts.'

'I prefer to pursue my information with my own men. I should like to make up for losing him in the first place by capturing him myself.'

I grinned. 'I see that you are quite back to your former ways, Nick.'

He laughed. 'Well, perhaps I do hanker after the old life. This business of selling poultry does not demand all my time and attention. I can spare a little for more interesting pursuits.'

'Supposing this Richard Upton is caught – do you think he will have any more idea than the other players why Sir Thomas Oxley dreamt up such an odd scheme? For it *is* odd. Stealing plays, hiring down-at-heel players, arranging performances for – what? Not seriously to start a rebellion?'

'We are going round in circles, Kit.'

'Indeed we are. I wish you success in catching Upton, but if you do, then you had better hand him over to Sir Rowland.'

'That I shall certainly do. I have not the same means of persuasion as do the men in authority.'

We both knew that this was a euphemism. It was the dark side of the work we did and I found it hard to reconcile with my true calling as a physician. A calling that seemed to be slipping more and more away from me. The weather was pleasant, neither too hot nor too cold, therefore not a breeding ground for either summer plagues or winter infections of throats and lungs. As a result, my private patients remained in the best of health and did not require my services, nor did they provide me with any income.

Master Burbage told me over supper the following day that I had now caught up with the backlog of copying his decaying old play books.

'There will be no further need of copying, Kit, until Will writes us another play. A comedy, of course.'

He looked meaningfully at Will, who rolled his eyes in mock despair, and helped himself to more of the stewed capon from the common pot.

'It has been my intention to write a further play about the reign of the sixth Henry,' he complained. 'All those troubled years last century, in our great-grandfathers' time, need more than one play to explore the whole of the forces at work. It is an important story, and one worth telling. My first Henry play leaves everything unfinished, unanswered.'

'Will, remember what Sir Rowland said. You must have a care.' Master Burbage waved an admonitory finger at him. 'A comedy's the thing.'

Will ran his spoon round and round in his dish glumly, but kept silence.

'Now, Kit,' Master Burbage said, 'although there will be no more copying work at present, I have not forgotten my part of the bargain. You shall share our supper every night until the playhouse closes for the winter.'

'I thank you,' I said, but I was worried.

Walking back to our lodgings that night with Simon, Rikki trotting behind when he was not distracted by interesting smells, I found myself giving way to an involuntary sigh.

'You have been silent ever since we left the inn, Kit,' Simon said, 'and now you are sighing like a lovelorn maiden. What ails you?'

'Money,' I said bluntly. 'I paid Goodwife Atkins three months' rent in advance out of my pay from the Muscovy Company. Those three months will run out shortly. My earnings from copying are little enough. They have paid for any additional food Rikki and I have needed, but I have been able to put very little aside, not enough for next month's rent. My wealthy patients are in the best of health. Even Mistress Dolesby, she of the imaginary illnesses, is mysteriously well. Once Master Burbage closes the playhouses, I shall not even have one meal a day.'

I stopped and lifted my foot, so that he could see the sole of my boot.

'I am even wearing out my shoe leather and cannot afford new soles for my boots.'

'Nearly worn through,' he agreed. 'What will you do? Sara Lopez helped you before.'

'I cannot go a-begging to her again. I know she is worried about Ruy, who is somehow caught up in the struggle between the Cecils and Essex, though he will not tell her how. I must not add to her burdens. I might try to find a clerking post.'

We had reached the Bridge and joined the regular evening flow of those who worked by day in the City, but lived more cheaply in Southwark. There seemed more folk than usual today. Perhaps there was to be a bear baiting south of the river.

'You could always take up Master Phelippes's offer of employment.' He suggested it tentatively, knowing my reservations about Essex.

I sighed again. 'I would need to be desperate and starving. But perhaps that is just what I shall be, come the winter.'

I looked at Rikki, who was now running ahead of us as we drew nearer home. He paused to lift his leg against a stout corner post of one of the Bridge houses.

'I would not let Rikki starve,' I said. 'But I might be forced to sell Hector. He would fetch a fine price. I could probably live on it for nearly a year.'

'You know that would break your heart.'

We ducked through the gates at the south end of the Bridge and turned right along the river, past St Mary Overy and Bessie Travis's whorehouse.

'Perhaps you must simply swallow your pride, Kit. Forget Essex. I doubt you would have much to do with him. He will just be financing this new intelligence service, but it will be Anthony Bacon who is running it – is that not what Thomas Phelippes has said?'

'Aye,' I conceded reluctantly, 'though it is not merely that I dislike Essex. He is, quite honestly, a pompous fool. Any scheme he touches ends in disaster. I shall never forget his posturing as we crawled away from Lisbon, starving and defeated, to make the march to Cascais and rejoin the ships. Essex threw a spear at the city gates and challenged them to send out a champion to fight him in single combat for the honour of the Queen. A stupid childish act of bravado.'

'What did they do?' Simon asked, curious.

'Laughed at him and kept their gates closed.'

As we climbed the stairs, shadowy in the twilight, to our rooms, I paused and laughed softly. We had reached the door of Simon's room.

'Do you remember what Sir Rowland said to us? As he was overseeing the removal of the arrested men from the Blue Boar, my lord of Essex rode up with a party of armed men, prepared to protect us all by putting down the riot. It reminded me of Lisbon. Empty bravado.'

'And he was far too late to do any good, even if we had needed him.'

'Exactly. I expect he hesitated over which plume to put in his hat, to make the best show, or whether he should wear the red velvet gloves embroidered with thread of silver, or the white satin trimmed with pearls.'

Simon snorted with laughter. 'He is not truly such a fool.'

I turned away and began to climb the next flight of stairs to my room. 'Oh he is,' I said. 'I fear he is.'

Sometimes I wonder whether certain events in our lives are pure coincidence, or if somehow we shape them, all unconsciously, ourselves. The next morning I took Rikki for a long walk along the river bank all the way to Lambeth, to his great joy. The trees were already beginning to turn, the first splashes of gold and crimson amongst the green, like the dabs of paint on an artist's palette. It was early for autumn colour, but I have noticed that if the summer is very hot and dry, the trees slip all the sooner into autumn, as if exhausted. We were no longer experiencing a drought, indeed the Thames was almost restored to its normal flow, but the trees had suffered a hard time of it during the dry weather. Even, in places, a few leaves had begun to fall.

As I walked, I kept turning Simon's words of the previous evening over in my mind. It *would* break my heart to sell Hector.

I had inherited from my horse-breeding grandfather a passion for the creatures, having learned to ride almost before I could walk. A poor refugee physician in London, I had never hoped to own a horse of my own, so that Sir Francis's gift to me of Hector had been a joy almost beyond words. But as matters stood at present, I should soon be penniless, and Hector would fetch a high price. Could I bear to part with him?

Simon was right. Why not swallow my pride and take work with Phelippes? If Anthony Bacon was in charge of the service, why need I have anything to do with Essex? Unlike Sir Francis, my lord of Essex would not condescend to involve himself in the actual day-to-day work. Something about that thought niggled at the back of my brain, but before I could catch it, it had darted away, like a trout in a stream. In any case, I was back at my lodgings and must think what to do with the rest of my empty day until it was time to sup with the players. I was not inclined to go to the Theatre today, and hang about like an unwanted stray dog.

I was no sooner through the front door than Goodwife Atkins came bustling out of the back premises where she had her larders and still room.

'Ah, Dr Alvarez,' she said, 'there is a message just come for you. You have missed the boy by no more than a minute.'

She reached into the capacious pocket of her apron and handed me a paper, folded and sealed. The wax of the seal was unmarked, but the writing on the front – *To Doctor Alvarez at the house of Goodman Atkins, Southwark* – was so minute that only one man could have written it. It was the unmistakable hand of Thomas Phelippes.

I nodded my thanks to Goodwife Atkins and carried the letter up to my chamber to read in private.

I had but to contemplate the possibility of working for Phelippes, and – behold! – here is a letter from him in my hand.

As Rikki drank thirstily from his bowl of water, I prised up the wax carefully with my penknife. Habits die slowly. Working for Sir Francis had taught me always to lift a seal carefully, even if I no longer needed Arthur Gregory to forge it. I read the tiny script within:

I bid you good day, Kit. While you have declined to join me and others in this new service for the good safety and security of Her Majesty and the realm of England, it would be as a great favour to me if you would call at the Customs House at your earliest convenience. We have intercepted a parcel of letters from Lisbon. The code is new and I believe them to be written in Portuguese. My Spanish is fluent, as you know, but not so my Portuguese. Moreover, the burden of work in hand is considerable at present. I do not ask you to take employment here, but your assistance in this matter would be seen as a great kindness to your friend,
*Th*os. *Phelippes*
You will find my office on the first floor, facing the river.

Well, I thought, your letter comes very apt, Th^{os.} Phelippes. I was not quite sure I could believe his deprecating tones about his knowledge of Portuguese. Phelippes was an excellent linguist, though of course his fluency in Spanish was not as great as my own, since for me it was virtually my second mother tongue. I was not certain we had ever handled any documents in Portuguese, since most of the enemy correspondence was in Spanish, French, or Italian, and occasionally Latin.

Should I accept this charmingly worded invitation? Reading what lay hidden behind the surface of the words, I suspected Phelippes was overwhelmed with work. I remembered times when our office in Seething Lane groaned under the weight of paper. I had nothing better to do today. Aye, I would go and make it quite clear that I would not accept permanent employment, however remotely under Essex, but I would be prepared to undertake occasional work, to be paid as Walsingham had paid me in the past.

I changed into my better doublet, but left my physician's gown and cap behind. I would just have to endure the sharp pebbles under the worn soles of my boots, but perhaps now I would be able to have them mended. I whistled to Rikki, who had installed himself on my bed.

238

'Come along,' I said. 'If Seething Lane had no objection to my dog, then neither shall the Customs House exclude him. You will soon see some old friends, my lad.'

I had never before been inside the Customs House, but I found it as busy as a bee skep. Clerks young and old rushed about, clutching bundles of papers. Several sea captains sat around glumly in the main hall, unmistakable with their wind-weathered countenances and that piercing squint all seamen acquire from peering over distant seas. I imagined they were waiting for their cargo manifests to be checked by these clerical watch dogs before their ships, moored at the Legal Quays, would be permitted to unload. Every hour lost is money lost to a captain and his merchant owners or his clients. The year was drawing on. If the ships were to put to sea for one more trading voyage before winter, they needed to unload one cargo and load the next without delay. I wished them luck with it. I have met men like those customs clerks, men whose delight in life is to enhance their own importance by causing as much difficulty and inconvenience to other people as possible.

I had no trouble in finding my way to Phelippes's office. He had been well provided. He occupied a roomy, airy office, off which two smaller rooms opened. There were large windows, facing in two directions, for this was a corner of the building. One looked over the river, with an excellent view of the quays and all the activity there; the other gave a view of the north end of the Bridge. Much of the traffic along the Bridge was, of course, hidden by the houses, but, should he wish, Phelippes could keep an eye on those entering or leaving the Bridge, information which might be useful at times.

'Ah, Kit!' Phelippes rose to greet me, holding out an ink stained hand. He had laid aside his spectacles, as he often did when engaged on close work, so that instinctively he leaned forward to see me the better. 'I am relieved that you find yourself able to come to my assistance.'

He waved his hand at a table piled high with tottering heaps of documents. I felt a sharp stab of recognition, despite the strange room. A room which even smelled different. At Seething

239

Lane, although our quarters were official, devoted to government business, they formed part of the Walsinghams' home, so that there always lingered in the air faint smells of good dinners and hot linen freshly ironed. The building here smelled of little but paper and ink – a great deal of paper and ink – but from the open south-facing window the scents of the river also drifted in – mud and sea water and a tinge of sewage. Also, I suppose from one of the ships unloading below, I detected something more exotic, pepper, cinnamon, and another spice I could not quite identify. It might have been mace.

'Good day to you, Thomas,' I said, shaking his hand. 'I was moved by your desperate plea.'

He smiled at my ironic tone.

'Indeed, matters are very nearly desperate, for my assistant decoder is taken ill of some unspecified malady, which may be the bloody flux, or may simply be bloody mindedness and a disinclination to work.'

'Therefore he is quite alone in the business of deciphering, for as you know I am far too slow and of little use.'

I turned and smiled. Arthur Gregory was standing at the door of one of the other rooms, which must have replaced his tiny cupboard at Seething Lane.

'It is good to see you, Arthur,' I said. 'How are your wife and baby?'

'Hardly a baby any longer, Kit. He is a fine upstanding lad of two years now, talking without pausing for breath, though the language he employs does not always resemble English very closely. Sometimes our house seems like the Towel of Babel.'

'You look well on it.'

'I thank you. Perhaps you are somewhat thinner. Did you find the months in Muscovy trying?'

I smiled. I had no intention of revealing, even to Arthur, the fact that I was now living on little more than one meal a day.

'Muscovy was quite an adventure,' I said, 'but I am recovered from any ill effects.'

'And I am glad to see that Rikki is as fine a fellow as ever,' Arthur said, squatting down to fondle my dog. Rikki responded by licking his chin. Arthur had always been a favourite with him, which might have had something to do with the fact that Rikki had often been given a share of Arthur's pasties and buns, which his wife packed up for him every day, fearing perhaps that he might perish of hunger before he reached home in the evening.

I turned to Phelippes. 'Before you explain what you would like me to do, Thomas, I think we should understand each other on what terms I am here. I do not wish for a permanent position.'

I did not voice the name 'Essex', though it hung in the air between us.

'However, I am content to work here while you are hard pressed, and to be paid on the same terms as when I worked for Sir Francis, if that is agreeable to you.'

Phelippes put on his spectacles, perhaps in order to judge my expression more carefully, then he nodded.

'Very well, Kit, I am agreeable. I understand that you no longer work at St Thomas's hospital?'

It was not surprising that he should be aware of this. Although most of his attention was concentrated on agents from abroad and traitors at home, he could not stop himself storing up every fragment of information that came his way. It was an intrinsic part of the man's nature. Sooner or later, Phelippes knew everything that was going on in London.

'I do not,' I said, 'although I have a considerable number of private patients now.' *Considerable* was an exaggeration, but Phelippes was not likely to know that detail. 'However, at the moment all my patients are in good health, God be praised, therefore I can spare you some time to tackle this.'

I gestured at the heaped papers.

'Excellent.' Apparently regarding everything as settled, Phelippes began to clear a table, piling the documents on the floor, for want of any other horizontal surface. Arthur brought in a spare chair from his room, and they found me ink, uncut quills, and paper.

'I recall that your collection of seals was stolen from Seething Lane at the same time as the files,' I said to Arthur, as I arranged the table to my satisfaction. 'Have you been able to make replacements?'

'It has taken a long time,' he said, 'but fortunately I still had my sketches of the designs, so I was able to start again.'

'Someone told me you had gone to work for a printer, as an engraver.'

'Aye, so I did for a few months, until Thomas set up this new office. Then I joined him.'

I began to sharpen a set of quills with my pen knife. 'Does Anthony Bacon take much interest in the business?' I asked, looking at Phelippes.

They exchanged a glance.

'He generally calls in once or twice a week,' Phelippes said, 'but he leaves the handling of despatches and the code-breaking to us.'

'And you have some agents working for you?'

'A few,' he said cautiously.

I realised I must be careful not to overstep the mark. Having said firmly that I did not wish to become a permanent member of this new secret service, I had best not probe too deeply. Nevertheless, it seemed to be poorly provided for, at any rate in terms of men. This large suite of rooms appeared to be occupied by just the two of them. A 'few' agents. What did that mean? Two? Three? Sir Francis had placed agents in every capital city of Europe and beyond, even in Constantinople. He must have had forty or more. I wondered how many agents Lord Burghley and Sir Robert employed, and where they were based. Did the merchants of our Marrano community still provide information obtained through their trading contacts, and pass coded messages from country to country? I decided I would not ask Phelippes, but Dr Nuñez might be willing to tell me.

In the meantime, there was work to be done.

'This is the bundle of despatches from Lisbon which we were able to intercept,' Phelippes said, handing me a packet of perhaps a dozen letters, tied together with a bit of green ribbon. 'As you know from your own experience, Portugal had been an ancient ally of England, ever since John of Gaunt's daughter married the Portuguese king. After Spain invaded and seized control of Portugal, it has become an enemy, a servant state of Spain.'

242

I compressed my lips. There was much I could say about this, but I would not.

'Of course, Spain was particularly anxious to gain control of Portugal's excellent ports on the Atlantic,' he said, 'very convenient for the exploitation of their colonies in the Americas.'

I nodded as I untied the ribbon holding the packet together. I lifted one of the documents and sniffed it. Arthur grinned at me.

'Taken at sea, were they?' I asked innocently.

The whiff of tar and sea water is unmistakable. Somewhere off those excellent Atlantic ports, then.

'They were,' Phelippes said shortly.

So at least one sea captain was working for the service. I doubted whether it would be anyone as distinguished as Drake or Raleigh, but there were plenty of lesser men, minor privateers, who would know that letters taken from an enemy ship might prove as valuable as other forms of cargo. I wondered how many came to Phelippes and how many, by contrast, went to the Cecils.

Arthur had already lifted the seals on the letters. Presumably Phelippes had studied them sufficiently to decide that this was a new cipher. That they were written in Portuguese he must have deduced from the circumstances of their capture. However, I did not need to know the details of how they were obtained. I was here to crack the code and translate the deciphered contents. I flattened the paper on the desk, drew a sheet of clean paper toward me, and studied the writing. Letters and numbers in groups of five. Arranged in neat columns, which might mean that the message was to be read vertically, either up or down, instead of horizontally. Anything was possible. I smiled to myself, and felt the little thrill I always felt when faced with tackling a new cipher.

Arthur had disappeared into his room, but he returned carrying an hour glass, which he placed on my table without a word.

I laughed. 'Very well,' I said.

Sometimes Phelippes and I would time ourselves against the hour glass, and race to see who could crack a code first. Sometimes we merely raced against our own best time. I was out of practice, but it would be good to see whether I retained any of my skill. I turned the hour glass over and began.

In the event, I worked in Phelippes's office for more than two weeks. The new code proved quite demanding to break. Partly, as I knew, because I was out of practice, but also because all the codes I had broken in the past were in Spanish, French, Italian, or English. Every language requires a slightly different approach. In addition, this was a double cipher. The message had first been encoded, then the coded message was rearranged by the rules of a second code. The second must needs be solved first, for in a sense the code breaker works backwards from the end to the beginning, the original message.

I succeeded at last, though I am not sure it was worth all my efforts, since the despatches were fairly factual reports of our own ships' movements along the Atlantic coast, which we knew anyway. Phelippes believed the despatches were on their way to the Spanish army in the Low Countries. So their value lay in the fact that we had prevented them reaching their destination, rather than in information they revealed about our perpetual enemy, Spain.

Once I had finished with the Portuguese bundle, Phelippes persuaded me to stay and help him with the backlog of other paperwork, mostly in Spanish, though there were some documents in Italian, concerning activities in the Papal court. I discovered that Phelippes was attempting to run a projection with a very dubious agent, William Sterrell, at the express request of the Earl of Essex. So far it had yielded little of any value. It was not that Sterrell was of dubious loyalty, like Poley. He was merely incompetent.

'His lordship is particularly anxious for a quick result,' Phelippes told me one day when he was in a confidential mood. 'He desires a *coup de foudre* to eclipse the Cecils.'

'You mix your metaphors,' I chided. 'Can a *coup de foudre* engender an eclipse?'

He shrugged. 'Do not play schoolmen's games of logic with me, Kit. And in any case, it will not be a *coup de foudre*. It will be about as lively as a barrel of sodden gunpowder left out in

244

the rain. He has not the patience to understand that these things take time, months, sometimes years.'

'That squares with what I know of the man,' I said.

He took off his spectacles and pinched the bridge of his nose, which bore a red mark where they rested.

'Like the affair at the Blue Boar,' he said.

I pricked up my ears at that and looked at him sharply. 'You mean the rogue players' company, set on by Sir Thomas Oxley to stir up treachery against the Queen?'

He gave a dry laugh. 'Oh, Oxley was merely the cat's paw, poor booby, and now must kick his heels in Amsterdam, while his lands are forfeit to the Crown and his wife and children made homeless.'

'How do you mean, a cat's paw?'

'Oh, there was never any serious intention to incite a real rebellion. There was to be a great deal of noise. Alarm! Panic in the streets of London! Then my lord of Essex would ride in on his destrier and quell the rebellion. To his great glory. Saviour of London! Of England! The Queen would be delighted, the other nobles prostrate with admiration.'

'I see,' I said slowly. 'Another *coup de foudre*!'

'Precisely.'

It explained a great deal. Glory for Essex. Never mind those who died or were injured. Or lost their family estates.

'And he failed. As always,' I said. 'By the time he arrived, a minor fight in the inn yard had been contained. It never even reached the street.'

Phelippes nodded and looked grim. 'Indeed. He failed. As always.'

Phelippes gave further evidence of his ability to ferret out information from every corner of London on the last day I was due to work at the Customs Office. I had made a diversion on my way to his office that morning, for Nick Berden had sent me a message to say that Richard Upton had finally been found hiding in a miserable tavern in Billingsgate and had been handed over to Sir Rowland.

'So honour is satisfied,' I said.

'Aye,' Nick said. 'I may have lost him at the Blue Boar, but I caught him at the Three Cocks. Is there some kind of metaphor in that? Anyway, he has proved eager to talk, if it will save him worse punishment. It was Sir Thomas Oxley he had dealings with, but on more than one occasion Oxley let slip that it was the Earl of Essex was behind it all.'

I told Nick what Phelippes had said about Essex's plan to play the hero, at which Nick doubled up with laughter.

'Then it was not by chance that he came riding up when the men were being carried off under armed guard. I wish I might have seen his face! What a disappointment for the poor fellow, after all that planning, and all that money spent.'

I thought it was as well that there was no one nearby to hear a peer of the realm referred to as a 'poor fellow', but I laughed and agreed.

On arriving at the Customs House, I told Phelippes that Upton had been taken, but he had already heard.

'Aye,' he said, 'no doubt he will blab all that he knows, which my lord will not like, but I doubt he can stop him. However, it will probably not be broadcast to the world. The Queen would not care for her favourite to be both blackened and humiliated.'

'Ultimately,' I said, 'Essex is responsible for those deaths. Oliver Wandesford, John Stoker, and the men who died in the fight at the Blue Boar. He ought to be made to answer for it.'

'But he will not. He will say that it was all Sir Thomas Oxley's doing. It will be his word against a disreputable player who has been in trouble with the law before. And Sir Thomas is not here to defend himself. It will be hushed up.'

'It is not justice,' I said.

'Justice is not always even handed. Moreover,' Phelippes took off his spectacles and used them to point at me, 'you need to watch your own back.'

'Me?' I was surprised. 'Why so?'

'It appears that my lord of Essex has learned that it was you who persuaded Sir Rowland Heyward that the theft of the plays was intended for a political purpose. Without your interference and Sir Rowland's presence at the play with his sergeants,

246

together with his alerting of the Watch and the constables, the planned riot would have gone ahead unhindered. My lord would have had his moment of glory. Instead, you deprived him of it. He is not a man who readily forgives any who thwart his little schemes. You would do well to remember that, Kit. And watch your back.'

I shivered.

'I will watch my back,' I said.

Chapter Fourteen

Some time after finishing my work for Thomas Phelippes, I learned the fate of the rogue players who had accepted employment under Sir Thomas Oxley so that Essex's foolhardy plan might be implemented. After their arrest, they had been sent for trial to the assizes, and although I had not heard the outcome, I was sure that Nick Berden would have done. I had taken to visiting Nick from time to time, where we would reminisce about our previous adventures, like two old cronies sitting over a tavern fire of a winter's evening. I felt myself over young to be thus hankering for a past life, while Nick cannot have been more than in his middle thirties at the time. Still, we had some enjoyable times. Danger is always more pleasant in retrospect.

It was almost the end of August, though it seemed like autumn already, with a chill in the air which we felt even in the shelter of his back garden.

'This is the last time we shall be able to sit out here, I fear,' Nick said. 'I think those who warned of a cold winter had the right of it.'

I nodded. One of his hens was scratching pointlessly at the dried earth by my feet. I could not see what she hoped to gain by it, but I suppose chickens have very small brains. She suddenly noticed Rikki, who was sleeping peacefully beside me, and ran off squawking, as if a fox were after her. Rikki opened one eye, then closed it again.

'Are you still doing any work for Master Burbage?' Nick asked.

'Not for some time now. I still usually sup with the company of an evening, but even so I have seen little of them these last weeks. I have been busy, working for Thomas Phelippes and also having taken on more of Dr Nuñez's patients. He has not been well. I fear that he is fading.'

I looked away. This was something I did not want to think about.

'Fortunately for the weight of my purse, some of these new patients have needed physicking. I would not wish them ill, but it is best for me if they have a few minor illnesses.'

He grinned. 'Aye, the wise physician keeps his patients always a little ill, but not so ill that they die, for what profit is there in that?'

'You are a cynic, Nicholas Berden, and I will not listen to you.'

'Indeed? Then you will not wish to know what became of those players from the Blue Boar.'

'You have heard something?' Nick might not possess as wide a network of informants as Phelippes, but he came a close second.

'I have seen nothing further of Sir Rowland,' I said, 'and none from Master Burbage's company has mentioned anything.'

'But you do not wish to listen to me.'

'Do not tease, Nick. What have you heard?'

'Well, it seems that between them Sir Rowland and the Master of the Revels persuaded the men to reveal all the details of the plot, including the involvement of the Earl of Essex. Because they had cooperated very readily, at the assizes they were spared the worst punishments. However, they were fined so heavily that I doubt whether they were left with two pennies to rub together out of the money they were paid by Oxley.'

'Ill gotten gains,' I muttered, seeing again Oliver Wandesford sprawled on the table at the Green Dragon, dying.

'Their leader, Richard Upton, was sentenced to the pillory for two days. As a kind of poetic justice, the pillory chosen was in Queene Hythe, very near to the Blue Boar. Those who had been injured in the fight at the inn, and those who had lost members of their families, pelted him all the daylight hours, and not just with rotten fruit. They threw stones as well, and I believe he was quite badly knocked about.'

'It's a pity that such a man should have followed an evil path,' I said. 'He had some talent. Given other circumstances, he might have done well in a London playhouse.'

'He has not my sympathy,' Nick said. 'He must have known there were likely to be deaths.'

'What of the other men?'

'Once the sentence of the pillory was over, the whole company was whipped at the cart's tail and driven out of London. I believe they were set on the road for Essex. That should be the last we see of them.'

'It hardly seems just that they should suffer so much, when the man responsible for it all rides like a royal prince through the streets of London. Though I suppose if they had been found guilty of treason, they would have been hanged.'

Nick merely shrugged. Like Phelippes, I think he took a poor view of justice which operated differently for rich and poor. As for the Earl of Essex, he clearly believed himself to be above the law.

Now that I had a few more chinks in my purse from my private patients, Simon urged me to rent a better lodging, but I was saving my money carefully. Thrice in my short life already I had been left a beggar. I would not let it happen a fourth time. For some reason I could not fathom, he had taken against living in Southwark. The Atkins house was no palace, but it was as clean as any lodging in London could be expected to be, and a good deal cheaper than anywhere north of the river, unless you found lodgings in the eastern 'suburbs', as they were called, rough areas grown up outside the City wall, beyond Aldgate, places like Poplar and Ratcliffe, which were a good deal worse than Southwark. Goodwife Atkins and her husband were decent folk, not drunkards, as some who rent out rooms can be. Indeed Goodman Atkins had something of an inclination towards the Puritan view of the world.

For a short while Simon moved out of the house where we both roomed, and shared lodgings with Kyd and Marlowe. It was during the time I worked for Phelippes and just afterwards. I missed him sorely, much more than I wanted to admit to myself. I think at that time he dreamed of becoming a poet and maker of plays, as Kyd and Marlowe were, and hoped that somehow in their company he might absorb some of their talent. Yet his own true talent was rather to stride upon the stage and live the parts they created. I always watched him fondly in the playhouse, loving the way he came alive before an audience, creating for us the reality of the people who had existed before merely as the poets' inky scribbles upon the page.

After three weeks or so, he was back in Southwark, his room fortunately not having been rented by anyone else in the meantime. He was not prepared openly to admit why he had returned, but I gathered something from hints he dropped. Although he had always admired Marlowe's talent, I suspect that sharing lodgings with him was a less than pleasant experience. Marlowe had a violent temper and was a bully. Rubbing shoulders with him every day may have opened Simon's eyes a little.

'Kyd is a good fellow,' he said, leaving me to deduce that Marlowe, perhaps, was not. 'Most of the time he ends up paying, for food and suchlike, though I do not believe he has much money.'

'You are far better here,' I said. 'With your own room. You can come and go as you please, spend what you will. Independence has much to be said for it.'

I would not admit openly how pleased I was that he was back, though I think he sensed it. We spent more time together, taking Rikki for long walks before the weather turned too cold. Even once, like naughty urchins, climbing the wall into a Lambeth orchard and scrumping enough apples to fill our pockets and my satchel. In the evenings we often sat in his room or mine, playing chess or cards or reading, or simply talking. I was very happy. He had given no further hint that he had guessed who I really was, so that most of the time I was at ease. Though – sometimes – I wondered.

Early in September, one of Dr Nuñez's servants arrived on my doorstep as I returned very weary from visiting my patients amongst the City merchants. There had been an outbreak of measles affecting the children in the neighbourhood, and the parents were very worried. It is a dangerous disease. If the child does not die, it may be left blind or deaf or simple-minded. When the servant appeared, I had just passed through the Great Stone Gate at the south end of the Bridge before it was closed and I was more than ready for my bed.

'I have a two-man wherry waiting, Dr Alvarez,' the servant said. 'The mistress does not think Dr Nuñez will live till morning, and he is asking for you most urgently.'

I could not refuse. I shut Rikki in my room and went with the servant at once to the landing place by St Olave's, whence we were swiftly rowed across the river to St Botolph's Wharf near the Customs House, which was a short walk from the Nuñez home in Mark Lane. Once inside I was hurried upstairs to Dr Nuñez's bed chamber. I could see at once how it was with him. His skin had the ashen tint of a dying man, and his face was sheened with fine sweat, though he shivered under the covers. I sat on a chair at his bedside and took his hand in both of mine. It was cold and clammy.

His heavy eyelids lifted, and he smiled gently. 'Ah, Kit, thank you for coming.'

For a long while he said no more, then he roused himself.

'I have told my wife that you are to have as much of my medical equipment and my medicines as you can use. Over there on the chest,' he made a feeble movement of his head, 'is my small collection of Arabic medical texts. I have never owned as many as your father, but I want you to take them all. You must work at your Arabic and study them carefully. Take any other of my medical books. Those you used when you were studying for your licence.'

I thanked him and could not keep the tears from running down my cheeks. He freed his hand from mine and brushed them away.

'Now, Kit, you must not weep. I am past seventy and have had more than my share of life.'

He laid his hand on my bowed head.

'Bless you, dear girl. May the Lord keep you safe.'

I lifted my head and stared at him in astonishment. His face and the whole world around me seemed to shift and take on a new shape.

'You knew!'

'My dear child, I could not share that journey on the *Victory* with you, for all those weeks and all we lived through on the Portuguese expedition, without discovering your secret, which I had suspected for some time. But take care who else learns it.'

Several things that had puzzled me for many months were becoming clear.

'Did you tell Sir Francis?' At last I was beginning to understand.

'Aye. We thought you needed someone to care for you, living so dangerously near the edge. After your father died, I took him into my confidence. You were alone, with no one to protect you. We wanted to see you safe.'

He smiled.

'I have always regarded you as a daughter, and for Sir Francis, with only one surviving child, you became, as it were, a secret sister for his Frances. So he told you that he knew, did he?'

'Not long before he died. When he gave me his horse.'

'Ah, that horse! Horace, is it?'

So he could even tease me when he was dying.

'Hector,' I said gently.

'Aye, that's it. Hector. A Trojan hero.'

'He is indeed heroic. Like others who share his name.'

'Sir Francis always had a great regard for you, you know, Kit.'

He lay quiet for a time.

'Sir Francis told me Phelippes did not know,' I said, 'nor anyone else in the service.'

'No one else. It was safer for you that way. Except, of course, Pyotr Aubery.'

'*Pyotr* knew!' I stared at him, amazed, yet perhaps, not quite. 'I always thought there was something . . . But why did you tell Pyotr?'

'We were sending you into a dangerous country. You needed someone to keep a watch over you.'

'And I thought he was up to no good in some way.'

His eyes crinkled in a smile.

'Did a little private trading with Muscovy, did our Peter, through his family there. Nothing major. We turned a blind eye.'

'He was a brave man, in the end,' I said. 'He saved my life. At the time, everything was confused, but I realised afterwards that he had deliberately put himself between me and the crossbow. Poor man.'

'Redeemed.'

He began to cough, so I slipped my arm beneath his shoulders and helped him to sit up. There was half a cup of brandy caudle beside the bed, and he was able to sip a little.

Dame Beatriz came in, but was so distressed that one of her sons put his arm around her and led her away. He motioned to me to stay.

Dr Nuñez said little more, although he slipped into speaking Portuguese and rambled a little about his childhood and a dog he had once owned.

He died before the dawn.

The same servant escorted me back to Southwark by wherry. The autumn sunrise was just tinting the river reddish copper as I reached my lodgings and stumbled upstairs. I flung myself on my bed, holding Rikki close, and wept.

In the weeks after Dr Nuñez's death, I felt as though the whole world had turned dark. I think perhaps I had never quite realised how much he had meant to me. I had never told him, and now I never could. I attended his funeral, which was modest but respectable, a more worthy funeral than Sir Francis's hasty interment by night at St Paul's. It was held in the local parish church, St Katherine Coleman, according to Anglican rites, but for all I knew, the family may have conducted a Jewish service at home beforehand. In my childhood, when we had first come to England, my father and I had attended the clandestine services held at the Nuñez house, but since his death I had become slack in my attendance. Neither Dr Nuñez nor his wife had ever mentioned this to me. It was difficult for those of us in the younger generation to know where our loyalties and faith lay. We were more English than Portuguese, more Christian than Jewish, but above all without clear direction. Perhaps in time we would each make our choice, find our individual path into a future which, at the moment, was unclear.

The Nuñez family arranged for the books and medical equipment to be delivered to my lodgings, but Dame Beatriz was so prostrate with grief that I did not trouble her with visits after the funeral. I knew that the two of them had known each other since childhood and had travelled to England soon after they were married – long before my father and I had come – having seen the rising danger from Spain and the Inquisition. She must be feeling that her entire world had fallen apart. I know I felt as though the firm ground under my own feet had begun to quake like quicksand.

Simon was sympathetic and kind, but he had not known Dr Nuñez well, and he had all his fellow players about him as a surrogate family. I knew I was always welcome amongst them, but their world was not quite my world. Dr Nuñez had shared my native land, my mother tongue, my debatable heritage, and my profession. To lose him was like the severance of a limb.

It was nearly a month later that Guy greeted me as I walked into the Cross Keys to sup with the players. Now that there was no copying work to be done, I felt somewhat ill at ease to be enjoying my free meals, but Master Burbage had assured me more than once that he was happy with his end of our bargain. It had turned very cold, more like the end of November than early October. Shivering as I crossed the Bridge, I wondered at such a change after the almost unbearable heat of the summer. The playhouses would be forced to close soon and my dinners would end as well.

'Good e'en to you, Kit,' Guy said. 'Come in beside the fire. We are all toasting our frozen limbs and you looked perished with cold.'

'Had you an audience today?' I asked. The citizens of London are hardy folk, but standing in the pit of the Theatre for three hours demands a strong devotion to the playhouse.

He shook his head. 'Barely half full. We have perhaps two weeks more, three at most. Then we must close.' He handed me a mug of steaming spiced wine, that Will was tending in a pot at the side of the hearth.

'However,' Guy went on, 'we have some good news.'

'You will be doing a winter season here again?' I said.

'Nay, nothing is decided as to that, but we have some private performances bespoken.' He grinned broadly. 'We are bid to Hampton Court for the Christmas Revels, more than one performance. Will is busy scribbling away at a new play. You would not care to join me in a lute duet again, I suppose?'

I laughed. 'I think not. When I did so before it was to serve a greater purpose.'

'What could be greater than giving pleasure to Her Majesty?'

'What indeed? Except, perhaps, preserving her life. That will set you up well for the winter.'

'The Master of the Revels is mindful of our part in exposing and destroying the plot to incite rebellion by means of those rogue players, so it is partly by way of a reward.'

'How thoughtful of him.'

I confess to a small stab of jealousy at this. It seemed that the Master of the Revels had forgotten that, while the players had wished merely to recover their plays, it was I who had first suspected the subversive intentions of the company at the Blue Boar. Still, Thomas Phelippes had warned me that my part in the affair had endangered me with Essex, so perhaps it was to my advantage that it should be forgotten.

'Moreover,' Guy said, 'we have other engagements.'

It seemed he had not noticed the lack of warmth in my last remark. I smiled and tried to make up for my lack of enthusiasm.

'More private performances?'

'Aye, and you will never guess where.'

'I am sure I shall not.'

'At Somerset Place. Lord Hunsdon has commanded us for a week of performances in early December, a different play every night.'

'Lord Hunsdon?' This did surprise me. 'I should have thought he would have wished to have no more to do with Lord Strange's Men, after Master Wandesford's poisoning and that unpleasant inquest.'

'It seems not. Perhaps he realises that we suffered for it, and has some sympathy with us. Though to tell you the truth, Kit, I believe our notoriety has helped to boost the numbers in our audiences since the affair. Also, I believe Lord Hunsdon is still of a mind to persuade Master Burbage to come under his patronage.'

'Master Burbage will not do so, will he?'

'Nay, it would be a scurvy trick. Lord Strange has treated us well and made few demands, unlike some noble patrons. Our season at Hampton Court will be of benefit to Lord Strange as well as to us, improve his standing with Her Majesty.'

'I shall never understand the manoeuvrings of courtiers,' I said. 'Essex thought to gain by putting down a rebellion he himself had stirred up. Yet all he has done is to escape punishment.'

'We are not supposed to know about that, or at any rate to speak of it. It seems that Her Majesty has laughed it off as a young man's jape.'

'How old is the Earl?'

'About six and twenty, I believe,' Guy said.

'Old enough to know better.'

'Very true. In any case, what I was about to tell you is that Lord Hunsdon has invited us to another dinner, this time at Somerset Place, where his own cooks can ensure that no *belladonna* is used to spice the food.'

I raised my eyebrows at this. 'I am even more surprised that he should ever want to dine in your company again.'

'Not only ours but yours. He has specifically invited you as well, since it was you who detected the murder of Oliver Wandesford.'

'He has forgiven me, then, for his summons to the inquest?'

'It would seem so.'

'Then I graciously accept. When is it to be?' I said.

'The day after tomorrow. Six o' the clock at Somerset Place.'

'I shall wear my best finery.'

Guy laughed. He knew I was already wearing it.

Simon, Will, and I shared a wherry to Somerset Place, disembarking at the watergate where Master Burbage and I had struggled across the exposed mud of the foreshore all those weeks before. This time the wherry was able to land us at the very gate, which saved our clothes from the Thames. For the moment, Will was still in lodgings in Southwark, but talked of moving north of the river again. It would be nearer the Theatre, he said. I felt that, like Simon, he was beginning to find that Southwark was too rough. Now that he was earning substantial fees for his writing, he could afford something better.

We were greeted at the watergate by a liveried servant, as before, and escorted through the garden to the house. The garden looked very different now, in the autumn dusk. Apart from a few faded blooms clinging to their stems, the roses were over. No flowers adorned the lavender that edged the path, and the bees had already gone into their winter hibernation. The copper-coloured leaves on the pleached limes rustled in the sharp little wind that strewed their fellows about our feet. Clearly the gardeners had been hard at work earlier in the day, sweeping away the fallen leaves, for leaves lay in great heaps under the brick garden wall, but at this time of year it is an endless task, like Penelope at her weaving. Overhead a thick layer of black cloud threatened rain before night.

The house, however, was bright with an abundance of candles in candelabra which hung from every ceiling and stood in wrought iron formation along every wall. So abundant were they that the room grew hot with the flames and the air was filled with the scent of perfumed beeswax. I thought I could also smell frankincense, but could not believe such extravagance. I must be mistaken.

Many of the players, I noticed, had raided the costume baskets for this visit to the great man's house. Master Burbage was ever lavish with his costumes and the players had a childlike delight in dressing up. In law, mere players were forbidden to wear the luxurious fabrics except on stage, but it was a law more often broken than observed.

'Meanness in dress is more damaging than meanness in speech,' Master Burbage had declared in my hearing more than once. 'The groundlings will look up to us if we dress like nobles. Nobles will look down on us if we do not dress as well as they do.'

Many of the costumes had indeed come from noble houses. When a garment is no more than six months out of fashion, your noble lord or lady will pass it down to a servant. Now, a servant cannot go about in this finery, but such clothes are worth much in chinks, and players' companies are eager to buy. Master Burbage's company had an excellent seamstress in Goodwife Blakely, who could alter and refurbish such garments, so that they looked fashionable and new once more. I do not know whether any noble lady or gentleman noticed their last year's clothes adorning this year's players, but it would not surprise me.

Simon and Will had helped themselves to elegant outfits, and had even offered to find something for me, but I declined.

'I should feel like a conjuror's monkey,' I said. 'I thank you, but must refuse.'

They may have been a little hurt, but it did not last for long.

Now, in the lavish apartments of Somerset Place, with the sheen of satins and velvets glimmering in the candlelight, the sparkle of buttons set with semi-precious gems, the subtle glint of a gold earring here and there, Burbage's Men were transformed from mere jobbing players into some company of courtiers from an ancient tale. The hall where we were received was hung with a vast Flanders tapestry depicting not the usual scenes of Biblical tales but a hunt through a green forest. Nobles on fine-limbed horses galloped between the trees, their dress that of two hundred years before. Following on foot, their servants held back eager pursuivant hounds on delicate chains. Nobles, servants, and dogs all strained eagerly toward the end of the tapestry. I walked down the room, following after them, curious to know what they were pursuing.

There, at the far edge of the tapestry, poised with one foot raised, was a pure white stag, his head turned as he regarded the hunt with a certain glorious confidence. He knew, however hard they chased after, he would always outrun them.

'You are admiring my lord's newest tapestry?'

The voice came from behind my shoulder and caused me to start, for I was so absorbed in the scene before me that I had almost forgotten where I was.

I turned. It was Aemilia Bassano. If the company of players had become a court of nobles, she was transformed into Queen Mab. She wore immaculate white satin, sewn all over with pearls, white on white. Her hair was elaborately looped and braided with more pearls, which gleamed against her dark tresses. She wore no ruff, but one of the fashionable wide collars, which rose stiffly behind her head, and lay softly spread out on her shoulders, allowing the low-cut bodice to display the curve of her breasts. I had a sudden sharp vision of her as the white deer, hotly pursued, but I feared she would not be fleet enough of foot to escape the hunt.

'My lady,' I said, with an appropriate bow.

Her eyes lit up with laughter, and she swept me a mocking curtsey. 'Hardly,' she said.

For a moment we both regarded the tapestry, the deer for ever pursued, the hunt for ever pursuing. As we turned away, she tapped my arm.

'I remember you, doctor, from that other unfortunate dinner. You do not disapprove of education for women. Even agree, as I recall, that women may be as intelligent and learned as men.'

'I do believe that,' I said, with a secret smile of my own.

'Such wisdom in a beardless youth!' she said, running her finger down my cheek.

Indeed, I was beardless. Although many young men in England only grew beards in the middle or late years of their twenties, I realised that the time could not be long in coming when some might regard my smooth cheeks with a speculation

260

that could spell trouble for me. As it was, Aemilia looked very thoughtful as she touched my cheek. I was at a loss how to respond, but at that moment Lord Hunsdon approached us and I was able to bow deeply, thus hiding my confusion.

'Dr Alvarez,' he said, in a friendly tone which gave no hint of any lingering annoyance at the unpleasantness he had endured at the inquest, all owing to me. 'I am glad to welcome you to my home in happier times.'

We began to speak of trivial matters and moved away from the tapestry, but I did not lose the dreamlike feeling that had come over me as I followed the hunt through the forest. The candle-lit hall, the glittering company, the distant music which now crept in, perhaps from the chamber where we would dine, seemed more illusion than reality. I felt as though I was watching the party as it was enacted on a playhouse stage, myself moving invisible amongst the players.

This strange sense of dream and illusion wrapped me round for the whole evening, and although I felt somehow apart from the rest of the company, I also found my vision and hearing sharper than usual. I caught snatches of Master Burbage's conversation with Lord Hunsdon from the far end of the table, Lord Hunsdon not pressing his case to become patron, but praising the plays and performances of Burbage's Men. As before I was sitting near Will and Aemilia. I saw him take her hand and heard him whisper in her ear. She blushed, but did not draw her hand away. I wanted to warn Will against such dangerous dalliance, but as happens in a dream, I seemed unable to speak. And how could I speak, in company?

The food, too, was dreamlike. Larks' tongues and little singing birds on spits. Swan, which only the greatest nobles may serve. Whole turbot and salmon, laid on a bed of pickled samphire. Haunches of venison. Sides of beef. Sucking pig. Pies of layered meats tricked out in fantastical shapes, as castles, mountains, busts of the Caesars. Exotic fruits, pineapples and pomegranates. I saw Aemilia pricking pomegranate seeds on the tip of her knife and feeding them to Will. I glanced along the table to Lord Hunsdon, but he was deep in conversation with Master Burbage and another guest I did not recognise.

Rich red wine of Burgundy. Canary sack. Rhenish wines from Germany.

It was growing hotter and hotter. The faces of all my fellow guests were flushed and I could feel my own cheeks burning, though I had drunk very little. Simon too had stopped after his third glass was poured and it remained undrunk, in his goblet of fine Venetian ware. I noticed Will was abstemious in both food and drink, his attention too much focussed on Aemilia. She was indeed lovely, with a quick, well-informed mind which would entrance him, but she belonged to another. I tried to direct a warning look at him, but I seemed to be invisible. Perhaps, after all, this was a dream.

The overabundance of food, after my weeks on narrow rations, was beginning to make me nauseous. Now there were speeches by both Lord Hunsdon and Master Burbage, but I paid them no heed, concentrating on maintaining control over my heaving stomach and spinning head.

'And now,' Lord Hunsdon said, 'the sugar banquet. My love, will you lead to way?' He glanced sharply at Aemilia, and I wondered whether he had noticed the byplay between her and Will.

We all rose, and I realised that Lord Hunsdon was one of those nobles who had erected a separate banqueting house where his guests might conclude the feast. For feast it was, no simple dinner. It was as if this lavish spread was intended to wipe out any memory of that other occasion when we had dined together, although this time there were other guests, in addition to the players. I had been too absorbed in my thoughts to notice them fully before. Other courtiers, by their looks, and a number of women amongst them, one of whom swooped down upon Simon and began talking animatedly. Perhaps these were all patrons of the playhouse, enjoying a little wicked thrill at dining with such vagabonds and rogues as played upon the stage.

I was glad I had not agreed to wear stage finery.

We were conducted out of the house and over to the far side of the garden, where I had not been before. Here there was an artificial mound with a banqueting house erected atop it, which might perhaps serve as a pleasant summer house on quieter days.

We climbed the steps to the upper floor, where a table was laid out with all kinds of sugar confections. Cups made of sugar. Playing cards painted with kings and queens, the kings looking remarkably like the Queen's late father. Tiny sugar birds in sugar cages. Sugar hares crouching on sugar forms. Sugar fans, delicate as lace. Even the plates were sugar. In the centre of the table, a fairytale sugar castle, a Camelot three feet high.

As other guests exclaimed over the banquet I turned away, feeling sickened again, and walked to a wide window facing the river. The casement had been thrown open and I welcomed the cold breeze on my hot face. Out on the water, wherries rowed up river and down, their lanterns dancing over their own reflections like will-o'-the-wisps. Someone out there was playing a lute and singing, too far away to be heard clearly, but snatches drifted in with the wind off the water.

'Beautiful, do you not think, Kit?'

It was Will, no longer close by Aemilia's side. Glancing over his shoulder I saw that she was standing with Lord Hunsdon, talking to some of their noble guests.

'Be careful, Will,' I murmured. 'She belongs to Lord Hunsdon.'

'But I refer to the river, of course, and the night. Look, the clouds are clearing and the stars come out, looking as though they have been cut from candle flames and sprinkled over the dome of heaven.'

'Aye,' I said, wryly, 'it is become a beautiful night. And, aye, she is beautiful. Do not try to divert me with fine words, Will.'

'I know you mean me well, Kit, and I shall be careful. But I am become as a moth, and may singe my wings a little.'

'Take care it is no more than a little.'

Simon joined us by the window. 'Some are beginning to leave. What say you two? Shall we find a boat? I am told a whole fleet has been bidden to await us at the stairs.'

'I am happy to leave,' I said. 'Too much food and too much sugar!'

'Look,' Simon said, 'they are lighting torches all along the path to the watergate.'

I turned back to the window. The torches set up amongst the pleached limes added to the strange illusory sense of the evening, as if by passing through the flaming tunnel we would pass from one world into another.

'Will?' Simon said.

'I'll stay awhile,' he said, his eyes on Aemilia still. 'But I'll not delay you.'

Simon grinned at me and raised his eyebrows. He too must have noticed Will with Aemilia.

We gave our thanks to our host with many bows and pretty speeches, then descended to the garden again. When we reached the path to the watergate, I saw that the torches were placed apart at a safe distance, but the wind which had blown away the rain clouds was causing the flames to stream out like comets' tails, scattering sparks amongst the dry leaves on the ground. I stamped out one with my boot, thankful that I no longer walked on paper-thin soles.

There was indeed a fine cluster of wherries at the watergate, so we were soon launched on the river, where the cool air, like a splash of water in my face, dowsed my feeling of unreality and brought me back to the workaday world.

The tide was on the ebb, so with the tide and the river current we swept past the other great houses north on the Strand and Lambeth Palace on the south bank. The round shapes of the bull baiting and bear baiting in Southwark were dark against the sky, but there were lighted windows on both sides of the river.

It seemed the wherries had been paid for by Lord Hunsdon, so we climbed out of the boat at St Mary Overy with our purses no lighter. Bessie's improved playing on the hurdy-gurdy flowed out of the whorehouse, punctuated with shouts and laughter. There was a light showing at a downstairs window at our own lodgings.

Before Simon and I could climb the stairs, Goodwife Atkins waylaid us.

'That lad Eddi from the hospital has brought a message for you,' she said, handing me a folded paper. 'He's still here if you want to send an answer. Having a bite to eat in my kitchen. I don't believe they feed them enough at the hospital.'

I was aware that Eddi, like all the staff at St Thomas's, would be very well fed, for Superintendent Ailmer knew that he should keep his employees strong and healthy in order to run a successful hospital. Still, growing boys are always hungry.

'Wait a moment, Simon,' I said. 'They may need me for an emergency. You will have to fetch Rikki from my room.'

'No need,' said Goodwife Atkins. 'I brought him down, for he was crying, left alone.'

And there he was, wagging an apologetic tail.

I slipped my penknife from its sheath and lifted the seal. The message was short, but changed my life.

My greetings to you, Dr Alvarez.
(He had never called me Kit.)
I have received word from Dr Wattis that he wishes to resign from his post at St Thomas's, having found a more lucrative and less arduous position elsewhere. He will not be returning. I have spoken to the governors, who authorise me to offer you your former position again, with a small increase in your remuneration. If you are willing to accept this offer, will you please inform me immediately, and report for work tomorrow morning?
Your ob^{dnt} servant,
Roger Ailmer, Superintendent

I looked up and smiled at Simon. The dark autumn evening was suddenly brighter.

'I am back at St Thomas's,' I said. 'They want me to return.'

He shook his head in mock sorrow. 'No longer a member of Lord Strange's Men? Copyist extraordinary?'

I laughed. 'Only when you are in desperate need.'

I bent down to rub Rikki behind his ears, but in truth to hide the tears in my eyes. 'We're back at St Thomas's, lad,' I said.

When I straightened up, I saw that Simon was smiling at me affectionately. He threw his arms round me and hugged me.

'A fine ending to our evening,' he said.

'Not an ending,' I said. 'A new beginning.'

Historical Note

It was a cutthroat business, the theatrical world of Elizabethan London. The purpose-built playhouses of the period could hold as many as two thousand people. Although London was unimaginably large compared with all other English towns at the time, and larger than all European towns apart from Paris and Naples, its population was only around 200,000. Therefore, to run a successful business and fill their playhouses, the players' companies had to tempt the London playgoers to return again and again, preferably more than once a week.

The inevitable result was that a constant supply of new plays was needed. A professional company would stage around twenty new plays each season, together with about twenty plays which had proved popular in previous years. The feats of memory on the part of the actors were prodigious. There were hack writers, turning out unmemorable plays which died rapidly. There were the 'university wits', who wrote clever plays – sometimes obscure, sometimes scurrilous – but most of them had died young by the early 1590s.

Then there were the two giants – William Shakespeare and Christopher Marlowe. We know that plays were stolen, including theirs. Those feats of memory could be employed to 'record' a play performed by one company, which would then be performed illegally by a rival. Sometimes a player might move from one company to another, taken the memorised play with him.

Despite their immense popularity with the London public, as well as with the Queen and the Court, the playhouses were under constant attack by the city authorities and rampant preachers. They were places of ill-repute, the haunt of whores, pickpockets, and tricksters. The crowded conditions were a breeding ground for disease. Above all, the plays themselves were dangerous, pernicious things, apt to stir up trouble and feed the common man with subversive ideas.

Whenever epidemics of disease broke out in London, the theatres were closed. All theatres were shut down after a riot on

12 June, 1592, in Southwark was alleged to have begun at a playhouse. Apart from these closures ordered by the Common Council of London or the Privy Council, the regular means of control and censorship was in the hands of the Master of the Revels, the only person who could license a play for performance. For much of the Elizabethan period, the office was held by Sir Edmund Tilney, who scrutinised every play for any insults to the Queen or the nobility, and above all for any trace of heresy, blasphemy, or treason.

All of these aspects of the world of Elizabethan theatre lie behind *The Play's the Thing*. Another strand draws on events of ten years later. I have imagined that what happens here was a form of dress rehearsal for what the Earl of Essex attempted in 1601. It was also convenient that the supposed date of the plays *I Henry VI* by Shakespeare and *Edward II* by Marlowe (both concerned with the overthrow of kings) was 1591, a time when the atmosphere in London was uneasy, almost paranoid. After the death of Sir Francis Walsingham there was a struggle for supremacy between the Earl of Essex and the Cecils (Lord Burghley and his son Sir Robert Cecil). With Walsingham's intelligence service gone, the government must have felt extremely vulnerable. Moreover, with the Queen now past child-bearing and refusing to name an heir, many were nervous about the future. It was an atmosphere apt to trigger fears of rebellion.

Law enforcement at the time was somewhat piecemeal. Every parish throughout England (including London) elected parish constables who were responsible for controlling and reporting crime. These men were amateurs, ordinary untrained citizens, serving unpaid for a year. Shakespeare himself makes fun of them. There was also the Watch, who patrolled the streets at night, armed, carrying a lantern, and accompanied by a dog. They checked that premises were locked, arrested vagrants and criminals, and called out the hours with their 'All's Well' (if it was). In addition, anyone could summon the 'hue and cry', a gathering of all able-bodied citizens to pursue and capture someone seen committing a crime.

In London, the city was run from the Guildhall, under the Lord Mayor, the Sheriffs, and the Common Council, with its subsidiary body the Court of Aldermen (made up of the aldermen from all the twenty-six city wards). The Guildhall employed a large number of city clerks, officials, and specialist servants, including a number of sergeants. The coroner's office was located in the Guildhall, and the coroner plays a considerable part in *The Play's the Thing*. Unfortunately, the names of the coroners from this period do not survive. However, a survey of the history and function of the coroner, written some two hundred years later, states that the Lord Mayor of London was, *ex officio*, the coroner. Given the heavy burden of duties carried by the Lord Mayor, it is likely that he may well have delegated this task to a suitable deputy on occasion. However, I have assumed that in this case the current Lord Mayor, Sir Rowland Heyward, undertook to act himself.

A coroner's inquest was required by law in any instance of unlawful killing. A famous case was the inquest held after the death of Marlowe in 1593. I needed to ascertain the exact details of a Tudor inquest, and in this I have been given enormous support and encouragement by Nicholas Rheinberg, Senior Coroner for Cheshire, who has hunted out details I could never have found for myself, for which I am most grateful.

Did this particular conspiracy take place? Perhaps not. But it might have done.

Praise for Ann Swinfen's Novels

'an absorbing and intricate tapestry of family history and private memories … warm, generous, healing and hopeful'
VICTORIA GLENDINNING

'I very much admired the pace of the story. The changes of place and time and the echoes and repetitions – things lost and found, and meetings and partings'
PENELOPE FITZGERALD

'I enjoyed this serious, scrupulous novel … a novel of character … [and] a suspense story in which present and past mysteries are gradually explained'
JESSICA MANN, *Sunday Telegraph*

'The author … has written a powerful new tale of passion and heartbreak ... What a marvellous storyteller Ann Swinfen is – she has a wonderful ear for dialogue and she brings her characters vividly to life.'
Publishing News

'Her writing …[paints] an amazingly detailed and vibrant picture of flesh and blood human beings, not only the symbols many of them have become…but real and believable and understandable.'
HELEN BROWN, *Courier and Advertiser*

'She writes with passion and the book, her fourth, is shot through with brilliant description and scholarship...[it] is a timely reminder of the harsh realities, and the daily humiliations, of the Roman occupation of First Century Israel. You can almost smell the dust and blood.'
PETER RHODES, *Express and Star*

The Author

Ann Swinfen spent her childhood partly in England and partly on the east coast of America. She was educated at Somerville College, Oxford, where she read Classics and Mathematics and married a fellow undergraduate, the historian David Swinfen. While bringing up their five children and studying for a postgraduate MSc in Mathematics and a BA and PhD in English Literature, she had a variety of jobs, including university lecturer, translator, freelance journalist and software designer. She served for nine years on the governing council of the Open University and for five years worked as a manager and editor in the technical author division of an international computer company, but gave up her full-time job to concentrate on her writing, while continuing part-time university teaching in English Literature. In 1995 she founded Dundee Book Events, a voluntary organisation promoting books and authors to the general public.

Her first three novels, *The Anniversary*, *The Travellers*, and *A Running Tide*, all with a contemporary setting but also an historical resonance, were published by Random House, with translations into Dutch and German. *The Testament of Mariam* marked something of a departure. Set in the first century, it recounts, from an unusual perspective, one of the most famous and yet ambiguous stories in human history. At the same time it explores life under a foreign occupying force, in lands still torn by conflict to this day. Her second historical novel, *Flood*, takes place in the fenlands of East Anglia during the seventeenth century, where the local people fought desperately to save their land from greedy and unscrupulous speculators. The next novel in the Fenland Series, *Betrayal*, continues the story of the search for legal redress and security for the embattled villagers. *This Rough Ocean* is a novel based on the real-life experiences of the Swinfen family during the 1640s, at the time of the English Civil War, when John Swynfen was imprisoned for opposing the killing of the king, and his wife Anne had to fight for the survival of her children and dependents.

Currently the author is working on a late sixteenth century series, featuring a young Marrano physician who is recruited as a code-breaker and spy in Walsingham's secret service. The first book in the series is *The Secret World of Christoval Alvarez*, the second is *The Enterprise of England*, the third is *The Portuguese Affair*, the fourth is

Bartholomew Fair, the fifth is ***Suffer the Little Children***, the sixth is ***Voyage to Muscovy*** and the seventh is ***The Play's the Thing***.

She now lives in Broughty Ferry, on the northeast coast of Scotland, with her husband, formerly vice-principal of the University of Dundee, and a rescue cat.

www.annswinfen.com